First Friends

Also by Marcia Willett

A Week in Winter

A Summer in the Country

The Children's Hour

The Birdcage

First Friends

Marcia Willett

Thomas Dunne Books

St. Martin's Griffin   New York

THOMAS DUNNE BOOKS.
An imprint of St. Martin's Press.

FIRST FRIENDS. Copyright © 1995 by Marcia Willett. All rights reserved. Printed in the
United States of America. No part of this book may be used or reproduced in any
manner whatsoever without written permission except in the case of brief quotations
embodied in critical articles or reviews. For information, address St. Martin's Press, 175
Fifth Avenue, New York, N.Y. 10010.

www.thomasdunnebooks.com
www.stmartins.com

Design by Jane Adele Regina

ISBN-13: 978-0-312-30662-5
ISBN-10: 0-312-30662-8

First published in Great Britain by Headline Book Publishing, a division of Hodder
Headline PLC, as *Those Who Serve*

First U.S. Edition: August 2006

10 9 8 7 6 5 4 3 2 1

To Roddy

Acknowledgements

My thanks to Cate Paterson, my editor, who acted as midwife to the birth of this book and encouraged me through the labour pains.

First Friends

Prologue

1981

Cassandra Wivenhoe stood at the foot of the open grave and watched her daughter's coffin being lowered into the Devon earth. She thrust her hands into the pockets of her dark grey wool suit and swallowed several times. She simply must not think of Charlotte, lying there, alone and unprotected: soon to be abandoned to the windy moorland churchyard.

'Thou knowest, Lord, the secrets of our hearts . . . '

The secrets of our hearts! She looked up and into the eyes of Kate Webster, her oldest and closest friend, whose compassionate gaze stiffened Cass's spine and gave her a small measure of courage. She blinked back tears, remembering Kate's words: 'If you go on playing Russian roulette, one of these days you'll get the bullet.'

But I didn't want anyone else to suffer, Cass cried silently. Not my children! Not Charlotte! She was only fifteen!

' . . . to take unto Himself the soul of our dear daughter . . . '

Despite herself, images superimposed themselves on the churchyard scene. Charlotte; as a baby, as a small child playing with Kate's twins, as a bigger girl learning to cook in a too-large apron—her face serious and intent—on her pony, and then, as a teenager, shy and awkward . . .

No! screamed the voice inside Cass's head. I can't bear it! It is simply not to be borne!

' . . . earth to earth . . . '

Handfuls of damp black moorland soil thudded softly on to the wooden lid, breaking into crumbs.

She jerked her head up and met Kate's eyes again. She saw that Kate's own hands were balled into fists and she knew that Kate was willing her some of her own strength.

Cass swallowed, her face twitching pitifully and gave Kate an infinitesimal nod.

' . . . in sure and certain hope of the Resurrection . . . '

MEMORIES CROWDED UNBIDDEN INTO Kate's head: so many scenes and conversations, a whole way of life that had finally brought them to this graveyard on a wild autumn afternoon. Through unshed tears and a whole shared past, Kate looked back.

Part One

One

1964-68

The Isle of Wight, ghostly and featureless, seemed to float on a sea of liquid glass. A faint, thin pencil line of silver indicated the horizon where it merged with a sky of a uniform grey-white. There was a brightness, a gentle glow to the late-autumn afternoon, a promise of sunshine yet to be fulfilled. Kate, scrunching slowly across the beach at Stoke's Bay, was gradually adjusting to her new surroundings. Accustomed to the sandy beaches, rocky outcrops and towering cliffs of the West Country, these shingly flat shores and broad esplanades, with the worn stretches of grassed areas behind them, seemed tame to her. Even the behaviour of the sea itself was much more domesticated here. It lay placidly against the land, retreating calmly, advancing demurely, quite unlike its boisterous, wild poundings on the north Cornish Coast.

Kate glanced into the shelters that were placed at intervals along the esplanade. She was beginning to recognise the elderly regulars who sat there like so many spiders waiting to trap the unwary victim with friendly little nods and bravely pathetic smiles. They were lonely, of course, and so was she, but she knew that if she went too close she would be drawn in by the flying strand of a casual greeting and caught in a web of gently banal conversation which would wind inexorably around her independence, curtailing the freedom of her walk. Almost it was tempting. There would be a certain companionship in sitting idly, half anaesthetised by the gentle hum of reminiscences, knowing that any half-hearted struggles to escape would be obstructed by the sticky flow of talk flowing over and around her.

Kate hardened her heart and turned her head away. Her husband, Mark, had gone to sea for seven weeks and it was early days. Remembering all the advice and warnings that she had received from well-meaning friends on her wedding day nearly two months before, Kate stuck her chin out, thrusting her fists more firmly into her duffel coat pockets. She had no intention of admitting defeat and rushing home the first time that the submarine sailed although it would have helped to have known a few other people in Alverstoke before Mark had left. He didn't know anyone either. How could he when he had come straight from Britannia Royal Naval College and Fourth Year Courses to *HMS Dolphin*, the submarine base at Gosport?

Watching the Isle of Wight ferry ploughing out from behind the sea wall, Kate let herself realise how much she missed her closest friend. Cassandra and she, both twelve years old, had first met at boarding school on the north Somerset coast on the edge of the Quantock Hills. The friendship had meshed smoothly and firmly at once. Kate, coming from a home overflowing with brothers, a sister and dogs and presided over by two loving generous parents, had listened, eyes stretched, as Cass, an only child, talked about nannies and Army quarters and her father—now a General—at his wits' end after her mother's death in a car accident.

'Rumour has it,' disclosed Cass, biting into a forbidden doughnut, 'that she was eloping with her lover.'

Kate's eyes grew rounder.

'Gosh!' she breathed. 'But can you elope if you're already married?'

Cass shrugged, the details were unimportant. She licked up some jam. 'Ran away, then. Anyway, the car was a write-off. I can't really remember her. I was only two.'

'Your poor father.'

'Devastated, poor old dear. And he simply doesn't know what to do with me now I'm growing up. That's why he's sent me out here, to the back of beyond, for the next five years. He thinks I'll be safe from temptation.'

Even the way she spoke the word gave it a flavour of excitement and promise. Something to be sought rather than avoided.

The five years had passed, punctuated with crushes on Cliff Richard and Adam Faith followed by agonising infatuations with other girls' brothers. They had played lacrosse and tennis, rode and swum, passed examinations by the skins of their teeth, chaffed over puppy fat and spots and then, one day, they had woken up and it was all over. The schooldays that had stretched so endlessly ahead were now a thing of the past.

'But we'll stay in touch.'

They stood together in the study that they had shared for the last year, their things packed, shelves and desk tops emptied, and looked at each other.

Cassandra, blue-eyed, tall, full-breasted, her long fair hair twisted into a French pleat, was elegant in a cashmere twin set and a navy blue pleated skirt, pearls in place.

Kate grinned. 'D'you remember sneaking out to see *Expresso Bongo*?'

'And that year I got twelve red roses and a Valentine card from Moira's brother and they were confiscated?'

They roared with laughter.

Kate, with her mop of unruly brown curls and grey eyes, was shorter and stockier than her friend and made no attempt at elegance. She wore honey-coloured tweeds; going-home clothes.

They hugged and hugged.

'You must come and stay. We'll have lots of fun.'

They separated. Cass went to her father's flat in London for a year of relaxation and to think—very vaguely—about getting some sort of job. Kate went to her home in Cornwall to think—very reluctantly—about attending a course on cookery or shorthand typing. Both thought very seriously indeed about falling in love and getting married.

At a party barely a year later, Cass met Tom Wivenhoe, a midshipman in his final year at Britannia Royal Naval College, and shortly afterwards Kate received a telephone call.

'S'meee. How's the typing course?'

'Awful. Terrible. How are you?'

'Never better. Listen, I've met this smashing chap. Now! How about coming to the Summer Ball at Dartmouth? You know, the naval college.'

'Are you serious? The tickets are like gold dust!'

'Aha! Trust your Fairy Godmother. You shall go to the ball, Cinderella.'

'But who shall I . . . ?'

'Tom's got a friend called Mark Webster. His partner's broken her leg or something and he's at a loose end. He's nice. Honestly. A bit quiet but tall, dark and handsome. What about it? We'll book a double room at the Royal Castle. It will be just like school. What do you say?'

'Oh, Cass . . . '

A year later, after Fourth Year Courses and a continual round of balls, ladies' nights and parties, they were both married; Cass and Tom in August with Kate as bridesmaid and, two weeks later, Kate and Mark, with Cass as Matron of Honour. In a rapture of white silk, the thunder of the organ in their ears and a vision of married bliss in their dazed eyes, they passed beneath the arches of naval swords and out into the sunshine of Happy Ever After.

On their return from honeymoon, Kate and Mark had moved into a furnished ground-floor flat in a lovely Georgian terrace in the village of Alverstoke, one road back from the beach. Kate had spent many happy hours making it as cosy and homelike as she could with their few possessions whilst Mark, now a Sub-Lieutenant of sufficient standing for the single gold stripe around each cuff to have lost its obvious newness, went daily into *Dolphin* to complete his submariner's specialisation course.

Cass and Tom were in Alverstoke too. He was the only other married man on the course and he and Mark were drawn together, more by their newly-married status and the long-standing relationship between the girls than by any similarity of character or outlook. They started to adopt a more serious and responsible air than the rest of the course who were living in the Mess and whose main topics of conversation were still parties and girls and arrangements for drinking sessions in the pub in the evenings. The four of them often got together for informal suppers at Kate and Mark's flat or at Cass and Tom's cottage and sometimes met late on Sunday mornings in the Anglesea Arms for a pint. Tom and Cass often had other members of the course round at the cottage for curry suppers but when Kate tentatively suggested that they might do the same at the flat, Mark said that he had quite enough of them during the day, thanks very much and, although Cass and Tom seemed to have a great deal of fun, Kate was pleased that Mark seemed content with her company.

For Kate, being a naval wife was endowed with far more glamour and responsibility than being any other sort of wife except, perhaps, a doctor's or a vicar's. Her mother—and others—had warned her about the loneliness of her life to come, the difficulties involved in dealing with emergencies and moving households from one base to another, often all alone. She had felt pride that she would be 'doing her bit' and making sacrifices herself in order that Mark might do a demanding job involving national security whilst having the comfort and support of a home and family in the background to which he could return.

Even so, Kate was beginning to realise how very long a day could be. It was so difficult to spin things out. She had always been an early riser and found it impossible to laze on in bed in the mornings. She would deal with the solid fuel stove and take as long as she could over her bath and breakfast. If it was as late as half-past nine when she'd finished, she felt that she'd done well but there were still twelve long, empty hours to be filled before the bedtime routine could be embarked upon. She made so little work all on her own that after a while she tended to let things mount up so that the jobs seemed worth doing. Preparing food took minutes—it wasn't worth cooking elaborate meals just for herself—and took even less time to eat and she spent every mealtime with a book propped up in front of her plate. She had mentioned the possibility of getting a part-time job when the boat sailed but Mark had vetoed that at once: he wanted a wife at home when the boat was in, not off somewhere, working.

Surely she could cope for a few weeks alone? he had said. After all they'd see little enough of each other as it was. And Kate, anxious to pull her weight—and who, at that point, had never been alone in her life—agreed that she could manage perfectly well and shelved the idea of a job at once.

At the end of this course, Mark was appointed to one of the older conventional boats as Fifth Hand: Casing Officer and Correspondence Officer. It was a proud and a solemn moment—Real Life had started at last. Within a few weeks of Mark joining, the boat had sailed for Norway to 'show the flag'. Tom's career, thus far, had followed an identical pattern and when his boat had sailed for Middlesborough, Cass had hurried down to Devon to help her father, now retired, settle into his new home on the edge of Dartmoor.

Kate trudged on. Mark's letters arrived intermittently and she learned that it was difficult to get letters away from a submarine unless it was in port. Occasionally a helicopter would rendezvous with the boat to collect and deliver mail and then there would be a letter from him telling her how much he missed her and how he was looking forward to coming home. He wrote very little about his life on board but Kate didn't mind that. It was so lovely to hear from him, to see the envelope with the familiar handwriting lying on the hall floor. She would carry it with her when she went out, to read it over and over, sitting in one of the shelters on the front or in the little cafe in the village. It made her feel less lonely, as she watched other women gossiping with their friends over coffee, to bring out Mark's latest letter to read yet again.

Coming back to the present, Kate realised that she was hungry and, turning her back on the sea, she headed for the road which swept along the sea front and curved back into the village. As she turned into the Crescent a small car passed her and pulled up at her gate. Kate quickened her step. The driver of the car was getting out, opening the gate and going in. It could have been a visitor going to one of the upstairs flats or to the basement but Kate prayed that it was someone for her. To talk to someone other than at a shop counter or on a bus would be bliss. She hurried up the road. Hearing the gate clang open, the woman glanced back. She was short and slight, with sandy feathery hair and a dusting of freckles on her pale, small-featured face. She wore sailcloth trousers and a jersey and to Kate's nineteen years she looked very mature, twenty-eight at least.

'Hi!' She was turning back from the front door, smiling. 'Could you be Kate Webster? Do say you are. Oh, good!' as Kate nodded breathlessly. 'My mission is to track you down and take you home to tea. I've only just heard about you.' She made it sound as though Kate were a new species, just invented. 'I had a letter from Simon this morning saying that no one knew you were here. It was too bad of Mark to go off like that without introducing you to the Wardroom but he's a new boy so we'll have to forgive him. I'm Mary Armitage.'

Kate was aware that her hand was being pumped briskly up and down and that Mary's smile had a fierce frowning quality, rather quizzical and assessing. Behind this, however, she felt a real anxiety. Simon Armitage was Mark's First Lieutenant and, if Kate knew that submarine Captains were God to their junior officers, she also knew that First Lieutenants were the Archangel Gabriel. She prayed that Mary wouldn't want to come inside. Housekeeping had ceased to be important with Mark at sea and she could imagine Mary reporting the cobwebs, the pile of unironed clothes and the lack of cake or biscuits to Simon. Mary, however, was moving back down the path.

'Can I carry you off with me? I've got to pick my son up from school and I daren't be late. First term and all that. Then we can go home and have tea. I can drop you back later although, to be honest, you could walk it in ten minutes.'

Kate found herself in the car and being driven away, schoolwards.

'This is very kind of you,' she began, rather shyly. 'I've been looking forward to meeting some other wives. I wasn't sure if there were any living near the base.'

'You poor child. You'll soon learn the ropes.' Mary, sounding like a very senior Girl Guide, patted Kate's arm. 'There's lots of wives to meet, all like you with husbands away. No need to be lonely again.'

———

'But, honestly, Cass, that's what she said. "Learn the ropes!" I thought: it'll be tying knots next. It's the way they talk.'

Kate's relief at the sight of her old companion had been overwhelming. Cass and Tom were living in a tiny cottage near the church in the village and as soon as Cass had returned from Devon, Kate had rushed round to see her. Her new friends were very ready to integrate her into their society but Kate could already see a requirement to conform that was rather terrifying. The sight of Cass, piling a most unsuitable-looking tea—crisps, sausage rolls and shop-bought chocolate cake—on to the old deal table that was squashed into the corner of the sitting room, was immensely comforting. Kate thought of Mary Armitage's home-made scones and cakes and jams and experienced a sense of release from pressure. Being with Cass was like taking off a tight corset or kicking off a pinching shoe.

'I know exactly what you mean.' Cass crammed some crisps into her mouth. 'Tom says it's a wonder that some of them don't have stripes on their handbags. You know, the ones who start a conversation: "And what is your husband?" Not even "who" you notice. Oh, well. We'll probably be just like them when we're old.'

'I hope not!' Kate looked horrified. 'What a terrible thought. I just wish there were more wives of our age.'

'Tom and Mark have married very young. It's not at all usual. Anyway, much more fun like this. Just think of all those spare men! What bliss when Tom's at sea!' Cass disappeared into the tiny kitchen to make the tea.

'You've only been married five minutes.' Kate leaned against the door jamb to watch her.

'I know that, but you must remember the Navy rule. Be prepared!'

'That's the Boy Scouts.' Kate wandered back, sat down at the table and took a sausage roll.

'Oh, well. Same thing.'

'You're hopeless. And you've eaten all the crisps, you pig.'

'I haven't.' Cass put the teapot on the table. 'Here they are. Listen. It's Happy Hour at *Dolphin* tonight. Why don't we go along?'

'What? Without the boys?'

'Can't go with them, can we, lovey? They're hundreds of miles away.'

'But we can't just go on our own.'

''Course we can. Lots of wives were there on their own when we used to go with the boys. Why not? All their friends are there. That's one of the good things about having *Dolphin* just down the road. It's somewhere to go when the boys are at sea. Like the curry lunches they have on Sunday after church. Everyone understands if you turn up on your own. It's what it's all about. Like having a big family round you. I'm not going to start behaving like a nun just because Tom's at sea.'

'But will there be anyone we know now that the specialisation course is over? All the boys on the course have joined boats and none of them were married. Everyone will be terrifyingly senior.' Kate was very sure that Mark would be deeply disapproving.

'George Lampeter will be there for one. I saw him in the village. His boat is in for a few weeks, apparently. He told me that it would be fine. He'll be coming for us later to take us in.'

'Oh, well.' Kate hesitated. George had been at BRNC with Tom and Mark and they were all good friends. Surely Mark wouldn't object? The evenings were so long and empty and it would be rather fun.

'Well?' Cass raised her eyebrows. 'Squared it, have you?'

'Squared what?'

'That terrible conscience of yours. It must be hell having to worry all the time. Thank God I haven't got one!'

MARY ARMITAGE INSISTED THAT Kate come with her to meet the boat when, finally, it docked at *Dolphin*. By this time, Kate had discovered the hard way that an ETA was truly only an estimated time of arrival and not by any means something to be relied on. Much to her surprise and delight, she had learned that the submarine was due back on Mark's birthday and had decided that she would make his homecoming very special indeed. On the day before he was due home, she walked into the village with the birthday supper shopping list: steak, mushrooms and a bottle of Mark's favourite wine. She went into the butcher's shop.

'I'd like some fillet steak, please. Enough for two.'

'Well, you're going it, aren't you?' The butcher beamed at her, used to her orders for half a pound of mince, one lamb chop or a few slices of ham. He was a fatherly soul and always felt sorry for these young naval wives, miles from their homes and families, struggling to manage alone. He leaned across the counter, resting his weight on hands almost as red and raw as the meat in his window. 'Celebrating, are you? Old man coming home?'

'Yes. Tomorrow.' She beamed back.

'Been away long?' He flopped the steak down, cut two thick slices and threw them on the weighing machine.

'Two months.' She tried, unsuccessfully, to hide her pride in managing for such a long time alone.

He winked at her as he passed her the parcel and her change. 'Don't go overcooking it,' he said.

Back home, Kate put the food away and cleaned the flat thoroughly. She put clean linen on the bed and laid the fire in the grate in the sitting room. Like Cass, she only had this one big, elegant room but at least her kitchen was big enough to eat in. For this occasion, however, Kate polished the big mahogany table in the sitting room and went to find her candlesticks. When everything was ready, she bathed and washed her hair and then wandered from room to room wondering if she'd forgotten anything.

She went to bed early to lay awake almost sick with excitement. She felt terribly shy at the thought of seeing Mark again. It was as if he had become a stranger to her and she could hardly bring his face to mind. She remembered their first meeting in the bar at the Royal Castle in Dartmouth when he and Tom had arrived to escort them up to the College for the Ball. They had looked so formal and glamorous in their Mess Dress uniforms. Mark had gone to get drinks and Tom and Cass had chattered away like old friends. Kate thought that Mark, with his tall, sleek, dark good looks, was much more dashing than Tom who was short and solid and whose brown hair was thick and tended to curl. Mark was much the quieter and more serious of the two and Kate felt rather flattered that he should find her interesting. Having been through three years of military training, these young men seemed years older than their contemporaries in civilian life. Her subsequent meetings with them underlined this impression although never in the year before their marriage did Kate spend enough time with Mark to enable her to discover what lay beneath the veneer that the Navy had given him. She and Cass had been to balls and parties, all imbued with an aura of glamour and a sense of sacrifice and even danger. They were so proud to accompany these young men who were prepared to give their lives for their country.

Kate remembered, too, their first clumsy attempts at lovemaking. Mark had once bragged about his various sexual exploits in Sweden which hadn't helped, serving only to make Kate feel more shy, afraid that unfavourable comparisons were being made. It was only afterwards that she realised that it couldn't have been of much benefit to Mark either since he seemed as inept and nervous as she was. She tried now, staring into the dark, to imagine him beside her but it was quite impossible. It would be like starting all over again from the beginning. A guest at the wedding had said that all the homecomings would be like lots of honeymoons which, at the time, had sounded exciting. Now it seemed merely terrifying.

She slept fitfully, waking suddenly at intervals having dreamt that she'd overslept. Finally, wrapping herself in her dressing gown, she went into the kitchen to make a cup of tea and to struggle with the solid fuel stove. It was just six o'clock.

By eight o'clock, she had prepared all the vegetables, made a pudding and had even set the table for dinner lest there should be no time later on. She dressed carefully and forced herself to eat some toast while she wondered how early she could telephone the base. Mark had told her that although the date of the submarine's return was known, no one would know the time that it would actually arrive until the last moment. The form was, he explained, to telephone the hall porter in *Dolphin*, tell him who she was and give him the name of Mark's submarine. He would give her the latest ETA to which she must add an hour to allow Mark to get away from the boat and reach home. He had not suggested that she should come to meet him.

By nine o'clock she could contain her impatience no longer. She pulled on her old duffel coat and walked out to the telephone box at the end of the road. The hall porter's voice was brisk and efficient as he took her call.

'That's right, ma'am,' he said. 'She's due back any time, isn't she? Hold on a moment.' She could hear the rustle of papers. 'Here we are. Oh, dear.' His tone changed to one of regret. 'I'm sorry, her programme's been changed and she's spending forty-eight hours in Middlesborough on the way down. She won't be in for another two days.'

Kate tried to grapple with this totally unforeseen situation.

'Hello? Are you there?' The hall porter sounded concerned. 'It's very disappointing but you'll get used to it, ma'am. Didn't your husband warn you that they rarely keep to their first ETA?'

'No. No, he didn't mention it.' She barely recognised her own voice. 'Thank you so much. I'll telephone on Thursday.'

She went back home, barely aware of her surroundings. This moment had been the focal point of her existence for the last few weeks and the shock of the disappointment had the power to make her feel as though she had stepped into thin air, all her sense of purpose gone. In the hall she stood quite still, listening to the silence.

How could she possibly exist through another two days? And why did two days seem so much longer and more impossible to survive than the two months she had already lived through? She went into the sitting room and put away the table settings and then changed out of her smart clothes, pulling on an old tweed skirt and a Guernsey. Finally, letting herself out of the flat, she walked slowly towards the sea.

'YOU'LL GET USED TO it,' said Mary nearly a week later when, after more delays and disappointments, they drove along the sea wall and up to *Dolphin*'s main gate. 'I'm kicking myself for not warning you. Never mind.'

The sentry popped out of his little box and Mary showed him her pass. The car also had a pass which was stuck permanently on to the windscreen. The young sailor bent to peer in at Kate.

'New wife,' said Mary briskly, with her fierce frowning smile. 'Hasn't had time to get organised yet. I'll look after her.'

The sentry nodded, saluted and swung up the barrier.

'I hope Mark won't mind my coming.' Kate felt nervous.

'Mind? Why on earth should he mind?' Mary drove past the museum and the little church and Kate looked with interest at the midget submarine displayed opposite the museum, wondering, as usual, how anyone had dared to go to sea in it. 'It's very good for wives to meet the boat. Good for morale. Mark will soon get the hang of things. Very young officers are often afraid of stepping out of line.' She parked the car neatly in the square outside the wardroom windows.

Crossing over tramlines and avoiding cranes, they made their way to the edge of the dock where, below them, the submarines lay at their trots, rocking gently on the water in the dusk. A little group, including the Captain of the submarine flotilla and his senior officers, had already assembled. Mary approached them with confidence and Kate found herself shaking hands with Captain SM who seemed delighted that she'd turned out. Kate heaved a sigh of relief. If someone of such unbelievable eminence was pleased at her presence, who was Mark to take exception to it? She was aware of the tension as people glanced at their watches, talking in quiet voices as the water lapped gently below them and the dusk deepened.

'Here she comes!' It was a sort of exultant, shouted whisper.

The cigar-shaped hull moved silently, dark against the oily, glinting sea. She turned slowly in from the main channel. The casing party, their white jerseys gleaming in the fading light, moved to and fro, sure-footed. Up in the fin, on the bridge, stood the Captain and his First Lieutenant who passed instructions to the engine room and the casing party.

Slowly, surely, she slid alongside, some of the casing party jumping ashore to fasten the mooring lines. The hum of the engine was suddenly quieted and Kate realised that she'd been holding her breath, struck by the menacing quality of the submarine as it had slipped so quietly through the water. For the first time she really thought about what it must be like to be hundreds of feet beneath the sea, totally cut off, and of the close-knit unit of men dedicated to this way of life, and she felt a great surge of pride that Mark was amongst those to come ashore and that she was here to meet him. Presently, the Captain appeared at the gangplank and came ashore to shake hands with the senior officers. He acknowledged his wife with a smile and rather formal kiss on the cheek and Kate realised that restraint was the form here and determined not to display her emotions when Mark should appear. When this finally happened he affected not to see her and Mary was obliged to draw her forward, explaining that she had brought her along. Kate felt that she might suffocate with shame and disappointment and knew that she had been right to assume that Mark would not want her to meet him.

As soon as Mary turned away, he looked at her, his face unreadable in the dark.

'So how are we getting home?'

'I suppose with Mary and Simon.' She felt that she had managed somehow to ruin everything. But how?

'That will be fun!'

His tone was heavily sarcastic and she turned away to gaze across the water to the lights of Portsmouth in an effort to hide the trembling of her lips.

Two

Cass curled up in the corner of the sofa, watching her father blowing life into the fire with an ancient pair of bellows, and felt enormous relief that he looked so well and was evidently settling happily into his new home. It was a rather tiresome journey from Hampshire to Devon by train and she didn't get down as often as she would have liked.

'This is fun, my darling. Quite like old times. When's that husband of yours going to get a submarine that runs out of Devonport? Then you could come and see your old pa occasionally.'

General Mackworth piled some logs on to the fire in the wide stone fireplace and sank back into his comfortable old armchair. His study was a charming room full of the treasured possessions that had been accumulated throughout his military career. Firelight gleamed on well-polished wood and the leather backs of much-read books and sparkled on cut glass and porcelain. Heavy brocade curtains shut out the damp February evening. In this room Cass felt a child again and she sighed with pleasure.

'It would be lovely, Daddy, wouldn't it?' She sat, smiling at her father, wondering for the thousandth time why her mother had run away from him. She adored her tall, fair, handsome father who was such fun to be with and who was so popular with the ladies. Perhaps too popular? It might be rather horrid to be married to someone who stole all the limelight, thought Cass, and felt a tiny twinge of guilt. She tended to do the same herself. It was such tremendous fun and she so enjoyed the admiring glances, the attention, the flirtations. She felt quite sure that Tom didn't mind a bit, in fact it boosted his ego, which was why he treated her conquests as huge jokes.

'So how do you like being a naval wife? Bit lonely at times?' The General leaned forward to knock out his pipe against the stone. He started to pack the bowl with aromatic weed, his penetrating dark blue eyes fixed on his daughter.

'Bound to be.' Cass shrugged it off. 'But when the boat goes away you've got all the other wives who are on their own too. It's not so bad, really, and lots of fun when it's in. Parties and ladies' nights— you know the sort of thing. I'm getting used to it.' She gave him a grin. 'After all, the men in my life have always gone away and left me! And how are you enjoying village life? Are you happy with your cottage?'

'Love it. Got lots of space, plenty of room for all my things. And there's a wonderful woman comes in to look after me.'

Cass arched her brows. 'That didn't take you long.'

'Nothing like that. Nice little woman, lives by the church. Mrs Hampton. Her husband works up at the big house. Her cooking has to be tasted to be believed. In fact, we've got one of her casseroles for supper. When she heard you were coming she said that you must have something sensible to eat. Her husband is helping me to sort the garden out. I feel I've really landed on my feet.'

'That's wonderful, Daddy. Perhaps I'll meet them while I'm here. Can't stay too long, though. Tom's back next week.'

'Well, I must make the most of you. And how's that dear Kate?'

'A great comfort, as always. I'm terribly jealous of her at the moment.'

'Why's that?'

'She's pregnant. Oh, Daddy, I would so love a baby.'

'Natural feeling, I should have thought. Can't see Tom objecting to that. What does he say about this business in Vietnam?'

'What business?'

'Never mind. Let's have a drink before supper.'

Later that evening, before she climbed into bed, Cass opened the bedroom window and leaned out, snuffing up the cool damp air. The night was misty and quiet and she could hear an owl up in the woods behind the Manor. Her window at the back of the cottage looked out over the garden to farmland beyond but little was visible except the smoky swirling mist.

She shivered a little, hugging her dressing gown round her, and remembered how surprisingly envious she had been when Kate had told her that she was pregnant. It had been tacitly agreed that neither of them was going in for motherhood for a while: they were still very young and the boys were feeling the way in their careers. Now she felt in some obscure way that Kate had stolen a march on her. After all, it had always been Cass who had led and Kate who had followed—whether it had been in terms of fashion, pop stars or even husbands.

To Cass, being a naval wife meant a life of change, variety and freedom. Because one's husband was away didn't mean that one shut oneself off from pleasure. It had never occurred to Cass that her husband would be the alpha and omega of her existence—she wouldn't have wanted it. Her image of herself was too clearly defined, too complete, to imagine it as a half or a part of another person. She wanted a husband who would provide the framework, the protection, from which she would operate and who, in return, would receive certain rights and privileges, and she was delighted to be a part of a life which offered so many opportunities. She realised that Kate was unlikely to avail herself of these opportunities and that to start a family was probably the most sensible thing she could do. At the very least children would keep her busy and fill the long days when Mark was at sea. For Cass herself, a family was not quite such a priority: nevertheless she was filled now with an inexplicable determination to follow Kate's example.

Tom was likely to prove the stumbling block. He had already showed surprise at Kate's news and had reiterated his opinion that he felt that it was silly to tie oneself down so early on. Since this had been Cass's view too, she had been obliged to agree with him. Now her mind worked busily on how she could persuade him to change his ideas. Tom was no less jolly and fun-loving as a married man than he had been as a Midshipman. He liked to have his friends around him and had a very definite eye for a pretty face. This pleased Cass. She was far too secure in her own beauty and popularity to look upon other women as threats. Rather she regarded them as fellow adventurers in pursuit of a common prey—man! She had also grasped the principle that, if she planned to break the rules, it would be to her advantage if Tom were breaking them likewise. No recriminations or reproaches if anything came to light: both of them in the same boat was how she wanted it to be. How, though, to present the idea of a baby in a new and interesting light?

The rabbit's scream as the owl dropped upon it out of the dark broke the train of her thoughts. Turning her back on the night, she dropped her dressing gown on to the floor and climbed into bed.

'COME ON!' MARK CAUGHT Kate by the arm and ran her across the road. 'I can see the top of it over the hedge.'

'I can't go any faster.' Kate stumbled beside him, gasping. 'Got stitch.'

'One last sprint.' He put his arm around her to hurry her along. Their arrival at the bus stop coincided with that of the bus and Kate climbed aboard and collapsed thankfully on to a seat. Her pregnancy, still in its early stages, was going well but this hadn't been one of her best days. Gradually she began to regain her breath although the pain in her side showed no sign of subsiding.

'Well done!' Mark swung into the seat beside her. 'I do hate to miss the start of a film.' Kate nodded, too breathless to speak, and they remained in silence for the short journey until the bus stopped opposite the cinema in Gosport.

Throughout the film, a war epic, Kate was aware of the pain in her side. She couldn't concentrate on the screen where khaki-clothed men shouted and fell, shot and were shot at whilst tanks and lorries rumbled and throbbed and guns roared and smoked. She dwelt on the thought of the coming baby; she could still scarcely believe in the miracle of its being. After all, there was no evidence of it yet although, out of sheer pride and excitement, Kate had taken to wearing a loose pinafore and sticking her stomach out.

She shifted a little in her seat to ease the discomfort and looked at Mark who was absorbed in the film. Expressions passed over his face reflecting emotions that were being acted out before him: his eyebrows lifted, his lips twitched into a smile, a grimace, his shoulders lifted in a shrug. He was absolutely involved although remaining unaffected by scenes of the most horrific violence. 'Man was made for war,' he was fond of quoting, 'woman for the recreation of the warrior.' She tried to relate the two sides of him that were beginning to emerge—the vulnerable, unconfident man and the insensitive and sometimes cruel man—struggling with the dichotomy of a character that reacted strongly against criticism of himself whilst taking pleasure in undermining other people. She realised that she was staring at his unsuspecting face in an attempt to read something of his character from it and looked away, feeling that in some unfair way she had been spying on him.

She had been surprised at Mark's willingness to embark upon parenthood, having prepared herself to meet opposition and even flat refusal. She had felt that it was only fair to point out that it might prevent them from doing certain things together but he had agreed that, since he would be at sea for most of the next twelve years, it was really quite sensible to start a family. In the first place it would keep Kate from loneliness and secondly they would still be young enough to enjoy life when the children were grown up and off their hands. Kate was delighted at his response and even more delighted to find herself pregnant at the first possible opportunity. So was Mark. It seemed that his virility was well and truly established and his peers were impressed and even envious and Kate was made much of when he took her into *Dolphin*. If she had hoped for any physical consideration, however, she was to be disappointed. He had pointed out that pregnancy was not a cause for special pleading: women everywhere were doing it and he even told her of peasant women who had their babies in a hedgerow and went back to work in the field the same afternoon. Kate retorted that she wasn't a peasant woman but when Mark began to look irritated she had decided that it was best to let the matter drop.

When the programme finally ended, Kate made her way to the ladies' cloakroom. She dragged down her knickers and experienced a moment of shock followed by panic. Holding her breath, she stared at the blood. Without waiting to pee, she dragged them up again and hurried out, into the crowded foyer.

'Mark.' She almost fell against him as she clutched his arm. 'I'm bleeding! I'm going to lose the baby!'

'For goodness' sake!' He glanced about him involuntarily to see if anyone had heard. 'Don't make a scene. Come outside.'

They went down the steps, Kate taking little choking breaths. He led her to the bus shelter and pushed her down on the bench.

'What shall I do?' she asked, staring up at him and trying to control her panic.

'The bus goes right past the surgery.' He made an effort to control his instinctive reaction of distaste at any real human emotion. 'We'd better go in and see the doctor. Thank goodness we came to the early performance. Do try to pull yourself together.'

Kate huddled in her corner and tears slid down her cheeks. Horrified by this lack of restraint, Mark lit a cigarette and moved away to stand at the kerb feeling resentful that she was making him an object of interest. Passers-by stared curiously at them. Kate was past caring. All that mattered to her was that she might lose her precious baby. She sat shivering in the cold wind, her leg and stomach muscles clenched as though she would hold the baby in by force.

When they arrived at the surgery, she was taken straight in and examined by her doctor. Because of her stress and fear, she found the examination even more painful than usual but he was fairly quick and when he had finished with her he turned away to peel off his rubber gloves, motioning her to get dressed.

'Will I lose the baby?' She slid off the couch and put her clothes straight.

'No, I don't think so.' He was sitting at his desk, writing on a pre-
scription pad, and she wondered what he would do if she flung her
arms around his neck and kissed his balding head in gratitude and relief.

'These tablets should do the trick. But you must go to bed and stay
there. I'll come in to see you tomorrow. You say that you were running for a bus? Mmmm. Haven't been making love too fiercely, have
you? Doesn't help at this stage, you know.'

Kate was silent. Mark had certainly been very passionate on his return from sea. The doctor watched her for a moment, looking at her
over the top of his half-moon spectacles.

'Well, none of that for a bit now, I'm afraid. I shall send your husband down to the late-night chemist to get this made up and then you
must take a taxi home and go straight to bed. I'll be round in the
morning.'

At last, having gulped down one of the precious tablets, Kate was
able to slide between the sheets. Mark stood at the bottom of the bed,
his face worried. She smiled at him.

'Don't worry. I'm fine now and so is the baby, thank God. Aren't
we lucky?'

'Yes, of course.' He smiled a little but the anxious look quickly returned. 'It's not that. I'm just wondering how I shall manage with you
in bed.'

Kate looked surprised. 'It won't be too bad, surely? It's not as if
you've got to go to sea or anything. You've got another week's leave.
I should be OK by then. We'll manage.' She smiled at him encourag-
ingly.

'Yes.' He didn't return her smile. 'Do you want anything to eat?'

'No. Don't bother. But I should love a cup of tea.'

She lay listening to him moving about in the kitchen and, after a
while, began to relax as the realisation that the baby was safe took
hold. Presently she dozed and was woken by the sound of the front
door closing.

'Mark?' she called. 'Is that you?'

'Don't worry.' He put his head round the door. 'Only me. You nodded off so I thought I'd do the tea when you woke up. It probably did you good to sleep.'

He was looking much more cheerful and Kate felt relieved.

'Where did you go? Did you run out of ciggies?'

'No. I went and phoned Mother. Father is driving her down tomorrow to look after you.'

'*What?*'

'You know that I'm no good at this sort of thing. I didn't marry you to be a nursemaid,' he said, reacting instantly and defensively to her exclamation of dismay. 'Mother can look after you properly. I can't cook or do anything.'

You could learn! thought Kate, resentfully. I had to.

'Well, you'll have to clean up a bit.' Disappointment, that at the arrival of their first real domestic problem he had gone running to his mother rather than giving the two of them the chance to attempt to deal with it together, made her sharper than usual. 'The bathroom's terrible and you'll have to make up the spare bed.'

'Whatever for?' Mark stared at her in surprise. 'That's why Mother's coming.'

Kate hauled herself up in horror.

'You can't let her see the place like this. Please. She'll think I'm a slut.'

'Who cares?' He laughed, comfortably. 'She'd have a fit if she thought I was dashing round like a maniac. She'll be perfectly happy to take charge. I'll go and make that tea.' Delighted to have shed the domestic difficulties, he went whistling down the passage and Kate felt a wave of mortification engulf her.

She felt the helplessness of her situation and knew in a brief moment of enlightenment that Mark would never put himself out just to make her feel happier—not even at a time like this. She began to weep hurt and frustrated tears but, feeling an echo of that earlier pain, stopped abruptly, frightened.

I simply must relax, she thought. The baby's safe. I mustn't put him at risk again. She began to take deep breaths, waiting for the pain to subside. Presently she slept.

'Tom?'

'Mmmm?' He continued to read *The Sunday Times*.

'Did I tell you that Kate nearly lost the baby?'

The conversation was taking place late on a Sunday morning in early-March in Cass and Tom's bedroom. The rumpled bed was littered with newspapers and empty mugs and crumby plates stood on the bedside tables and the floor.

'No!' Tom came right out of the paper, looking shocked. 'Is she OK? How did she manage that?'

'She was running for a bus.'

'Whatever for?'

'They were going to the cinema. I expect that Mark was afraid he was going to miss the cartoons.'

'Oh, honestly, darling.' Tom chuckled in spite of himself.

'Perfectly true. Poor old Kate was almost deranged. It was while I was down in Devon for a few days and she told me all about it when I got back. The steam was still coming out of her ears. She had to stay in bed and Mark persuaded his parents to come and look after her. She was furious.'

'Quite sensible, surely? Would she have been OK on her own?'

'She wouldn't have been on her own. Mark was on leave. But he couldn't cope with cooking a few meals and making the odd cup of coffee so he sent for Mummy! Kate said that the flat was in a terrible mess and Mark refused to do any cleaning up or make up a bed for them or anything. Kate was totally humiliated. Said that the old bat went round sniffing and tutting about the cobwebs and the ring round the bath and things, while Mark stood looking pathetic and making faces behind her back. Poor old Kate. She was extraordinarily cross, for Kate.'

'But she's all right now? What about the sprog?'

'Both perfectly all right now. Tom?' she added, as he showed signs of returning to his newspaper.

'Mmm? Any chance of any more coffee, darling?'

'Oh, all right.' Cass, clad only in one of Tom's shirts, slid her long legs out of bed, picked up the mugs and padded to the kitchen.

Tom stretched and reached for a cigarette. This was much better than being cramped into a little bunk, snatching four hours' sleep between watches. There was no doubt that married life had a lot going for it. And Cass was wonderful! Tremendous fun to have around, no nagging and whingeing about the separations, and as for sex . . . Tom inhaled deeply and grinned to himself. All his oppos were green with envy. A few of them were sniffing round though. Tom frowned a little. He was quite sure that though Cass loved to flirt it amounted to nothing more than that. Nevertheless . . . He flicked some ash in the direction of an overflowing ashtray. He remembered her dancing with Tony Whelan at a recent party and knew that he may not be able to trust the bastards while he was at sea. He drew in another lungful of smoke and thought about Mark bragging about his incipient fatherhood. Good enough chap, bit serious and anti-social for Tom's liking but OK in his way. Perhaps, after all, he'd been a bit too quick to pooh-pooh the idea of starting a family. It would certainly tie Cass by the heels and it might be fun to be a father . . .

When Cass returned, he studied her appreciatively. The long blonde hair fell about her shoulders and his shirt hung open allowing glimpses of her superb breasts. As she stood his mug of coffee on the bedside table, he reached out for her, sliding his hand up her long, smooth flank.

'Watch out,' she giggled. 'Mind the coffee!'

She collapsed on top of him, only just managing to stand her mug in a safe place first. 'Tom?' Her mouth was against his.

'Mmmm?' His hands were exploring the now familiar and excitingly delicious curves and he rolled so that she lay beneath him.

'I've been thinking. I know what we said about not having a family yet but don't you think that it would be nice to have a baby, darling?' She ran her hands down his back and, drawing up her knees, wrapped her legs around him. 'It would be such fun.'

'A baby? Mmmm.' (Mustn't sound too keen. She might suspect

something.) 'But I thought we agreed . . . Oh, Cass. Oh, that's nice.'

'Mmmm, isn't it?' (If I can turn him on enough he'll agree to any-thing and it'll be too late afterwards.) 'Yes, a dear little baby. Oh, do let's, darling.'

'A baby . . . Oh, darling. Well, if it's what you really want . . . Christ Cass! Don't stop!'

'Oh, it is, Tom. Is that nice . . . ?'

'Oh, yes. Yes, it is. If you like then. Why not? Oh, Cass . . . '

'MARY HAS SUGGESTED THAT I come up to Newcastle when the boat goes up. You know that she's driving up? Her parents live out near the moors, Hexham or somewhere. It's quite a good idea, isn't it?'

'Mmmm?'

The conversation was taking place in Kate and Mark's bedroom on a Sunday morning in June. Kate had made early-morning tea and brought it back to bed for them. A little later she had satisfied, as best she could with the present restrictions, Mark's passion. As soon as it was over, he had immersed himself in the newspaper. Kate sighed inwardly. She knew now that Mark's 'Mmm's' were time-buyers but she didn't want to upset him by snapping 'You heard!' The idea of a trip to Newcastle after months of being alone was too thrilling for words.

Reluctantly he lowered the newspaper and looked at her.

'I said,' she felt nervous now and it sounded ridiculous repeating it all, 'Mary Armitage is driving up to Newcastle when the boat goes up for your visit and she's asked me if I'd like to go with her. What do you think?'

'I think it's terribly silly.' Mark's tone was dismissive.

'But why?'

Mark gave a sigh which prayed for patience and shook his paper. 'What are you going to do in Newcastle all by yourself for a week—six months pregnant at that? It's different for Mary. She's got her family. And I shall be too busy to spend any time with you, I promise you. It's not some great party, you know. A great deal of work goes into these "Show the Flag" visits.'

'I know that.' Kate was disappointed but resigned. 'I wouldn't be in your way. Mary has asked us to stay with her family so I'd have company in the day and you could go in and out with Simon.'

'Oh, thanks very much!' Mark's irritation rapidly became annoyance.

'Well, what's wrong with that?' Kate pushed aside the bedclothes and got out of bed. She felt that she could argue her case better on her feet.

'If you think I'm staying with the First Lieutenant and sucking up to his family you've got another think coming. I've got some pride, you know.'

'But they've asked everyone to stay,' explained Kate. 'Apparently they've got this huge house and . . . '

'Forget it! Andy and Paul can stay if they like. They're not married so it's different.'

'Why is it different?' she asked, trying to understand him.

'It just is. And, anyway, it's crazy rushing around the countryside in your condition. I thought you said the doctor told you that you had to take care. Especially now he thinks it's twins.'

'Well, he did. But I'm not planning to walk to Newcastle,' cried Kate in exasperation.

'And how will you get back?' Mark raised his brows and smiled in an irritatingly superior manner. 'The boat's going on to Rosyth. You know that, don't you? From what I've gathered, Mary's staying up north until the boat's due back in Gosport. Are you sure that they'll want you for three weeks?'

'Well, she didn't actually say how long . . . '

'Quite. It's my guess that she wants company on the way up and a nursemaid for those sprogs of hers. Once there, you'll be on your own and then you'll have to fight your way back on a train. She probably can't find anyone else to go with her. I can't see the Captain's wife wanting to slum it in Newcastle.'

'No,' said Kate reluctantly. 'Angela's not going. She's got something on, apparently.'

'I bet she has.' Mark gave a snort. 'She's no fool. She knows what these trips are like.'

'Mary made it sound like fun,' said Kate wistfully. 'She said there were parties and things . . . '

''Course she did! She needs your help. It's a long trip up. Once you're there you'll be cast off like an old boot. Take my word for it.'

'Well, it'll be a bit embarrassing now.' But Kate knew that she'd lost the battle. 'I more or less said that I'd go.'

'Well, tell her you've got to go home. Got to see your mother or something,' said Mark impatiently, preparing to return to his newspaper.

'But it's almost as far to St Just as it is to Newcastle and I'd have to fight my way on a train then.'

'But you won't actually go, will you?' Mark's exaggeratedly patient tone made him sound like a schoolmaster trying to instil information into the head of a particularly dim pupil. 'You'll just tell Mary that you're going. You can still stay on here. We're only away for three weeks. Now,' he shook his newspaper open, indicating that the conversation was closed, 'are we having any breakfast this morning or aren't we?'

Three

Cass pottered in her little cottage feeling relieved that Tom had gone back to sea. It was really so much easier just to have herself to worry about now that her pregnancy was advancing. Less than three months to go now and love-making was a bit uncomfortable and she didn't feel up to washing and ironing Tom's voluminous white cotton naval shirts or worrying about organising evening meals. Much nicer to laze about, eating and sleeping when she felt like it.

She poured herself a glass of milk and stretched herself out on the sofa. Tom had been thrilled about the baby. He'd fussed over her like an old mother hen: she mustn't do this and she mustn't do that and she must put her feet up after supper while he brought her a cup of coffee. She knew how lucky she was. She took a sip of milk and grimaced to herself when she thought of poor old Kate stuck with her in-laws at that flat. Mark's boat had just sailed for Nova Scotia and he had arranged for his parents to come and stay with Kate who had about a fortnight to go now before the babies were due.

'The doctor says it's almost certain to be twins,' Kate had said, 'but Mark won't let me buy two of everything just in case it isn't. His parents are coming to stay for the last few weeks so that, if it is two babies, they can rush off and duplicate everything while I'm still in the nursing home.'

Cass sipped some more milk and shook her head. She'd like to have seen Tom wishing his father on her, twins or no twins. The trouble with poor old Kate was that she was too busy trying to please everyone around her. Having that grumpy old man with her was enough to make her miscarry and Cass had told her so. Not to mention that fussy old wife of his. It was no wonder that, with parents like that, Mark was such a wet. Cass had nearly said that, too, but had restrained herself in time. She sometimes felt guilty that it was she who had introduced them. She was beginning to feel that she didn't like Mark and it wasn't just because he didn't flirt with her and flatter her like all the others. At the start she had put it down to the fact that he was simply one of those quiet clever types but she had come to see that this was not the case. He had got lower marks than Tom at BRNC and on the Fourth Year Courses and there was nothing highbrow about his conversation—when he took enough interest to make any.

Cass tried to analyse her feelings about him. There was no life in him, she decided, nothing to him and yet one never felt at ease with him. He wasn't a jovial, friendly man like Tom—who was never happier than when he was one of a crowd—nor was he a devoted family man. He never did anything in the flat to make it more comfortable for Kate or gave the impression of being a companionable husband. He was often quite rude to her in public in a nasty sarcastic sort of way which Kate always tried to turn off with a laugh but which made Cass seethe.

She finished her milk and sighed. Perhaps fatherhood would change him. Meanwhile it would be a kindness if she were to go round to see Kate and help to lighten the load with the in-laws. She picked up a magazine. But not today. They would barely have arrived and, after all, they would be there for another two weeks at least. Cass stretched herself comfortably. No, not today.

THE TWINS ARRIVED TWO weeks early and the Websters had only been in the flat for forty-eight hours when Kate went into labour. It had been a hot September day and they had taken a trip to Bournemouth. When Kate woke in the night with backache, she had assumed that it was due to walking up and down the promenade, queuing endlessly for lunch and the long uncomfortable car journey. After a while, she got up and wandered into the stuffy sitting room. It was so hot. She had tried to persuade Mark that it would be sensible to move now that there were babies on the way. The flat, charming in summer, was hard work during the winter. Rising damp, an old-fashioned and temperamental solid fuel stove, nowhere to dry clothes; all these things had made Kate's life difficult during the last winter.

She was thankful that her pregnancy had happened through the summer so that she hadn't had to hump coal and ashes. Mark managed to avoid all household tasks.

'You have to do it whilst I'm away,' was his argument. 'You may as well get used to it. I don't ask you to come and do my work on the boat.' This was undeniable. As to moving, his answer was simple. 'I'll be leaving the boat some time next year. I shall have done two years by then. I might get a boat anywhere: Devonport, Faslane, anywhere. No point in moving twice.'

Kate sat down heavily on the sofa in the dark, put her head back on the cushions and closed her eyes. Goodness, how her back did ache! Pregnancy might have been such fun if there had been someone around to share her excitement, cosset her and cater to her occasional cravings. For a brief disloyal moment she envied the few civilian wives she'd met at the clinic, whose husbands came home every evening and who—apparently—were taking such an interest in the whole procedure. Presently she felt water trickling between her thighs. Her eyes flew open. She raised her head, stared into the growing light of early morning and clenched her stomach muscles. The water trickled on.

'Hell's teeth!' she said softly.

CASS, DRESSED IN A flowery cotton smock and wearing a floppy linen hat on her fair head, strolled along the esplanade at Stoke's Bay watching the holiday makers. She especially watched the very young children, enjoying their absorbed concentration on their games and the way they moved about.

They're like little clockwork toys, she thought. What fun it will be to have one of my own! I'm glad that Kate and I are having them at the same time. If we have girls they can go to St Audrey's together.

She smiled to herself at the thought and then paused. Did she recognise the girl sitting on a huge striped towel rubbing sun lotion into her thin brown arms? Surely it was the one who had married Mark Mainwaring. Cass and Tom had been invited to the wedding and George Lampeter had been best man. Cass racked her brains for a moment before she remembered that the girl's name was Felicity. She also remembered that she had appeared to be totally lacking in humour and charm and if she had been like that on her wedding day she was unlikely to prove a congenial companion. Nevertheless, she was now a naval wife and if Mark had gone to sea his wife might be lonely. Cass made her way down the steps and across the shingly sand.

'Hi!' she said. 'Felicity, isn't it? I'm Cass Wivenhoe. We met at your wedding. Not that I'd expect you to remember. Tom's a very good friend of your Mark. How is he? I didn't realise that you were here already.'

Felicity Mainwaring, shielding her eyes from the sun, gazed up at Cass.

'Yes, I remember.' She recalled, amongst other things, that Mark and George Lampeter had behaved in a very silly manner with Cass. They'd kissed her and flattered her outrageously and left Felicity quite out in the cold. Not what a bride expects at her own wedding. 'I remember,' she repeated, rather flatly, surveying Cass's bump. 'How are you?' She did not invite Cass to share her towel.

Cass flopped down anyway, obliging Felicity to draw back her thin legs.

'I'm fine. Gosh, it's hot, isn't it?' She pulled off her linen hat and fanned herself with it. 'Poor old Kate must be feeling it. She's much bigger than I am. Any day now I should think. Do you remember Kate? She's married to another Mark and she came with us. Mark Webster. He's another friend of your Mark.' She giggled. 'We'll have to call them Mark I and Mark II. Where are you living?'

'We've managed to get a naval hiring in Privett Road. Quite nice, actually. A thirties semi with a good garden.'

'Oh, I know. What they call in Alverstoke "one of a pair." I shall come and visit. Is Mark at sea?'

'Yes,' said Felicity, quickly. 'He sailed yesterday.'

'Well, don't be lonely. I'm in the village. Want to come back and have some lunch?'

'No,' said Felicity, after a tiny pause. 'No thanks. Not today. I've brought lunch with me and I want to make the most of the sun.' Her eyes ranged over Cass's pale, pearly flesh. 'Must be infuriating not to be able to sunbathe.' She glanced complacently at her own tanned limbs.

'Not a bit,' said Cass cheerfully, getting to her feet. 'Nanny brought me up to think that it was terribly common. Don't want to end up looking like an old leather saddle. Pale and interesting—that's me! Really pulls the chaps. See you around. 'Bye.'

She pulled on her hat, waggled her fingers and made her way back across the beach. Felicity watched her proud, graceful progress, noticed the covert admiring glances—despite the lump—and gnashed her teeth. She thought of all the things that she might have said and dug her fingers into the sand with frustration.

Cass went on her way smiling serenely.

'FEELING TERRIBLE?' THE LARGE dark girl paused at the bottom of Kate's bed. The accent was definitely Australian. Kate tried to smile.

'Awful backache,' she admitted. 'They've shaved me and given me an enema but they don't really think I'm in labour.'

'What do they know about it?' The Australian girl leaned over the foot of the bed. 'Take my advice, sweetie, have it quick and get out. If you get it over before noon you get to go home one day early. I've been in here forty-eight hours already. Back home they'd give me something but not here! The Matron's a right cow!'

'Are you on exchange?' The nursing home was devoted almost totally to naval wives and Kate felt fairly certain that this girl was one.

'Yeah. My old man's in *Dolphin*. Where's yours?'

'At sea.' Kate gasped with pain.

' 'Course he is! Never there when you need 'em. And if they are, they're useless. Yesterday, one poor girl had her old man in with her. Come the interesting bit, he ups and faints right on top of her. The midwife drags him off and bundles him under the delivery table. When he comes to, he sits up suddenly and knocks himself out! Nothing but trouble, men.'

'Please don't,' cried Kate, weakly. 'It hurts to laugh.'

The Australian girl looked her over judiciously. 'Pain real bad, is it? Coming and going? You're in labour. No doubt about it, I'd say.'

Kate had to wait for the wave of pain to subside before she could speak. 'But do you know anything about it?'

'Sure do, sweetie. Back home I'm a midwife. Hang on, I'll get Sister.'

Kate closed her eyes and tried to breathe deeply as the pain laid hold and wrestled with her.

'Bloody hell, Sister. You're only just going to make it with this one.'

Kate opened her eyes. Sister and the Australian were leaning over her.

'She didn't say that she was having contractions,' said Sister, resentfully. 'Only backache. I'll get the trolley.'

As Kate was wheeled out, the Australian leaned over her.

'It's only just on eleven. You could still make it, you lucky cow!'

four

The submarine was notified of the birth of the twin boys through the usual naval channels but all Kate had was a brief telegram from Mark that arrived at the same time as a huge bouquet of flowers from the Wardroom. She was terribly touched by the latter—organised, of course, by the Captain's wife—and was aware of the feeling of camaraderie that existed in these close-knit naval circles whilst feeling hurt that Mark had made no further effort to communicate. After all, she had told herself as she watched flowers and telegrams and husbands arriving for the other wives, I suppose there's not much he can do when he's nearly three thousand miles away. But at the back of her mind doubts lurked. If the Wardroom could arrange to have the flowers delivered to her, then so could Mark. Or he could have made some arrangement with his mother to buy some and left a letter with her to give to Kate after the birth. In her disappointment, she hinted as much to Mrs Webster who was obviously embarrassed by her son's casual attitude although she hastened to Mark's defence. Fortunately, there were several wives in the same situation which made her feel less lonely. Her parents had rushed up from Cornwall to see her and had rushed back again although Mrs Webster had pressed them to stay the night at the flat.

"I simply couldn't cope with him,' admitted Kate's mother, having kissed Kate, admired the twins and settled down to chat. 'She's not too bad but he manages to make me feel completely superfluous. I'll come and stay with you when you get back home—if you want me to!'

'Oh, Mummy! You know I will! I'm sorry that they're here. It was Mark's fault. You know I'd much rather have had you with me.'

'Of course I know that.' Elizabeth Beauchamp held her daughter's hand tightly. 'But we must allow them their moment. After all, Mark is their only child and this is their first grandchild—grandchildren, I should have said. I'm an old hand, remember, although it's our first set of twins. Apparently, Mr Webster had a twin brother. Fancy there being two of them! His poor old mum!' They chuckled guiltily. 'Well, I suppose we must think of going soon.'

Kate's father had already left the ward, being constitutionally unable to survive for more than thirty minutes without a cigarette. The sight of all these lactating women and roaring babies had thrown him off his stroke and he had had to hurry out quite five minutes before his usual expiry time.

'Oh, Mummy.' Quite suddenly Kate felt that she simply couldn't manage to go on being brave if her mother was going to leave. The loneliness of those long months of pregnancy and the sheer terror of the thought of coping alone with two new babies was unbearable. She looked at her mother's beloved, worn, tired face and fear overwhelmed her. Elizabeth Beauchamp had a heart condition and Kate realised at that moment what it would mean to have to face life without this strong comforting love at her back. The tears she held back on other occasions, and especially in this last week, welled up and her chin shook. 'Oh, Mummy!'

Elizabeth gathered her close, ignoring the side glances of the other women in the ward. 'Brace up, my darling. You can do it. Mark will be back soon.' She wondered, as she had wondered before, why her warm-hearted, impulsive, sensitive daughter should have fallen in love with such a cold, undemonstrative and selfish young man. Should she have made more of her reservations? Kate had been so swept up in the romantic world of balls and parties and dashing young men in striking uniforms. 'He's the strong silent type,' she had insisted when her mother had tentatively voiced her anxieties, but meeting Mark's father had underlined Elizabeth's fears. Her arms tightened around Kate and she sent up a little prayer. After all, Mark was very young and struggling with a new and exacting career. She sighed.

Misunderstanding the sigh, Kate straightened herself and tried to smile at her mother. 'Sorry,' she said, 'I'm perfectly all right really and you mustn't worry about me. Come and stay when I'm back at the flat.' Not 'home,' her mother noticed. 'We'll have a lovely time. Tell Daddy to drive carefully.'

'I will. And we'll certainly come. Or, if you prefer, when Mark goes off again we'll drive up and pick you and the twins up and take you down to Cornwall.'

'Oh, yes please!' Kate's eyes shone. 'I'd love to come home. Just for a week or two.'

Noticing the 'home,' Elizabeth kissed her and stood up. 'That's settled then, you've only got to say the word. Now, look what we've brought you.'

She nodded to the window by Kate's bed. Outside, on the gravel, flirting with Kate's father and making him laugh, was Cass. Kate looked from Cass and back to her mother in amazement. 'But how super! I've longed to see her but she can't struggle about on buses in her condition. How will she get back?'

'Don't worry. We picked her up this morning and brought her with us. She's been sitting out there on a bench in the sun. Daddy's arranged, and paid for, a taxi to take her home. We didn't want to leave you on your own. I'm sure you'll both have plenty to talk about. Apparently, she suggested that the Websters gave her a lift but they've managed to evade it so far.'

Kate smiled through the tears that would keep forcing themselves into her eyes. 'They hate each other,' she said. 'She's very naughty to them.'

'Can't say I blame her! And now I really must go before she captivates my husband totally. I don't trust her an inch, even if she is seven months pregnant.'

By the time Mark was due back from Nova Scotia, Kate was already at home with her twin boys—Guy and Giles—and adjusting to

a completely different way of life. To be fair—although, as she later
said to Cass, 'Who wants to be fair?'—Major and Mrs Webster had
proved very helpful in the two weeks after the twins' birth. They had
erected two cots in the spare bedroom and had doubled up on all the
requirements necessary for the babies' welfare. They had even found
a huge pram, which blocked the hallway, in which they proudly
pushed the twins down to the sea every afternoon, insisting that Kate
should put her feet up. They moved into Kate's bedroom and she
slept in with the twins, grateful that Mrs Webster was within call
should an emergency arise. None did and, after a very short while,
Kate longed for them to be gone so that she might have her home—
and her babies—to herself. She felt nervous when she inexpertly
handled them under the critical eye of the older woman and, since it
was not in her nature to assert herself in the face of experience and
seniority, felt that the twins would become truly her own only when
the Websters had gone home. Mrs Webster was a managing sort of
woman who was delighted to have two new grandchildren and Kate
felt that her independence was being taken away from her. Major
Webster had no difficulty in containing his delight, muttering darkly
about the cost of two children whilst Mark was still so junior, and
seeming as relieved to set out for his own home as Kate was to see
him go. During that two weeks, Kate had become a little fonder of
Mark's mother. Nevertheless, when their big Rover had pulled away
from the kerb with Mrs Webster waving enthusiastically from the
window, Kate sighed a huge sigh of relief.

Within a few hours of their departure Cass was bundling in, to hug
Kate and to exclaim over the twins.

'Aren't they lovely! Who are they like, d'you think? Thank God
Frankenstein and his monster have gone! Tell me, Kate, does Mark's
father ever smile? And the monster! Fuss, fuss, fuss! Every time I see
them I try to imagine them in bed together. Quite impossible.'

They giggled hysterically, remembering whispered conversations in
the dormitory—d'you think so-and-so and whoever 'do' it?—and Cass
sank into a chair.

'Mark must be thrilled! When's he back? Imagine, he'll have missed a whole month of their lives. Oh, you are lucky to have got it all over and done with and to have these two gorgeous poppets to show for it!'

Kate glossed over Mark's 'thrilledness.' One telegram and a letter which dwelt more on the delights of Nova Scotia than it did on the arrival of his twin sons, hardly came under the heading of 'thrilled.'

'Must be sheer bliss,' said Cass, tactfully changing direction, 'to be able to cut your own toenails again and I see that you've squeezed yourself back into your jeans. Pig! Never mind. I'm determined to get back into my ball dress by Christmas.'

'Then you'll have to have the baby early, like I did,' said Kate.

Cass's daughter, however, made no effort to hurry into the world. Charlotte was born two days after Tom's birthday at the end of November. He was at home for the event and there were great celebrations.

'I'm sure,' said Felicity, watching Cass twirling languidly in George Lampeter's arms at *Dolphin*'s New Year's Eve Ball, 'that she shouldn't be out and about yet, let alone dancing. Much too soon!'

'Cass believes that it never harms you to do the things you want to do,' said Kate. 'Much worse for her, she says, to be frustrated in her desires.'

'I can certainly believe that!' snapped Felicity.

WHEN TOM'S SUBMARINE SAILED at the end of January, the General drove to Hampshire, packed Cass and his granddaughter into his car and drove them back down to Devon. Cass settled down happily to being spoiled by her father and Mrs Hampton whose son John was now grown up and working in Hong Kong. She missed him dreadfully and poured out all her redundant mother love on Charlotte whom she adored. She spent every moment she could with the baby thus giving Cass, who was only too delighted, the chance to relax and enjoy herself. General Mackworth took her round introducing her to all his new friends in the village.

It was a charming village, tucked away in a fold on the edge of the moor, with the church and its Georgian Rectory. There was a tiny shop with a Post Office, a cluster of old grey stone cottages, and several larger properties on the outskirts of the village. The Manor House with its farms and estate cottages stood farther out and had belonged to generations of Hope-Latymers as far back as anyone could remember. The present owner, William, a widower, was in his late-forties; his only son, another William, was just sixteen and away at school.

It was too damp and raw to enjoy the countryside but Cass charmed her father's friends and basked in their obvious admiration. Before long she began to be a tiny bit bored with the company of mainly elderly people and started to think of rejoining her friends and the social life awaiting her in Alverstoke. She told her father that perhaps she should be getting back. He was far too wise to show his disappointment or to attempt to stop her.

'Quite right,' he agreed at once. 'Got your own life to lead. And Mrs Hampton will spoil that child to death if you stay much longer.'

Overwhelmed by his generous and uncomplaining attitude, which made things so much easier for her, Cass flung her arms around his neck.

'It's been such fun,' she said. 'And we'll come again soon. We're going to try to find a bigger place so that you can come to stay with us. If only it wasn't such a bore on the train. Specially now, with the baby.'

'Ah!' He returned her embrace and gently put her from him. 'Wanted to talk to you about that. It's your twenty-first birthday this year. No, I hadn't forgotten. I think the best present I could give you would be a little car. Only a little one,' he added as Cass's cries of excitement threatened to drown his words, 'but you'll be able to get about more. No excuses then, mind, about visiting your old pa when Tom's away!'

'Oh, Daddy! It would be absolutely wonderful!'

'That's settled then. What d'you say to a trip to Plymouth tomorrow? See what's going.'

So Cass and Charlotte returned to Alverstoke, Cass driving them in a little Mini. Kate was quite green with envy.

'We shall share it,' declared Cass, as they sat together in Kate's sitting room, surrounded by babies. 'We can go shopping together and, in the summer, we'll have picnics and outings. Imagine the fun!'

But by the time the summer had come, Mark had been appointed to a submarine running out of Devonport and Tom to a submarine in refit in Chatham.

'IT'S PERFECT HELL HERE,' Cass wrote to Kate. 'There's hardly any submariners and we have to use *Pembroke*'s Mess. All dreary Supply and Secretariat people. Oh for dear old *Dolphin*! General Service people aren't a bit like us! Thank God I've got the car. The Medway towns are the end but Canterbury's lovely. And, of course, it's not too far from London on the train!

'Have you seen these wonderful nylon tights? No more boring old suspenders! Go and have a look in Plymouth. If you can't find any just let me know and I'll send you a pair. Just the job with skirts getting shorter!

'How are the twins? I'm glad they liked their presents. Just think what we were going through a year ago. I'm glad you're seeing my dear old pa. Give him my love and tell him that Charlotte and I will be coming down to see him soon. Tom's got to go on some course so I thought we'd pop down for a little visit! It will be wonderful to see you but I'll probably have to stay with him.

'It's lovely having Tom home but I do miss all the parties, etc. Never mind . . . '

But she did mind. For the first time she and Tom were thrown very much on each other for entertainment and they discovered that life ran along more smoothly with friends dropping in and various social events to look forward to. Tom, surprisingly, minded less than Cass. He was delighted with the year-old Charlotte and could spend hours playing with and reading to her. Cass was amused by this new aspect to his character and left him in charge now and then while she popped up to London. Their married quarter was one of a block of five houses built on the edge of a new housing estate on the outskirts of Rainham.

Only two other quarters were occupied, both by General Service Lieutenants, one attached to *Pembroke* and who was, therefore, a Supply Officer, or in Naval parlance, a 'pusser,' and the other to a frigate in refit. The submarine service considered itself the elite branch of the Service and the surface fleet—known as 'general service' whilst its men were known as 'skimmers'—to be definitely inferior.

'One "pusser" and one "skimmer," ' reported Tom to Cass after his first sortie. 'Never mind. Nice enough chaps and their wives seem fun. One's pregnant. I'm sure you'll get on.'

And with these and the only other young officer as yet appointed to the submarine, the Wivenhoes had to be content. Cass felt happier with a little court around her and, although she preferred to operate with larger numbers, she made the best of it. The pusser had come up through the ranks and was rather older than Tom and very free and easy. His wife Maggie, aware that Tom was 'Officer Entry' and Cass a real pukka memsahib, was rather deferential which Cass thought touching. Because Maggie made it clear that she knew her place, Cass never felt the need to put her in it and was able to ignore it and pretend that there was no difference in their status, thus enabling the relationship to proceed very satisfactorily. No such subterfuge was needed between the men. Tom ignored Jeff's broad Midlands accent and his confusion on occasions as to which knife to use and they got along splendidly. Jeff flirted outrageously and publicly with Cass, accompanied by shocked remonstrances from Maggie who feared that Cass might feel that he was presuming on the growing friendship and getting above himself. Cass merely laughed and responded in kind and encouraged Maggie through her pregnancy, taking her for little trips in the car and doing her shopping for her.

Richard and Annette were a slightly different proposition. They were a very serious couple who found it just the tiniest bit necessary to show that they felt that Jeff and Maggie weren't quite up to scratch, managing to do it in a very tolerant and understanding way that drove Jeff mad and upset Maggie. They had two young children and at the little supper parties at the Wivenhoes' Cass would send Maggie into fits of horrified mirth by giving huge pretend yawns behind Annette's head whilst she droned on about the latest amazing achievements of these two dreary children. Since Cass was constitutionally unable to resist charming any man who swam into her ken, she would listen with an absorbed expression whilst Richard bored on about the war in Vietnam and would make one or two relevant remarks culled from *The Times* or from Tom's conversations with Jeff. This caused Richard to remark to Annette later that Cass was quite an intelligent girl but that it was a pity her formal education had been so much neglected.

Cass and Tom would shriek with laughter after their guests had gone, feeling that little glow of complacency that sheds such a warm retrospective light on generous actions that have—supposedly— brought excitement into other rather dull little lives. They would clear up and go happily to bed, having drunk enough to feel pleasantly sexy and to enjoy themselves thoroughly before falling asleep. Neither was of the temperament to feel the least interest in exploring their own or their guests' reactions in depth. Enough to pass another evening in convivial company where they themselves were the hub and to look forward to the next time.

Before too long, however, Cass began to find her social diet lacking in spice. As the winter, cold and harsh on this east coast, closed in she longed more and more for the temperate climate of the south and the company of her old friends and the potential stimulation of some new ones.

KATE HAD BEEN DELIGHTED to learn that she and the twins would be going to Devon and had suggested that she and Mark hire a car and go to look around in the hope of finding a hiring or, if not, to look at the quarters. She had heard that one didn't have to live in Devonport and that there were actually quarters in a village called Crapstone on the edge of Dartmoor. The thought of living near or on Dartmoor had fired Kate's imagination and she hoped that Mark might be persuaded to take a weekend to explore. This, it seemed, was too much to expect: he was busy, they couldn't afford it, it would be difficult with the twins. He would apply for a quarter and see what came up. Devonport came up: there were no quarters available in Crapstone. By this time Mark had gone on ahead to join the boat, which had just come out of refit and was on 'work-up,' a testing process to make sure that all was in order before she went to sea, and Kate was left to follow with the twins as best she could. First, however, she would be obliged to go down to Plymouth to view the quarter before she was allowed to accept it. When this news was relayed to Cass, and Tom told her how much Kate would hate living in a small flat in Devonport, Cass told Kate to hold her horses and had then telephoned her father and apprised him of the situation.

'Dash about,' she told him, 'there's a duck! See if you can't find something they could rent near you. I just don't see poor old Kate stuck in a city with the twins. She'd love it on the moor. She's used to all that wildness after Cornwall!'

Accordingly, the General had dashed and finally, through the grapevine, had found a place on the outskirts of Dousland not much more than ten minutes away from his own village. The retired owner and his wife were planning an extended visit to New Zealand where their eldest daughter lived. They would be delighted to let the big colonial-style bungalow to a naval couple for eighteen months. An affordable rent was finally agreed after a bit of a tussle—but only after Kate had agreed to move out without demur should the owner or his wife return before the eighteen months expired—and a moving-in date was fixed.

'They're not a bit worried about the children,' the General assured her. 'I'm sure you'll like it.'

So was Kate. A roomy bungalow sounded like heaven after the cramped conditions that now prevailed in the flat. They didn't have too many possessions: their clothes, some china, linen and books but no furniture apart from the twins' cots and pram. There was too much to cram into a car but not enough for a furniture removal van. Kate's brother, Chris, came to the rescue. He hired a small van and, driving up to Gosport, packed everything into the back, including the twins propped up comfortably in their huge pram just behind the seats, put Kate into the front and drove her down to Dousland.

The General was waiting at the bungalow, the rooms dusted and aired and one of Mrs Hampton's casseroles ready to be popped into the oven.

'What do you think?' he cried, helping Kate from the van and assisting her up the front steps. 'It'll do, won't it? Do you like it?' Anxious for her approval, he hurried her from room to room. 'There's a wonderful garden and the moor's just behind you. Two minutes' walk—no more. What d'you say? D'you like it?'

'I love it. Oh, I just love it.' Kate gazed around with eyes already dazed and enchanted by the spectacular trip across Dartmoor. 'It's perfect. How clever of you to find it. Imagine! I could have been stuck in a gloomy little quarter in Plymouth. I simply can't thank you enough.'

The General exhaled a great breath of relief. 'Tea!' he declared. 'I know that women are always desperate for a cup of tea at times like this. Kettle's on. But first,' he led her back to the sitting room, 'wait here a moment.'

Kate, still bemused by the day's activities, wandered to the window. The twins were sitting in the pram on the lawn in the sun gazing at their new surroundings.

I must get them in and feed them, she thought. Where did I put the nappies? Oh, how wonderful to have a garden. I can't believe my luck!

A tiny doubt assailed her. It occurred to her that Mark would have been happier to be close to the base and to the shops and cinemas of Plymouth. She did not really know his views on the countryside. He had been perfectly happy to walk along the beach at Stokes Bay in the evenings but had showed no enthusiasm for the idea of actually living in the country. Of course, with no transport . . . Kate felt a real anxiety at the realisation that it would not be easy for Mark to get to the base when the boat was in. There were buses from the end of the road, she had checked that, but they weren't too frequent. On the other hand, there were plenty of naval people around and she knew from experience that they would be only too happy to give him a lift. Kate sighed. She also knew that Mark detested being under any obligation to anyone. He had used an old bike at *Dolphin* rather than accept favours. She would have to organise the lift for him before he returned, pretend that someone had offered and that it would have looked churlish to refuse.

She felt guilty and then her gaze fell on the twins, mesmerised by a friendly robin on the lawn. Her spirits rose again and she felt confident that she would be able to sort something out. Mark had a knack of viewing problems as though they were a direct result of Kate's incompetence or because she asked too much of life—or of him. The familiar look, a sullen stiffening of the features and a slight drooping of the eyelids, was enough to make her heart race. His tongue could be cruel and his temper frightening. She made every effort to sidestep scenes by dealing with problems herself rather than sharing and consulting, assuring herself that it was only whilst he was finding his feet and growing up a bit. It never occurred to her that she was in exactly the same situation—as well as being nearly two years younger—but without a book of naval rules and regulations to fall back on nor an experienced Wardroom all ready to help. Mark had been quick and clever enough to lay several things on the line from the start. No whingeing about his being away was the first thing: he got six weeks' leave a year, anything else was a bonus. No complaining about having to manage alone: the old naval joke 'if you can't take a joke you shouldn't have joined' seemed to sum it up. When he did come back home from sea he would be tired: it was no good expecting long lists of jobs or other problems to be dealt with—that was her department. And Kate, in the first flush of enthusiasm and with no yardstick to consult, had taken his rules to heart as if they had been written on tablets of stone. Now, as she turned away from the window, she was determined that her first task would be to resolve the transport problem. It shouldn't be too difficult. After all, Mark seemed to be home so seldom and they already had a tidy sum saved towards a car . . .

'Here we are.' The General bustled in carrying three glasses and a bottle of champagne. 'Where's that brother of yours? Give him a shout. That's it! Here she comes! Quick! Ready with that glass! There. Now. Here's to you, Kate. Let's hope that your stay here is a very happy one!'

IT WAS. UNLIKE CASS, Kate was perfectly happy to have a break from Service life and pottered around the bungalow, playing with the twins, working in the garden and pushing Guy and Giles up on the moor in a double pushchair that she found in a second-hand shop in Tavistock.

She did not analyse the sense of relief she experienced when Mark went to sea, the freedom from the strain of his presence. A feeling of holiday pervaded the bungalow and Kate merely congratulated herself on being of a temperament that could endure these separations so contentedly. She attributed a great deal of this to the moor which she was growing to love with a great passion and which the General was encouraging her to know.

On sunny days, he would appear in his car with Mrs Hampton who was only too happy to look after the twins and make up for Kate's somewhat dilatory and slapdash housekeeping whilst the General bore Kate off for trips over the moor and lunches in country pubs.

'I feel so guilty!' she said to Cass during one of their lengthy telephone calls. 'He never lets me pay for anything and when we get back Mrs Hampton won't let me pay either. And she's usually cleaned up and then, when they're gone, I come across all sorts of goodies in the larder.'

'For heaven's sake stop fussing,' said Cass. 'Daddy's absolutely loving it and he'll see that Hammy's OK, never fear! And she'll be loving it too. She's just the same with Charlotte. She misses her son dreadfully now he's out in Hong Kong so you're doing her a favour. And Daddy loves to have women around him, you know that, 'specially young pretty ones.'

'Honestly, Cass!'

'It's true. Try to see that you're doing him a favour.'

Kate tried but found it difficult. She invited him around to supper when the boat was in so that he could renew his brief acquaintance with Mark. The evening went very well. Mark could be very charming to older people, even if he did often spoil the effect for Kate afterwards by saying things like, 'Thank God that's over, boring old buffer!' or 'Daft old bat, what on earth made you ask her?' and she was amazed at his ability to deceive people into thinking that he was a charming, intelligent, young man.

On this occasion, he and the General reviewed several subjects, ranging from the general election that had taken place earlier in the year to the World Cup. The most recent topic on everyone's lips at that time, however, was the Aberfan disaster in which a hundred and sixteen children had lost their lives when the spoil and waste from the coal mines slid down a Welsh hillside and collapsed on to the small mining village in the valley below.

When she heard of the disaster, Kate had sat for a long while on her sofa, a twin in each arm, and had imagined the nightmare agony for the parents of those children who had choked, struggled and suffocated to death in the coal dust. She had sat, staring straight ahead, hugging the twins tightly, seeing their smooth limbs and blonde heads covered and crushed by the inexorable black waste.

'Won't go into that,' said the General, glancing at Kate. He'd popped in a few days before to find her listening to the news of the rising casualty numbers and shedding tears over the tragedy. 'Terrible thing! Mustn't upset Kate.'

She smiled at him gratefully and stood up to collect the plates.

'Oh, Kate always takes the troubles of the world on her shoulders,' she heard Mark say as she went into the kitchen to make coffee. 'Totally pointless. Got enough of our own problems without worrying about other people's. They never thank you for it.'

Only a few submarines ran out of Devonport and Mark and Kate were in much the same situation as Tom and Cass. The Captain and the First Lieutenant had both bought houses in Alverstoke and neither of their wives had moved down. Since neither of the other officers was married, there was no social life and they knew no one. The boat spent most of its time at sea and Kate was left with her own little round of children, garden, the General, and, all around her and dominating her world, the moor.

Through the following year she watched it change: the new bracken pushing up through the black, peaty soil in a tightly curled fist, growing to be waist-high in summer, the bright enamel yellow flowers of the gorse coming into bloom. She saw the cloud shadows darken the purple heather that covered the hills as the clouds raced before the wind and she caught her breath when the low late-autumn sun turned the dying bracken to fire.

She loved to see the rain clouds bellying blackly in the west and, when the storm had passed, to see the golden gleams of sunshine that followed behind.

Even when the rain poured relentlessly down, filling the great sponge of the moor to saturation so that dry watercourses became streams and small issues gushed with water, when the overspill thundered over the dam at Burrator and the rivers raced and foamed over the rocks, even then she loved it.

She saw the thorn and the rowan berries ripen and the beech leaves turn and knew that when the time came to leave it would be one of the saddest days of her life.

five

Kate and Mark went to Cornwall for Christmas and to the Websters' for the New Year.

'Never again,' said Kate to the General when they were back in Dousland and Mark had gone to sea again. 'Everyone was as helpful as they could be about transport but it's impossible with two small children. And I was so disappointed to miss Cass and Tom.'

'It was lovely to have them. Now where's that husband of yours gone this time?'

'Out to the Med. The boat's spending a week in Gibraltar. He'll be gone about five weeks. Two of the wives are going out when they get to Gib. In fact, the First Lieutenant's wife telephoned me to see if I was too.' She made a face and then laughed. 'It was a bit embarrassing, actually. At that stage I didn't even know where they were going and she seemed a bit surprised. Mark was cross when I told him. He felt I'd dropped him in it.'

'And are you going?'

'No. Mark's not very keen on the idea. He always says these visits are hell. The others seem to enjoy them . . . ' She paused and then shrugged. 'Oh, well. I'm sure he's right. And anyway, we probably couldn't afford it. The Navy doesn't pay for the wives. Some husbands squeeze them on to their subsistence allowance. They don't live on the boat when they're in harbour, you see. They get a set rate so they can stay at an hotel but if you don't mind a bed and breakfast place, the allowance more or less covers two of you. The Navy doesn't care.

If you choose to live less luxuriously and have your wife with you, it's up to you. The wives can hitch cheap flights out with the RAF but they have to wait for one that fits in and then, Mark says, if the boat's ETA is delayed all sorts of muddles happen. So . . . ' She smiled at the General. 'Anyway, I bet Gib's not as nice as Devon. Now tell me all about Cass and Tom. And how was Charlotte? Cass sent me some photographs and she looks an absolute sweetie.'

The General drove home thoughtfully. More and more lately he was seeing service life from a different angle, through the eyes of Cass and Kate as they struggled to come to terms with its problems. He longed to help them, to protect them, but he knew that his role could only be a peripheral one. He must not interfere or give advice, all he could do was to be at hand. He was full of admiration for the way they dealt with the crises, the loneliness, the anxieties, and found himself thinking of Caroline, his shy, silly wife who, unable to cope with a husband twice as old as she was, had turned to a boy of her own age and finished up crushed and mangled with him in his little car.

'He had his arm round her.'

Funny how that still had the power to twist his gut. The policeman had told him that afterwards and he had in that moment imagined quite clearly the two of them, wrapped up in their romantic ideal, fleeing into the night. The boy had been a subaltern and had seen himself, no doubt, as rescuing her from an intolerable marriage with a man old enough to be her father and an insensitive womaniser to boot. And Caroline, her head full of poetry and dreams, had encouraged him, seeing herself as the wronged heroine in one of those endless romances that she was always reading.

The General gave a small exclamation of self-disgust and struck the steering wheel lightly with the flat of his hand. Even now, more than twenty years on, his instinct was to belittle her. The fault had been his. Wrapped up in a brilliant career and then fully occupied by war, he had decided to take a wife at a time when he was established, experienced and absolutely in control of his life. He should have chosen from amongst his own circle, a woman of his own age, a widow—there were plenty at that stage of the war—or a divorcee. But he hadn't wanted another man's leavings; at least, not as his wife. He wanted a young girl who would give him children and blend willingly and gracefully into his well-established way of life. Caroline had seemed the perfect choice: barely out of the schoolroom, dazzled by the dashing, handsome Colonel who knew so well how to charm and flatter.

She had bored him quite quickly and he had left her to her own devices. There was still so much to be done just after the war and he had neither the time nor the inclination to realise that she was lonely and bewildered. His friends petted and patronised and then ignored her. Whispers of his reputation reached her ears, although since his marriage he had been perfectly correct, and she became even more lacking in confidence. When her baby was born, Nanny was installed and even Caroline's pretty child was gently but inexorably removed from her inexpert care. No wonder then that she should turn to young Hurley who saw her as a damsel in distress, used and humiliated by his wicked Colonel who was not always as tender of his young officers' feelings as he might have been.

Afterwards, the sympathy had all been for him. Even her parents— thrilled at her brilliant marriage—had been mortified by her behaviour and let him know that no blame could be attached to him. He had never been able to decide whether it had been an accident due to dangerous driving or a deliberate act.

'He had his arm round her.'

Now, as he watched Cass and Kate grappling with the difficulties of service life, he could see, here and there, the pattern repeating itself although in different ways and for different reasons. Sometimes it seemed as if he were being giving a second chance, an opportunity to redress the balance. Perhaps his support, a word of advice, may prevent these children from making the mistakes that he had made and in so doing he could find some measure of atonement. Forgive me Father for I have sinned. And what of Caroline and young Hurley, wiped out, extinguished between one breath and the next? What could atone for that? Had she been afraid?

'He had his arm round her.'

The General drove round to his garage, put his car away and went indoors.

IT WAS SPRING BEFORE Cass visited her father again. Tom was, at last, on the long awaited course and she drove the long distance from Kent—avoiding London—on a blowy March day. She glanced in the driving mirror at Charlotte who sat sucking her thumb and gazing stolidly at the passing countryside. She was such an easy child, so good-tempered and adaptable, and Cass felt a great wave of affection for her daughter, who looked so like easy, good-tempered and adaptable Tom. She loved them both dearly but, nevertheless, it was lovely to be free and independent and to be within a few miles of her father and her dearest friend. She had every intention of thoroughly enjoying her little holiday.

KATE WANDERED ROUND THE garden, eagerly waiting for the telephone call from the General to tell her that Cass had arrived. She had already had a call from her mother, who had just returned to Cornwall after one of her fairly regular visits and could talk of nothing but the *Torrey Canyon,* the oil tanker that had gone aground off the Isles of Scilly spilling a hundred and twenty thousand tons of crude oil into the sea. It was all too close for comfort, she had said.

'All the poor birds!' she kept crying. 'All the wildlife destroyed. It's terrible!'

Kate strolled on, the twins gambolling around her. She loved the garden. It was all mainly to the front of the bungalow: a long, long lawn edged with rhododendron bushes stretching down to the road. At present the lawn was massed with daffodils and she walked on the drive which passed up the side of the lawn and round to the garage at the back of the bungalow.

In the border beneath the wooden fence primulas bloomed and the starry flowers of the forsythia shivered a little in the cold wind. Although most people welcome the spring and find the autumn a melancholy time, Kate's experience was quite to the contrary. The great westerly gales of autumn, the blazing vibrant colours, the scent of wood fires and the silver and blue of crisp, frosty mornings seemed to make the blood sparkle in her veins and a sense of excitement, the thought of Christmas close on its heels, bubbled within her. But the spring, ah, the spring was different. Its promise was veiled in an uncertainty that was encapsulated in the vulnerability of a clump of pale early primroses in a wet hedgerow and the cruel sharp shower of hail descending suddenly out of a clear pale blue sky. The long light evenings made her restless, no longer content to huddle round the fire, yet it was too cold to be out of doors listening to the blackbird's evocative call and the thin, high, plaintive bleating of the lambs. The stillness of a spring evening was unlike the stillness of late-autumn or winter. Theirs was a stillness of fulfilment, of a deserved peace, of things drawing in and down into the quiet earth. The stillness of spring was a breathless stillness, anticipatory, waiting. There was a hopeful expectancy which might never be fulfilled: a promise of such magnitude that it must surely fail. It was this promise that encouraged the delicate blooms and tender shoots to unfurl in its gentle warmth only to be beaten down by heavy rains or withered by a late frost.

Kate turned back to the bungalow, thankful that she had the twins to save her from her melancholy. She was slowly and not always consciously coming to terms with the knowledge that Mark needed to keep his career and his family quite separate. She had been more hurt than she was prepared to admit, even to herself, that he hadn't wanted her in Gibraltar. It was necessary to reason with herself, to remember that he was not a social man, that he took his job very seriously. It was rather a desolate outlook for her but she still looked upon her role in the light of a job, as a support, and if that was what was demanded of her she must find her happiness with the twins and when Mark was at home. The trouble here was that he didn't seem to find pleasure in having the twins around and leaves had become rather stressful affairs. He was happiest when the twins were in bed or left with Mrs Hampton, and Kate, knowing that it was only for a fortnight and that he looked upon these times as holidays, felt that he must be humoured. She had not yet let herself dwell upon the unreality of a marriage developed along these lines. The whole point was that it was different to most marriages, that there were unusual strains and requirements. When he got a shore job there would be time to adjust.

She swung round at the sound of a fanfare at the gate: there was Cass, in her little car, waving furiously. Kate broke into a run to open the five-bar gate—always kept shut because of the twins. Cass drove in and Kate, having shut the gate behind her, dashed round to the driver's door.

'Thought I'd just pop in for two minutes,' Cass was saying as they hugged and hugged. 'It's been such an age. Oh, look at them. Aren't they sweet!' And she was on her knees before the twins who stood, round-eyed, watching this display of emotion. 'This one sucks his thumb just like Charlotte. Which is which?'

'That's Giles. Oh, Cass! How marvellous to see you. But you mustn't stay. Your father and Mrs Hampton have the most unbelievable tea ready for you.' Kate went to the car and looked in through the window. On the back seat, strapped into a little chair, was Charlotte, a sturdy, serious-looking child, dark-haired and brown-eyed. She stared solemnly at Kate. 'Goodness, Cass. She's so like Tom.'

'Isn't she? Must get her out for a moment. She's been as good as gold. Get the kettle on, Kate. There's time for a quickie. I won't eat anything, I promise. But I'm dying for a pee and, if I know my old pa, he'll know full well that I wouldn't be able to drive straight past your door when I haven't seen you for nine months.'

'THERE NOW, MY LOVER.' Mrs Hampton put Charlotte's plastic beaker on her high-chair tray and beamed at her. 'What about some porridge?'

She'd got into the habit of popping in every morning, once she'd seen Jack off to the big house, to get the General's breakfast, tidy up a little bit and see to it that he had some lunch organised. She knew that you couldn't trust a man to look after himself properly. The General, who had been looked after by orderlies or by his batman for most of his life, took it all in his stride and knew how lucky he was.

Charlotte nodded and looked round as the General came in.

'Good morning, my darling.' He dropped a kiss on Charlotte's head. ' 'Morning, Mrs Hampton. That daughter of mine still in bed, I suppose? Well, she didn't get back from Kate's 'til late. Porridge? Excellent.'

' 'Tis lovely to see 'em together.'

'They've been like sisters since they were children and now we've got the next generation coming along, growing up together. You're very fond of Giles and Guy, aren't you, my darling?'

'Chiles,' repeated Charlotte. He was definitely her favourite, 'Like Chiles.' She drank deeply from her mug.

' 'Tis a pity Kate's 'usband's not 'ome more, like Cass's Tom.' Mrs Hampton finished stirring the porridge and ladled it into two bowls. ' 'Tisn't natural for a young girl to be on 'er own so much. An' with two babies t'deal with, too. Real tired 'er looks sometimes.'

'Service life, Mrs Hampton! It's very tough on these young wives, always has been. On the positive side, it can keep the romance going much longer. Lots of honeymoons.'

Mrs Hampton's answering snort was expressive and the General raised his eyebrows. She put his porridge before him and tucked Charlotte's bib more firmly round the child's neck.

' 'Ere you are, my lover,' she said. 'Let 'Ammy 'elp you. What a lovely bowl. Now, where've all they rabbits got to? 'Ave to eat the porridge up to find 'em, we will.'

'Do I take it, Mrs Hampton, that you don't subscribe to that idea?'

Once it would never have occurred to the General to discuss personal matters with a domestic. Mrs Hampton, however, had never really quite fitted into that role. She had a dignity and a wisdom that had earned the General's respect from the beginning and, on one or two occasions, he had found himself seeking her advice. In her company he felt relaxed and, ludicrous though it may sound, safe. He knew that the twins and Charlotte felt it too. He watched the child's dark eyes fixed trustingly upon her as she spooned in the porridge.

' 'Tisn't lots of 'oneymoons that young mums want. 'Tis a bit of attention, a bit of fussin' over,' she said, at last. 'She gets like a strained look. That's right, my lover. All gone!' She wiped Charlotte's mouth.

The General looked worried. She was, after all, only voicing his own doubts. 'May improve,' he said. 'He's very young. There can be a lot of pressure on these young officers. It could be as simple as that.'

Mrs Hampton raised her eyebrows disbelievingly but was too polite to contradict him.

'How about a nice egg?' she asked. 'Go down well, would it?'

THE SUBMARINE BERTHED TWO days early and Mark got a lift home with the Navigation Officer who lived at Walkhampton. He was not at all pleased to find Cass in the kitchen when he arrived and even more displeased when she stayed until just before Kate served up supper.

'I had a letter from Dad when we were at sea,' he said when they finally sat down together to eat. 'He's going to buy us a car. He thinks it's crazy us being stuck out here with no transport. So it is, of course. Anyway, he suggested that I catch the train to Cheltenham and then we can go and choose it together.'

'How very generous of him,' said Kate, sipping her wine. 'It will be marvellous but can't he just send you the money?'

'You know Dad!' Mark grimaced. 'Thinks I'd buy a dud, I expect. I'll have to go up. It's worth it to have a car and, after all, they're not expecting us to chip in. He's told us to keep our money for something else. I'll only be gone a couple of days. No point in you and the twins dragging up on the train. I'll be able to come back in the car.'

'We could come,' said Kate. 'If it's only one way. I know your mother would like to see the twins.'

'Well, she'll have to put up with it, won't she? I'm not doing a four-hour train trip with two screaming brats.'

Kate was silent. You've been away five weeks, she thought, but even so you don't want to be with us enough to spend a few hours on a train

with us. And they're not screaming brats! She quickly drank some
wine to take the edge off her hurt.

'Anyway,' said Mark, smiling a little as he pushed his chair back,
'you'll have Cass, won't you?'

Kate looked at him quickly and knew that he blamed her for Cass's
presence when he had arrived back home and that her exclusion from
the trip to Cheltenham was, in some way, a punishment. He hated
anyone around when he first got in and Kate, who knew why, had
been delighted that Cass had been present so that she had a genuine excuse to become used to his presence again before they made love.

'I didn't know that you'd be in today, Mark,' she said reasonably,
answering his thought rather than his question. 'You weren't due for
another two days. You must admit that it's practically unheard of for a
submarine to be in early.'

He raised his eyebrows as if making note of the—unintentionally—
implied criticism. 'In that case we don't want to waste any more of this
unexpected and unusually precious time, do we? Shall we go to bed?'

A few hours later, she lay beside him staring into the darkness feeling
frustrated and used. There was certainly no mental communication between them. Mark withheld himself, his aspirations, his doubts, unwilling to let her into his own private self. Nor was he prepared to
make any efforts to get to know her as a person, being more concerned
in remaining remote and unapproachable. He seemed even more remote when he was with her than when they were apart for then she
was able to imagine him differently, more open, confiding and close.
His letters were very expansive for he seemed able to express himself
more easily in writing. Yet when he came home it was as if he were a
stranger. She tried to talk herself back into familiarity, hearing herself
gabbling on and on. She would offer him food and drink, still talking.
He would stand watching her, slightly amused, unhelpful, waiting
while she tried to talk away the strangeness and invoke desire, longing,
lust—anything that would help her through the painful act which, to
her, was almost rape. After any period of celibacy she could not feel

instant passion. She needed love first: tenderness, caring, an exchange of experiences during their separation and so on into the act of love-making as a form of communication when words failed.

She never got it. Sometimes he would take her on the sitting-room floor, sometimes on the landing and sometimes in the bedroom. It hardly mattered where to him. If they were in bed, Mark would roll away and be asleep in minutes, unconcerned as to whether or not her enjoyment was as great as his.

She avoided him as often as seemed reasonable when he was home for any length of time: getting up early in the morning, pretending to be asleep when he had finished reading at night. It didn't always work and he became angry if he suspected that she was trying to put him off. Then there was an element of real cruelty when the act, in-evitably, took place. She craved real affection, warm hugs and com-forting cuddles, but she had learned early that these things meant but one thing to Mark. It was better to do without.

She eased her taut muscles, rolled on to her side and concentrated on the idea of a new car: she would learn to drive and when Mark went back to sea, she and the twins would spend long happy days ex-ploring. The idea of such independence filled her with excitement and presently she slept.

MR WEBSTER INSISTED ON A sensible estate car much to Mark's disap-pointment. He fixed little chairs to the back seat for the twins and dur-ing that summer, when Mark had gone back to sea and Kate had passed her test, she explored the moors until she knew nearly every road and stream.

They picnicked at Bellever Bridge and at Cadover Bridge, where the twins paddled in the shallows, and on the sandy beach at Bigbury where the twins paddled in sun-warmed rock pools. They drove to Torcross and along the line with the sea on one side and Slapton Ley, that wonderful freshwater lake with so many different birds, on the other. When they went to Totnes or Dartmouth, Kate, never forgetful of earlier kindnesses, invited the General along and they explored the delightful old towns together, taking it in turns to push the twins in the double pushchair. On one occasion, Kate took Mrs Hampton to see her sister in Exeter whilst the General baby-sat and, while the two sisters gossiped over their tea, Kate slipped into the Cathedral and listened to Choral Evensong. And always, on her journeys home, when she saw the great outcrops of the moor, indigo against the golden evening sky, she felt her heart expand with a joy and gratitude that made her want to weep and laugh and her troubles and fears were swept away into a silent litany of thanksgiving.

Summer gave way to autumn and Kate's heart continued to rejoice and then, suddenly, it was Christmas and amidst the excitement of the puddings, the secrets and the decorations, here was Cass, arriving in Kate's kitchen and they were hugging and laughing and both talking at once.

'I must sit down,' said Cass, at last. 'I'm six months pregnant and the little bugger's giving me hell!'

Six

In the early spring, Mark was appointed to a submarine in refit in Portsmouth dockyard. She hadn't long started her refit so that it meant she would be in dry-dock for at least a year. This was a tremendous blow to Kate as the dockyard was on the opposite side of the harbour from *Dolphin,* the submarine base.

Kate hated the idea of leaving Devon although she had known very well that there would be little chance of Mark's staying on. At this time very few submarines ran out of Devonport and she had prepared herself for the move. She felt quite confident that a year together, leading a more normal life, was all that was needed to bring her and Mark closer together, to strengthen the bond as it were. And perhaps it would give him and the twins time to get to know one another. He never seemed to want to play with them and was uninterested in their new achievements and exploits. Of course, he was very young himself and busy with his career, Kate told herself. Nevertheless . . .

She had watched enviously at Christmas, looking on while Tom played with and read to Charlotte, hugged and kissed her and called her endearing names. The twins adored him, too, and he would lie on Kate's sitting-room floor while they swarmed all over him. Mark, meanwhile, looked on with a tolerant but disdainful smile and, with a tiny disbelieving shake of the head, would turn away to switch on the television which he had bought for himself as a Christmas present with the car money—an extravagance which had shocked Kate. Perhaps, she thought, he might behave differently with a daughter. Seeing Cass pregnant again had made her feel tremendously broody.

The move would bring her closer to Cass who was living in a married quarter in Anglesea Road at Alverstoke now that Tom had been appointed to a submarine running out of *Dolphin*. It meant, however, that Kate would have to make the long drive round the head of the harbour or take the Gosport Ferry whenever she wanted to see her.

'It's a pity that it's Portsmouth,' she said to Mark. 'It's so dreary on that side of the harbour.'

'Well, you don't have to come,' he said, displeased as always by any form of criticism of the Navy, direct or implied. 'You can stay here and I'll weekend.'

'But the boat's in refit, for heaven's sake!' said Kate. 'You'll be ashore for at least a year.'

Mark shrugged and lit a cigarette. He remembered walking in the park at *Mercury* the day before he proposed to her. He had weighed things up very carefully. Although he hadn't seen much of it, he had realised that he wouldn't like living in the Mess on a full-time basis: too social and too organised. Another thing was that he hated chatting up girls so that he could have sex; having to turn on the charm and deal out the flattery was so exhausting and he was not particularly successful at it. Fortunately, his good looks had got him by so far but he wouldn't want to have to find a new girlfriend each time he came back from sea. Emotional dramas were messy and tiring and casual sex was worrying—one might catch something. A wife was the answer and Kate had seemed so malleable to him that he was sure he would be able to train her to his ideas and that he would always be in control. So far that had been true but life had become less comfortable since the twins had arrived so that, for a moment, the idea of Mess life seemed positively attractive.

'Well, don't you want us with you?' Kate asked. 'Wouldn't you hate to be living in some shore establishment? We can be properly together, like an ordinary family. Refits are so boring for seaman officers, aren't they? You've said so yourself. Nothing much to do. It'll be lovely to have some time together. The twins hardly know you.'

'Then don't go on so much about how you hate Portsmouth! It's up to you.'

'Well, I can't stay here anyway, the lease is up soon. Of course we'll come. Where will we live?'

'Oh, there are loads of married quarters on the Portsmouth side of the harbour,' said Mark. 'That's no problem. It's not like Alverstoke. I suppose I'd better get in touch with the Married Quarters Officer.'

In due course, they received a letter with the address of an unoccupied quarter which they were obliged to inspect before they could agree to take it and early one morning they all set off to Portsmouth. It felt strange to return and to see the familiar landmarks. Kate hardly knew the Portsmouth side of the harbour. They had sometimes crossed by ferry to go to the Keppel's Head and during Fourth Year Courses she had stayed at the Nuffield Club for parties and a ball and then, on the Sunday mornings, they had explored the Old Town and walked along Southsea front before Kate had caught the train back to Cornwall.

The quarter, however, turned out to be at Eastney, a drab and dingy area behind the Barracks at the farthest end of the sea front where the road swings back inland. There were five or six concrete blocks of flats standing at intervals on the open grassy area of the estate, each block containing six flats, two on each floor. Kate sat in the car and stared at them with dismay. They appeared to have nothing to commend them. Each block was overlooked by another block, there were no gardens and no way to keep the twins off the road if they were to go outside to play.

Taking the key that they had collected from the Married Quarters Office, Mark went to check that this was indeed the right place. Kate's last tiny flicker of hope died when he reappeared and waved. She released the twins and together they went to look at the flat.

The entrance was cold, dark and cheerless. Their door was on the left, immediately opposite the door to the other ground-floor flat. The concrete staircase with its iron handrail led straight up and then turned left and out of sight. Kate shivered. Mark unlocked the door and they went in.

A long corridor led away from the front door. To the left was a small and very old-fashioned kitchen with cracked linoleum on the floor and grubby, yellowing paintwork. Next door was the bathroom, more linoleum and grubby paint, and opposite was a very large room which was evidently both sitting room and dining room. The bright covers of the three-piece suite made no attempt to harmonise with or even vaguely match the curtains or the square of carpet—all reproduced en masse in naval quarters all over the country. It was a scene that was to become depressingly familiar. Kate was to learn that she could walk into a quarter in Chatham, Faslane or Plymouth and be confronted by an identical scene. 'Oh, I had that suite, those curtains, that carpet in Smugglers Way . . . Otterham Quay Lane . . . Crapstone . . . ' visiting naval wives would cry and, plonking their offspring on the well-known carpet and getting out the cigarettes, would settle down to a morning's gossip.

Kate went back out into the passage. The three bedrooms opened up fan-wise from the far end of the corridor. The master bedroom was very large, the blankets neatly folded and piled on the bed together with the pillows. All except linen and towels was supplied. Everything was there waiting for the long and tedious task of checking against the inventory with the person from the Married Quarters Office: three blankets, double, one stained; one mat, coir, bathroom for the use of. On and on it would go until he had gone and one could pack it all away and bring out one's own possessions—only to drag it all out again many months later and display it ready for inspection, the sharp eyes searching for new cracks, chips or stains.

'What do you think?' Mark was watching her.

Kate hesitated. 'Are you quite certain that there isn't anything else available?' She saw the closed expression on his face and waited for the impatient tone in his voice. She was not disappointed.

'I've already told you that this is the only quarter available. We can take it or leave it. I have to give them our decision when we take the key back.'

'But you said there were plenty of quarters in Portsmouth.'

'There are. There are four more in this building alone. Naturally, I'd assumed that, with the twins to look after, you'd want to be on the ground floor. I also assumed that you'd like to be near the sea. Of course, if you'd prefer a grotty little flat in the middle of Portsmouth or to be stuck out at Drayton, I'm sure they'd be only too pleased to find you something.'

Kate walked to the bedroom window and looked out. Face it, she said to herself. Anything after Devon is going to be a let-down. Just over there is the sea and we can walk to the beach in minutes. And we shall all be together. That will make up for an awful lot. I mustn't spoil it by starting a row. She turned back into the room.

'OK.' She smiled at him. 'We'll manage. It'll be nice to be so close to the beach and we can drive into Southsea to shop.'

She was rewarded at once by his own smile; his relief was patent.

'Of course,' he said. 'I'm sure it'll be fine. The rooms are big, aren't they? Would you like us to take the twins down to the beach?' He'd already vetoed a visit to Cass, now living in a hiring in Alverstoke, saying that he must get straight back to the boat. 'I think they deserve a break.'

They looked at the twins who were standing, shoulder to shoulder, staring at themselves in the looking glass set in the door of the huge ugly wardrobe. Kate laughed.

'Why not?' she said. 'May as well start making ourselves at home.'

LEAVING THE BUNGALOW AND the moors was every bit as agonising as Kate knew it would be. The General was sad to see them go but bore up like the stoical old soldier that he was.

'Got a home here if ever you need it,' he said, shaking hands gravely with the bemused twins. "Only need to pick up the telephone. Come for a holiday.'

Kate flung her arms around him. 'Thank you for everything— finding the bungalow, showing me the moor, everything. It's been wonderful. I shall come and see you often and you must stay in touch.

Not just through Cass. You must write and tell me how the moor is looking . . . ' She swallowed back tears, her face buried in his rough tweed jacket.

He held her tightly. 'Oh, my dear.'

Mrs Hampton was in the kitchen waiting her turn. She gave Kate two little parcels. 'That's for 'em to open on the journey,' she said, her eyes suspiciously bright. ' 'Tis a long way for two li'l mites. They'll get bored. An' this is for you. No call to open it now.'

But Kate was already tearing away the paper and holding up an exquisitely hand-knitted Aran jersey.

' 'Tis nothin'.' Mrs Hampton brushed away Kate's stammered thanks. 'I'm always knittin' somethin' an' I know 'ow you always like to be in those old trousers with a great big woolly. 'Twill keep you warm up there by the sea.' She scrubbed away furiously at the spotless sink. 'Go on, now. Time you were off. Take 'em away or that 'usband of yours'll be wonderin' where you've got to. Come on, my lovers, let 'Ammy put 'ee in the car.'

They both stayed to wave goodbye and Kate set out, awash with tears, to drive across her beloved moors on her way to Portsmouth, following Mark who had set out earlier in a hired van with all their possessions.

PORTSMOUTH WAS A DISASTER from first to last. Neither of them had realised that they must notify the gas and electricity boards to have the supplies connected. The flat was cold and there was no way to heat or cook food. The twins were tired and hungry and Kate, distraught and longing for a cup of tea, finally persuaded the unwilling Mark to go out to buy some sort of camping stove whilst she dealt with the inventory and did her best for the twins with the remains of the picnic. The only other occupant of the building was the wife of a Supply Officer who had come up through the ranks and was, therefore, a Lieutenant like Mark but considerably older. Once Kate had completed the formalities with the representative from the Married Quarters Office and they had jointly inspected every item on the inventory, which took them nearly an hour, this kindly woman invited her in for a cup of tea and was heating some milk for the twins when Kate heard Mark return. She went out into the hall to find him empty-handed and disgruntled.

'It's early closing day,' he said resentfully. 'Everything's shut.'

'Bad luck.' Her heart sank at the sight of his face. 'Would you like a cup of tea? Mrs Richards in there,' she gestured towards the opposite flat, 'has just given me one and says you're very welcome. She's going to let me use her phone to get onto the gas and electricity people.'

'I don't want any bloody tea. I'll get on with the unpacking.' He managed as usual to convey that everything was her fault.

Kate settled the twins in their new bedroom with some of the toys that she had unpacked and hurried back across the hall to make her telephone calls, only to discover that neither utility could do anything until the following morning. Realising how much the General had taken on to his shoulders during the move to Devon, she went back to her own flat aware that she should have asked Mark for the moving-in instructions and checked them herself. No point in antagonising him now. She could hear his voice raised angrily as she went through the front door.

'Here we are,' she said cheerfully, smiling at a tearful Giles and pretending not to see Mark's cross face. 'Mrs Richards has given me a big flask of hot milk and another with boiling water. We should be able to manage now.'

The next few days passed in a muddle of packing away unwanted glass, china and cutlery and unpacking their own belongings. The twins, who missed the freedom of the garden and who were not allowed outside the door without Kate, grizzled. The weather was cold. The flat bleak and depressing. Mark was tired when he arrived home in the evenings from the dockyard and hinted that it would be nice if the twins were in bed by that time so that he could relax. Kate had envisaged happy moments: she and Mark bathing the twins, Mark reading them bedside stories and even playing with them while she prepared supper. She soon found that this was to remain a dream.

His object was to get home, switch on the television and slump in front of it, moving only to the table to eat his supper, one eye still on the screen. There were no intimate moments, no sharing of household tasks. He remained uninterested in the twins, ignoring them for most of the time and then suddenly playing fast and furious games that tended to end with either Guy or Giles in tears. Then he would get up, shrugging in disgust as if they were spoilt cry babies, unworthy of attention. If Kate took their part, he would look at her with a cynical half smile that made her feel that she was a fussing and overprotective mother. She felt frustrated, disappointed and confused.

Just after they'd moved in, Cass, about to produce her second child and finding the long journey round to Eastney difficult, bullied Felicity into driving her round.

'Now, you simply must come to Paul and Jenny's party tomorrow,' she said as she lay stretched out on Kate's sofa. 'They're dying to see you again. They said to bring the twins and put them upstairs to bed while the party's on. If they can't sleep they can play with their two. They're all about the same age. Or, even better, bring the twins to us first. They can share our baby sitter and you can spend the night. All the gang will be there so do say that you'll come. Any more coffee?' She stretched out a languid arm and passed her coffee cup.

Felicity took it reluctantly and put it on the table. 'Are you going to be up to it, Cass?' she asked, falsely solicitous. 'You look as though you might pop at any moment.'

'Sweet of you to be concerned.' Cass winked at Kate behind Felicity's unsuspecting head. 'Must make an effort, though. There's a few more days to go yet, you know. Anyway, old Tom loves a jolly and I've promised George I'll be there.' She watched Felicity stiffen. 'Isn't it funny how men find women so sexy when they're in pig?'

'It's the first I've heard of it.' Felicity couldn't quite prevent a certain shrillness from creeping into her voice. 'Quite the opposite, I should have thought.'

'Oh, no, no,' Cass protested sleepily. 'Ask Kate. Men can't leave you alone. You should try it.'

Kate poured the last drops from the coffee pot into Cass's cup, hiding her grin. She knew that Felicity suspected Cass of trying to seduce George, whom she regarded as her own property and with whom she had been having an affair for some months. It was naughty of Cass to tease but Kate could quite see how irresistible it must be. Felicity never failed to rise to the bait like a starving trout.

'I don't think you'd find my Mark agreeing with you,' she was saying. 'We've decided—no children! He finds the whole process messy from start to finish and so do I.'

'I should have thought the start . . . ' Cass yawned and snuggled into the old patchwork quilt that Kate kept on the sofa. 'Oh, well. All I can say is that I had quite a different impression from Mark. Still, you should know him better than I do. Old George just loves it, of course. Keeps cuddling me and putting his hand on my bump to feel the little bugger kicking. Mind you, I don't have to be preggers for George to fancy me.'

Felicity, already rankling at Cass's 'should,' looked as if she might implode and Kate took pity on her.

'I've got to make some more coffee,' she said. 'Charlotte or one of the twins is crying and if you're feeling well enough to go to a party, Cass, you're well enough to get off the sofa and go and sort it out!'

Three days later, Cass was brought to bed with her second child. It was a boy this time, blond, beautiful. Oliver.

WHEN THEY'D BEEN AT the flat for a month, Mark took a fortnight of overdue leave. Kate cherished great hopes of these two weeks. The weather was kind, warm and spring-like, and they explored the country inland, visited Porchester Castle and went to Winchester.

On the Wednesday afternoon, Mark received a telegram. It was a message instructing him to contact the Appointer (known colloquially as God since he held all their lives in his hands). When Mark returned from the interview, Kate was sitting at the dressing table drying her hair.

'I'm in the bedroom,' she called, when she heard him come in. 'Hello. What was it all about?' She looked at him through the mirror and then lowered her arms; he looked drawn and preoccupied. She turned on the stool to face him. 'What's the matter? What did he say?' For some reason she felt quite frightened.

Mark came further into the room. 'I've been pierhead jumped. He's sending me to another boat as Third Hand. They've had a personality clash and one of the chaps has been taken off which means that they need somebody in a hurry.'

'But why you?' cried Kate. 'There must be other people around with the same seniority.'

'Obviously not.' He didn't look at her. He could hardly tell her that he was delighted to be going back to sea and had jumped at the chance. 'I'm on a refit boat. I can be spared more easily and they're in a fix.'

Suddenly she knew why he would not look at her. 'Mark,' she said, getting up and going to him, 'does it mean that you're going back to sea?'

'I'm afraid so.' He lit a cigarette. 'I had no choice, you know. I couldn't just say no.'

You couldn't! thought Kate. I bet you didn't even try! She made a great effort to pull herself together.

'Which boat is it?' Her heart gave a wild leap upwards. 'It's not . . . It couldn't be based in Devonport, could it?'

'God, no. It's *Oceanus*. She's over in *Dolphin*.'

'Oh, well.' Kate sighed. 'I suppose there's no point in arguing about it. Let's just hope that she spends more time alongside than the last one did. How soon do you have to join? At least we've got another week of leave.'

Mark looked at her at last. 'I'm afraid not. She sails on Monday and we'll be away for three months.'

BEFORE MARK WENT TO sea, Kate begged him to find out if there was by any chance a vacant quarter in Alverstoke. It was the Friday morning and they were still at breakfast. They intended to make the most of their last free day—for the weekend would be taken up with washing his kit and packing—by taking a picnic to the New Forest, finishing up with tea at Lymington.

'You could dash out and telephone the Married Quarters Officer or we could pop into the office on our way to the New Forest.'

'We've got a quarter,' said Mark, eating his eggs and bacon. 'They won't give us another one.'

'But it's in the wrong place,' cried Kate as she cut up Giles' bacon. 'It'll be hell being on opposite sides of the harbour. How will you get to and fro when the boat's in? You'll have to catch the ferry from *Dolphin* to *Vernon,* obviously, but I'll never know which one you'll be on.'

'That's easy. You'll have to go out to the telephone box and phone the boat every afternoon.'

'Are you kidding? You should try it. First of all, the dockyard exchange is engaged for twenty minutes. Then you get through and the boat's engaged. And when you finally get through to the boat they tell you that the person you want is ashore—not even on board—and suggest you try again in half an hour! And, don't forget, I have to drag the twins out with me every time.'

'Well, you'll have to put up with it. Oh, for heaven's sake! Guy's dropping egg everywhere. Can't you do something, Kate? Having breakfast with these two is enough to ruin anybody's appetite.'

'That's Giles,' said Kate quietly, 'and you could try to remember that they're only two years old.'

'Yes, well. You know my views about that. I see no point to children until they're old enough to hold an intelligent conversation.'

'Then let's hope,' said Kate, 'that when that time finally arrives, they feel *you're* worth talking to.' She glanced at him. His face was bleak and closed and his eyelids drooped a little over his cold grey gaze. She felt a tiny flicker of fear.

'I've just seen the solution to your problem,' he said softly. 'Obviously, when the boat isn't in, transport isn't a problem. When it is in, I shall take the car. I'll drive round to *Dolphin.* It means that you'll have to do without it, of course. What a pity. Never mind. You managed without a car before and I'm sure you'll manage again.' He pushed back his chair and stood up. 'I've just remembered, I'm going to have to go out. Don't know how long I'll be. I'm afraid our day in the New Forest will have to wait!' He went out.

The twins looked at her expectantly.

'Daddy gone!' said Giles cheerfully. He always seemed happier when this was the case.

'Very true,' agreed Kate, trying to beat down the anger which she knew would frighten Giles who was very sensitive to the moods of those about him. She managed a smile. 'Eat up and then we'll go down to the beach.'

AFTER OLIVER WAS BORN, Cass returned to the fray, more beautiful and vivacious than ever. She obviously adored the child and, when people commented on his likeness to her and the complete absence of any of Tom's characteristics, she would smile.

'One each,' she'd say. 'Charlotte's all Tom and Oliver's all me.'

This was true. Even from day one, Oliver seemed to have his hands on all the ropes, avoiding all the traumas of babyhood and moving smoothly from one phase to the next. As for Cass, she realised that motherhood in no way impaired her charms or clipped her wings. She smiled to herself when she thought of Tom, who was fairly confident that she was now safely removed from the dangers of the hunting male. She often wondered if he was faithful to her. He would sometimes return from sea with some new technique or idea to be tried out in bed and Cass would wonder who had taught it to him. There were always plenty of girls around when submarines went on visits. The host town wanted to give the Navy a good time and there would be parties on board and in people's homes and plenty of opportunities for extramarital fun.

Once, after a particularly exciting session in bed, Cass had challenged him but Tom merely said that he'd been reading somebody's *Playboy*—an article on how to keep your sex life new and exciting. Cass had laughed and told him she was all for it and when Tom, in an ecstasy of gratitude, had risen from the bed and insisted on taking her out to dinner, she was even more amused.

She didn't even have sibling jealousy to contend with. Charlotte was very proud of her new brother and would bring him little presents or hug him warmly.

'You are lucky,' said Kate looking enviously at Oliver. 'I'd love another one but Mark won't hear of it. Says two are quite enough. Shall you have any more?'

'Oh, yes,' said Cass at once. 'Four at least, I think. Such fun, isn't it? And people make a fuss of you and dear old Tom gets so pleased with himself. Odd, that, isn't it? After all, animals are doing it all the time, and people of course, but Tom thinks it's a great achievement. Do you like Mark II?'

'Not much. And I have to say that I think it's too bad of you to make such passes at him.'

Cass burst out laughing. 'Don't look so po-faced. It doesn't suit you. You're thinking of that party last week on the Norwegian boat.'

'Yes, I am. You were all over each other and Felicity was nearly out of her mind.'

'She had George dancing attendance. Parties on submarines are so boring. Dancing round and round the dreary old periscope or being squashed into the Wardroom and having to go to the loo in those ghastly little holes that they call, for some reason, "heads." And that awful pong of diesel! I had to do something to liven it up a bit. Kate, why don't you just forget to take the pill?'

Kate stared at her blankly.

'If you want another baby!' said Cass impatiently. 'It's your life, too. If you want one, have one. Get pregnant before he goes to sea next time and don't tell him before he's well away, when it's much too late.'

'Too late for what?'

'An abortion. You don't think he'd let you keep it, do you, after he'd said no?'

'I'd never have an abortion!'

'No? Not even if Mark insisted?' Cass gave Kate a strange look. 'Shall I tell you something? Your Mark is the only man I've ever known who makes me feel afraid.'

'No, no!' This was something Kate was not yet prepared to admit, even to herself. 'He's just . . . It's really . . . '

'Well, it's an idea. That is, if you're really desperate to have another one. Listen. I've got a bottle in the fridge. Why don't we get pissed?'

If it had been left to Mark they would have continued to live at Eastney, with Kate and the twins more cut off from all the social life that was attached to the submarine as well as that relating to *Dolphin* itself.

Once the boat had sailed, Kate enlisted the help of the naval grapevine and sat back to await results. It was a fairly quiet three months. On sunny days she would pile the twins in the car and drive round to Alverstoke. She and Cass would sit in the little garden or take the children to the beach; Oliver lying in his pram, shaded by a parasol, whilst Charlotte and the twins would play quite happily together, building sand castles and making roads on which to run the twins' toy cars. The girls would lie on the sun-warmed rug, drowsing and making desultory conversation.

'Perhaps,' Kate said on one such afternoon, 'perhaps Charlotte will marry one of the twins when she grows up.'

'Mmmmm.'

'Which one, do you think?'

'Oh, I think Giles. She likes Giles best.'

'Do you think so? She's such a sweetie. I'd love a little girl.'

'Mmmmm.'

'What do you want, next time, Cass?'

'I shall have another boy. But just like Tom.'

'How can you be so sure?'

'I just can. Be a duck and get the picnic out. I'm dying of thirst.'

Quiet, happy, peaceful days that women share when their children are very young.

Seven

Oddly, it was Felicity who found the little house in Solent Way. It belonged to a naval couple who were being sent to Singapore and they were more than happy to let it to another naval couple. The system was that if there were no married quarters in the area to which a naval officer was posted, the Navy would give an allowance towards rented accommodation. If it were more expensive, as it invariably was, the difference had to come out of his pay. Felicity had sung Kate's praises to the couple with whom she had become very friendly and they were prepared to be as helpful as possible over the rent, relieved to have a reliable tenant and confident that Kate would be prepared to move out should they need to come back unexpectedly.

One sunny morning she went round to look at it with Felicity, leaving the twins with Cass. It was a fairly ordinary, comfortably furnished, three-bedroomed house with a long, secluded pretty garden. Kate could see that it was perfect for her. The house would not be difficult to keep clean, there was central heating and the garden would be wonderful for the twins. She let her enthusiasm show, pleasing the owners, and, over a cup of coffee, they struck an agreeable bargain.

'They're really nice,' said Kate as Felicity drove her back to Anglesea Road. She had been rather surprised that Felicity had put herself out to the extent of finding a house for her. 'And the house is lovely. I can't thank you enough. It will be terrific to get back to civilisation.'

'It was no problem.' Felicity shrugged off Kate's thanks. 'Anything I can do to help with the move, just say the word.'

'Bless you.' Kate was faintly suspicious at this sudden display of camaraderie. 'I'm hoping to do it in relays in the car rather than hiring a van. I shall need masses of cardboard cartons. Cass says she'll do a few trips and then have the twins for the day. It will be much easier without them.'

'Well, I can load up my car, too, if it's any help. It'll be nice to have you a bit closer. For one thing you might be a bit of a restraining influence on Cass.'

Kate's eyebrows shot up in surprise. 'Heavens! Does Cass need restraining? What's she been up to?'

'She's getting a reputation.' Felicity changed gear rather viciously. 'People are talking about her.'

'People have always talked about her,' said Kate soothingly, wondering if Cass had been flirting with Mark II again and sensing a possible motive for Felicity's goodwill. 'She's a shocking flirt but it doesn't really mean anything. You know that.'

'I'm not talking about flirting. There are rumours going around about her and Tony.'

'Oh, Tony!' Kate sounded relieved. Tony Whelan, who had been at Dartmouth with Mark and Tom, was teaching the specialisation course in *Dolphin*. 'Tony flirts with all of us.'

'I'm not talking about flirting,' said Felicity again. 'Jenny said that she went round the other day, rang the bell, no reply. The car was there so she went round the back and peered in and banged on the back door. And Cass appeared at the bottom of the stairs—you know how you can see them through the glass—doing herself up, Jenny said, hair all over the place. Anyway, she let her in, very casual, and then Tony appeared. Cass said he'd popped in to borrow a book on navigation that Tom had promised him. Tony said he must be going and went. Jenny said that Cass looked as if she was going to explode with laughter.'

'And did he have a book?'

'Well, he did as it happened. Had it in his hand when he appeared, cool as a cucumber, Jenny said.'

'Well, then.'

Felicity swung the car into Anglesea Road and pulled up at Cass's gate. 'The point is that while Tony was saying goodbye, Jenny managed to get a good look at the title.'

'And?'

Felicity turned to look at her. 'And the book just happened to be *The Wind in the Willows*!'

'BUT IT IS, DARLING! *The Wind in the Willows* is absolutely packed with information about navigation. Dear old Ratty, up and down the river all day long, showing Mole how to steer and things. Surely you remember?'

'I remember perfectly well and I can't imagine for a single moment that Tom would give Tony a copy of *The Wind in the Willows*.'

'Lend, darling. Only lend. Heavens, Kate! For a moment then you looked just like dear old Nanny. Now, promise that you're not going to become all stuffy or I shan't be able to tell you things. Look, Guy has drawn you a lovely picture of a submarine—just what you need!—and Giles has made you a plasticine man. Now come and have a drink and tell me all about it. Charlotte's done you a picture, too. It's your new house and these are all the flowers growing around it. They've all been so good and quiet.'

Kate admired all these works of industry and imagination with great enthusiasm and followed Cass through to the sunny little terrace at the back of the house. The children, delighted by her appreciation of their efforts, suddenly became very noisy and excitable and rushed out on to the lawn where various outdoor toys stood. They began to throw themselves about, shouting and showing off. Kate put the drawings and the little figure on Cass's garden table and sat down in one of the wicker chairs beside it. Oliver's pram stood at the far end of the lawn, beneath the flowering cherry. Presently Cass joined her, carrying a bottle and two glasses.

'So what's the house like? Tell me all. Do I gather that Felicity thought that she might be polluted if she came in?'

'The house is great.' Kate began to laugh rather helplessly. 'Oh, honestly Cass! *The Wind in the Willows*! Couldn't you do better than that?'

'Well, to be honest, it was all rather spur of the moment stuff. There was old Jenny, ringing and hammering away, and Tony couldn't find his knickers and we were dashing about, thinking up reasons why he'd come and the book was just lying there. Charlotte often comes into my bed in the mornings and I read to her for a bit. Thank goodness I'd taken the paper cover off but even so. Old Eagle Eye Jenny must have been really peering. Thank God it wasn't Beatrix Potter!'

They both rocked with laughter.

'But Cass, Tony . . . '

'He's such a sweetie. He just popped round, you know, being friendly and the children were asleep and it was all hot and sleepy and sexy. You know the sort of afternoon. We had a little drink and, well, I'm sure you can imagine the rest.'

'But what if Tom finds out?'

'Well, he won't! Don't start going all dreary. Remember, it's me who's Cassandra and supposed to foretell gloom. Not you!'

Kate sighed. 'OK. But every time I look at Tony now I shall imagine it.'

Cass topped up their glasses. 'I found his knickers when I went to bed that night,' she said, musing. 'All wrapped up in the sheets. Thank God Tom didn't come home unexpectedly! Now! Do tell me all about the new house and then we'll have some lunch.'

ON HIS ARRIVAL BACK in Gosport, Mark was delighted to find that all problems had been solved and that Kate and the twins were installed in a jolly little house in Alverstoke. His relief at not being called upon to take any of the decisions—or to do any of the work—made him quite expansive. The boat was now alongside for a maintenance period and for the remainder of the summer they were able to enjoy the social life as much as possible, given that Mark was by no means a social animal and always made some difficulty or other about every event. Kate met the rest of the Wardroom and persuaded Mark, after quite a round of parties, that they must give one of their own. He became very taciturn until Cass suggested that they make it a barbecue. She would lend the equipment and Tom, who cooked a mean steak, could be assistant chef.

That did the trick and Mark was able to anticipate the event without too much anxiety. It was a great success although they held it not a moment too soon for that September was the wettest for many years and there was a tremendous amount of flooding.

Kate, guided by Cass, had started to pay more attention to her appearance, which she had neglected in Devon. She let her brown curls grow longer and wore pretty cotton shift dresses, although she clung to her jeans for ordinary daily wear. Having the twins to look after kept her slender and by the time the summer was over she had almost as many admirers as Cass. Felicity, not to be outdone, had a Mary Quant haircut and wore very short miniskirts that looked well with her thin, tanned legs. With her almost black hair and eyes she was an excellent foil for Cass's tall, fair voluptuousness.

The boat was due to sail to Gothenburg just after the twins' third birthday and there was the usual end of maintenance party on board. On the way to the boat, Kate found herself puzzling as usual as to why submariners were so keen to hold parties on board. She had got used to going carefully down the gangplank—purgatory in high-heeled shoes when sober and hell after a few drinks—on to the casing of the inboard submarine, crossing by another gangplank to the next and so to the host boat. She let Mark precede her down the hatch and then climbed down herself by means of the vertical ladder which only descended so far before she had to turn to step across the hatch so as to continue down the other side. This procedure, accompanied by the threat of diesel oil—death to evening clothes—had now become part of her life and, as such, familiar.

Descending into the warm and smoky atmosphere humming with voices, Mark standing at the bottom of the ladder so that no passing sailor could look up her skirt, Kate felt the usual small thrill of anticipation.

She was manoeuvred into the Wardroom, designed to hold six officers in minimal comfort and now packed with at least twenty people,
and was hailed by Tony Whelan who presently fought his way to her
side bearing a gin and tonic in either hand. He passed one to her and
hugged her with his free arm. She hugged him back, perfectly able to
understand the attraction he held for Cass. He had an easy charm and a
ready sense of humour and the knack of making a woman feel fatally
attractive. Kate, who considered this to be a perfectly admirable trait,
enjoyed it to the full whilst knowing that it meant nothing. She par-
ried his advances, laughed at his jokes and went to dance with him in
the crowded control room, circling the periscope in his intimate embrace and ignoring Mark's displeased face. Mark hated dancing and,
although he rarely danced with Kate, rather resented anyone else who
did. They circled the periscope yet again and Kate, beginning to suspect that Tony had at least six hands, caught sight of Mark, watching
her now with something like distaste.

She remembered that during the time she had left to her before the
boat sailed she was still hoping to convert Mark to the idea of another
baby and reluctantly pushed Tony away.

'Come on, octopus,' she said. 'Let's go and find something to eat.'

When the boat sailed, Kate took Mark into *Dolphin,* wondering
why submarines always went to Harbour Stations at seven in the morning, hugged him goodbye and drove away. He discouraged her from
waiting to see the boat sail although some wives went into *Dolphin*'s
Wardroom and out on to the balcony to wave the boat past as it went
down the river to the channel. Sometimes, if the weather was fine,
Kate would take the twins to the beach and they would watch from
there until the black hull was no longer visible. Today, since it was
raining and Mark would not know—or care—if they were there or
not, Kate drove straight home and put the kettle on. Strange how
the smell of diesel seemed to cling. It was a smell that all through her
life would instantly remind her of submarines, brown canvas holdalls,
starched white collars just back from the laundry in cardboard boxes,
windy dockyards and the poignant sense of waiting. Always waiting.

Waiting for the boat to come in. Waiting for the leave to start. Waiting for the shore job.

As KATE WAS FINISHING the washing up after lunch a tiny plan formed in her mind. Perhaps she would take a trip to Cornwall to see her family and, on the way, she would stop off to see the General. Tom's boat would be sailing soon so Cass might like to come too. It would be such fun to go together, just for a week or two. Her heart lifted at the thought and she went to the telephone and dialled Cass's number. It rang for some time and she was about to hang up when there was a click and Cass's voice said: 'Hello.' At the same time a man's voice could be heard clearly in the background.

'Hello, Cass,' said Kate. 'Is that Tom I can hear? I thought he had to go to London today. Is he OK?'

'Can I call you back?' Cass sounded as if she were trying not to laugh. 'Bit of a crisis. I'll speak to you later.'

There was a click as the receiver was replaced. Kate stood puzzled, thinking hard. Giles started calling to her from the landing and she put the receiver back on its rest and started to climb the stairs. It was only later that she realised that she had recognised the man's voice. It was George Lampeter's.

WHEN IT SEEMED THAT both Tom and Mark were going to be at home for Christmas, it was agreed between parents and grandparents that the children would be happier in their own homes and the trip to the West Country became a compromise between a little holiday and a pre-Christmas visit.

The girls decided to travel together in Kate's car, Charlotte squashed between the twins' seats and Oliver in his carrycot on the seat by their feet. They were all very uncomfortable but immensely excited and took it in good part. It was arranged that the twins should take turn and turn about with Charlotte and that regular stops should be made for leg stretching and refreshment.

'Thank God Mark's father insisted on an estate car,' said Kate as they packed their luggage as well as Christmas presents and a picnic into the back. 'If the kids get too uncomfortable with Oliver crammed in front of them, we'll put his carrycot in here.'

They set off in good spirits but it was well into the afternoon when Kate turned on to the Moretonhampstead road out of Exeter. As it began to climb up to the moor she felt her spirits climbing with it. It was a quiet day, warm for December, and the clouds moved lazily before the wind that blew gently from the south-west. Today the moor was a study in pastels: chalky browns for the bleached grasses and dying bracken, soft charcoal grey for the granite tors smudged against creamy slow-moving clouds, the hills, unfolding mistily into the distance, a soft muted blue. Kate pulled off the road, released the children who ran to look at the little stream, and stood gazing about her. Cass brought her a mug of coffee, the last of the picnic.

'Glad to be back?' she asked.

'Home,' amended Kate. 'I feel as if I've come home. I can't imagine how I ever managed to leave it.'

The General and Mrs Hampton underlined this feeling. They hurried out to greet the travellers, exclaiming over how much the children had grown and hugging the two girls. Mrs Hampton crooned admiringly over Oliver, who took all such tributes in his stride, and hurried off with him, Charlotte beside her.

'Just like dear old Nanny,' said Cass, stretching mightily and slipping her arm through her father's. 'You're looking terrific, Daddy. Younger than ever. Are you going to be able to squeeze us all in?'

'It certainly is going to be a squeeze,' he agreed, 'but the more the merrier. You two are in the bigger bedroom with the cot, and the boys and Charlotte are in the little one. In the end I decided to buy some bunk beds. Two sets. If you go on like this, I'll be needing them and it saves space.'

'The twins will be out of their heads with joy,' said Kate, taking his other arm. 'Their one ambition is to sleep in bunk beds. Let's go and show them.'

'First things first.' The General was unable to contain his excitement.

'Get the children together. I've got something to show them in the drawing room.'

They all trooped in and stopped short with little cries of pleasure. In one corner, to the right of a blazing log fire, stood a Christmas tree, its coloured lights twinkling softly. The baubles and decorations shimmered and flashed in the firelight as they swung and beneath the tree was a pile of brightly wrapped mysterious looking parcels.

The children, who were too young to remember previous Christmases, were rendered quite speechless as they gazed with wondering eyes upon the magic of it and the General, watching their faces with delight, was amply rewarded for all his efforts.

Kate found that she was clutching his hand and when she looked across at Cass she saw tears in her eyes.

'I thought that we'd celebrate early, my darlings,' he was saying. 'After all, the Queen has two birthdays, why not the Christ Child?'

Mrs Hampton, carrying Oliver and holding Charlotte's hand, nodded. ''Tis right pretty,' she said, her eyes bright. 'We got mince pies made, too, an' a cake an' a sizeable old chicken in the fridge. 'Twas too early to get a turkey but 'e'll do us. Now, what about some tea?' She bore the reluctant children away to be cleaned up.

'It's absolutely perfect,' said Cass.

'Did you see their faces?' Kate smiled. 'They'll never forget that as long as they live. Neither shall I.'

The General looked pleased. 'It went down very well,' he agreed. 'Now, all that we need to do is to choose which day to have as our own private Christmas. We may want to wait until Kate and the twins come back from Cornwall. Meanwhile, what about that unpacking? Come and see what we've done upstairs and then we can all relax.'

'It's funny,' said Kate, as they drove home again a week later. 'I find it harder to say goodbye to your father than I do to Mark! And I always hate leaving Devon.'

'Perhaps Mark'll get another boat down here,' suggested Cass, deciding to ignore the first half of the remark. 'You never know your luck.'

But when the time came and they were appointed as First Lieutenants, it was Tom who was given a boat running out of Devonport, while Mark was sent to Faslane, the submarine base built at the head of the Gare Loch on the west coast of Scotland.

Part Two

Eight

1972-75

Both Tom and Mark were recommended out of their First Lieutenants' jobs for Perisher: the submariners' Commanding Officers Qualifying Course. They were both exultant—and terrified. The Perisher lasted overall for about six months and now, with Mark's appointment to Faslane coming to an end, the question of where to live arose. Once an officer had passed the course, he was given a submarine to drive and no one could possibly guess which of the three bases that submarine might be running from.

Kate had enjoyed Scotland, revelling in the wild, beautiful country north of the small town of Helensburgh which stood at the end of the Gare Loch. Mark had been at sea for most of the two years and she and the twins had explored the country together and had been made to feel at home in the base which looked out over the loch to the mountains beyond. Nevertheless, she was very glad to be back in the West Country and delighted and relieved that Mark had succeeded thus far. Her suggestion was that they move to Alverstoke so that she would be able to give him some moral support for the first part of the course. The Attack Teacher was at the Submarine School at *Dolphin*. Mark wasn't so keen.

'I shall be revising like mad to begin with and in the Attack Teacher most days. Then I shall be here at Faslane for the periscope time. It would probably be more sensible if I get a cabin in *Dolphin*. I can concentrate better on my own. No distractions. If I pass, I could get a boat anywhere. Couldn't you go down to Cornwall for a bit?'

The Attack Teacher was a simulated submarine control room where the Perishers practised attacks of all types before spending six weeks on a conventional submarine doing it for real with an obliging frigate.

It was during these six weeks that tempers frayed and people tended to crack up. If an officer failed, it was generally during this period. They would be tactfully taken aside, informed that they had failed and taken quietly off the submarine without the others knowing.

Kate, knowing how Mark would react to failure, prayed fervently that he would pass. Meanwhile, where would she and the twins go since he didn't want them at Alverstoke? After all, they had to live somewhere.

When Mark left the boat at Faslane, he was given a fortnight's leave and they went down to Cornwall. While Mark was out sailing with her brother Chris, Kate told her mother the problem.

'He doesn't really want us in Alverstoke,' she said, as they stood together chopping vegetables and preparing the dinner, 'and I can understand that. This is vitally important to him: his whole naval life has been leading up to this and if he fails, his career in submarines will be finished. That's why it's called Perisher—so many do! It seems so unfair that they just get sent back to general service as failures, especially as you have to be exceptional to be recommended for Perisher in the first place. I think it's very important that he plays it his way and it's not easy to study and revise in a small house with two active children. The trouble is, wherever I go, you can be sure that Mark will be posted somewhere else if he passes. I shan't be allowed a married quarter if Mark's not there and I'm not sure that I'll be able to rent anywhere for just six months. And I've got to get the twins back into school. They were just nicely settled in Helensburgh. It would be awful to put them somewhere for six months and then move them on again.'

'You're always welcome here,' said her mother. 'You know that. But it won't solve the problem of the twins' schooling. We'd love to have you but Daddy's got something up his sleeve. He wanted to tell you himself but he won't be home until the weekend so I'm sure he won't mind if I spill the beans.

'The thing is that he's sold some land on the edge of the village. Managed to get planning permission on it so he was able to ask a very respectable price for it. He wants to give the four of you a sum each—don't worry, it leaves a tidy bit over for our old age!—but the stipulation is that you all use it for something sensible. James and Sarah are putting it towards a new roof and Chris is going to buy himself a decent car. Penny's too young really. She's trying to wheedle us into buying her a pony.

'Now, Daddy wondered whether you might like to use it as a deposit on a little house. You know his maxim: never rent if you can buy! What d'you think? I shan't tell you the amount, I'll leave that to him, but it will be enough for a very reasonable deposit, I promise.'

The idea took Kate's breath away for a moment. Her mother smiled and went on chopping and presently Kate found her voice.

'It's unbelievable! We've thought of it, of course. We can afford a small mortgage but it's always the deposit that kills it. I can never seem to get the budget organised well enough to save anything. Oh, I can't believe it!' She dropped the knife and hugged her mother. 'Oh, thank you! I can't wait to tell Mark.' She paused.

'Yes?' Her mother saw the thoughtful look returning. 'What now?'

'Well, it still doesn't answer the question of where. That still remains the same.'

Her mother picked up the chopping board and swept the vegetables into a large casserole dish.

'It ought to be near one of the three submarine bases,' she said. 'Then you've got a one in three chance of living in your own home, and plenty of people wanting to rent if you have to move. But which one is up to you. I hope not Faslane. Scotland's so far away. It's between Gosport and Devonport, I should think.' She smiled at Kate's expression. 'I'm sure that I don't need to guess which you'll choose.'

'Oh, Mummy! We could buy a little cottage on Dartmoor, couldn't we? Just a small one.'

'If you can get a mortgage. It's always more difficult on older properties, remember. Still, you might be lucky. You could have a look when you go up to stay with Cass and Tom at Crapstone. Get the General to keep his eyes open. Anyway, it's a thought.'

'KATE AND MARK ARE going to buy a house,' announced Cass when Tom arrived home that afternoon. 'Kate phoned, she's absolutely out of her mind with excitement. She wants us to keep an eye open for a nice little cottage on the moor or as near as possible.'

'What's brought that on?' asked Tom, swinging Charlotte up and giving her a smacking kiss and ruffling Oliver's fair head. 'Bit sudden, isn't it?'

'Her parents are giving them the deposit. They've sold some land or something.'

'Well, it has to happen sometime. We ought to be thinking about it, I suppose.' He sat down at the kitchen table with Charlotte perched on one knee while Cass peeled potatoes at the sink. 'The trouble is, where does one decide to live? Not to mention finding the deposit, of course. I should have thought that it would be more sensible to wait 'til after Perisher. At least they'd know where Mark was going. If they buy here you can bet your boots he'll get a boat in Faslane.'

'You think he'll pass then?'

'Oh, I should think so. He's good at his job. Not what I'd call popular but he's a good submariner.'

Cass wrinkled her nose and shrugged.

'Oh, I know you don't like him,' acknowledged Tom, 'but you women are so personal. He's OK.'

'He doesn't want Kate and the twins with him while he's on Perisher. Thinks he won't be able to concentrate.'

Tom strove to be fair. 'Well, you're not coming up either, are you, love? There really isn't any point in moving twice. We'll only be in *Dolphin* for a couple of months before we go north. We'll move when I know where I'm going. I've arranged with the married quarters people that you can stay on here 'til then.'

'That's fine. I can see that it's the obvious thing to do. But poor Kate has nowhere to go for six months and she's got to get the twins back into school. She's going to buy here and hope for the best.'

'Well, they may be lucky.' Tom nuzzled Charlotte's neck. 'And how was school today?'

'It was all right.' Charlotte had been following the conversation closely. 'If the twins come to live here they can come to my school, can't they?'

'Probably. If they're close enough to Meavy. Would you like that?'

'Oh, yes.' Charlotte beamed at him. 'You must get a submarine here, Daddy. I don't want to move any more.'

Cass and Tom's eyes met briefly and Tom gave Charlotte a hug.

'I shall do my very best. Goodness! Is that the time? Come on, I'm missing the Magic Roundabout!'

MEANWHILE, THERE WAS THE question of a dog. For a long time, Kate had been promising the twins—and herself—that they should have one. Perhaps, if they were going to have their own home at last, that time had come. Finally the breed was decided on: it was to be a golden retriever. A name was discussed ad nauseam. The twins, besotted with *The Hobbit,* wanted Bilbo. Kate havered. She felt that they should first find the puppy and then name it.

'She's right,' nodded Cass, with whom they were staying at Crapstone. 'You need to see puppies—and babies—before you can decide on names, or you can get it wrong. Imagine if I'd called Oliver "Bert," say, or "Sid." It wouldn't be him, would it?'

The twins roared with laughter. Bert and Sid seemed such wildly improbable names. Oliver smiled serenely and ate a cup cake. Kate, not for the first time, had a strange feeling that he was older than all of them, herself included.

'And what does Charlotte think?' she asked, retrieving the last cup cake and giving it to her as she sat, quiet as always, listening and watching. 'What would you call a puppy, Charlotte?'

'Huckle,' returned Charlotte, who was a Richard Scarry fan.

'And why not?' Kate smiled at her. 'It's a jolly nice name. What do you say, Oliver?'

Oliver deftly took the cake from which Charlotte had removed the silver paper and ate it.

'Dog,' he said with his mouth full. 'I'd call it dog.'

THE SUMMER BALL AT HMS *Drake,* the shore establishment at Devonport dockyard, saw them all gathered together again.

'Quite the old gang, isn't it?' Cass slid into her place and put her evening bag on the table. 'Nice to be at a ball again. Who's the dark girl dancing with Tom? I haven't seen her before, have I?'

'She's called Harriet,' said Mark II, following Cass's gaze. 'She's Ralph Masters' new girlfriend. He's just come down from *Dolphin.* Seems he's an old friend of Tom's.'

'That's right. They were on *Optimist* together. What fun. I must meet her.' She smiled round the table and reached for a bottle of wine. 'Just think! By the time the Summer Ball comes we could all be Captains' Wives. Think of the glory! And about time, too! What's that line? "They also serve who only stand and wait." Well, that's us. To be honest, I think we deserve it almost as much as they do.'

'I must say,' said Felicity, sipping contentedly at her wine, 'that I'm enjoying every minute of it. I do hope Tom makes it, Cass. The failure rate seems pretty high at the moment. The relief when Mark phoned to say that he'd passed, I can't tell you! They'd been drinking all the way in on the James Bond boat and he was pissed as a rat when he got to the phone. Mind you, everyone said that he'd pass. Who's Teacher now?'

Teacher was the examining officer in whose hands the Perishers' careers were held.

'Jess Hoxworth,' said Cass unperturbed. 'He's an absolute sweetie. Great friend of mine.'

Kate could almost hear Felicity gnashing her teeth and grinned to herself. Poor old Felicity hated it when Cass claimed friendship with

Senior Officers to whom Tom should be almost too overawed to speak. Before she could intervene, however, George was rising from his seat further along the table and gesturing that Felicity should dance with him. She went without a backward glance and Cass sighed with pleasure.

'Felicity-baiting should become a national sport,' she sighed, 'such fun.'

'I see she's still got George on a lead,' observed Kate. 'I gather that your little fling with him didn't last too long.'

'You know me, lovey! Variety is the spice of life and all that.'

Beautiful as ever, elegant in her long gown, Cass seemed untouched by the passing years and yet another baby.

'I must say, Cass, that you don't look like a mother of three,' said Kate enviously. 'How on earth do you do it?'

'It's because I never worry about things. I take everything as it comes. After all, what a life! Who'd be a naval wife? Still, it has its compensations.' Cass smiled reminiscently.

'Does it?' Kate snorted. 'Name one: always moving house, separations, ghastly cocktail parties, everything made as difficult as possible. For instance, why does the Navy always go to Harbour Stations at seven in the morning? Why not lunchtime? Three in the afternoon? No. We all have to be up at dawn, seeing them off . . . '

'And the bloody boat breaks down just outside the breakwater, they all arrive back unexpectedly and you have to do it all over again the next day.'

They burst out laughing.

'I remember that happening three times with one boat. Which one was it, Cass?'

'The third time it was very embarrassing,' she said thoughtfully. 'I really didn't think that it could happen the third day running and . . . Well, it was very embarrassing.' She grimaced. 'Ever played Russian roulette, Kate? It's very exciting. So what do you think of my new baby? He's just like Tom. Told you he would be, didn't I?'

They looked at each other for a long moment.

'One of these days, Cass,' Kate said at last, 'you're going to get the bullet!'

IN THE END, MARK had left for Gosport before Kate found her cottage. She finally tracked it down on the edge of the moor behind Walkhampton, a small stone house with a slate roof and just enough accommodation. Fortunately, the owners had re-wired and re-plumbed it. It had a beamed sitting room with a wood-burning stove, a fair-sized kitchen with a Rayburn and another smaller room that could double as a study and dining room. There was a very basic lavatory in a lean-to at the back. Upstairs there were two good-sized bedrooms, also beamed, the third having been sacrificed to make the bathroom and loo. It had a small but delightful cottage garden in the corner of which stood two adjoining stone outbuildings; one was the log store and garden shed, the other was just big enough to house a car. Kate fell in love with it all at once and plunged headlong into mortgages, solicitors, surveyors and all the other horrors of buying a house. She loved every minute of it because she never imagined that anything would go wrong or that she would be thwarted in her desire to own it. And she was right. Beginner's luck!

She wrote reams to Mark, who had hurried down for a quick approving glance and was now totally absorbed in Perisher.

Thank goodness that it's such a small house, she thought, as she hurried round buying second-hand furniture at bargain prices, and that it's got so many cupboards. She threw bright rugs over worn armchairs, arranged their few precious pictures on the walls and bought a brand new double bed. The twins had their own bunk beds now and painted chests of drawers. Her greatest find, though, was an old pine dresser on which she arranged pretty china and ornaments and this, with an old scrubbed deal table and some rickety chairs, made her kitchen complete.

' . . . add as we go along,' she wrote to Mark, 'but at least we've got the essentials. Bookshelves are a problem. I hope you're good with a drill! I can't wait for you to see what I've done. Thank goodness all the walls were painted white. I can go to town on the colours for other things. It would be lovely to see you for a weekend if you could get away like Tom did but I know how busy you must be. Don't overdo it . . . '

He came down for a weekend before he went to Faslane to join the submarine that had been chosen to carry out the Perisher running. He looked pale and strained and was smoking very heavily. His interest in the cottage and how the twins had settled in to school was cursory and his preoccupation and anxiety were patent.

They left home on the Monday morning, Mark driving, to drop the twins off at school and then to Plymouth station where he was to catch the train. When they arrived he jumped quickly out of the car, taking his grip from the back seat. When Kate joined him on the pavement, he gave her a perfunctory kiss and turned to go. Everything had been said already and, as usual, they were like strangers, polite and distant.

'Good luck, Mark. I'll be thinking of you.'

He smiled pitifully, his face set and pale, waved and set off towards the ticket office.

Kate watched him go. She felt exactly the same as she had when the twins had gone into their classroom on their first day at school: anguish, fear and a longing to rush in and take them away again, to shield them from any hardship or danger.

She climbed into the car and set off back towards Walkhampton. As usual she felt muddled and confused. Mark was obviously an efficient officer. He had risen in his career from job to job, been all over the world, handled crises and air travel and managed in many foreign countries. Why, then, should she feel the need to protect him?

When it came to dealing with anything outside the Navy with its rules and regulations which provided him with a framework in which he felt comfortable—and, as far as Mark was concerned, that included married life—he buckled at the knees. That strange mixture of vulnerability and cruelty was so difficult to combat. She was coming to the conclusion that he was a bully. He kept up a campaign of psychological warfare designed to keep her off-balance. But why? Why couldn't he simply trust her and relax in her love and loyalty? Perhaps he was afraid that she may demand too much in return. She was beginning to realise that she was the stronger character and yet she feared him.

The next few weeks seemed endless.

Kate stayed at home as much as possible in case Mark should telephone. He sometimes did this if he found himself ashore for an evening's relaxation. Their conversations were strained and monosyllabic: yes, he was fine; yes, it was tough; yes, a few more had been thrown off the course. He told her that if he hadn't phoned by eleven o'clock that meant he had survived another day and she took to waiting up until ten past, twenty past, just in case. She knew that he could survive until the final day and still fail. Teacher gave them the maximum opportunity to get it right. Kate began to rehearse conversations, practising how she would respond if he failed whilst feeling disloyal to be even contemplating it. One morning, as she returned from taking the twins to school, she heard the telephone ringing. She raced into the cottage and seized the receiver.

'Kate?' It was Mark's voice. It sounded slurred and strange.

Kate's heart seemed to stop beating altogether and her brain leapt hither and thither trying to remember her rehearsed replies.

'Hello. Yes, it's me. Are you all right?'

'Oh, Kate, I'm through! I've passed! Isn't it fantastic?'

He sounded as if he might burst into tears and Kate realised that she was nodding wordlessly, her eyes tight shut with relief.

'I can't believe it. Can't . . . can't seem to take it in.' Mark seemed to be having difficulty with his words and she guessed that he was drunk.

'It's wonderful!' she cried, finding her voice at last. 'It's terrific, fantastic! Oh, I'm so proud of you. You deserve it. Well done.'

'We've only just been told. Old Tom's made it, too. We've just come in on the James Bond boat and we've been drinking all the way.'

Well, that explained the voice. And why not? He deserved it after all the months of strain.

'There's one thing though. We've been told where we're going.' He gave a sort of snort. 'It's typical! I've been given a boat in *Dolphin*.'

Kate felt a great stab of dismay. She had so hoped for a boat running out of Devonport so that they could stay in their new home. Resolutely she pushed her disappointment away. He had passed and that was all that mattered. She said so.

'I knew that you'd see it like that.' His voice was ebullient now. 'I don't care where it is. I've got a boat to drive and that's all that matters to me. Look, I've got to go now. There's a queue forming. I'll phone you later.'

Trembling from head to foot, Kate replaced the receiver. She suddenly realised how tense she had been for the last few weeks and, sinking into the nearest chair, she burst into tears of relief.

Nine

The turning point came when Kate found that Mark didn't want her around when he passed Perisher and was given a submarine to drive. He would be putting up his half stripe in the autumn and was obviously delighted at the way his career was going. It was confirmed that he would be given a boat running out of *Dolphin* and he put his foot down firmly, refusing to allow her and the twins to join him in Alverstoke.

She couldn't believe it. It was the first real reward of his naval career and she wanted to share in it. Cass was right when she said that by this stage the wives had earned a bit of glory, too. Tom had been given a submarine running out of Faslane and although Cass was dreading the move to Scotland she was very pleased at the idea of being a Captain's wife. She was still at Crapstone at the end of the summer, Tom being away, with Mark, on a course.

The girls were at the General's. Lunch was over and the children were playing in the garden. The General had made some excellent coffee and they sat lazily on at the table, Cass nibbling at some little chocolates that he had produced.

'When does Mark take over?' she asked. 'Tom doesn't go until just after Christmas. Plenty of time to get a quarter sorted out. Smuggler's Way, I suppose. I must remember to pack my kilt! Maybe you'll get a quarter in Alverstoke this time, Kate. I can't wait. Can you? Just think—the Wardroom hanging on our every word, all the young wives falling over themselves to get into our good books. Not to mention all those chaps playing up to us. Yum, yum! Frankly, I think that we enjoy it every bit as much as they do. It's our ego trip as much as theirs. I suppose you'll let the cottage?'

Kate was silent. How could she explain that her presence wasn't required and that Mark had said quite clearly that he didn't want the distraction of his wife and children?

'After all,' he had said cheerfully, 'if I'm driving a boat I'm damned if she's going to spend much time sitting beside the wall!'

'But you'll have to be in sometimes,' Kate had protested. 'Surely it would be fun to be together then? There're bound to be parties and things on the boat and in *Dolphin*.'

'Not if I can help it.' Mark's smile died away. 'It's not some bloody Sunday School picnic. When I'm on leave I can come home. It'll be nicer for me to come here than to be stuck in Gosport in a quarter, and if there's anything special on, you can come up for it.'

For once, Kate tried to make him change his mind but it was soon made clear that, even if she insisted and moved to Alverstoke, Mark was more than capable of turning it into a very hollow victory. She imagined the tiny public snubs and put-downs of which he was a master, all done with a smile under cover of being 'just a joke,' which she found so hurtful and damaging to her confidence. Anyway, who would want to go where they are so obviously not wanted?

She realised that Cass and the General were staring at her.

'What's up?' Cass was now studying her closely. 'Beastly for you to have to let it when you've just moved in but I expect you'll find a nice naval couple who would leap at it.'

'I expect so,' Kate attempted a light laugh. 'The thing is, we haven't quite decided whether I shall go or not.'

Cass put down her coffee cup. 'You mean Mark doesn't want you,' she said brutally, ignoring her father's exclamation.

'It's not quite like that,' protested Kate. 'You know Mark. He seems totally unable to run his marriage and his job together. He's always preferred to keep them in separate compartments. Driving his own boat is terribly important to him. He wants to be able to concentrate on it, give it his all, you know? Not have to worry about . . . well, anything else.'

'For Christ's sake, Kate! When did Mark ever think about anything but Mark? He's never worried about you or the twins in his life. You give him everything on a plate! What about you?'

'Darling.' The General tried to remonstrate with his daughter, distressed by the sight of Kate's white face. 'Please. It's not your business . . . '

'It is my business!' Kate had never seen Cass so angry. 'Kate's my friend. Mark is a selfish, idle bastard who plays on her love for him and uses her disgracefully! All the other chaps take their wives with them. What's so special about him? He never lets her go on the visits abroad, deliberately doesn't tell her about Ladies' Nights and parties and then tells people that she's anti-social and won't go. He's a liar and a cheat. He even refuses to let her have any more children . . . '

To everyone's surprise, she burst into tears. After a moment Kate, who had been sitting as if turned to marble, pushed back her chair and went to her.

'Come on,' she said, putting her arms around her. 'Don't get upset. You know the old naval motto—If you can't take a joke, you shouldn't have joined. Anyway, why should I want to go and live in a grotty quarter all on my own when I can be in my dear little cottage with your father just along the road? Much nicer.' She smiled at him over Cass's blonde head and was horrified to see that he had tears in his eyes too.

Cass gained control of herself and sat up. 'Sorry,' she said. She scrubbed at her face with the napkin by her plate. 'I'm sorry, Kate.'

'Forget it.' Kate went back to her seat. 'I shall miss you terribly so you must come down for visits, mustn't she?' She looked at the General, willing him to smile, to be happy. 'We'll have lots of jollies, won't we?'

'Absolutely. At least we shall all be here for Christmas.' He smiled back at her. 'And I can tell you now that Mrs Hampton is already making plans for it.'

' . . . THINGS GO ON MUCH as usual here,' Kate wrote, 'and we're having some wonderful late-autumn weather. The twins go for the entrance exam to Mount House next week. I'm so glad that you are settling in and that you've got a good Wardroom.

'The car has failed its MOT and Bob says that he can't bodge the rust again. I suppose that we can't complain. After all, she's done awfully well given her age. I've found a garage that will do a part exchange on a newer one, so I think we'll just have to do that . . . '

She put down her pen and looked around the kitchen for inspiration. None came. Standing up, she reversed the Ella Fitzgerald tape in the cassette player and went to fill the kettle. How many letters, she wondered, had she written to Mark over the last eight years? Not a single shore job in all that time although it wasn't his fault that the refit in Portsmouth had been such a disaster. She brushed a few geranium leaves into a corner of the window sill and removed a few dead leaves from the plants. Soup bubbled gently in a saucepan on the Rayburn beside which, in her basket, Kate's new puppy, Megs, was sleeping. The twins would be home from school before the contentment of the day turned to boredom, the quiet stillness to loneliness, but how would it be when they went off to boarding school?

George Lampeter had popped in once or twice since Mark had gone. The last time he had had rather more than usual to drink and had suggested that he take her to bed. She had resisted but suspected that he might make another attempt and her thoughts were confused. She was fond of him and attracted to him physically—but could she sleep with him? She felt that he might be a tender lover and already felt at least as close to him mentally as she did to Mark. Kate had never found sex a good enough sport on its own to want it for its own sake but maybe with George it would be different: maybe she would discover just what it was she seemed to be missing with Mark.

She leaned against the Rayburn and closed her eyes. She was in bed with George and he was kissing her, stroking her, touching her breasts. Kate dragged her eyes open and groaned. This was terrible—perhaps making love could be as good as other people, books and films all implied. If it were, could she bear to miss out? Perhaps this time sex, just for the sake of it, would be good enough to outweigh her conscience. But was she capable of having a brief affair with George and then resuming her married life as though nothing had happened? If love-making was that good, would she be able to continue with a man who treated her like a machine? Again she groaned. If only she could be carried away by her emotions and just do it without all this soul searching! Like Cass.

'Why shouldn't I?' she asked the kettle. 'I've spent the last eight years waiting for boats to come in, waiting for Mark to come home, moving house, going nowhere, doing nothing. Most wives go abroad when the boats are going to nice places—they have a week in Gibraltar, a few days in Malta, time in the States. Mark obviously doesn't want me to go. He never asks me and when I suggest it he gets cross. He never tells me about Ladies' Nights or about parties I later find we were invited to. Two nights a year I go out—the Christmas Ball and the Summer Ball: and that's only if the boat's in!'

The kettle remained silent.

She could feel self-pity, that dreaded emotion, welling up inside her as she looked at her life slipping by while she waited—but for what? Leaves that were always an anti-climax? The shore job? That was supposed to be the answer: time with Mark, time to communicate, time to understand each other, time to become close so that even sex would be good.

The kettle began to sing.

She realised that she couldn't just sleep with George: she must give her marriage every chance and if Mark were to find out that she had been unfaithful—quite likely knowing her luck and thanks to the naval grapevine—what chance would it have then? Mark would never be able to trust her again. He might divorce her and then what would happen to the twins? How could she hurt them? And all for George!

The kettle boiled.

Kate made some coffee and, taking it back to the table, sat down, pulling her writing paper towards her. She read through what she had written, sipped some coffee and picked up her pen.

'I was very sorry to hear that you won't be home for Christmas but I quite understand that, since you may not get the chance to drive another boat, you want to make the most of this one. At least you know the run to Nova Scotia and you always enjoy Halifax, don't you? How kind of Liz and James to offer to put you up. When does their exchange finish?'

THE BREEDER HAD ADVISED Kate to buy a bitch puppy. Kate planned to mate her in due course and then keep the pick of the litter so that she would have two really good breeding bitches. She wondered whether to take the new puppy to shows as soon as she was old enough so as to start building up a reputation.

'Well, I do hope you're not going to turn into one of those tweedy women, with sensible shoes and hairy chins,' said Cass, when Kate told her these plans. 'You seem to be getting rather serious about all this.'

'That's because I *am* serious, Cass. Look, I've got to do something with my life. I probably see Mark, on average and not consecutively, for about twelve weeks of the year. What am I supposed to do for the other forty? Go to coffee mornings? Raise money for charity? Do meals-on-wheels?'

'Sorry, Kate.' Cass was contrite. Since her outburst she had been very wary on this subject. 'It's just that I didn't realise you were such a doggy person. That's all.'

'We were always knee deep in them at home. We used to walk hound puppies and my mother used to train retrievers to the gun. I might do that later on.'

'It's a pity you haven't had any more children. What did actually happen about that? I thought that you were just going to stop taking the pill.'

'I did in the end. I took your advice. I thought it would be so nice to have a second baby, well, third, of course, but knowing all the pitfalls.

In a way, the twins were a nightmare when they were small. All through that winter in that terrible flat with no heating, no washing machine. I had to wash everything by hand and drape it round the kitchen to dry. All those nappies! And that awful stove! Humping coal and ashes to and fro. I got so tired. If one cried, the other would start up. I remember walking up and down in the night, freezing to death, trying to carry both of them. Often I'd cry with them. I must be crazy even to think of wanting more. I used to be so anxious, so terrified that they were ill. They'd cry for hours and then, suddenly, they'd go to sleep and I'd think "My God! They've died!" and I'd go and poke them and they'd wake up and start crying again.'

'Poor Kate.' Cass couldn't help laughing. 'I was lucky. I had Tom around, on and off, and Charlotte was very good. I can't somehow see Mark being good with babies.'

'He hated it! He simply couldn't cope with them crying. He said he could sympathise with people who bash babies' heads on walls to make them shut up. So even when he was at home, I didn't dare trust them to him and he couldn't bear to have his nose put out of joint for a second. The relief when he went back to sea was enormous. But when they got to about six months, it all changed and I loved it. I feel that I'd be much calmer with a second—well, third. You know what I mean?'

'Oh, definitely. I was much more relaxed with Oliver. But how long have you been off the pill?'

'Oh, years. Since that Christmas when we came down and stayed with your father and he had the Christmas tree. I was so happy; all the children and Oliver a baby. And I went on down to Cornwall and James and Sarah had just had their second, little Lizzie. They were there as well. And I had this terrible ache, you know? I longed for another one so much. But nothing happens. It's very odd. It was practically first time off with the twins.'

'Perhaps you're too anxious. After all, they're away so much, aren't they? Then they dash in for a week, or it may be two, and it's the wrong time of the month or you're so uptight that it doesn't work.'

'Perhaps you're right.' Kate sighed. 'The thing is, the twins are nearly seven now and I'm beginning to wonder if it's a bit late.'

'Well, you could try a bit longer. After all, you'll be pretty lonely when the twins go away next year. I'm lucky to have a girl as the eldest. When I send Oliver I shall still have Charlotte. I plan to have another girl soon so that when Saul goes off I still shan't be alone.'

'I should have thought you might find it quite convenient to be without your children hanging round you,' remarked Kate mischievously.

Cass smiled blandly at her. 'What can you mean? I adore my children. Plenty of time for amusement when they're in bed or at school. Which reminds me. It's very quiet upstairs, isn't it? Do you think that we should go and see what our offspring are up to?'

BY THIS TIME, KATE and the twins were perfectly capable of enjoying a Christmas without Mark. Nevertheless, Kate was delighted to receive an invitation to the Ball at the Britannia Royal Naval College at Dartmouth.

George Lampeter had been invited and was looking for a partner.

'Could you save my life?' he asked her on the telephone. 'I know Mark's away but I'm sure he wouldn't mind if you took pity on me, would he? I can't think of anyone I'd rather escort.'

Kate bit back the retort 'What about Felicity?' and accepted with pleasure. 'Who else is coming?' she asked.

'Well, Felicity and Mark,' he replied, dead on cue, and added some others whom Kate knew well. 'Should be fun. Bless you, Kate. Listen, I'm staying with friends in Dartmouth and the snag is getting you over here. Would you mind coming with Felicity and Mark or is that too much to ask?'

'My dear George,' said Kate, amused, she was sure that Felicity—who would not want George appearing with a glamorous dolly bird—was behind the invitation, 'I'd hardly expect you to act like the lovelorn swain. That'll be fine. I haven't been to the college since the Passing Out Parade and Summer Ball with Mark all those years ago. It'll be a marvellous treat.'

So Kate went, bundled into the back of Mark II's car, listening with half an ear to his and Felicity's bickering, and thinking about the strangeness of life.

The college, en fête, was wonderful as always: a splendid buffet supper, the marquee with the jazz band, the disco with its whirling lights and the ballroom where the more sedate officers and wives circled to the strains of a decorous waltz.

Nothing really changes, thought Kate, sitting at a large table on a balcony that was probably called the Poop Deck. Bottles of champagne popped while jovial, handsome men—smart in their Mess Dress—and laughing, pretty, scented women—elegant in their ball dresses—moved up and down the stairs, calling to each other, embracing friends. She thought of Mark, nine years before, tall and darkly handsome, striding these very corridors and halls, and herself, excited and overawed by it all and quite sure that life had nothing more to offer. She remembered standing in the soft air of that July evening with the lights twinkling on the river below and listening to the Royal Marine Band playing Beat the Retreat on the Quarterdeck with the tears prickling at the back of her eyes.

How romantic and glamorous it all was, she thought. I suppose it isn't Mark's fault that I saw him as something on a film set. What a turn-on that strong silent approach was! That wonderful feeling that love conquers all. Perhaps it's as well that the young never think about the stark realities of life. It's essential that they feel that they can cope with anything it throws at them. How else would they have the courage to go forward?

She remembered her own high ideals, the part she'd hoped to play in Mark's life and the aura of excitement that had surrounded the Navy and particularly the submarine service.

It was like being presented with a big beautiful box, she thought, only to find that when the paper was torn off and the ribbons undone, the bloody thing was empty!

'You're looking far too sad.' One of the men was bending over her, filling her glass. 'Cheer up, your old man will be home before too long. Come on, let's go and swing a leg!'

IN THE NEXT EIGHTEEN months, Kate found Dartmoor a tremendous solace. She rediscovered old haunts and found that the wild contours and rolling landscape were a constant joy. Its vast spaces kept her problems in proportion; beside such immensity and timelessness it seemed that nothing could be so terribly important. Out walking with Megs and the twins, her heart was soothed and uplifted and she understood the psalmist's cry: 'I will lift up mine eyes unto the hills.'

With the twins at school she was free to spend more time on jaunts to Dartmouth and Totnes, often accompanied by the General. He was an unexacting, easy companion to whom she often found herself talking about her anxieties. It was a relief to voice her thoughts, to look at them calmly and rationally instead of arguing round and round inside her head. The General listened thoughtfully. He was fair and sensible and yet she knew that he was on her side. Kate found this immensely comforting. Her mother had the same approach but she had been unwell of late and Kate was too frightened to burden her with her own problems on her visits to St Just. Her mother rarely made the trip to Devon now. Her father was closer to his sons and Kate had never been intimate with him. She had no idea how seriously the General took his role of confidant, how he mulled and brooded over their talks and worried in case he was in any way misjudging the situation. It was not so much a question of advice but more of allowing her to talk things through and he prayed for guidance.

Mrs Hampton was another good friend. Wise and motherly, she had the same effect on Kate as the General had already remarked on himself and the children. She made her feel safe. In her company she could relax, shed her responsibilities. This was an enormous luxury for Kate who had no one to turn to when pipes froze, the children were fractious or she was ill. There was no one to make her a cup of tea, take the twins off her hands or dig the garden. No one came home in the evening to share anxieties about money, laugh over some amusing incident or advise her about bringing up two boys. Mrs Hampton was an invaluable ally and Kate tried to repay by taking her for trips in the car. They would go Tavistock most Fridays to explore the market where Kate would pore for hours over the second-hand books whilst Mrs Hampton pottered about inspecting the home-made goodies and fresh vegetables and fruit. When she had made her purchases, Kate would help her carry them back to the car and then they would go and find some coffee.

Tavistock was Kate's local town and she would often go there to shop and visit the library, stopping off at the Bedford Hotel for coffee or for lunch, a great treat for the twins when they were on holiday. Gradually she began to make a few friends but, even so, it seemed odd to be living without the framework of the Navy after nearly nine years within it. She missed the life in the base and felt a strange sense of loss that she no longer had the support and companionship of other naval wives.

Only once did Mark invite her up to *Dolphin* to a party on the boat. The Wardroom greeted her with a certain amount of deference and some reserve and Kate, remembering Cass's words, wondered how Mark had represented her to them: as some potty woman living in the wilds of Dartmoor, unsocial, uncaring, wrapped up in her own life?

He paid a great deal of attention to one of the younger officer's wives as if to imply to Kate that he had been obliged to make the invitation but was resentful that she had accepted it. The girl was very flattered by his attentions and giggled and squirmed a great deal. Kate waited for her to say: 'Oh, you are awful!' It seemed that she had been made much of when she went out to Nova Scotia during the boat's visit, this much being made clear to Kate by veiled hints and allusions and sidelong glances. The young officer, delighted to see his Captain so en rapport with his wife, encouraged and took it all in good part.

In the end she found herself talking to Ralph Masters, the First
Lieutenant, a very pleasant and serious young man who clearly disap-
proved of Mark's behaviour but was doing his best to hide his feelings.
He went to fetch her a drink and returned with a tall, dark girl.

'I can't remember whether or not you have already met Harriet?
We're engaged to be married now,' he said.

Kate smiled. 'Yes, we met at the *Drake* ball, didn't we?' Suddenly
she had a vision of Cass at that summer ball in the base at Devonport
saying ' . . . we could all be Captains' wives. Think of the glory . . . '

That night in their room at Anglesea, Mark had had enough to drink
to be sexually aroused but not enough to make him incapable. Kate,
who after months of being alone longed for love, was disappointed.
All she got was sex; brief, unsatisfactory and degrading.

She drove back to Devon, tired and dispirited, put the car away and
let herself into the cottage. Before the kettle had boiled there was a
knock at the door. The General stood outside.

'How lovely,' Kate dragged him inside. 'I've just got back. The kettle's on.'

He followed her into the kitchen and surprised her by taking both
her hands firmly in his.

'You must be very brave, my darling,' he said. 'Your father telephoned me earlier when he couldn't get an answer from you. Your
mother died this morning. It was her heart. She died, suddenly and
painlessly, as she sat up in bed to have her morning cup of tea.'

Kate stared at him uncomprehendingly. It was simply not possible
that her mother should die. Despite the fact of the deterioration in her
health, Kate had not seriously considered that she could be left without
the solid wall of unconditional love and support that had been at her
back since memory began. She thought of the beloved face, worn with
pain but still serene, and pictured quite clearly her mother's hand,
holding her own, touching the twins, soothing pain, drying tears. Never
again would she see that smile of welcome or know a safe place of
shelter. Kate shook her head and her face crumpled like a child's. The
General gathered her to his breast, comforting and consoling her, as if

she had indeed been one of the children. With her cheek against his heart, her hands clutching the rough tweed of his coat, Kate tried to imagine a world that no longer contained her mother. Her mind baulked and shied away from the idea. It was totally unimaginable. Presently the kettle boiled and, placing her gently in a chair, the General made the tea.

'What shall I do?' she asked helplessly at last. 'I need her.'

'Oh, my dear.' The General put the mug beside her and she looked up at him. Today he looked his age and Kate's heart contracted with terror. One day all those whom she loved and needed would die and she would be left to go on alone. Interpreting her look correctly the General put his hand on her shoulder, his long fingers gripping the rounded bone.

'Don't dwell on the inevitable,' he said and his voice was firm. It was almost an order. 'You are stronger than you can possibly imagine and I am here. For the moment that will have to be enough.'

Ten

'I 'ear the Rectory's comin' up for sale.' Mrs Hampton put a plateful of aromatic kippers before the General and looked to see the effect her news might have.

'I'd heard some rumours about that.' The General shook out his napkin. He rarely volunteered information related to the village although he heard a great deal from his old crony, William Hope-Latymer. 'I don't suppose that the Tanners will be too heart-broken. It's a big place for a middle-aged couple with no children. And, of course, the church can't afford to keep it repaired and I'm sure the Rector can't afford to heat it properly. They'll probably be better off in a smaller modern place.'

'Old Tukes' place,' nodded Mrs Hampton, making toast. 'Very nice so I've 'eard. Everythin' all built-in. 'Twill be a change but does seem funny to me.'

'Why's that?' The General attacked his kippers with relish.

'Rector 've always lived up at the Rectory. Don't seem proper, 'im livin' in old Tukes' place.'

The General reflected that the new house at the end of the village would probably always be known as 'Old Tukes' Place.' Old Tukes, a solitary and unsavoury ancient, had lived in a falling-down disgusting shack on that spot for time out of mind. Now that he had been carted off to a modern hygienic institution where, no doubt, he'd be dead within months, the owner of the plot had sold it to a local builder and in the place of the old ruin, like a Phoenix from the ashes, had risen a sparkling little modern box.

'Times change, Mrs Hampton.' The General shook his head. 'And not always for the better. I expect the Rector will be happy enough—happier perhaps. And we may get a young family at the Rectory who can afford to put it to rights, as it should be. It's a lovely house and it would be good to get some young blood in the village.'

''Tis funny you should say that.' Mrs Hampton busied herself with the coffee. 'I was sayin' to my Jack only last night, what we need is a nice young family up at the Rectory, just like the General's Cassandra and all 'er little 'uns.' Mrs Hampton sighed wistfully and peeped at the General out of the corner of her eye. 'Twould be just the ticket.'

The General had sat bolt upright and, neglecting his toast, was staring thoughtfully at the wall opposite.

'An' my Jack said,' continued Mrs Hampton somewhat mendaciously, Jack's actual contribution to the conversation having been a series of 'ar's,' ''e said, "Can't be right draggin' they children from pillar to post. No settled 'ome."' Mrs Hampton shook her head regretfully. 'An' that little Charlotte. 'Ow she do love bein' 'ere. Do seem cruel, some'ow. And Kate's twins off to boardin' school next term. She's gonna miss 'em somethin' terrible. 'Twould be lovely to my mind to see both they girls settled 'ere, close like.' She placed his coffee beside him.

'Mrs Hampton, you're a genius,' said the General slowly. 'This is quite the most brilliant idea!'

Mrs Hampton bridled a little at the unprecedented success of her ploy.

'I wonder who the agent will be?' The General was almost talking to himself. 'Perhaps William will know? I must speak to Cass. Should be able to get it for a song.'

''Tis in a terrible way, so I 'eard,' volunteered Mrs Hampton. 'Needs lots doin' to it.'

'That's all right.' The General was pushing back his chair, his coffee untasted. 'First things first. Before we do anything else I must sound Cass out. Mustn't look as if I'm trying to take over. Now where have I put her telephone number?'

CASS REPLACED THE RECEIVER and sat for a few moments staring at nothing. Her father's suggestion had come as a tremendous surprise and she needed some time to assimilate it.

It was well worth thinking about. Only recently, she and Tom had been discussing the possibility of buying a house and putting down roots. After all, schooling was likely to become a problem now. Charlotte was already on her second primary school and had made a great fuss about having to leave Meavy school and her friends to come north. She hated Helensburgh and couldn't understand the speech of the local Scottish children and Cass dreaded the next move which would probably plonk her down in Alverstoke to start all over again. Oliver would begin school in the autumn and it would be very sensible to go back to Devon and put them in Meavy school where they could stay until they started to board.

Besides, it would be lovely to have her own home. Cass gazed round the unexciting married quarter and imagined how wonderful it would be to have one's own choice of decoration and furnishings. She was beginning to realise that she could have just as much fun in a set-tled situation—if not more. After all, Tom would still be going away and as well as naval friends she could at last develop a circle of civilian ones, knowing that she would be staying long enough to make it worthwhile.

Of course *Dolphin* was the best base for a submariner's family to live near but now that nuclear boats were running out of Devonport there would be much more going on. And there was the usual one in three chance of Tom being based there.

She felt quite sure that he would be all for it. Her father's offer was amazingly generous but she was certain that he would not have been prepared to be quite so helpful if the Rectory hadn't happened to be half a mile from his own front gate. And that, too, in Tom's eyes would be another advantage. There had almost been an incident a few weeks back when he'd come home unexpectedly and found Cass with another officer. Fortunately, everything had seemed quite innocent and the officer had been very quick with an excellent reason for being there. Nevertheless, Cass had felt a tiny suspicion still dwelt in Tom's mind. To have her under her father's eye would be—to Tom—a plus factor. After nine years of quarters and hirings, a large Georgian Rectory with an acre of garden would be quite impossible to resist. And she would be near Kate. Without stopping to think any further, she reached out and picked up the telephone receiver.

'IT'S GOING TO BE such fun,' said Kate cheerfully. 'Lots more things to do, lots of boys to play with. You know quite a few of them already and you'll be playing rugby and football and cricket. Before you've been there five minutes it will be time to come home for the first Sunday out. And then there's exeats and half-term. With me being only ten minutes away across the moor we shall be able to make the most of every minute.'

The telephone rang and Kate picked up the receiver with relief. She felt exhausted.

'Hello. Oh, hi, Cass. How nice to hear you. How are you?'

The twins raised their eyebrows at each other and, with one accord, rose and strolled out into the garden.

'I'm fine.' Kate lowered her voice a little. 'Just doing one of those confidence boosting "of course you're going to love school" chats. I think Guy will. Not so sure about Giles but they'll have each other and they know a lot of the service families with boys there . . . Oh, I know. Mount House is a super school and it's not as if I'm far away, although they're very strict about taking them out. Quite properly . . . I know we did. I tell them that but we were twelve when we went, not eight . . . Yes, I've got the "wonderful opportunity for the best education" bit to go yet. I'm not really worried about them. It's me who will be devastated . . . What? . . . I don't believe it! Oh, Cass, that would be magic . . . Is he? Oh, what a duck he is! When? . . . Oh, I see. Yes, of course, so you'll be coming down to look over it. It's the best thing I've heard for years. How's Tom? . . . '

In the garden, Guy stooped to tie his shoelace.

'D'you think we'll like it?' asked Giles.

'Should think so. Charlie Blackett says it's brilliant.'

'Yeah. I know.'

'The Head's got a dog like Megs. He's called Winston.'

'Matron calls him Poops.'

They began to laugh immoderately, pushing and barging into each other. They started to wrestle half-heartedly and, as suddenly, fell apart.

'Paul says it sounds like prison. He says he'd hate not to be able to go home to his mum after school.'

'That's 'cos he's a sissy,' said Guy nonchalantly. 'A mummy's boy. Anyway, his dad couldn't afford for him to go. He's jealous, that's all.'

'Shall we get our bikes?' suggested Giles, feeling happier. 'Mum will be hours if she's talking to Cass.'

'MY DEAR GIRL, YOU must be exhausted.' The General brought Cass a drink as she sat in her usual place in the corner of his sofa. 'What a journey!'

'Well, it was.' Cass sipped appreciatively. 'I suppose that it was madness to drive all the way down but Tom's at sea and it was a heaven-sent opportunity to have a little holiday. Scotland is very beautiful but it's an awfully long way from home.'

'It's wonderful to see you.' He sat down opposite and raised his glass to her. 'Mrs Hampton was quite beside herself at the thought of seeing all the children.'

'Well, I must say that if I hadn't known that she'd be here to take over I might not have brought them. Nearly ten hours on the road with three Smalls, not counting the stops, is one hell of a trip!' Cass shook her head. 'Mind you, Charlotte would never have forgiven me if I'd left her behind. She hates Scotland and school and she misses Tom. I can't think why. Apart from those two years in Chatham, he's hardly ever been around but, to be fair, he does spend a lot of time with her when he is. Anyway, you look wonderful! Full of beans! This really is a terrific scheme and it's awfully generous of you.'

'Not a bit. Not a bit. Got something put by for just this sort of thing. Been waiting for the right moment. What does Tom say?'

'He was absolutely thrilled. He says he can cope with the mortgage and he's more than happy to pull his weight getting the place to rights when he's home.'

'Well, that's what I want to talk about.' The General put his glass on the slate hearth and felt in his pocket for his tobacco. 'I want to make sure that the basics are right. It'll almost certainly need rewiring and replumbing. Thank God the church had the roof done when they did—about ten years ago. Heating may be a bit of a problem. It would be nice to fit proper central heating but I'll have to do my sums first. No point you and the children living there in misery. We'll go and have a look at the place tomorrow. You may hate it.'

'I think that's most unlikely. Have you ever been inside?'

'Once or twice. The Rector invites me up for a glass of sherry. There's a lovely drawing room and a very cosy study. Haven't seen anything else but it's quite big.'

'Sounds like heaven.' Cass stretched luxuriously. 'Shall we leave the Smalls with Hammy?'

'Probably a good idea. Don't want to raise false hopes. Anyway, you can concentrate better without them.'

'So what's been going on? What's the gossip?'

'Well.' The General brought his mind to bear on the few local happenings that might interest her. 'Young William got married, as you know. He was very disappointed that you couldn't make it. So was I. His father and I travelled up together. Spent the night in my club. Marvellous wedding. You won't like my saying this, my darling, but the Army does that sort of thing so much better than the Navy.'

'How was, um, what's she called . . . Annabel, is it?'

'That's right. Abby they call her, for some reason. Such a pity. Annabel's such a pretty name. They came down after the honeymoon for the weekend. Seemed happy enough. Now, what else? Well, the Rector and his wife are going to be rehoused at Old Tukes' place. They're thrilled at the idea that you may buy the Rectory. She's looking forward to showing us around tomorrow.'

'Poor them, having to move from a beautiful Georgian house to a ghastly modern box.' Cass made a face and raised her glass. 'I simply can't wait for tomorrow. Any chance of another one and then I might be in a fit state to crawl upstairs and organise bedtime?'

'I WISH YOU'D BEEN with us. I shall have another look before I go and you simply must come then. It's a super house,' said Cass as she sat on Kate's lawn with Saul staggering around, picking daisies and dropping them into her coffee. 'Don't do that, you beastly child.'

'How he's grown.' Kate watched enviously. 'He's very like Charlotte was at that age, isn't he? It's lovely to see them all together again.'

The twins and Charlotte, sharing the two bicycles, were playing in the adjoining meadow. Their shouts and laughter echoed through the stillness of the hot July afternoon. Oliver swung himself to and fro on the swing under the apple tree.

'It's terrific to be here.' Cass lay back and shut her eyes. Saul fell across her midriff and she gave a grunt.

'And what's this I hear,' said Kate, standing Saul upright and giving him a quick hug in passing, 'about naughty goings-on with Mark II when his boat was in Faslane? Still playing Russian roulette?'

'Good heavens! Where on earth did you hear that?' Cass smiled to herself. 'No, don't tell me! Could it have been the Wicked Witch of the north?'

'Felicity herself!' agreed Kate. 'It's a wonder that the paper didn't go up in flames. Tell your mummy that she's a naughty girl,' she said to Saul, who was now clambering on to her lap and trying to push the daisy heads up her nose. He chuckled as she tickled him and buried her mouth in his soft neck to blow raspberries.

'Why is she naughty?'

Kate looked up into Oliver's blue eyes. 'You made me jump,' she said.

'Yes, but why is she?'

Kate sat up and, giving Saul a biscuit, turned her attention to Oliver. 'Your mum,' she said, circling him with her arm, 'is very shaky on the principle regarding "mine" and "thine." Do you see?'

Oliver looked at Saul who was regarding his biscuit thoughtfully. Pushing him backwards on to his well-padded bottom, Oliver took the biscuit and smiled blindingly at Kate. 'Yes,' he said, above Saul's anguished roars. 'I see.'

IN THE AUTUMN, THE twins went off to preparatory school. Dressed in their grey corduroy shorts and high-necked navy blue jerseys, they looked even younger and more vulnerable than usual. The long grey stockings made their stick-like legs stretch on for ever and the new regulation sandals rendered their feet enormous. With a quaking heart, Kate drove them, their trunks, tuck-boxes and overnight cases across the moor, up the long drive and round to the stables to unpack the car. It all went off much better than she had dared to hope. Charlie Blackett was waiting for them and the trunks were carried off. The dormitory was inspected and beds chosen with teddies—owners' name tapes securely sewed to the pad of one foot—placed proprietorially on pillows. By the time their pocket money had been handed in, the twins were quite ready to be hurried away by small friends that they had known for years.

Feeling faintly superfluous, Kate hugged them, promised to write, assured Giles that it really was only two and a half weeks to the first Sunday out and drove away. She kept blinking her eyes furiously to drive away nightmare visions of them being ill, being bullied, being frightened and unhappy. Thanking God that there were two of them and talking determinedly to Megs, she made her way home completely oblivious to her surroundings. For once the moor failed to soothe and comfort. Her eyes were inward-looking and she was unaware of the autumnal beauty all around her.

She put the car in the shed, released Megs and looked around; no muddy boots in the porch, no bicycles thrown down carelessly on the path. She went straight indoors and automatically pushed the kettle on to the hotplate. The cottage seemed unnaturally quiet.

No more quiet than on an ordinary school day, she told herself firmly. She stood staring out of the kitchen window; no blond heads bobbing about, no shrieks or the thump of a football being kicked.

Fatally she went upstairs and looked into their bedroom. It was very tidy, the twins having decided that when they came home it should be just as they would like to find it waiting for them. There was no Lego scattered on the carpet, no books open on the beds.

She picked up a golliwog from Guy's pillow and stood holding it, realising that for the first time for eight years she was all on her own again: no one to cuddle, no one to care for, no one to chat to about the day's events. It was as if their childhood was over. She could only pray that, for the twins, boarding school was the sensible choice. It was simply not fair to keep moving children from school to school every two years. This would give them a stability and continuity in their lives which was important with boys whose father was rarely at home. Perhaps it was true that a boy needed a firmer discipline than he would get from a mother on her own. Since it was apparent that Mark was very happy to pursue his career without Kate being close at hand, she had given serious thought to staying put and letting the twins go to a day school. Nearly everyone had advised her against it: The Navy paid for them to have a first-class education, it was one of the perks, it would be selfish to deny them the benefit of it. Guy showed promise of being good at sport and Giles had a tendency to cling. She had to put them first, try to decide what was truly best for them in the long run. After all, they were hardly any distance away and they had so many friends there. But did the advantages of a first-class boarding school outweigh the benefits of being in your own home with your own family?

Kate didn't know the answers. She only suspected that, by the time one knew whether one had got it right or wrong for one's children, it was too late to do anything about it. Replacing the golliwog she went slowly downstairs. The long evening, the night and all the lonely days stretched endlessly ahead.

AT CHRISTMAS CASS, FOUR months pregnant, travelled down with her family and moved into the Old Rectory.

'And that,' she said to Kate, 'is that! No more moving, no more quarters, no more changing the children's schools. I've done it. Had it! I intend to settle down. Tom can come down for leaves and weekends. He's perfectly happy about it.'

And so he was. Cass had been quite right in thinking that Tom would jump at the offer. He felt that the time had come for Cass to settle down in her own home, suspecting that her time would be better occupied in bringing together and looking after a large house and garden than twiddling her thumbs in a cramped quarter. He knew very well that Cass liked a certain amount of social activity and, being of like mind, totally sympathised. He hoped that she would build a circle of friends that would satisfy her need for amusement and the fact that her father and best friend lived on the doorstep would put a brake on any little plans she might have regarding extramarital dalliance.

He wouldn't have been human had he not imagined—with a certain amount of satisfaction—himself as owner of a substantial property. He saw them throwing parties, giving intimate little dinners and enjoying long lazy summer days in the garden. Cass would make a perfect chatelaine and it would be wonderful for the children. He had been very concerned at the distress Charlotte had suffered during the move to Scotland and it seemed now that several birds could be killed with one stone. He knew that he would miss Cass waiting when the boat came in but sacrifices would have to be made. The General's help meant that they would be starting well up the home-ownership ladder and ever since his father had married again—to a much younger woman—Tom had known that he could count on very little future assistance from that quarter.

He would miss his family but he must make every effort to get appointed to his home port and make the best of the rest of it.

'Apart from anything else,' said Cass, 'he fancies himself as a man of property.'

'I can't say I blame him. Or you. Moving from pillar to post must be hell with three and a half children. You are lucky to be pregnant again, Cass. What's it going to be this time?'

'Oh, a girl. Just like me.' She grinned. 'No bullets yet. I live a charmed life. It's going to be great to be together again.'

But in the spring, Mark was given the news of his new appointment: a First Lieutenant's job on a nuclear boat in refit in Chatham.

'You can't go!' wailed Cass, when she heard. 'You'll hate Chatham. What will you do there?'

'I must go. It's our first shore job. I've got to give our marriage— what's left of it—a chance. I hate the idea of being so far from the twins and all of you but we really need something to bring us back together. We've never had time alone. I must make the effort.'

'What about the cottage?'

'Well, Felicity has said that George would like to rent it. He wants a little more freedom and space, she says.'

Cass grinned maliciously. 'And we can all guess why. Mark's up at the MOD now, isn't he? Felicity can pop down from London on the pretence of visiting that old bat of a mother of hers whenever she wants to. How she dares talk about me, I really don't know. She and George have been at it for years.'

'Honestly, Cass . . . '

'Perfectly true. But never mind her. I'll look after the twins, take them out and so on, you know that. And you can stay with us when you come down to see them. Where does the boat go when she comes out of refit?'

Kate grimaced. 'Faslane.'

'Hell's teeth!'

'I know. I'm not thinking about it. One step at a time. Let's get Chatham over first.'

KATE DISLIKED THE MEDWAY towns on sight and nothing happened during her stay to make her change her mind about them. Canterbury she loved and, although it was quite a drive, spent many hours pottering there, drinking coffee and roaming around the cathedral. She loved to see the little boys hurrying between school and cloister and to listen to their high, pure voices in choir practice. They reminded her of the twins, whom she missed intensely, and she could be often found, during Choral Evensong, sitting hunched behind a pillar crying her eyes out.

Chatham was like no naval base that Kate had ever known. Gosport and Faslane, of course, were purely submarine bases and here Kate felt most at home. Everyone knew everyone else and being in the Mess at either of those places was like going back to an extended family and carrying on where you left off. Devonport was rather different but there were now enough submarines based there to feel fairly at home in *Drake*. At Chatham, the shore establishment was *Pembroke*, which was the Supply and Secretariat School, and they didn't particularly want submariners in their Mess. Moreover, the submarine's Wardroom was nowhere near complete, no point yet, so apart from the Engineer and Electrical Officers, both of whom were complete strangers to Kate and whose wives had remained in Scotland, and the Captain, who rushed back home to his family in Hampshire at every opportunity, there was nobody to make friends with and no social life. Kate felt very isolated.

She now learned the difference between being lonely with Mark away and being lonely with him at home. The latter was infinitely worse in her eyes. She realised that she was married to a man with whom she had nothing in common and who was not really interested in her or their children. It was a dreadful blow. She knew now, without any doubt, that it was not the continual separations that had caused the rift between them, although they hadn't helped, but simply that as a couple they were incompatible. The spark that had ignited their love

had been made up of youth and beauty coupled with the glamorous
naval whirl and set ablaze by the usual biological urge.

He was one of the most boring men that she had ever known. He
never wanted to do anything except watch television and bang away in
bed. Conversation as entertainment was out of the question. He never
spoke of the Navy. The movements and developments of his career
were on a strictly 'need to know basis,' as he put it, and she had become used to finding things out from other friends rather than from
Mark. This was humiliating but she had learned to live with it. Regarding ordinary conversation, the sort that oils the wheels of daily
life, his response was simple: 'If you haven't got anything intelligent
to say, keep quiet.' Any reference to the twins and the response was:
'They'll be OK. Stop fussing.'

Kate was a great chatterer. She talked to the twins, to the dog, to
lonely people on trains and in cafes and to her friends. Being away
from her usual round, shut with Mark into a silent world of boredom, made her want to scream and cry. She cried, privately, quite
often in despair and fear. She thought of her life stretching emptily
away before her, a speechless old age with Mark, and calling to the
dog, she would hurry out to walk for miles in the hop fields. Her only
pleasures were her trips to Devon to see the twins and to stay with
Cass.

Mark was always too busy to go. Either the First Lieutenant or the
Captain must be within a few minutes' drive of the submarine and, as
this Captain was hardly ever there, Mark had the perfect excuse for
never leaving the boat. Kate went alone, driving herself, and the journey was a bore but she looked forward to these weekends away, little
oases of joy in a desert of loneliness and boredom.

'I TOLD MARK THAT this was an exeat weekend,' said Kate, as she sat at
Cass's breakfast table on a lovely, blowy, blue and white spring morning. 'He would think it completely crazy of me to come down just for
a "Sunday out."'

Cass moved round the table, distributing food to Charlotte and Oliver and attaching a bib to Saul, who had been promoted to two cushions on a kitchen chair and was driving a truck slowly and intently around his place mat. Cass's fourth child and second daughter, the ten-month-old Gemma, was wedged by cushions into the high chair.

'We'll have a nice quiet day,' said Cass. 'Give you a chance to relax. And then, in the morning, we'll all go to church at school and collect the twins.'

'I wish that they could come out before church. It makes the day so short.'

'Never mind,' said Cass, sitting down at last. 'We'll cram in as much as possible. Charlotte is going to make some lovely cakes for their tea.'

'Are you, Charlotte?' Kate was touched. 'That's very sweet of you.'

Charlotte smiled and then, suddenly shy, hid her face in her mug of milk.

'Poor Charlotte is horrified that the twins have to be shut away up there without their family,' said Cass, smiling at her eldest child. 'Aren't you, my poppet? If she had her way they'd be out every week-end.'

'Don't worry.' Oliver ladled honey on to his toast with great panache. 'Next year, I'll be going and then I can look after them.'

'Ollie!' Charlotte glanced at Cass and Kate, scandalised by his presumption.

'Oh, he's probably right, Charlotte,' said Kate, laughing. 'Oliver is capable of anything.'

Oliver beamed at her tolerantly, his cheeks bulging.

'He can't wait to get up there and start organising them,' said Cass. 'Mr Wortham won't know what's hit him.'

On Sunday, as she stood at the window, watching the children racing about in the garden, Kate wondered how she would ever be able to make the effort to leave the twins and drive back to Kent—not home, it wasn't home—and Mark. She had been terribly envious when Cass had produced yet another child, a beautiful blue-eyed girl, and had prayed that she might yet be lucky herself but there had been no sign of a baby on the way, despite Mark's sexual energy. Her hopes that the shore job would bring them close, solve the differences and strengthen the relationship, so that those past lonely years would be given a point, had been dashed and she knew that she'd been living with a dream. She also knew now that another child would not be, had never been, the answer.

'They always remind me of your brother. I met him once. Chris, isn't it? The absolute image of him, aren't they?' Cass stood at her shoulder looking out into the garden.

Charlotte had fallen and the twins were helping her up. Guy was brushing her down while Giles had his arm around her, comforting her. Oliver strolled up eating an apple and held it out casually, offering her a bite.

Suddenly, uncontrollably, Kate began to cry. Great tearing sobs shook her body. Tears spurted from her eyes and rolled down her cheeks. She turned blindly and Cass took her into her arms, quietly, comfortingly, and stood holding her, watching the trees that danced and bowed in the wind beyond the window.

'How STRANGE LIFE IS,' mused Kate, some weeks later, as she drank an after-dinner cup of coffee. 'It seems to go in cycles. You spend a period of time in a certain place with a set group of friends, shopping in a particular town, and you feel that this is how it has always been and always will be. You look back on other parts of your life and think "Was that really me? Did I do those things, know those people?" but you feel that the "you" of now is the only one that really counts. Then, suddenly, the kaleidoscope is shaken, the pattern shifts. Everything changes and you start all over again and the "you" that really counted becomes the past. Do I make any sense?'

Mark turned a page of his newspaper. 'Mmmmm?'

'It doesn't matter,' sighed Kate. 'I was just thinking that I seem to have lived in Chatham for ever and I'm thinking of going home.'

There was more silence broken by a sudden shout of laughter from Mark.

'Oh, what a scream! There's a Frenchman here. He's ninety-one years old, been driving for seventy-five years without a single accident and he's just been killed in a car crash. Don't you think that's funny?'

Kate stared at Mark for a long moment. 'I don't think it's the least bit funny. I think it's rather sad.'

He lowered the paper and looked at her. She watched his expression change and set, as though his features were stiffening under ice, and, as usual, felt as though she were looking at a stranger.

'I said that I was thinking of going back to Devon,' she said.

Mark raised his eyebrows in a mental shrug. 'Why not? We'll be going to sea soon. Trials and so on. You may as well be down there as on your own here.'

'I didn't mean it quite like that. I think that I was thinking of a more permanent separation. After all, there's not much point in continuing our marriage, is there?'

Mark folded the newspaper and put it aside without taking his eyes from hers.

'Oh, I think there is. What about the embarrassment of telling people, for a start? You're just feeling a bit depressed.'

'I don't think so.' Kate shook her head. 'It's so much more than that, Mark. There's nothing left as far as I'm concerned. The only thing to show for the last eleven years is the twins. Perhaps if we'd had another child . . . '

'Oh, don't start on that one again,' he said impatiently. 'Children are much more likely to wreck a marriage. You know my feelings about that.'

'Yes. Yes, I know.' Despair gave her the courage to confront him at last. 'I think I'm going to have to tell you what I really think about our relationship. You see, being married to you has been so different to what I always imagined marriage was about. It's like being married to a lodger or a paying guest who has sexual rights over my body—to someone who isn't really a part of me or interested in me. I used to put it down to the fact that you were young and trying to carve out a difficult career for yourself and I decided that we would have to wait until you matured a bit and got far enough up the ladder to feel secure. But that was going to take years and the only way I could have got through those years was to have more children—so that I had something to live for, too.

'I thought it was morally wrong of you to deny me those children, so I came off the pill. Because I didn't tell you, that was morally wrong of me and I know that two wrongs don't make a right—but what else could I do? I know that children aren't the answer in the long run—but I thought we'd sort ourselves out, given enough time, and that they would have been the answer in the short term. I know now that it goes deeper than that and that we just don't have a marriage and never would have had one even if I'd had another baby. Perhaps it was lucky that nothing happened after all.'

'Oh, hardly.' Mark had been leaning back in his chair while she talked, regarding her with amused contempt. Now he smiled a little and continued to stare at her.

'What d'you mean?'

'I don't believe in trusting to luck. Did you honestly think that knowing how much you wanted another child I'd trust you to go on taking the pill? Oh, no.' He laughed aloud. 'No. I had a vasectomy.'

Kate felt as if she had been dealt a heavy physical blow. Her heart began to beat with thick heavy strokes and she could hardly breathe. She seemed to stagger under it and Mark laughed again.

'I knew I couldn't trust you. You were droning on about it one summer—oh, years ago now. The boat went to Sweden and someone told me where I could get it done, no questions asked. I thought it was sensible and I see now that I was right.' Still smiling, he watched her for a moment and then picked up his newspaper. 'I think it's a very good idea for you to go back to Devon. It's getting very busy now and I shall be perfectly happy in *Pembroke*. There's no point in your coming to Faslane when the boat goes up, but listen very carefully . . . ' the smile had gone and the familiar threatening, heavy-lidded look had taken its place ' . . . I have no intention of advertising our differences to the Navy and neither will you! I'm sure you want me to continue to support you and the twins and to meet the school fees and the mortgage, don't you? Naturally, I shall come down if I feel like it. And I shall expect you to come up to the Commissioning.'

He stared at her for a moment longer and then shook out the newspaper and buried himself in the pages. Presently Kate got up and left the room. A week later she was back in Devon.

Eleven

'Felicity! This is an unexpected pleasure.' Cass, her baby daughter astride her hip, stood at the top of the Rectory steps looking down at her. 'To what can I possibly owe this honour?'

Felicity took her bag from the car, shut the door and advanced to meet her.

'Quite a spread you've got here, Cass. Very impressive. I hear your father bought it for you.'

'Some people will say anything.' Cass stayed where she was and Felicity was obliged to stop a couple of steps below, feeling at a distinct disadvantage.

'I've really come to see Kate.' Felicity abandoned any pretence. 'I understand she's staying with you.'

'She's not here at the moment,' lied Cass, with an ease of manner that would have shocked and disappointed her father. 'Can I take a message?'

Realising that Cass intended to conduct the whole interview on the front steps, Felicity felt her temper begin to rise.

'George tells me that she wants him out of the cottage. It's quite ridiculous. I feel that it's most unreasonable of her to come rushing back after a few months and expect him to go.'

'But that was the arrangement, Felicity. George had it on very reasonable terms, and all her nice things left there to make him feel at home, on the understanding that if she needed to come back unexpectedly he would leave.'

'Nice things! What nice things?' Felicity looked scornful but decided to let it pass. 'But why does she need to come back? The boat doesn't commission for another three months and then she goes to Faslane.'

'What a lot you know, Felicity.' Cass watched an unbecoming flush stain Felicity's thin cheeks. 'You have been busy. And you must forgive me for asking this question but what on earth has any of it to do with you?

'George feels extremely upset . . . '

'Oh, balls!' said Cass impatiently. 'Kate went to see George yesterday. We both went. He was absolutely sweet about it. Most understanding. We were there for hours. He's going to move back into the Mess. Odd, actually,' mused Cass, 'I almost felt that, for some reason—can't imagine what—he was relieved to have an excuse to go. Very odd.' She gave a little laugh. 'Oh, well. So you don't have to worry about him anymore. Really touching, your attitude to old George, Felicity. Just like an old mother hen with one chick but then, you're rather older than he is, aren't you? Well, than all of us! You mustn't worry about him so. I always did feel that you should have had children . . . '

But she spoke to thin air. Felicity had gone. The car door slammed, the engine burst into life and gravel spurted as she turned the car and sped away down the drive.

'You're very naughty.' Kate joined Cass on the steps.

'She is the ultimate cow. Good job we saw her coming.'

'You shouldn't have said that about George.'

'It's probably true. He welcomed us with open arms, didn't he? Even though he knew we were going to ask him to go. He's great fun on his own. Felicity has the most terrible effect on him. I think he's frightened of her.'

'It's going to be a bit embarrassing,' said Kate, as she followed Cass back into the house. 'Everyone's going to wonder why I've come back so suddenly. You won't tell anyone, will you, Cass? Not about the vasectomy?'

'Of course I won't! What do you take me for? And no one will wonder anything. No one needs an excuse for getting away from Chatham, for God's sake, and lots of wives of our ages are beginning to stay put now. Stop worrying. What d'you say we wander down to the village and go and see my old pa? Charlotte and Oliver go in and see him on their way home from school. Hammy's always got some little treat on the go. Saul can just about make it and we'll put Gemma in the push chair. Then we can all come back together.'

'The twins will be breaking up in a few weeks,' said Kate, taking Saul's hand as they set off down the drive. 'We'll be able to take them all to the beach.'

'So long as you don't sit on your own, moping.'

'I wish I could finish it properly. I shall feel in a sort of limbo but the idea of divorce fills me with horror.'

'Perhaps he'll die,' said Cass cheerfully. 'Fall under a bus or something. Trip off the casing and drown.'

'Don't think I haven't thought of it,' said Kate guiltily. 'I was imagining it myself last night in bed. How many ways he could come to a painless end. I don't want to go on with it dragging round my neck for ever. But where would I live?'

'Well, it was your pa who gave you the deposit for the cottage.'

'Yes, but it's Mark who's been paying the mortgage. If I was qualified for anything I could get a job and take it over. I must look into it. But what about the school fees? The naval grant doesn't cover it all, you know, and it's even worse when they go to second school. It would be a pity to take them out just when they've settled so well. They've been moved about so much and so many of the friends they've known all their lives are there. It would be a terrible upheaval. I couldn't possibly hope to earn enough for all of it.'

'Well, Mark would obviously have to make some contribution anyway. They're his children too and he can certainly afford to. Oh, look, there they are!' They all waved as Charlotte and Oliver appeared round the lane at the other end of the village. 'I see Charlotte's got both satchels as usual. That boy!'

'Just like his mama,' laughed Kate, as Saul set off at a run to greet his siblings. 'He has that same knack of making one feel that it's an honour to do things for him.'

'Darling! How sweet of you to say so. Hello, my poppets!'

'Good heavens! What's all this?' The General had appeared at his gate. 'Looks like the Eighth Army arriving. Let's hope that the provisions can cope with this invasion.' He stood back to let them file in, returning his daughter's peck and giving Kate a brief hug. 'Lovely to see you back, my darling.'

He made no mention of her sudden return—having been primed by Cass—and she smiled at him gratefully.

'I did suggest that we should warn you.'

'Nonsense, nonsense. Always welcome.' They followed the others up the path. 'It's quite extraordinary how Mrs Hampton seems to pop over when school's finished. Incredible coincidence! I wouldn't be a bit surprised if she's in my kitchen even now. I get my tea very much earlier these days. Good afternoon, Mrs Hampton. Now this is very nice. We've got the hungry hordes visiting us, I hope there's an old crust to give them.'

'Old crust!' exclaimed Mrs Hampton, bustling out. 'An' a chocolate cake just out the oven. In you come, my lovers. Well now, what's this?' Charlotte had already dropped Oliver's satchel and was rooting in her own. 'Well now! That's a right pretty li'l box. An' you made it all yourself? I never! For me? Well now, I don't know what to say. And me sayin' only last night to Mr 'Ampton: "If only I 'ad a li'l old box to put my special things in." I reckon a little bird must've whispered in your ear. 'Tis lovely. I'll put it 'ere, safe, where I can see it while I gets the tea.'

'Blue Peter,' sighed Cass, as the adults headed for the drawing room. 'That programme has a great deal to answer for. The things you can make out of two egg boxes and a bog roll simply have to be seen to be believed!'

The twins were delighted that Kate had returned to Devon and the summer holidays got under way in high spirits. The moor was a huge playground right on the doorstep and Kate knew the places least likely to be discovered by the grockles. The twins had entered a war-like phase and Kate, after some thought, felt that it was best to let them get it out of their systems. Wearing cotton camouflage boiler suits and green plastic helmets, they raced up and down the granite tors firing toy machine guns and emitting loud explosive noises. With Megs stretched in the shade of some overhanging rock, Kate sat in a sheltered corner with a picnic and her book although, all too often, her eye was drawn away from the printed page to the scene laid out before her: the green bracken, waist high, the shimmer of heat over the short-cropped turf that was starred with tiny gold and white flowers. Sheep moved slowly, barely distinguishable from the grey boulders, and a cluster of grazing ponies would, for no apparent reason, set off at a gallop, hooves clattering over the scree. Skylarks mounted up and up against the infinite blue, singing and singing until, suddenly, they shut their wings and dropped silently back to the heather.

The twins would appear, flinging themselves down at her feet and demanding sustenance and, after lunch, they would pack the detritus into the car and take Megs for a walk across the springy turf and down to a stream where she could drink the cold, peaty water. And so back to the car and home along the white ribbon of road to the cottage.

Sometimes they would drive to the coast: Bigbury was the favourite with its golden stretches of sands and its warm rock pools. The twins would plunge in and out of the long rolling waves and, when the tide was right down, they would walk out to Burgh Island and climb the cliffs to stare out over the sea. On these occasions Megs was left at home and after she had put the twins to bed, Kate would stroll up to Huckworthy Common, Megs quartering the ground ahead for interesting smells, letting the silence of evening envelope her and watching for the first faint twinkling of a far-off star.

She felt as if she were suspended, poised between the past and the future. If her life up until this point had been a waste, at least it had, until now, had a point. There had been the on-going hope that the shore job, time together, would miraculously put things right, fuse the relationship. Now she knew that it was all over, but what next? She had no intention of living in limbo. The marriage was finished, no more life could be breathed into its corpse and she wanted to bury it, put it aside and start on whatever future she might have. She simply didn't know how it was to be done. Divorce was the obvious and accepted way but on what grounds? The whole idea of it filled her with distress.

She'd had a letter from Mark telling her that he was spending his leave sailing with a friend who wanted help to take a boat over to France. He confirmed the date of the Commissioning and said he would let her have the details at a later date. It hung over Kate like the sword of Damocles. If only she could be free of it all.

They went down to see her father who was selling the house in St Just and moving to Wiltshire to live with James and Sarah. Kate was worried for him. Her sister-in-law was a rather managing person, although James had always been his favourite child.

'I'm so lonely, you see, with Penny away at school so much,' he told Kate, 'and she spends most of the holidays with Sarah, anyway. Life seems so utterly pointless. At least I shall be useful and little Lizzie is a sweet child. I see Elizabeth in her so much. It'll be OK. Penny and I will have a little annexe of our own.'

He gave Kate a few possessions that her mother had wanted her to have and presented each of the twins with a little memento to remember her by. Telling him to come to stay whenever he wanted to, Kate hugged him goodbye.

She drove sadly home. She didn't feel too badly that the house would be sold for they had only moved to St Just at the beginning of Kate's life at boarding school. It was, nevertheless, the end of an era. It made her mother truly dead. There was nowhere now for Kate to go where her mother had loved and worked and had her being. Her possessions were split up; her presence dissipated.

She drove out of Plymouth and through Roborough. As they climbed up to the open moor, a harvest moon—the colour of rich egg yolk—swung above the horizon. The moor lay silent and mysterious beneath it, the mist rising and spreading out over the low ground. Kate felt an upsurge of longing for some spiritual experience that would enclose her in serenity and certainty and lift her above the nagging anxieties of daily life. Ignoring various disturbances from the back of the car, she tried to concentrate on a kind of communing, of prayer. A verse of psalm slid into her mind: 'Oh Lord, our Lord, how excellent is Thy name in all the earth! who has set Thy glory above the heavens.' Wonderful! How did it go on? Something about out of the mouths of babes and sucklings?

'Mum.'

But what came after that? Ah, yes: 'When I consider Thy Heavens, the moon and stars which Thou hast ordained.'

'Mum.'

And what a moon! 'What is man that Thou art mindful of him? Thou hast made him a little lower than the angels and has crowned him with glory and honour.'

'Mum!'

'What is it, Guy?'

'Megs is being sick. And it's all gone down inside Giles' gumboot!'

THE TWINS' TENTH BIRTHDAY fell two days before term started and Cass gave a party for them at the Rectory. Mrs Hampton, who now went two mornings a week to help Cass out, was in her element: jellies were made, cakes baked, sandwiches cut.

'But not too much, Hammy,' said Cass, who was packing the twins' presents. 'Remember we shall be having the barbecue in the evening.'

Mrs Hampton pursed her lips.

'It will be fun, Hammy.' Charlotte, who was wrapped in a huge apron, perfectly understood Mrs Hampton's silent disapproval. 'Daddy's got all the things ready and we're going to have beefburgers and sausages. And we're going to wait 'til it's dark.'

'You'll need a good tea first,' said Mrs Hampton firmly. ' 'Tisn't a birthday without there's a proper birthday tea.'

'Quite right,' said Tom, who had just come in. He winked at Cass. 'I can't wait. The barbecue's just a bit of fun. It's the tea that counts. I hope you're making plenty.' He stuck his finger into Charlotte's mixing bowl and licked it. 'Mmmmm!'

'Daddy!' cried Charlotte. With her lips primmed but her eyes sparkling, she looked at Mrs Hampton.

'Worse than the children,' announced that worthy. 'You'll find that, my lover, when you grow up. Men aren't nothin' but trouble.'

'Not Giles, though,' murmured Charlotte, painstakingly placing spoonfuls of mixture into little paper cups.

Mrs Hampton sucked in her breath and shook her head. 'All on 'em,' she pronounced. 'Never known one different.'

'Nor Grandfather.'

'The General's a wunnerful man, I'll give 'ee that.'

'Nor Daddy.'

'All on 'em!'

THE COMMISSIONING TOOK PLACE two weeks after the twins went back to school.

' . . . and make sure you are here by mid-day,' Mark had written. 'There is absolutely no point in your coming the night before. I shall be far too busy to have time for you and I can't find anywhere for you to stay. I have been able to book a cabin for you for the night of the Commissioning. Make sure you arrive on time and . . . '

It was the General who insisted that she should drive up on the previous afternoon and put up at an hotel on the way.

'You'll be quite exhausted otherwise,' he told her. 'You'll have to get away at about five in the morning and, if I know anything about that sort of military set-up, it will be a long and tiring day.'

'It'll be hell,' agreed Kate. 'It starts at mid-day and goes on until about two the following morning. First of all there'll be a big buffet lunch with all the Wardroom and their wives and families, not to mention the Personage.'

'The Personage?'

'Usually Royalty. Someone who's been selected from a host of applicants to chuck the bottle of champagne at the submarine. Well, after lunch, we go over to the dockyard and stand in the pouring rain or a force eight gale while the sailors fall in for the service. Then the Padre does his little bit and we all sing "Eternal Father, strong to save," while the dockyard workers look on making ribald remarks. Then the Personage wishes the boat bon voyage and chucks the bottle and looks a fearful idiot when the wretched thing won't smash!'

'What a delightful word picture you paint,' murmured the General.

'Well then,' said Kate, warming to her theme, 'there's a cocktail party on the boat so that all the people who have helped with the refit can come and get stoned out of their minds and have to be carried up the gangplank afterwards. By this time, your head is bursting and your feet are killing you but it simply isn't done to be seen sitting down at a cocktail party, even if you've got varicose veins and gangrene is setting in. After all, the shock might kill FOSM!'

'FOSM?'

'Flag Officer Submarines. Everyone talks in capitals, General. You should know that. So then it's far too late to find anything as civilised as a cup of tea—steward's off duty, kitchen's shut—so you go back to change for the Ship's Company's Dance and that's hell on wheels. It's held in some draughty hall or other somewhere near the dockyard and all the sailors have enough to drink to tell the officers what they think of them—all discreetly forgotten the next day—and their wives sit in little huddles glaring at the officers' wives. If we go and talk to them they think we're patronising and if we don't they say we're snobs. And all to the background of your local dance band "Sid Biggins and the Astronauts" with the floor awash with beer.'

'It does sound rather grim,' admitted the General.

'Grim?' Kate snorted. 'If that's the best you can do then all I can say is you have a very poor command of the English language!'

Kate arrived at Chatham in a state of terror. The thought of confronting Mark, not to mention the Wardroom and all their wives, was totally unnerving. He was waiting for her in full uniform on the steps and looked forbidding.

'You're late,' he said, as she got out of the car.

She stared at him. 'You said mid-day. It's not quite ten to. I have just driven all the way from Devon.'

She walked past him towards the Wardroom. The usual hubbub of clinking glasses and voices greeted her. Inside the door, she hesitated for a moment, trying to pick out a face she knew. A small dark woman detached herself from the crowd and came towards her.

'You must be Kate,' she said. 'I'm Janet Anderson.'

'Oh, hello.' Kate remembered the Engineer Officer, a rather pleasant Scot.

On a nuclear submarine, the Senior Engineer Officer, like the Captain, has to be a Commander and Kate knew that she, as Mark was only a Lieutenant Commander, must be properly submissive.

'How clever of you to know me,' she said, taking a glass from a steward who was circulating with a tray of drinks.

'Well, you were the only wife not here. Mark says that you're always late.'

Kate looked at her quickly and in some surprise. The note of censure was unmistakable.

'I had a long way to come . . . ' she began but Janet put a hand on her arm.

'Just a word. I'm sure you'll take it in the right spirit. It was rather noted that you couldn't be bothered to come to the Ladies' Night last night. It was a very special occasion, you know, and Mark is the First Lieutenant. He did his best. He explained that you hate socialising. But there are times, my dear, when we have to put our husbands first.' She patted Kate's arm. 'A word to the wise,' she said. 'Must circulate.'

She disappeared and Kate stood quite still. It was as if she had received an electric jolt to her system, a charge that had split open the chrysalis of her fear of Mark, respect for the Navy and her loyalty to their marriage. She seemed to have been looking at her life through a thin membrane that had distorted and confused and now it was torn from her eyes at last. The little tears and cracks had given way and she saw things clearly and knew that she was free and strong. Mark materialised beside her.

'You bastard.' Kate spoke in a low tone but a social smile was pinned to her lips. 'Why didn't you tell me about the Ladies' Night?'

He looked profoundly embarrassed.

'And all those other lies you've told? What a shit you are, Mark! And what a coward. Well, you've had it your way for eleven years and now it's my turn.' He made a move towards her but she stepped back. Still she smiled at him. To any observer they might have been having a pleasant if private chat. 'No more talk. It's much too late for that. This is my ultimatum, Mark, so listen carefully. These are my conditions. One. You will continue to provide for the twins.'

A steward appeared beside them. 'Drink, sir?'

Mark waved him away. Kate swallowed her drink, exchanged her empty glass for a full one and continued to smile. The steward moved on.

'Two. You will pay the mortgage until I get something sorted out. Three. You will not consider it your home although you can see the twins whenever it's reasonable.'

'Any hitches, Mark? Nice to see you, Kate.' It was the Captain this time. He looked a little on edge.

'Everything under control, sir. FOSM's due any time now.'

'Good. Well, better circulate.' He nodded and left them.

'If you don't agree, I shall get up on that chair and scream. And when I've got everyone's attention, I shall tell them a few truths. Especially the one about the vasectomy. If you do agree, I shall go through with this farce although it will be for the last time.'

'FOSM's car just approaching, sir.' A steward thrust his head between them.

Mark nodded to him.

'If you renege, Mark, I swear to you that everyone will know all the facts. Otherwise, you can blame the break up on me. You can say whatever you like and I promise I shall never deny it.'

'What goes on here?' The Electrical Officer, already a little the worse for wear, blundered between them. 'Can't have this! Canoodling in corners? Especially not with your own wife. Shocking bad form!'

'Is it a deal?' Kate raised her voice as Mark was forced to step back. She laughed and sparkled at him as though they had been making some delightful pact but Mark saw the determination and contempt and knew that, for the first time, she had taken control away from him. For one moment, his true feelings showed in his face and Kate caught her breath. How he hated her at that moment!

'Definitely a deal!' he cried gaily, murder in his eyes. 'Every bit. You can trust me, I promise!'

She raised her glass towards him. 'I'll drink to that,' she said. She took a sip, her eyes still locked with his. 'Goodbye, Mark,' she said and her voice was almost inaudible and infinitely sad. Turning away from him, she pushed her way into the throng of laughing people.

Part Three

Twelve

1976-78

On a July day during the hot summer of 1976 Annabel Hope-Latymer wheeled her thirteen-month-old daughter, Sophie, down the long drive from the Manor, past the church and through the village. Abby had adjusted slowly to life in a rambling, draughty manor house on the edge of Dartmoor but now she was beginning to enjoy the feeling that there was more to country life than she had first imagined. Here Cass had made quite a contribution. She and Abby had much in common, not least their light-hearted approach to life, and Abby and William had been included in Cass and Tom's social round just as, in turn, they had been enjoined in the friendships which the Hope-Latymers had with the local landowners. The small Sophie's growing attachment to Gemma had strengthened the bond which easily surmounted the eight-year age gap between the two women.

William had taken on the responsibilities of running the estate very willingly and, although there was very little ready cash available and the Manor was in fairly urgent need of repair, the Hope-Latymers managed with all the philosophical optimism of youth. They were very happy together, the relationship containing a great deal of camaraderie and easy-going give and take rather than overwhelming passion, and they appeared to be a well-matched couple.

It was early but already the crushing weight of the heat was beginning to make itself felt. No current of air stirred the stillness and the flowers in the cottage gardens were beginning to wilt and fade; the patches of lawn burnt to a dull ochre. The hosepipe ban was beginning to take effect.

The General, immaculate as always in a linen jacket, raised his Panama hat to her. In his view, Abby didn't look old enough to be a mother. There was so much of the waif, the gamine, about her. She had such a frail look with her dark spiky hair and the grey eyes, huge in the tiny pointed face. She was like a kitten, he thought, in a sudden flight of fancy. A kitten that had been left out in the rain. She might purr happily if you picked her up and petted her: on the other hand she might just as easily scratch your hand to ribbons. Amused by his fanciful thoughts, he strolled over to his gate.

'Good morning,' he said. 'Taking your constitutional early, I see. Very wise. Going to be another hot one.'

'I love it,' confessed Abby, 'it can't be too hot for me. Sophie feels it, though.'

The General smiled at the child in the pushchair who waved her fists and then tore off her linen hat, casting it to the ground. Abby picked it up resignedly.

'That's how it's been all the way down. She hates this hat. I never have any trouble with her blue one but she simply won't keep this one on. I couldn't find the other one.' She put it back on Sophie's dark head.

'Amazing things, women.' The General shook his head. 'Shall never understand them. Know what they want from the cradle. And generally get it.'

Abby laughed as Sophie gave a loud shriek and flung the offending article away from her yet again.

'You try,' she said, picking the hat up and offering it to the General. 'Perhaps she'll wear it for you.'

The General let himself out of his gate, took the hat and gently but firmly placed it on Sophie's head.

'Very beautiful you look,' he told her. 'A hat always does something for a woman.'

The child surveyed him thoughtfully and gave him an angelic

smile. Abruptly, she put her thumb in her mouth and closed her eyes.

'Well!' Abby raised her eyebrows. 'I can see that I shall have trouble with her later on. Obviously she likes older men.'

'Beginner's luck,' said the General, rather taken aback by his success. 'Care for refreshment? Coffee? Something cold?'

'You are kind but I'm on my way to see Cass. We're making plans for Saul's birthday next week. Maybe see you later?'

He nodded, smiled at her, raised his hat again and returned to the contemplation of his roses.

Abby strolled on along the lane where the cow parsley, crumbly with pollen, stood almost head high and the muddy ruts made by tractors' wheels were baked hard as rock. In at the Rectory gate she turned and up the rhododendron-lined drive to the big open space before the front door. The drive wound on away to the left into the old stable yard where cars were kept. Lawns, still flanked by rhododendrons, stretched away to the right. Abby pushed the chair to the bottom of the steps. Sophie appeared to be sleeping and, leaving her where she was, Abby trod up the wide shallow steps and peered through the open door into the cool dark interior.

'Hi,' she called. 'Cass?' She went in.

To the right of the hall was the door to the long gracious drawing room. To the left was the much smaller study and the cloakroom. Abby walked past them to the back of the house and put her head round the kitchen door. As she did so, Cass came in from the utility room opposite.

'I didn't hear you arrive,' she said. 'I was hanging out some washing. Where's Sophie?'

'She fell asleep on the way up. I didn't want to wake her so I left her in the pushchair. She's in the shade.'

'Gemma's napping too. She was awake at dawn. At least, it felt like it. Let's have some coffee. I'm sure you're gasping. It's exhausting, walking in that heat. I'm sure we'll hear her when she wakes.'

'No fear of that,' said Abby, grimly, sitting down at Cass's huge and ancient kitchen table and pulling some cigarettes out of her canvas shoulder bag. 'Your pa put a spell on her. Persuaded her to wear her hat and then sent her to sleep. D'you think he'd like to come and live with me? Or even better, I could go and live with him. He's so much nicer than William!'

Cass burst out laughing and pushed the kettle on to the Aga's hot-plate. 'You can keep your hands off my pa! I need him! I've already had offers from Kate.'

'How is she?'

'OK. She's beginning to get on top of things at last. I hardly see her these days, she's so busy.'

'I never know quite what to say to her. Does she ever see her husband? It must be awful living in that sort of limbo for so long.'

'It's nearly a year now since they separated but I think it's been very hard for her to come to terms with it.'

'She never mentions him. What's he like?'

'He's a shit! She's better off without him but it's difficult to start again when you're thirty—especially when you haven't been brought up to fend for yourself. Mark supports the twins but Kate won't take anything for herself except that, to begin with, he continued to pay the mortgage. Her father had already paid half the cost of the cottage in the deposit and in the end Kate borrowed the other half from him and is trying to pay it back.'

'Well surely her father won't make life difficult?' Abby accepted her mug of black coffee. 'Or is he hard up?'

'Not particularly. But Kate's got two brothers and a sister and she feels that it isn't fair on them. When he gave her the deposit, they all had equal amounts but this is rather different. Kate looks upon it as a loan, which is why she took that job with the bookshop in Tavistock and breeds dogs on the side. She doesn't make that much, I suspect, but she likes to pay bits off the loan whenever she can.'

Abby sighed. 'Poor Kate. She's such a sweetie. She must find it a bit much trying to do it all.'

'I think she does in the holidays when the twins are home. But the chap who owns the bookshop is super to her. Gives her time off and lets her adjust her hours. She rushes home at lunchtime to let the dogs out. To be honest,' Cass hitched her chair forward conspiratorially, 'I think he fancies her.'

'Oh?' Abby put her elbows on the table, eyebrows raised. 'Is he available?'

Cass shook her head vexedly. 'I don't know. Kate's very cagey and I don't want to probe too much. She's been hurt quite enough.' She grinned. 'He's rather dishy, though. Have you seen him?'

Abby shook her head. 'I'm not even sure where the bookshop is. You don't mean W.H. Smith's, do you?'

'No, no. This is a little antiquarian bookshop round the back. He sells old prints and things, too. He's very tall. Lean and sexy. Wears gorgeous cords. Casual but right. You know?'

'Mmm.' Abby sounded appreciative as if Cass were offering her a cream cake. 'I do indeed. Perhaps I'll pop in and buy a book!'

'Honestly. First my old pa and now Kate's boss! There's a name for women like you! Anyway, you haven't got a hope. He'd find out in the first two minutes that you never learned to read!'

ALEX GILLESPIE PULLED AN old bookcase into position outside his shop window and went back inside to fetch some books. He came back out with a cardboard boxful and began to arrange them on the wooden shelves. Although it was barely half-past ten, the town seemed already to sizzle with heat and the sun beat on his back, burning through his shirt. He picked up the empty box and paused for a moment before going to fetch more books. Kate had just rounded the corner and was making her way towards him, walking slowly. She paused to look into the newly opened boutique. Alex studied her. She wore the denim skirt that she had worn all summer and one of the several cheese-cloth shirts that she possessed; this one had faded blue and pink stripes. Her legs were bare and on her feet she wore flat leather sandals. Her brown curls were cut short, emphasising the angle of her small square jaw.

She's too thin, he thought, and felt the usual wave of frustration.

He'd been terribly surprised when she'd walked into his bookshop nearly six months ago in answer to his advertisement for an assistant. She'd been in once or twice and on one occasion bought an antique print of Plymouth Hoe for her husband. They'd chatted a bit and he'd found himself very attracted to her but she was obviously married and Alex, whose own marriage had failed some years before, left married women severely alone.

She had an unusual quality of openness and friendliness without being in the least coquettish and he thought about her quite a lot after she'd left the shop. He found himself looking out for her in the town. She had told him that she came in mainly on market days and he would wander through the old Pannier Market, busy with both locals and visitors crowding around the stalls. Skirting trestle tables and avoiding loitering grockles, he looked over the tops of heads for a glimpse of her. Only once he had seen her and had been rather taken aback at the way his heart had speeded up. He had contrived to bump into her 'accidentally' at one of the second-hand book stalls and her smile of pleasure had buoyed up his spirits for days. He had persuaded her to join him for a cup of coffee, taken her into The Galleon and they had talked about books. She was well read although she knew nothing of his trade in antiquarian books and they spent a very happy half an hour. It was some time before he saw her again and then she had the twins with her and it had been little more than a passing greeting. When she walked into the shop and had asked very tentatively about the job he had been so delighted that for a moment he could hardly speak and she had taken his silence for disbelief that she could be seriously applying for it.

It was then that he began to get the inkling that her confidence had been damaged and he spent long hours wondering how. He gave her the job at once and found her willing to learn although a little diffident about her abilities. She was marvellous with his customers and very reliable but although they maintained a friendly easy relationship, he was no further on than he had been six months before. She had told him that her husband was in the Navy and away a great deal and now that the twins were at boarding school she was rather lonely which was why she had decided to get a job. But Alex was sure that there was more to it than that. She often wore an inward-looking expression and she had lost weight. In the whole six months she had never mentioned that her husband had been home. In fact she never spoke of him at all and he longed to ask her outright what the truth of the matter really was. Something always held him back but it was becoming increasingly difficult to keep his emotions at bay.

At that moment, Kate turned to walk on, saw him and raised her hand. He waved back at her, feeling that funny little pain that told him exactly where his heart was located.

'Hello.' She had arrived beside him. 'Am I late? Megs and Honey were having such fun that I couldn't get them back.'

'Not at all.' He smiled down at her and clutched his box more firmly lest he should fling it away and pull her into his arms. 'Just in time to put the kettle on. I'll get the other bookcase out.'

'The trouble is,' said Kate, going into the shop, 'it's simply too hot for people to be wandering around. They dash out early, gather up the necessities and dash home again. Still, it is market day so we may have a few grockles around.'

She dropped her basket on the floor by the little chair near the table which she used. Alex had a big desk at right angles in the corner. There was only the one big room with a small kitchen next door to a lavatory right at the back. Another door opened on to the staircase which led to the flat above where Alex lived alone.

The walls were lined with bookshelves and three tables held boxes which contained old prints, none framed—many of them local scenes. Kate went through to fill the kettle.

'There's talk of standpipes if it goes on,' she said, wandering back into the shop. 'You wouldn't believe it, would you? We have month after month of rain and then after just a week or two of hot weather we have hosepipe bans and standpipes.'

Alex carried the second bookcase outside and Kate came to help him stack it with books. He looked down at her thin brown hand and the bright gold of her wedding ring.

'I've been here nearly six months,' she said. 'Amazing. The twins break up next week but Cass says she'll have them as much as possible. Did Susie say she'd be able to do some extra hours like she did at Easter?'

'Yes.' Alex looked at her. Her slate grey eyes were worried. 'That's no problem. We're going to sort it out on a weekly basis. She's only too pleased to be able to earn some extra money.'

Kate looked at him with gratitude. 'You're very good to me,' she said. 'It's so difficult to find a job that fits in with school. I'm really grateful.'

'Kate,' he began, but as he spoke a voice called from behind them.

'Alex! And where were you last night, you rotten devil?'

He experienced a stab of frustrated anger before he turned resignedly. An opulent woman whose fair hair owed a great deal to artifice was bearing down on them.

'Good morning, Pam,' he said and Kate slipped past him into the shop. 'I'm sorry. I wasn't in the mood. I'm sure you all managed without me.'

'I missed you.' She pouted a little and wriggled her heavy shoulders. 'Living alone isn't good for you. You're getting to be a miserable old bachelor.'

'Chance would be a fine thing.' But he laughed to take the sting out of his words.

'Well, don't forget that you're taking me to the Mallinsons' barbecue tomorrow. Come early and we'll have a little drink before we go. See you then.'

Alex sighed and went into the shop. Kate was sitting at her table, her head bent over a catalogue.

'Coffee's on your desk,' she said without looking up.

'Thanks.' He hesitated. She turned a page, engrossed, and after a moment he went to his desk and sat down.

———

KATE CARRIED A RUG into the garden and spread it on the hard-baked lawn. The dogs no longer greeted her return from the bookshop with the boundless vigour that demanded exercise but went to lie beneath the apple trees at the bottom of the garden, tongues lolling. Kate went round opening windows, hoping for circulation of air, and then taking a cushion wandered out again and lay down on the rug. The early-evening sun still had great power and she could feel it almost nailing her to the rug, its tremendous heat sapping all that remained of her energy.

Her brain, hopping about like a tired bird, pecked at anxieties. Money was a continual nagging pressure. She mentally reviewed the contents of the larder, praying that they would stretch 'til the end of the month. She'd have to get some petrol tomorrow but that was OK as she'd got a few pounds in her purse. She'd miss her pay from the bookshop when the twins were home but they'd manage somehow. They might need new clothes, of course . . .

She stretched and turned her cheek on the old cushion, idly plucking at the dry grass and letting her brain fix on the subject that dominated it now for most of the time: Alex. To take the job had been so tempting. He was so easy to talk to; there were no strains and stresses, no having to think one thought ahead in case what you were about to say might be construed as criticism or complaint. It had been such a novel experience, going to the bookshop most days, learning how things were done, talking to customers. It seemed almost amazing to be actually paid for doing it. Sometimes at lunchtimes they would shut up shop and wander out for something to eat. At other times they would buy sandwiches from the baker at the corner and eat them at their desks with a cup of coffee. There seemed so much to talk about. This, realised Kate, was what had seduced her as much as anything else, this companionship. They spoke the same language, shared the same interests, laughed at the same things. It was fatal. He was interested in what she thought, how she worked, which was an utterly new experience for her. She was in love with him before she'd realised it and when she did, she panicked. Gulping back the first heady draught of friendship, she had not noticed that it also contained a fairly sizeable love potion. She caught herself watching his hands as he handled the old books, looking at his mouth as he talked and smiled, and she would experience strange and disturbing emotions. She was terrified that he might guess even though it was very clear that he was interested in her and prepared to be more so. But where would it lead? Slowly, semi-drugged with sun and weariness, she started on a long drawn out fantasy and presently she slept.

'Kate?' Her shoulder was being gently shaken. 'Kate!'

'Good grief! Tom! You really made me jump.' Kate rolled over and sat up.

He squatted beside her on the rug.

'Sorry, love. You were dead to the world. Didn't mean to make you jump.'

'That's OK. Is Cass with you?' She knelt up. The two dogs weaved about them, tongues lolling, tails waving. 'Wonderful guard dogs, you are!' she told them.

'They welcomed me in. Would have shown me where the silver was if I'd asked.'

Kate laughed. 'They're useless,' she said. 'But, Tom, whatever are you doing here on a Friday evening? Surely you've only just got down from London? How do you like driving a desk?' She struggled to her feet, shooing the dogs away, and then paused. 'Is Cass OK?'

'She's fine. No problems.' Tom stood up too. 'She sent me over to tell you off. She says you're being a stubborn old moo about the Mallinsons' party tomorrow night.'

'Oh, hell. Don't say she sent you over just for that? Not after a long train journey in that sweltering heat? It's too bad of her.'

'I got home early,' said Tom, following her into the cottage, his eyes on her hips and bottom. Like Alex, he thought her much too thin but Tom's opinion, however, was based on purely lustful grounds. 'I popped over while Cass gets supper ready. Now, why won't you come?'

Kate stood in the kitchen, resting her weight on her fists as she leaned against the table, her head lowered. After a moment she turned to face him. 'Do you ever see Mark?' she asked him.

The suddenness took Tom off guard. He shrugged a bit, raised his eyebrows, grimaced a little. Kate watched him.

'Occasionally,' he said, at last. 'Now and then. Not so much now I'm at Northwood.'

'And what do the gossips say about us? What's the buzz?'

Tom looked embarrassed. 'Heavens, Kate!' he blustered. 'Why should there be any? I haven't heard anything. It's nobody's business, after all.'

Kate continued to watch him. After a bit she sighed. 'I hoped that you might tell me the truth. I've heard murmurings, of course. I went to one or two parties and George invited me to the Christmas Ball at *Drake,* much to Felicity's fury. There was a certain amount of drawing aside of skirts, you know. I told Mark that he could make up any reason he liked to account for our separation and I wouldn't contradict it. It seemed a small price to pay to get out and have the twins looked after. Now I'm not so sure. There's a lot of Navy round here and I didn't realise how much I'd mind. I just wish I knew what reasons he had decided to give.' She smiled at Tom who was looking profoundly uncomfortable. 'Sorry. It's not fair to ask you. It's just easier to know what you're up against. The trouble is, it's given me a dread of going to naval dos. I'm getting a bit morbid, I suppose, but I wonder what people are saying about me. I expect that there'll be quite a strong naval contingent at the Mallinsons.'

'He's a skimmer,' said Tom dismissively, as if that made everything different. 'You mustn't shut yourself off. You've got to get out there and show people you don't care, otherwise they'll think you've got something to hide. Come on, love.' He went to her and took her by the upper arms. 'The people who know you will guess the truth—the others don't matter.'

'It's horrid being alone,' she said, knowing at once it was the wrong thing to say to Tom who would certainly misconstrue it. He was the sort of man who was quite sure that any woman living alone was frustrated and lonely and only too grateful for a man's attention. He tried to draw her a little closer.

'You don't have to be lonely,' he murmured. 'Beautiful girl like you.'

'Tom.' She tried to laugh as she held him off. 'What are you saying? And Cass my best friend! All right, I'll come. No. I'll drive myself over to the Rectory. You can tell Cass she's won. I never could resist a handsome man.'

She got him out at last and went back to the lawn. As she folded the rug she thought of the other reason for refusing the Mallinsons' invitation. Clutching the sun-warmed rug to her breast, she stared across the garden into the lengthening shadows.

You fool, she told herself. You stupid bloody fool!

'WHAT'S ALL THIS ABOUT rumours?' asked Tom, as he and Cass prepared for bed.

'It's that cow Felicity,' said Cass without preamble as she sat at her dressing table and unscrewed her ear-rings. 'When Kate came back it meant that it was the end of her secret idyll with George in Kate's cottage. And George has invited Kate to one or two things. So she's putting it about that Kate's sleeping around.'

'Oh, come on love! Kate? Not quite the type, is she? If it was you, now!'

'Thank you, darling.' Cass smiled as she began to brush out the long thick blonde hair. 'Sweet of you to say so.'

Tom bent over to kiss her, his hands sliding the narrow straps of her nightdress over her shoulders.

'Why are you wearing this stupid thing?'

'But, darling,' Cass stroked his hair as his lips slid down to her breasts, 'what is Mark saying?'

'Mmm? Oh, I don't know. Why don't you take it off?'

'But what?' Cass stood up and stepped out of the offending garment. 'I can't believe you don't know.'

'Mm. Oh, Cass. What? What does it matter?'

She let him half carry her to the bed.

'Oh, darling, That's nice. Tom? Does Mark say that she's sleeping around?'

'What? Well, no, not exactly.' Tom stood up and started pulling off his clothes. 'Says she's been having an affair with some chap down here. That's why she wouldn't go to *Dolphin* while he was driving. Had to drag her up to Chatham and then she ran out on him to come back down here.'

'Oh!' Cass frowned.

'Come on, darling,' he said as he rolled on to the bed and pulled her to him. 'Forget it, can't you?'

THE MALLINSONS' COTTAGE WAS set all alone at the end of the lane that joined the road that ran past the church out of the village. The footpath that led from the churchyard skirted its boundaries before crossing the fields at the back.

The terrace where the barbecue was laid out and the lawn below it looked across the fields to the moor and was a perfect setting for an al fresco evening. By the time the Wivenhoes arrived, having had an argument as to whether they should drive or walk, the party was well under way and the lane was full of parked cars. Tom, who had wanted to walk, lifted up his voice at once, complaining that by the time he had driven half a mile back up the lane to the nearest space he may as well have walked.

'True, darling,' said Cassandra sweetly. 'How well it's worked. You wanted to walk, after all. Now you can. You can drop us here, at the gate. Now we're all happy.'

'Honestly, Cass,' chuckled Kate, as Tom drove away muttering imprecations. 'How you get away with it I simply don't know. And don't think I've come just to keep Tom occupied while you pursue some man or other!'

'What an idea!' Cass arched her brows and led the way in. 'Really, Kate! Hello, Carol. How lovely it all looks. Whose clever idea was it to string those coloured lights in the trees? Oh, hello, Paul. Yes, please. White wine will be lovely. Good heavens! So many people.'

Kate, keeping well back, looked around. At last she saw him. He was standing in a group of people, staring down into the glass he held. Pam stood beside him, laughing and gesticulating. She looked up at him and Kate watched Alex bend his head to hers and smile. She felt a little twisting pain in her heart and tried to look away. He looked up and straight at her. Kate looked back, wide-eyed, and they stared at each other for a moment until Paul Mallinson stepped in front of her and gave her a glass.

'Don't stand here on your own,' he said. 'I'm sure you know lots of people. Where's Tom?'

'He's parking the car.' Kate took the glass and swallowed some wine. She smiled up at him. 'Thanks. Are you settling in?'

'Definitely. We shall hate having to leave it if I get appointed away. The down side of having your own home, of course.'

'Hello, Lizzie,' said Kate, smiling at the little girl hovering behind him. 'Poor Charlotte is green with envy that she couldn't come.'

'Mummy said she could come,' volunteered Lizzie. 'And she could have stayed the night. We could have gone to bed when we got tired but Charlotte's mummy said "no." ' She offered Kate a bowl of crisps and then disappeared with Paul into the crowd.

Kate raised her eyes cautiously and saw Cass talking to a slight, brown-haired man: he looked familiar. Kate frowned, racking her memory. Suddenly he burst out laughing and memory shifted back and the pieces fell into place: Tony Whelan.

Hell and damnation! thought Kate. No wonder she didn't want Charlotte around. Cass prefers to play the field unhampered by her offspring. So that's why she was so keen for me to come, the cow! She jumped violently as Tom slid an arm around her waist.

'Tom! Did you park OK? Shall we find you a drink?'

'Hi, Tom!' It was Paul. 'Great. Now what will you have to drink? I'm relying on your expertise with the steaks, remember. Come and get a drink.'

They disappeared together and Kate took another gulp of her wine.

'Hello, Kate. This is a surprise.' (How pretty she looks in that strange blue colour.)

'Hello, Alex. Is it?' (How does he always manage to look so relaxed?)

'Is your husband with you?' (How would I be able to be polite to him if he is?)

'No. No, he isn't. I came with the Wivenhoes. Do you know them?' (Cass is probably just his type.)

'Name doesn't ring a bell. I wish I'd known you were coming.' (I would have to be with Pam.)

'Why?' (Please let me stay cool.)

'I would much rather have been with you.' (Well, that's done it.)

'Would you?' (Then why are you with that beastly blonde tart?)

'Kate?' (Does she mean . . . ? She looked for a moment as if . . . ?)

'So there you are, Alex. You see, I can't trust him for a moment. I go off to the loo and he's immediately chatting up another woman. Living up to his reputation again!' Pam slipped her arm possessively into Alex's. 'Oh, it's Kate! Hello, my dear. I warn you, don't trust this man for a moment.'

'Tom,' said Kate with relief as he reappeared beside her. 'Tom, this is Alex Gillespie. He's my boss and this is . . . ' She hesitated, her pride making her pretend that she didn't know or couldn't remember Pam's name. 'This is Tom Wivenhoe.'

Pam held out her hand, introducing herself, smiling archly—every male must be a conquest.

Kate glanced quickly at Alex and as quickly away from the bleak look on his face. Tom was bending over Pam's hand, making flattering observations, and she was shrieking with delight.

Kate found that she was clutching her glass tightly and when Alex put out his hand for it his long fingers lightly touched hers. All her feelings of awareness were so heightened that the blood seemed to sing in her ears and she couldn't look at him. She knew that she was behaving like any teenager with a crush but she seemed unable to handle the situation. It had been so long since she had been possessed by this foolish illusory magic and part of her didn't want it. Life was complicated enough as it was. She should have stuck to her guns and, knowing that Alex and Pam had been invited, simply stayed away. It was all so much more controllable at the shop.

She released the glass but he didn't move. She was going to have to look at him but she knew she simply mustn't. And then Cass was there, wonderful beloved Cass, sweeping up, dragging Tony with her, breaking things up.

Alex went to get some drinks and Kate looked at Tony. He grinned at her. 'Long time no see.'

She nodded and then began to laugh. Her nerves were on edge and somehow she simply couldn't stop laughing.

'What's so funny?' Tony, infected by her laughter, was smiling.

'You are. Read any good books lately?'

'Books?'

'What are you talking about?' Cass, having abandoned Pam to Tom, was back.

'Books,' said Kate. 'I was just about to tell Tony that Tom's grown up a bit since we were all at *Dolphin*. This time you'll have to do better than *The Wind in the Willows*.'

Thirteen

All through that summer, Kate held the twins as a shield between her and any possible developments in her relationship with Alex. After the barbecue, she adopted the attitude of one who was in a permanent rush: rushing in, having taken the twins to Cass; rushing home, so as to pick them up to take them to the beach or for a picnic; rushing out at lunchtime, to buy something for their supper. Guy was struck by a whole series of Arthur Ransom's books—he adored the water and boats—and Kate was overwhelmed when Alex presented the set to him for his eleventh birthday. To Giles he gave two charming pen and ink sketches of the old town of Dartmouth, suitably framed. Kate was speechless and gave thanks that her own thirty-first birthday in August had passed in a well-kept silence. Fortunately, Alex had been away a great deal at that time, buying and attending auctions, and Kate's furious threats to the twins should they so much as breathe a word about it were almost unnecessary.

She was horrified to find that, even with the twins for company, she missed Alex most dreadfully. His presence, even when it was casting her into fits of apprehension, had become necessary to her well-being. She missed the companionable chats, the shared excitement of newly discovered books and prints, the occasions when they shut the shop at lunchtime and strolled over to the Bedford for sandwiches and beer.

The evening of the barbecue had changed all that. Tacitly, certain things had been admitted and Kate knew that Alex was only biding his time before making a further move. She spent hours trying to decide whether she wanted him to: she really knew so little about him. He was very popular, so much was obvious. There were always women telephoning and asking for him and some of them came into the shop. He was in great demand as a spare man and as an escort—and, she was sure, more—to the little clique of divorced women, one of whom was Pam. Kate was well aware that her arrival at the shop had been greeted with interest and even suspicion and Pam and a few others were making sure that she didn't trespass on their territory. Certainly, there had never been any sign of anyone staying with him at the flat, even overnight, and she had seen no evidence of feminine habitation when she had gone to collect some new stock which Alex kept in a room upstairs.

She blushed when she remembered how she had tiptoed along the carpeted passage, peering into his other rooms, one ear cocked lest he should come upstairs. The flat was one floor of a Victorian house, high-ceilinged and airy, the rooms opening off a long passage. Kate had taken in as much as she could in the brief time allowed her: a large bedroom furnished with almost austere sparseness—but containing a double bed!—with built-in hanging cupboards, a heavy mahogany chest of drawers—no photographs!—a bentwood rocking chair and a bedside table piled high with books: a delightful sitting room, the pale walls almost papered with water colours, more built-in cupboards on either side of a pretty Victorian fireplace and several huge, comfortable armchairs: a small bathroom with shaving things in evidence—no creams or lotions!—and a very masculine dressing gown tossed over a wicker laundry basket: a practical kitchen with a breakfast bar and two high stools, with a row of cacti on the window sill. The only other room contained the stock and, gathering up her requirements, Kate had hurried back downstairs conscious of Alex's quizzical look when she reached the bottom. Later, it had occurred to her that he had suggested that she should go upstairs—usually he went himself— so that she could check it out and the thought made her blush in earnest.

Poor Kate. Even her beloved moor betrayed her that summer. The drought transformed it into a huge scorched wasteland over which the sun hung, a burning ball of brass. Cracks and fissures opened in the ground, the streams dried up and the ponies and panting sheep crowded under the few areas of shade that remained in that shimmering, pitiless glare. Even the skylarks seemed to have lost heart and only the ravens were in evidence, strutting over the parched grasslands, their stiff-legged gait slow and purposeless, before taking aimlessly to the airless heights, their wings flapping with a slow dispirited beat.

Kate took to walking very early and very late but even then there was no respite from the inexorable heat. She was grateful for the cool of her thick-walled cottage and for the first time let the Rayburn out and had to buy a small camping stove. It was too hot to eat much and she and the twins spent a great deal of the summer lying beneath the apple trees in the garden, grateful for their shade. Even the beach, shadeless and glaring, with the sea, blazing like a mirror beneath the near white sky, was no place to be in this weather.

As the lack of water became a serious problem, the locals began to resent the tourists who poured down on holiday, using up precious resources and starting fires in their carelessness, and for many it was almost a relief when the heat wave came to an end and the rain fell.

CASS WAS ONE OF the few who would have liked the sunshine to go on for ever. Lazing happily and wearing as little as possible in her large cool house and shady garden, she managed to conduct an affair with Tony right through the summer and under the noses of her family and friends. Even the heat conspired with her.

Deceiving Tom, who was away at Northwood from Monday to Friday, wasn't difficult and, indeed, she almost looked upon it now as a necessity as much for his benefit as for hers. Over the years she had managed to persuade herself that it was her little flings that kept her happy and contented in his absence. Thus there was no strain on the marriage from the separations or possible loneliness and when Tom arrived home it was to be met with a loving wife ready to minister to all his wants. She uttered no recriminations or complaints—difficulties and traumas were related as huge jokes—and a blind eye was turned to any little philanderings of his that filtered down to her through the grapevine. Some wives who were jealous of Cass's beauty and success, and whose husbands were serving with Tom, were only too happy to let some little remark slip. Hastily they would pretend to gloss over or withdraw it, hoping, nevertheless, that the tiny dart of poison would find its mark. Generally, and to their chagrin, it would be met by a smiling Cass who dealt with it at once by a light remark. 'I'm so glad that my dear old boy's enjoying himself.'

On the few occasions when Tom had quoted gossip that he'd heard she would look sorrowful and talk of the spitefulness of jealous women and the humiliation of rejected men and then turn the subject slightly to some event or visit where Tom had not been quite so honourable as he might have been. Baffled, he would withdraw, only to be flattered and charmed back into the magic circle that she made for him, until everything else receded to the edge of his consciousness.

His hope that Cass's father would be a restraining influence had not been realised. In fact, the General had quite unconsciously proved a tremendous help. Now in his seventy-fifth year, he had a slight heart attack and the heat had kept him more or less housebound but he was well enough, with Mrs Hampton's help, to have the children to visit. They would walk down after lunch in a little chattering group, the twins often taking it in turn to give Saul a piggyback, to spend an hour or two with the doting pair before sitting down to the sort of tea that most children see only on very special occasions. Only two-year-old Gemma stayed with her mother.

Often, on these afternoons, Tony's car might have been seen nosing its way up the drive and pulling round out of sight behind the stables. Slipping in through the back door he would find Cass, smiling, warm, waiting, and they would climb the stairs giggling like naughty children and shushing each other lest Gemma should wake out of her afternoon slumbers. Several times this happened and Cass slipped away from Tony's protests to bring the child back and set her on the bedroom floor with toys and books before climbing back on to the bed to continue where they had left off. Once Tony, crying out in an ec-stasy of fulfilment, had collapsed across Cass's breasts only to find himself gazing into a different, if almost identical set of wide blue eyes. Gemma, who had pulled herself up by the quilt, gazed back gravely.

'Christ, Cass!' He had rolled away in ludicrous prudery, dragging the quilt over his naked loins, and Cass, shaking with silent mirth, had carried Gemma away so that Tony might dress in private.

On one afternoon Mrs Tanner, the Rector's wife, had arrived and Cass, descending calmly—yes, she had been having a little nap—had given her tea whilst upstairs Tony lounged naked amongst the crum-pled sheets, smoking and reading Tom's latest Wilbur Smith.

'Still playing Russian roulette, Cass?' asked Kate, who arrived un-expectedly early one afternoon to collect the twins.

Tony, looking slightly sheepish when Kate asked him if he'd come to borrow a book, had slipped away and the two girls lounged on sun beds drinking cold drinks.

'Can't resist, darling.' Cass stretched lazily. 'It's such fun. How's the gorgeous Alex?'

'Away buying,' said Kate coldly, and Cass burst out laughing.

'No good looking po-faced, my sweet. Anyone with half an eye can see that he's potty about you. Why don't you relax a bit and enjoy it?'

'I'm afraid to,' said Kate quietly. 'I'm not like you, Cass. I only wish I were. It would make life so much easier. Can't you see how wonderful it would be to get rid of all my frustration by rolling about in bed with someone who meant nothing to me?'

Cass sat up and looked at her. 'Oh, dear. Fallen for him?'

'I might have done,' said Kate miserably. 'I don't know any more. I can't afford another mistake. But I'm not going to be just one more in a long row of conquests, either.'

Cass raised her eyebrows. 'Like that, is he? I'm surprised. I always find him rather distant.'

'Well, I suppose there are, conceivably, one or two males on this earth who might just be impervious to your charms,' said Kate, somewhat acidly—and then laughed. 'Sorry. It's just that he's got all these bloody women who come into the shop and want to tell me about his reputation.'

'I should have thought that you of all people would know better than to believe that sort of rumour,' remarked Cass, and felt remorseful when Kate coloured slowly under her tan. 'Surely you know him well enough to judge him by now without listening to a pack of jealous women. What do *you* think?'

'I don't know!' cried poor Kate. 'If only I did! I think I'm going mad.'

'Bring him to dinner one weekend. I'll invite Abby and William. We'll give him the works.'

'I don't doubt it.' Kate began to laugh. 'I can just see it. Thanks but no thanks. I'd as soon join Daniel for a bite in the lions' den!'

TOWARDS THE END OF the holidays, Mark's mother telephoned Kate and asked if the twins could be spared for a few days to stay in Cheltenham. Mark, she said, would be there for a week of his leave and it seemed a good opportunity for a get together. Kate had seen the Websters once since the Commissioning. They had driven down just before Christmas and a white-faced Mrs Webster had begged Kate to reconsider her decision. It was plain that she didn't believe in Kate's mythical lover although the Major continued to stare at her as if she were a rather undesirable species quite beyond his comprehension.

Feeling a complete brute, Kate tried to explain that she and Mark were utterly incompatible and that a reconciliation was quite out of the question but that it need make no difference to Mrs Webster's relationship with her grandchildren. Kate knew full well that Mark would make no effort to see his sons unless there were a third person at hand to cope with all the boring bits. She also knew that his latent streak of cruelty would be kept under control with his mother around.

So it was that the unwilling twins were dispatched to Cheltenham, the only bright spot in their opinion being that they would be travelling by train unaccompanied. The Websters, who were going down to Cornwall on holiday, would bring them back by car. Kate drove them to Exeter St David's where they would catch a train that went straight through to Cheltenham and praised God, as she often did, that there were two of them.

She drove back across the moor, sombre now in a soft grey mist, and stopped to give the dogs a run on Crockern Tor. As she climbed the Tor behind them, getting very damp in the process, she thought about the twins, wondering how they would cope with Mark. She decided to use the tactic she had used when they were very small and asking questions: answer only what they ask, as truthfully and briefly as possible. Children, she had found, asked only as much as they were capable of assimilating. If one droned on, they became confused or bored and, though it was sometimes tempting to take them one stage further on, she generally resisted it. So it was now. They rarely asked after Mark and when they did she said that he was at sea. They knew the boat was based in Faslane and she assumed that they felt that life was following a fairly normal pattern. Mark had never written to them as some fathers wrote to their children and when he communicated with Kate on some financial matter she would always tell them that she had heard from him and that he sent his love. When she had told them about the proposed visit to Cheltenham they were surprised. Why Cheltenham? Kate explained that Mark only had a week and felt that he must try to see his parents. Giles had asked why she wasn't coming to Cheltenham and she had explained that she had promised to be at the shop because Alex had to go away. She pointed out that she could see Mark when they were at school, implying that this sometimes happened, and they accepted it readily enough although she was well aware that Giles would have been happier if she had been going too.

Giles is not as self-sufficient as Guy, thought Kate, stopping to get her breath and turning to look down on Parson's Cottage, set among some trees. She suspected that there was more than a touch of Mark in Guy and although it was tempting to think of this with alarm she knew that, tempered with other qualities, it need not be worrying. Giles was much gentler by comparison, more inclined to self-doubt, more openly affectionate. She wondered what Mark's approach to them would be and was glad that his mother—who adored the twins—would be on hand. She whistled to the dogs and started to descend to the car, praying that the week would pass without problems.

She dropped down into Tavistock to do some shopping and had got as far as the pavement when she realised that it was early closing day. So it was that Alex saw her standing beside her car, irresolute and dejected, her hair covered in misty droplets. He hesitated only for a moment.

'Kate!' he shouted and saw her head come up and round. For one glorious second he saw the unmistakable expression on her face. He ran across the road. By the time he reached the pavement she had regained her composure but he took her cold hands and she made no effort to prevent him.

'Come and have some tea,' he said. 'Please. I need to talk to you. We can't just go on like this.'

He drew her a little closer but before she could speak, a voice spoke from behind him.

'My dear Alex! You're a positive menace to the female sex. It was three o'clock when I finally levered you out this morning and here you are making up to poor Kate in broad daylight in the middle of Duke Street. There should be a law against you!'

At the sound of the hated voice, Kate shook herself free and, climbing into her car, set off at speed, leaving Alex and Pam standing on the pavement.

CASS, SELECTING HER CHEESES in Creber's, heard a familiar voice and glanced round.

'Well, well,' she drawled. 'If it isn't Felicity. How are you?'

Felicity, who was obviously more than able to restrain her delight at the sight of her old sparring partner, raised her eyebrows. 'Bit early in the day for you, isn't it, Cass? I didn't realise that you knew that the day started before eleven o'clock.'

'And me with four children?' Cass's eyes swept Felicity's spare, bird-like form. 'Still barren, I see.'

Felicity glanced around, scandalised, and met the sympathetic glances of at least two of the shop assistants.

'You know very well . . . ' she began furiously, in a lowered voice.

'And I hear that you're spreading terrible lies about Kate.' Cass did not lower her voice. 'I know she ruined your little extramarital affair with George but you shouldn't be vindictive, Felicity. There is such a thing as slander, you know. Love to Mark II. Special love, of course.'

She went out, smiling graciously upon the young man who hastened to open the door for her.

Felicity saw that the glances now were not so sympathetic and her lips thinned. Boiling with rage she went to the cold-meat counter. She was damned if she'd be made embarrassed enough to feel that she had to leave. 'I want some ham,' she said and did not add the word 'please.'

Cassandra sauntered along Duke Street smiling to herself. Damn, she thought, I didn't get my cheese! Ah, well, coffee, I think.

She paused for a moment and then, crossing the road, made her way by side and back streets to the bookshop. Alex looked up as she came in. He looked tired and preoccupied and there was no sign of Kate.

'I was hoping to carry Kate off for a cup of coffee,' she said when they had exchanged greetings.

'She's not in,' he said, rather abruptly. 'She phoned to say that she'd got a migraine.'

'Oh?' Cass looked concerned. 'Of course. She took the twins to Exeter yesterday, didn't she? She's probably worried sick that Mark's going to beat them up or something.'

Alex looked so patently puzzled that Cass smiled.

'Sorry. Just thinking aloud. Are you OK? You look pretty rough yourself.'

'Just tired. What did you mean?'

Cass looked at him for a long moment. 'I'm going to do something quite unforgivable,' she said at last. 'I'm going to interfere. I suspect that you know next to nothing about Kate's marriage or what the situation is between her and Mark? Or what she thinks about you?'

'I know she thinks I'm the biggest philanderer since Casanova,' said Alex bitterly. He thrust his hands into the pockets of his cords and stood, head bent, jingling the coins in his pocket. 'I saw her yesterday,' he said eventually without looking at her. 'She was just standing there in the rain looking so vulnerable and alone. I called her and when she looked at me . . . I could swear there was a look on her face that . . . ' He shrugged. 'Well, I just grabbed her, you see.' He took his hands from his pockets and rubbed them over his face. 'Should I be telling you this?'

'Definitely!' said Cass firmly. She moved over to the door and turned the OPEN sign round so that it said CLOSED. A woman peering in looked affronted and Cass beamed at her before turning back to Alex who was watching her, nonplussed. 'I see that I have much to say to you. Kate's migraine is obviously an excuse not to face you this morning?'

'Obviously.' He shrugged again. 'What can I say to her? She stonewalls me at every turn and yet, underneath, I was so sure that there was something. And yesterday . . . ' He sighed. 'I've read enough between the lines to realise that there's not much of a marriage there but she tells me nothing. I suppose that she thinks that I'm hoping for an affair but it's not just that. I've let her know that I'm divorced, have been for some years now, and there are no children. There have been women in that time—why not? But she seems to view me as a local Don Juan and herself as the next scalp on the list.'

'I can see that I'm quite right to interfere. Now, why don't we go somewhere where we can have a long, quiet chat? I've been Kate's closest friend since we were twelve years old and you've got an awful lot of catching up to do.'

'THE TROUBLE IS,' SAID Kate as she followed the General into the kitchen, 'that I'm just so afraid of trusting to my own judgment. Let me make the coffee. Are you really better?'

'Perfectly well,' he assured her. 'And Mrs Hampton leaves every-thing ready as you can see. She's up at the Rectory this morning. You sit down at the table and tell me all about it.'

'It's not fair to burden you.' Kate sat down on one of the Windsor chairs. 'I just thought that, being a man, you may know how his mind is working. He knows I'm married so I can only assume that he must be thinking about having an affair. Is that logical?'

The General put the kettle on to boil and added another cup and saucer to the tray. 'Of course, there is such a thing as divorce,' he said, cautiously. 'He may well be thinking of marriage. He must have gathered that Mark plays no part in your life. Have you talked about that to him?'

Kate sighed. 'It would have been so much easier if Mark had been unfaithful to me or beat me up. Mental cruelty is so insidious. How do you explain to people what it's like to live with someone who chips away at your confidence, puts you down in public? It's so difficult to verbalise without sounding like a wimp. Eleven years of small, unre-lated incidents calculated to keep you in your place. I realise now that Mark worked on the Gamesmanship principle—if you're not one up you're one down. I think he really believed that.'

She put her elbows on the table and rested her chin in her hands. Af-ter a while, she spoke again, so quietly to start with that the General could hardly hear her.

'He asked me to go up to Faslane when he was driving, you know. The boat went in for a week and he wanted the car rather than be stuck in the base. I was rather excited about it even though the im-pression was that the car was more the object than I was. I hoped that Mark was finally beginning to gain confidence and might see that I could be allowed to share in his life. I packed some pretty clothes and drove up.'

Kate paused and looked up at the General.

'It took me about ten hours and when I got there he'd forgotten to arrange with the gate sentries for me to get in. Can you begin to un-derstand how I felt? Me, saying all happy and excited, "Oh, hello. I'm

Mrs Webster. My husband's expecting me," and him, looking at his clipboard, very puzzled, saying, "I'm sorry, ma'am, he hasn't notified me. No arrangements have been made."

'I felt such a fool. It's a very high security base and there'd been a lot of problems, a lot of IRA bomb threats and so on. There were two sentries. One kept walking round and round the car, peering in, as I gave the other chapter and verse and tried to persuade him to phone the boat to check with Mark. At long last he agreed. I was kept waiting at the gate until, finally, he tracked Mark down who said that he'd forgotten I was coming. The sentry stood talking into his telephone and staring at me and the car, saying things like: "Do you authorise her to come into the base, sir?" "And what model, please, sir?," "Registration number, sir?," "What colour hair?," "What colour eyes?," "How tall?" and things like that. He smiled at the end and when he'd put the phone down he said, "Your husband doesn't know the colour of your eyes, ma'am. I shouldn't let him get away with that!"

'Even then it wasn't all over. They searched the car and then realised that I had Megs with me. Dogs just were not allowed but Mark hadn't bothered to tell me that either. Suddenly I felt very tired, I remember, and I very nearly decided not to bother; to go and find a hotel, have a rest and drive back home again. I kept telling myself how busy Mark was and that he wasn't very good at details. Anyway, after a lot of fuss they agreed to let me through providing that Megs wasn't let out of the car for even a second because of all the guard dogs on patrol. I remember wondering how on earth I was going to cope with taking her in and out of the base for exercise and so on. If Mark had told me I would have left her with someone in Devon. It would have been so easy.' Kate smiled at the General, who seemed to have forgotten all about the coffee. 'I'm sure you would have had her for me, wouldn't you?

'Anyway, I drove round to the Mess and a steward took me up to Mark's cabin. He was down the boat and the hall porter phoned him to tell him I'd arrived although he knew that anyway having spoken to the sentry. He said he'd be up in about half an hour. I rushed about, had a bath, put on my fancy gear and sat down to wait. The hall porter sent me up some tea. When more than an hour had passed, I phoned down to the hall porter and asked if a problem had come up. He sounded very surprised and told me that Mark was in the bar. I wondered whether to go down but I was too shy. It's a totally masculine world. So another hour passed and then he strolled in, very casual.

'I was really upset by then and I asked him where on earth he'd been and whether he'd got my messages. One doesn't speak to Mark like that. He paused just inside the door, raised his eyebrows and told me that he'd been drinking in the bar with a man he hadn't seen for ages—his life assurance man who'd come all the way from Glasgow. I pointed out—somewhat heatedly—that he hadn't seen me for ages and I'd come all the way from Devon!

"He stood there and looked me up and down, took in the special clothes, all the trimmings, and smiled with a sort of amused contempt. When he'd let it sink in he said that he was going back down to this chap. When I'd pulled myself together and could behave myself I could join them downstairs in the bar. Then he walked out.' She paused and laughed mirthlessly. 'My humiliation was complete. He always liked me to know where I stood in his life.'

There was silence apart from the sound of the kettle boiling, which neither of them noticed, and the steady tick of the old clock on the mantel.

Kate stood up and walked towards the window. 'It was just one of so many similar incidents,' she said. 'How do you explain to people, that after eleven years of that sort of thing, you get to the point where you have to get out to hold on to any self-respect that you may have left? If he'd formed any sort of relationship with the twins I might have hung on but he's totally uninterested in them and they don't like him. I was just wasting my life!'

She returned to the table and sat down.

'Oh, my dear,' said the General at last. 'I am so sorry.'

'Oh, it doesn't matter any more. Not really. The trouble is that

Mark left my sense of self-worth on the floor and I simply can't bring myself to take another chance with Alex.'

'All men are not like Mark,' observed the General grimly, suddenly realising that the kettle was boiling. He had felt a terrible and impotent rage during Kate's recital and tried to calm himself. He must remain detached if he was to be of any real use to her.

'You see, I couldn't bear to be just another woman he tires of like that awful Pam.'

'If he's been alone for a while there would naturally be women in his life,' suggested the General, making coffee. 'If he's like me, he enjoys their company. Nothing wrong with that. And if women like him it's a good sign, I should think. Is Mark popular with women?'

'Gracious, no! He doesn't like them and they can sense it and leave him well alone.'

'Well,' the General shrugged, 'speaks for itself. What you want is time to get to know each other. Could you tell him that?'

Kate remembered the previous afternoon and her reaction to Pam's sudden appearance. The General watched the flush creep up her cheeks and prayed for guidance. He put her coffee before her and passed her the sugar.

'I'm afraid that I shall lose what reputation I've got left if I'm seen around with him,' she said. 'There's so much Navy around here and there are enough rumours about why I left Mark.'

She explained that she had given Mark carte blanche and her suspicions that he had told everybody that she had been unfaithful to him. The General was deeply shocked.

'The man's a bounder!' he said and Kate smiled.

'He's taking revenge for hurt pride. But I worry in case Alex has heard these rumours and thinks I'm easy pickings. And then there are the twins. I'm afraid that someone at school may pick something up. I suppose that in some ways it's lucky that Mark's not interested in them and that they're afraid of him. Well, Giles is.'

'Afraid?'

'Mark's what I describe as an arm-twister,' said Kate, after a short pause. 'A bit of a bully. An inflicter of little pains, bodily as well as mental. All in the way of fun, of course—can't you take a joke?—and one is made to feel pathetic and inadequate if one actually feels hurt. He seems to enjoy creating that tiny touch of fear. Turns him on. You learn to cope with it yourself but you can't bear it for your children. It teaches you to hate.'

She saw the General's expression and pulled herself up short.

'I don't really know why I am telling you all this. Oh, let's forget it—it's not important any more. I shouldn't have phoned Alex this morning and said I had a migraine, then I wouldn't have felt guilty and come and poured out all my sorrows on you. Running away won't help and I need the money.' She grinned at him. 'Now, if only you'd asked me to marry you when I left school, none of this would have happened! We were all in love with you, you know. Cass's dashing father roaring up the drive in that sports car! All the mistresses rushing about and powdering their noses and the sixth form hanging out of the windows!'

'Oh, my dear!' The General began to laugh and Kate felt a wave of relief.

I simply must not burden him, she thought. It really isn't fair.

'Well, there's still time,' she said, making eyes at him across the table. 'Don't you think I'd make a wonderful step-mother for Cass?'

fourteen

The barbecue to celebrate the twins' birthday was held on the Saturday before they went back to school. This term Oliver was going with them. He showed no signs of first-term nerves but viewed the proceedings with his usual calm poise and expressed tolerance for adult flap and anxiety. Giles was to be his 'escort'—an older boy who was chosen to guide the new boy through the first difficult weeks—and it was obvious that he intended to take his duties seriously.

'I'm glad it's not me,' said Charlotte as she helped Mrs Hampton to prepare the statutory birthday tea. 'I'd hate to go away. But Giles will look after him.'

' 'Course 'e will, my lover,' said Mrs Hampton, comfortably. 'No need to worry about either on 'em.'

'He's going to have some presents when the twins have theirs. I've got him an address book. It's dark blue leather. Mummy's got him a writing case with a zip and Daddy's giving him a special pen.'

'Sounds as if 'e's goin' to be doin' a whole lot of writin'.'

'He has to write home once a week on Sundays. Mummy bought a pencil case for Saul to give him with pencils and rubbers and things in it. It's really nice.'

'And what about Gemma?'

'Well, she's going to give him a toy. They're allowed to take a few, you know. It's a helicopter. A proper naval one and it's got a hook on a string that winds right down so that you can hook people on the bottom to rescue them out of the water. There's a little rubber boat with two little men in it. You can put them on the hook and wind them up and then they go inside through the little door.'

'Well!' Mrs Hampton put the cake tin into the oven and straightened up. 'No prizes for guessin' which o' they presents 'e'll like best!'

'I WAS GOING TO invite a few grown-ups this year,' said Cass to Kate as they stood watching Tom cooking sausages and beefburgers with Charlotte, wrapped in a large apron, in attendance. 'But it's a bit early in the evening and Tom said that it wasn't fair on the Smalls so I've decided to give a lovely big party when Oliver's gone.'

'Sounds like fun. Any special reason?'

Cass shrugged. 'Does one need a reason? I just felt like it. You'll come, of course? Bring Alex.' She glanced out of the corner of her eye. 'How's it going, by the way?'

'Well. Fine, actually.' Kate sounded puzzled. 'It was quite strange, I had a bit of a scene with him the day I took the boys to Exeter and I was really upset. In fact the next day I pleaded a migraine. You weren't here and I went and drained all over your pa. I felt really bad about that afterwards. Anyway, I went in the next day and Alex was super. Made no mention of, well, of anything. He was just friendly and nice and it was like it had been before.'

'Well, that's good then.'

'Ye . . . . es.' Kate sounded doubtful.

'So what's wrong now?'

'Do you remember I told you about when the twins were little? When they cried I worried and prayed that they'd stop and go to sleep and when they did I thought they'd died? So I'd prod them just to make sure and then they'd cry again?'

'Yes, I remember.' Cass chuckled. 'What a twit you are. What's that got to do with Alex?'

'Well, it's the same principle, you see. I felt that he was getting quite keen and I lost my nerve and didn't know how to handle it. And now he's backed right off and I wonder if he's lost interest which, if I'm really honest, hurts a bit.'

'And now you'd like to poke him just to make sure that he does feel the same but you still don't want to wake him right up and make him start crying again?'

They both burst out laughing.

'That's just about right,' said Kate ruefully. 'Why is life such hell?'

'Speak for yourself, duckie. I still think you should invite him to my party.'

'That's only because you fancy him yourself. You can keep your hands off him. It's bad enough having the Blonde Bombshell crawling all over him.'

'She's still around, is she?'

'Well. No, actually.' The puzzled note was back. 'She hasn't been around lately. And she phoned one day and he told me to tell her that he was out. She sounded very pissed off. It's just odd. I was wondering if he'd found someone else.'

Cass smiled to herself, the bleak note was not lost on her.

'Why not give him a tiny prod, sweetie? Just a really small one. Not enough to wake him right up—just enough to get him along to my party!'

'I wasn't expecting you this afternoon, Mrs Hampton. I thought that you were preparing the church for the wedding tomorrow.' The General helped her off with her coat and hung it on the back of the kitchen door.

'Well, 'tis that Saul's first day at school, as you know, General. An' Charlotte will've 'ad 'er 'ands full, I don't doubt, looking after 'im.' Mrs Hampton rummaged in her capacious basket and brought forth a cake tin. 'I felt somethin' special was called for, see. They'll be along presently. Church's all done. Lookin' beautiful, it is. Autumn's difficult time for flowers but Jack give me plenty of Michaelmas daisies an' dahlias an' Jane brought lots of stuff along 'erself.'

'Is that the bride?' The General sat himself down at the table, grateful that the tea was no longer his responsibility, and prepared for some gossip.

'Thass right. 'Er mother was cook up the 'ouse an' 'er dad was cow-man. 'E died but 'er mum still 'elps out on special occasions. She's doin' well for 'erself is Janie. She was all set to settle down with one o' the lo-cal boys, young Philip Raikes, then 'e moved away an' she decided to better 'erself. Moved into Plymouth an' got 'erself a job in Deb'nams. She's been sharin' a flat with another girl an' it was 'er that introduced Janie to Alan. Alan Maxwell 'is name is. 'E's a Petty Officer. Fine, up-standin' young man. Better than that young Philip. Nought but a waster 'e is. Alan's got a bit saved so Janie tells me, an' they're thinkin' to buy a li'l flat. 'E's in they submarines like the Commander. 'E's only got a few days' leave so it's been fixed up quick like.' As Mrs Hampton bus-tled to and fro the General suddenly noticed that the glossy brown hair was now seasoned with grey and the serene face had lines that he had never noticed before.

'Do you know, Mrs Hampton, that I've been here now for over ten years?'

Mrs Hampton's hands were stilled for a moment, her mind under-standing and accepting the change in the conversation.

'That's so. 'Appy years. All they littl'uns growin' up. We've been very blessed.'

'That's so.' The General sighed heavily. 'You'll have to keep an eye on them for me when I've gone.'

'An' oo's talkin' of you goin' anywhere?' Mrs Hampton bristled alarmingly, hiding her stab of fear. He'd looked so frail in the sum-mer. Not even Jack had known how worried she had been. 'Never 'eard such nonsense! There now. That's the children.'

The door opened and Saul, wearing Oliver's old satchel across his chest, burst in followed by a harassed-looking Charlotte. They were alike, these two—Tom's children.

'I did a picture for you, Grandfather,' he said, brushing greetings and questions aside. 'Look!' He delved into his satchel and plonked the sheet of paper before the General.

'It's a tank,' explained Charlotte quickly lest there should be any misunderstanding and Saul's feelings hurt.

'It is indeed,' said the General, looking appreciatively at it. 'A Centurion, is it?'

'Yes.' Saul scrambled up beside him and they were plunged instantly into technicalities.

Charlotte looked at Mrs Hampton.

' 'Ow did 'e do, my lover? Didden cry, did 'e?'

'No.' Charlotte shook her head. 'He was really good and ate all his lunch.' She was keeping something back, something exciting.

'What else, then? I c'n see there's somethin'. Tell 'Ammy.'

'Oh, Hammy!' The brown eyes were shining. 'I'm head girl! We all had to vote and I came out top. I've got a badge. Look!'

'Well now. I never! Head girl! I'm that proud! Wait 'til you tells you ma. I c'n see that this is a very special day. Good job I brung along this cake. Now you tell your grandad while I get the table laid. Head girl!' And turning away under the pretence of fetching some knives, Mrs Hampton buried her face in the teacloth and indulged in a few tears of joy and fear.

ABBY PICKED UP THE post from the doormat, crossed the hall and pushed open the door of the little business room where William sat at a desk, riffling through papers.

'Coffee, darling?' She opened a large white envelope. 'Oh, goody!' She waved a stiff square of cardboard at him. 'Cass has got her act together at last.'

'What is it?' William raised a reeling head. The business side of the estate was a nightmare to him but he was enjoying it on the whole and had no regrets about leaving his regiment. On the contrary, he was glad that he had come out while he was young enough to adapt to a world that had none of the safety nets of service life. The Army may be run by rules and regulations which, at first sight, seem to cram its people into straitjackets; nevertheless, it is all too easy first to tolerate, then accept and finally embrace those confines and be unable to function without them. William had seen it happen and was glad that he was outside, with the power to mould his life to his own design and, hopefully, with the courage to face up to the consequences in the process.

'It's Cass and Tom's party. She's been waiting to fix the date. There's a nuclear sub due back from sea and she wants to invite a few people from the Wardroom. Should be fun.'

'Good.' He smiled at her, suspecting that Abby missed Army life much more than he did. There were few people of their ages locally and Abby was not naturally a country girl. He gave her full marks for the positive way that she too had grasped at this new life and his smile was full of affection. 'Black tie?'

'Absolutely. The full works. I may need a new dress, darling. Long and elegant. What d'you think?'

'Sounds good to me. You'll have to have a day in Exeter. Check my DJ, will you?'

She grinned at him and disappeared.

'And don't forget my coffee,' he yelled after her.

'Coming up!' shouted Abby as she ran up the passage into the kitchen where Sophie staggered on uncertain legs behind a horse on wheels. 'I'm going to a party,' she cried, picking up the surprised Sophie and dancing her round. 'And I'm going to have a new dress. Oh, what fun it's going to be!'

ALEX, WHOSE POST ARRIVED a great deal earlier than Abby's, was still gazing at his invitation with misgivings when it was time to open the shop. He was quite certain now that Cass's advice concerning Kate had been sensible. He was giving her time to get to know and trust him and it seemed to be working. Kate was opening up a little, talking about the twins, volunteering information about herself. They kept their relationship strictly to the shop, although they lunched together occasionally if Kate wasn't hurrying home to let the dogs out. He had cooled off his relationship with Pam, which was nowhere near as close as her hints and comments had led Kate to believe, and had become less available generally. He was working towards creating a situation where he could be with her, socially, informally, without arousing her alarm and now it seemed that just such a situation had arisen. What was Cass up to? he wondered. Did she know something that he didn't? He wondered whether to telephone her to find out and then realised that he should have opened up downstairs.

It was a sharp, bright November day and Alex started to set up the bookcases. Just as she had on the hot summer day four months before, Kate appeared round the corner coming towards him. She waved and he stood watching her. She wore a dark brown cord skirt now, in place of the denim, with a navy blue Guernsey and navy tights finishing in flat brogues. He realised that he'd never seen her in high-heeled shoes and never known her wear any make-up.

We're wasting time, he thought. It's so silly.

She smiled as she came up to him and he decided to plunge straight in before he lost his nerve.

'I've had an invitation,' he said.

'Oh?' Kate looked at him for a moment and then went into the shop. Alex followed her.

'It's from your friend Cass. An invitation to a party.'

Kate put down her bag. Alex crossed his arms and wished that he hadn't given up smoking. He looked at Kate, inviting some response, and she frowned a little.

'And will you go?'

Alex raised his eyebrows. 'Well, I don't quite know. It came as a bit of a surprise. Shall you be going?'

'I suppose so. She'll be hurt if I don't.'

'Are you . . . ' he began diffidently. 'Will you be going with any-one?'

Kate shook her head, not looking at him. 'I doubt it. I expect that I shall know most of the people there.'

'Well, since I won't, I suppose you wouldn't take pity on me and let me take you?'

'Yes, of course.' After a moment, Kate raised her head and looked directly at him. 'Does the invitation suggest that you bring a friend?'

'No. Does yours?'

'No.'

'Well, then,' said Alex, lightly, when the silence had begun to feel uncomfortable. 'Perhaps she felt that we would pair up together.'

'Yes,' said Kate, grimly. 'Perhaps she did.'

GEORGE LAMPETER SPENT SOME time, sitting at his desk in the dockyard, thinking about his invitation. He noticed that he was not asked to bring a partner and wondered for a moment whether Felicity would have been asked, rejecting the idea almost as it occurred. He knew very well that to accept would be a very disloyal act in Felicity's eyes and yet why shouldn't he? Tom was a very old oppo and he'd always had a very soft spot for Cass. He remembered a past summer in Alverstoke and smiled a little to himself. After all, Felicity didn't own him, dammit! Before he could weaken he pulled some paper towards him, wrote his acceptance and threw it in the Post Tray. He slipped the invitation into his pocket and pulled his 'In Tray' towards him.

'WHAT'S THE BIG ONE?' Ralph Masters was eating his breakfast. A good trencherman was Ralph and he forked up some bacon and munched away whilst Harriet opened the big square envelope.

'Oh,' she said and fell silent.

'Oh what?' Ralph gulped down some coffee. 'Come on, chuck it over. What is it?'

'It's an invitation.' Harriet passed the card and picked up her own coffee.

'From Tom Wivenhoe! That's really decent of him. He must have found out that we've just got down here. You remember Tom, darling? We were on *Optimist* together. Of course, he's a two and a half now. We must go. We'll still be in then. Yes, Saturday week. Great! Write and accept, will you, darling? Hell, is that the time? Must dash. Sure you don't want the car? OK, I shan't be late back.' He kissed her and went out.

Harriet sat at the table. Presently she picked up the invitation card and, staring at it, ran her fingers over the embossed wording.

'Damn,' she said to herself. 'Damn, damn, damn!'

TONY, NOTICING THE PTO written at the bottom of the card, turned the invitation over. On the back Cass had written: 'For God's sake bring a woman, darling!' He looked at it but there was no flicker of the amusement that he would have felt a few weeks earlier. Cass was behaving oddly and he was beginning to suspect that she had found a new fish to fry. He would be going to sea soon and he had the feeling that it might be 'out of sight out of mind' so far as Cass was concerned.

Later in the day he made a telephone call. 'Liz? . . . Hi, it's Tony . . . Are you well? . . . Good. Listen. Like to come to a party on Saturday week? . . . Thrash at the Wivenhoes . . . Yes, it should . . . Oh, black tie so wear something special . . . Super. See you.'

He replaced the telephone and strolled thoughtfully into the Mess.

'CASS?' KATE STOOD IN the hall and listened. She could hear the sound of the television coming from the study and Saul's voice. Cass appeared at the drawing-room door.

'Kate! How lovely. Come and have a drink.'

Kate followed Cass into the elegant but comfortable room. A fire crackled in the grate and Kate went to warm her hands.

'This is not a social call,' she said severely as Cass lifted a bottle and held it questioningly. 'Why did you send Alex an invitation to your party?'

'Because I thought he might like to come. Why not?'

'You might at least have warned me.' Kate sounded cross.

'But then you'd have had all sorts of excuses at the ready.' Cass poured two drinks. 'You'll enjoy it, sweetie. You know you like my parties.'

'That's not the point. You did it to stir up trouble. After all, you hardly know him. Why should you invite him?'

'You've made him sound such an interesting person. And anyway, I thought we'd agreed.'

'Agreed what?'

'A very tiny prod, we said.'

'You said.' Kate grimaced. 'Well, it's too late now. He's asked me to come with him. But I still think that you might have warned me.'

'Nonsense. You'll be quite safe with all of us. It's going to be great fun. Now, stop droning on and have a drink.'

'Who else have you invited?' Kate sank into the armchair beside the fire and accepted the glass.

'Oh, just the usual gang,' said Cass, evasively. 'Abby and I are going to Exeter to buy ourselves new dresses. No good suggesting that you come too, I suppose?'

'It would be fun,' admitted Kate rather wistfully, 'but I just can't afford it at present.'

'I'm flush at the moment,' began Cass but Kate shook her head.

'No thanks. It's sweet of you but I've plenty of things really. And Guy needs new rugger boots.'

'Doesn't Mark take care of that?' Cass sat opposite. 'Surely you don't let him off scot-free?'

'No, no. He pays a monthly allowance which is supposed to take care of all that. It's a very generous one. But now and then lots of things come together and I hate asking Mark for more. We only communicate by letter now and it's like dealing with a stranger—everything's queried.' She shivered. 'It's rather horrid, really. The twins never hear from him but they think that's because he's at sea all the time. We hardly ever talk about him. It's odd. It's as if he never really existed.'

'Oh, well. All over now. Don't think about him—think about my party. If you're not going to buy anything new, go and look out something really special! Promise you, it's going to be a great evening.'

THE EVENING OF CASS's party was cold and clear. Lights blazed out from the house and the women in their flimsy clothes were delighted to see the log fire burning in the drawing room.

Tom and Cass were in their natural element: expansive, welcoming, generous, they presided over the evening determined that everyone should have fun. Not all their guests were quite so relaxed.

Kate had been slightly overset by the sight of Alex in his evening clothes. She had been wandering around ready for at least half an hour before he was due, part of her wishing that she'd taken Cass up on her offer of a new outfit. Another part was determined not to deck herself out in an obvious way—as Pam might—and in the end she'd put on her long black skirt of crushed velvet with a grey silk shirt and tied a black silk scarf around her neck. She wore grey stockings and narrow, flat black pumps and knew that Cass would be cross with her for not making more effort. When she opened the door and saw Alex, elegant, tall and unfamiliar in his dinner jacket, she'd experienced a moment of panic. He seemed in that moment to be a complete stranger and, feeling gauche and underdressed, she had seized her cashmere wrap and hurried out. In the car she had said, lightly, 'You look very dashing.' And he said, thoughtfully, 'And you look just as I thought you would.' She didn't quite know what he meant and immediately felt dull and dreary. All ease between them seemed to have fled and Kate thought how odd it was to be back in the world, as it were, an unattached woman. She reflected that a second relationship was probably even more fraught with difficulty than one's first because one would take all the hang-ups from the first one into it. And then she had to direct him to the Rectory and a moment later they were turning in at the gate.

Kate paused at the door of the drawing room, taken aback at the sight of so many people. She had envisaged a fairly intimate dinner party of probably eight or ten at the most and she glanced at Alex to see his reaction.

He smiled down at her. 'I hope that you're not planning to abandon me at this point to hurry off and talk to all your friends?'

Before he could answer Cass, dressed in floating blue silk, emerged from the throng, kissed Kate lightly on the cheek and then did the same to Alex.

'How nice of you to come,' she said to him. 'You must meet all these people but not all at once. So pointless, you'll never remember their names. Is Tom getting you a drink? Good. When you get your bearings Kate can introduce you a bit. You're next to me at dinner.' She twiddled her fingers at him and turned away.

'I'm sure that she meant that to be comforting,' murmured Alex as Tom approached with their drinks. 'Why can't I sit next to you?'

'Cass never lets her guests sit by their partners,' said Kate, who had only just remembered this mildly disturbing fact. 'She thinks that it's more fun to split them up.'

She took her drink from Tom and, while he talked to Alex about the antique print of Devonport that Alex had found for Kate to give him for his birthday, Kate let her gaze roam around the room over the other guests. Her heart gave a little jump as she saw George's handsome sleek head bent towards a red-headed girl and she instinctively looked for Felicity before she pulled herself together. As if Cass would have Felicity in her house! There was Tony, cigarette in hand, talking to a short brown-haired girl and a tall dark striking-looking girl who was faintly familiar. She had an inward look as though only part of her mind was on Tony's story. No good! Kate shook her head. Maybe it would come later. Abby, dressed in slinky black, was talking animatedly to a tall, fair man with his back to Kate while William stood by listening with an amused look on his face.

'You know Ralph, don't you, Kate?' Tom was saying and the man on the edge of the group was turning to smile at her.

'Of course.' Kate remembered Mark's First Lieutenant who had been so kind to her at that ghastly party and smiled with real warmth. 'How nice to see you, Ralph. And now, of course, I remember! It's Harriet over there. I knew I recognised her. Wasn't she studying to be a Chartered Surveyor or something?'

'Yes, she passed her finals just before we moved down,' said Ralph. 'We've got a quarter at Shit-a-Brick.' He smiled and Alex looked puzzled. Kate laughed.

'This is Alex Gillespie,' she said. 'He's an expert on antiquarian books and prints but he doesn't understand crude naval language. Shit-a-Brick, roughly translated,' she explained to Alex, 'is Crapstone. And this is Ralph Masters.' She noticed Ralph's enquiring look and knew at once what he was thinking. 'Alex is my boss,' she said, lightly. 'I'm a working woman now, you know.'

She hardened herself to go through the same procedure with George and Tony and was relieved when Cass announced that dinner was ready and they all moved into the dining room.

Mrs Hampton and her niece Jinny, who had come down from Exeter for the weekend, had been helping to prepare the house and cook the dinner and they stayed on to wait at table. It was all beautifully done and everybody was suitably impressed. They sat down fourteen to dinner and Kate looked with interest at Cass's seating plan. Two wives— Belinda and Pat—whose husbands were at sea, pairing off, as it were, with George and another submariner called Stephen, whose wife lived in Alverstoke. Tom, flanked by Harriet and Belinda, sat at one end of the great oval table and Cass sat at the other with Alex on one side and Stephen on the other. Kate had been placed between Tony and Ralph, looking directly across to Pat who had William and George on either side. She was interested to see that George and Pat seemed to be old, if slightly embarrassed, friends and she wondered what Cass was up to. She looked at Alex who was unfolding his napkin, his head inclined towards Cass, and then at Stephen who was talking to Abby on his left. At that moment, Jinny stepped between them to fill Abby's glass and a quick look flashed between Cass and Stephen which made Kate sit up and take notice. She glanced involuntarily at Tom whose attention was taken up by Harriet who was fiddling with knives and forks and looking very odd. Kate tried to analyse her look: it was conscious, excited and controlled. She turned to Tony, who was staring at Cass with an intense but unreadable expression, and as she did so caught a look of despair on the face of the girl called Liz. She was puzzled and a feeling of dread began to weigh on her; a sensation of something being created that would have some future drastic effect on all their lives, as a stone tossed into a

pond causes waves and ripples long after it has sunk to the bottom.
There was an electric quality of overcharged emotions as if thought
waves were beating the air like wings: people saying one thing and thinking another.

'Yes, it's a lovely house. Absolutely lends itself to parties . . . '
(What fun this is! Mustn't let anyone guess, though. His wife would
be down on us like a ton of bricks.) Cass: talking to Alex and thinking
of Stephen.

'I hear that you're a terribly important person now with letters after your name. Now that you're down we must see lots of you . . . '
(She's a real sweetie. Terribly shy, though. Lovely legs.) Tom: talking
to Harriet and thinking about her in a different light.

'Still a hoary old bachelor, I'm afraid. Still waiting for some kind
lady to take me on. Living in the Mess at the moment . . . ' (I wonder if Cass heard that rumour about me and Pat. I wouldn't put
it past her. Still, it's rather fun to see her again. Wonder how long
her husband's away.) George: talking to Belinda and thinking about
Pat.

'Oh, of course. I know who you are. I bought a wonderful book
from you for my mother . . . ' (I wonder which one of them it is that
he fancies. Oh, God. Why can't it ever be me?) Liz: talking to Alex
and yearning after Tony.

'How refreshing to meet someone who isn't Navy. Do you live in
the village?' (It's madness! What risks she takes! And so do I. I'm like
a lovesick teenager. I can feel her leg under the table. Christ! Her old
man's looking straight at me!) Stephen: talking to Abby and thinking
about Cass.

'So when's John back? Haven't seen him around for a bit . . . '
(She's bored with me. I knew it. I wonder which of the bastards it is!)
Tony: talking to Pat and thinking about Cass.

'I hadn't realised you weren't Navy. Do you live locally?' (Oh, what
shall I do: I love him. I love him.) Harriet: talking to William and
thinking about Tom.

'Delicious pâté. My compliments to the chef.' (At least I can sit and look at her. She's not with us—in another world.) Alex: talking to Cass and thinking about Kate.

As Jinny came round collecting empty plates, Kate shook her head as if to rid it of some fantastic thoughts and looked at Alex. He was leaning back in his chair, one hand in his pocket, the other idly turning his wine glass round by its stem. He was watching her and, as their eyes met, he raised his glass to her.

'WELL, THEY CERTAINLY KNOW how to give a party!' Alex negotiated the turn in the lane and headed for Walkhampton.

'They're experts.' Kate was huddled into her shawl, pleasantly re-laxed now having had rather more than usual to drink. Her emotions were heightened and disturbed by the atmosphere of the party. 'They really love it, of course. I'm glad you enjoyed it.'

'Yes, I did. It was nice to be with you in a non-work situation. May we do it again?'

'Well, I don't know when Cass will be having another party . . . ' began Kate innocently and Alex laughed.

'I asked for that,' he said as he drove down the hill and over the lit-tle hump back bridge that spans the River Meavy. 'But you know per-fectly well what I meant.'

'It was fun,' admitted Kate and, for a blissful moment, forgot about being married, her reputation locally and how gossip or a divorce would affect the twins. She put out her hand and touched his knee. 'Thank you for coming.'

He covered her hand at once with his own and held it. 'It's a won-derful night,' he said. 'The moon's up. Do you want to go straight home? We could take the Princetown road and go up to the top. The moor looks so unearthly by moonlight.'

Kate stared at him in amazement. They had reached the Burrator Hotel and he waited at the crossroads, eyebrows raised.

'I . . . I should love it,' she stammered. 'It's a wonderful idea.'

'Good.' Alex turned right and they drove in silence until they reached Walkhampton Common.

Kate drew in her breath as Alex swung the car into one of the parking areas and switched off the engine. The flat white disc that was the moon bleached everything of colour: the granite boulders and the grass, sparkling in the grip of frost, created a silver-white background against which the gorse bushes and thorn trees were etched black.

'Shall we get out?' suggested Alex after a moment. 'I've got a rug here somewhere. You could wrap yourself in that. The air will be unbelievable.'

Kate got out and Alex came round to wrap the rug around her. He left an arm there afterwards and held her close against his side. Their breath smoked in the sharp singing air and the stars glittered with such brilliance that it seemed that they too must be touched by the frost. Kate's teeth chattered, partly from the cold and partly with excitement. She realised that she was trembling from head to foot and he held her closer and turned her chin up with his free hand.

'I can't imagine a better time or place to tell you that I think I love you,' he said. 'I know you're not free. I know there are all sorts of problems. But do you want to try to resolve them so that we can have a chance? Or is it still too soon for you?'

She looked up at him at last. 'I'm afraid,' she said, almost inaudibly. 'If I start, I'm afraid that I shan't know how to stop.'

'That's what I thought,' he said, with a sigh of relief, and he bent to kiss her.

The rug and shawl fell unheeded to the ground as they held each other. They were disturbed by a heavy lorry that lumbered by, the driver banging derisively on his hooter and they drew apart. Kate stared up at Alex, her eyes blind with moonlight, and began to laugh. She was shivering violently in her thin silk shirt and he gave an exclamation and, bending down, picked up the rug and her shawl and wound her up in them.

'Come on,' he said. 'I'm going to take you home.'

OTHER TINY RIPPLES WERE beginning to spread.

On their way home, Ralph and Harriet had a row: a silly affair that blew up out of nothing. Ralph had enjoyed his evening and said so. He enthused about the Wivenhoes, their home, the food, and went on at some length about what a great chap old Tom was, remarking more than once about how glad he was to see Harriet getting on with him so well.

At last Harriet, more infatuated by Tom than ever and torn by feelings of irritation and guilt, snapped at him, saying that it was a pity that he couldn't have sat by Tom himself if he liked him so much and that he seemed to be doing very well with Abby.

Ralph was shocked into a surprised silence and after a moment or two decided to be hurt rather than finding out what, if anything, lay behind this rather uncharacteristic outburst. He had had just enough to drink to feel pleasantly martyred and when one or two other things of a cutting nature had been said on either side, they both subsided into silence. Ralph's was a surly resentful silence: Harriet's a guilty desperate one. They went to bed—each pointedly on his and her own side—still in silence, Ralph to fall at once into a heavy sleep whilst Harriet lay beside him across the icy sheet, staring into the darkness and wishing she were dead.

LIZ TRIED TO IGNORE her heavy heart and chattered to a silent Tony on the way back to Plymouth. When he stopped outside her flat, he looked at her properly for the first time that evening and felt the prickings of guilt. He was surprised at how upset he'd been to realise that his affair with Cass was over. They'd been friends for years and he knew the score and had been as happy with the arrangement as she had. Why then did he feel jealous and miserable?

He looked at Liz—a little brown girl: brown skin, brown eyes, brown hair—who was always prepared, even at disgracefully short notice, to be used as a stop gap and smiled at her.

'Sorry, Liz,' he said. 'What a lout I'm being and what an angel you are to put up with me. I suppose there wouldn't be a cup of coffee if I came in?

Liz's spirits soared and she smiled at him with such radiance that her plain little face was quite transformed. Taken aback and seized with an even greater sense of remorse and also with a confused feeling of paying Cass out, he pulled her into his arms and kissed her thoroughly and with great expertise. Her arms went round him and he began to feel more than the prickings of guilt.

'Come on,' he said, his lips against her hair. 'Let's go inside.'

fifteen

As Cass embarked upon her affair with Stephen Mortlake, so Kate plunged into hers with Alex. She had been right in saying that once she started she would be unable to stop. Constitutionally unable to do anything by halves, she started the relationship with a whole-heartedness with which she had begun her marriage with Mark. It was as if she had been living in another world for the last twelve years, a sort of limbo existence, which had suddenly shattered leaving her free. She spent every available moment with Alex, revelling in the new freedom which had the effect of a powerful drug. Physically she was indeed drugged by his power over her body. If it had begun as a friendship, a meeting of minds, it was now balancing out with a vengeance. Having known only unsatisfying sex with an insensitive man, she now learned what making love was all about. And she simply couldn't get enough of it. Night and day she burned for the physical contact of a man whom she loved and desired, knowing that her passion was fully reciprocated. Love-making was a leisured, happy, earth-moving experience and Kate was totally disorientated.

Alex was moved, amused and delighted in turns. However, he was still cautious about pushing her into anything and recognised that she needed a period of freedom to enjoy what they shared as herself, Kate, rather than to have to think of herself in connection with the twins or Mark.

For a few blissful weeks this was the case and then the twins came home for Christmas and Kate returned to earth with a bump. The real difficulties of the situation now presented themselves forcibly to her and Alex waited to see how she would react. To begin with, they could spend far less time together and certainly not at night. The dogs had often proved a bit of a problem here and since Kate had preferred, during week nights, to be in Alex's flat rather than at the cottage, Megs and Honey had got used to sleeping at the flat and being taken for early-morning runs on the moor on Kate's way home. They were obliging, good-natured dogs and had settled quite happily to this new routine. At weekends Alex came to the cottage. Up to this point, Kate had been fairly relaxed about being seen in public with him. In Tavis-tock it was accepted as a working relationship and with the dark win-ter evenings hurrying everyone indoors, it was unlikely that anyone would be around at the crucial moments to see Kate's car still parked in a back road or to see her emerging very early to take the dogs for a run before she hurried home. She would reappear at the usual time to start work and no one was the wiser. They were never disturbed at the cottage and it had been one of the happiest times of Kate's life.

Now, driving the twins home across a sullen sodden moor, brooding under heavy rain clouds, Kate realised that her brief visit to paradise was over. She listened to their chatter and answered their questions whilst trying to imagine herself explaining the situa-tion to them. She had been fairly certain that the separation from Mark would not be distressing for them. The visit to Cheltenham had not been a happy one and Mark had felt it necessary to try to be-little Kate in their eyes and had been short-tempered; Kate was glad that she had never criticised him to them or justified her own ac-tions. She knew that she had no need to, Mark was more than capa-ble of doing all that was needed himself. An affair with Alex or a divorce were quite different issues. She had heard that the twins' headmaster had decided views on the subject of divorce and she knew that the boys would hate being both the objects of discussion and in the minority. So far as she knew, there was only one divorced couple with a boy at the school. No, divorce was quite out of the question, even if Mark agreed to it. And on what grounds would it be? Her infidelity with Alex, thereby proving that Mark and the gossips had been right after all? Would she be allowed to keep the boys if she had been committing adultery? Maybe they would be put in Mark's care, living with the Websters while he was at sea. Her hands, gripping the wheel, turned icy at the thought. She saw herself in court under Mark's cold disgusted gaze and shivered: out of the question until the boys had finished school or at least left Mount House.

So then, did she explain to the boys that she loved Alex and that she was having an affair with him? How would they react? Somehow it seemed quite impossible. She tried to imagine herself with Alex, laughing, talking, hugging, kissing—with the boys looking on. It simply didn't work. They would still see each other, of course. Cass would continue to look after the twins some days whilst Kate went to the shop and maybe Alex could come round from time to time. The twins liked him and were used to seeing him. They'd just have to be very careful. The boys simply must not suspect. And nor must anyone else. It struck her for the first time that Mark could all but destroy her if everything came out and she felt her old fears returning. Thank goodness she worked for Alex and that he lived above the shop. At least, during the working day, they could continue to live and love.

Kate caught herself thinking that, for the first time ever, the school holidays were going to seem very long indeed!

CASS WAS HAVING HER own problems. Stephen was proving to be a rather demanding lover, prone to turning up unexpectedly on weekdays and telephoning at unsuitable moments. He had fallen very heavily for Cass, finding her light-hearted attitude, her great beauty and amazing generosity a complete contrast to what he was used to from his own wife. He fell for her hook, line and sinker and simply had no idea how an affair of this sort should be conducted. Cass was flattered, amused and then concerned. She had made the fatal mistake of assuming that his anxiety lest his old bat of a wife should discover his infidelity would encourage him to exercise restraint. But this was not the case. After a few visits he was pleading that they should throw caution to the winds and set up home together. Cass, torn between a desire to shriek with laughter and very real terror that he might drop her right in it, pointed out that she had no intention of abandoning her four children or Tom and that if he didn't calm down, she wouldn't see him again. This brought him to his senses but he was still unreliable and Cass, feeling that for once she had seriously misjudged the situation, was deeply relieved when Christmas approached and Stephen was obliged to return to Alverstoke to the bosom of his family.

ALEX HAD TO BE content with the days Kate spent in the shop. He missed her very much and felt it very hard that his feelings must be put on a back burner. He knew quite well that it was the only way and, being far more intelligent than Stephen, was prepared to wait patiently for the time being. Kate's surprised gratitude for his love, his patience, his good humour and concern for her well-being gave Alex a very good idea of what she had been used to with Mark and he experienced, from time to time, a desire to seek him out and wring his neck. Alex, who liked women and made a great effort to understand them, knew that Kate would put the twins first all the time that they were dependent on her for their happiness and he was trying not to make her feel guilty about it. He did not approve of emotional blackmail and since he saw that Kate was always ready to take guilt to herself— as he suspected Mark had been quick to notice and very ready to exploit—he made every effort to keep their relationship free of it. At least the boys were away at school. They must be grateful for what they had.

IN THE NEW YEAR, the ripples had turned into little waves big enough to rock a few boats.

When Tony got back from sea there was a letter waiting for him from Liz asking if he would get in touch. He was faintly surprised for it was generally he who did the running but he turned up at the flat a few days later, on a mild February afternoon, and Liz let him in. It was a very pleasant flat in an Edwardian terrace: one big bedroom, one big living room, a small kitchen and a bathroom. It was on the ground floor and there was a little courtyard area outside the French windows. The decorations were simple, almost austere, and in her favourite colours, white and a sharp lemon with touches of cool green. It was a very restful place. Tony sank into the corner of the big white sofa and looked at her. She looked pinched and tired but she poured him his favourite Scotch and smiled at him.

'Good trip?'

'So so. What's all this about? You look a bit fagged.'

'I am a bit.' She rested an arm along the white-painted mantelshelf and stared down at the electric fire that had been fitted into the grate. 'It's no use prevaricating. I've been practising how to say this and there's no easy way. I'm pregnant.'

From the corner of her eye she saw his shocked reaction. After a moment Tony set his drink carefully on the low glass coffee table.

'Is it mine?' he asked and immediately felt ashamed.

Liz straightened up and looked directly at him. 'I've only ever been with you,' she said simply.

'I'm sorry,' he said at once. 'That was unforgivable. It's just a bit of a shock. I'm sorry.'

'It was after Cass's party,' she explained. 'You may remember that we . . . well, we got a bit carried away and we didn't use anything.'

'I remember.' Tony felt a savage blast of bitterness against Cass, followed by remorse for having used as her stand-in the girl who stood before him. 'Well, we must think about this, mustn't we?'

If she had hoped for more from him, she didn't show it but continued to look at him. 'I shan't have an abortion,' she said quietly. 'I just want to tell you that. I haven't told my parents yet. I thought that it was only fair to tell you first.'

Tony looked quickly at her to see if there was any hint of blackmail but she continued to regard him steadily.

'Yes.' Tony thought about her father, a serving Rear Admiral who, much against his will, had set Liz up in her own little flat so that she could finish taking her accountancy exams in peace and quiet and without too much travelling. Tony felt his heart sink and the bars begin to close in. 'Look, can you give me a minute or two to think this over? Get my bearings, as it were?'

'Of course. I realise that it's come as a dreadful shock to you. I've had time to think it over.'

Tony imagined her, all alone, coming to terms with it over the past weeks and his heart smote him. What a bastard he was! He'd used her as a smoke screen through the long hot summer of his affair with Cass and again afterwards in his hurt at Cass's defection. She loved him, he knew that, giving everything that she had and asking nothing in return. He stood up and went to her and gathered her rigid body into his arms.

'We'll get married,' he said. 'If you'd like to? If you'll have me?'

And, as she burst into tears of relief and he held her closer, he thought of Cass and felt despair and anger and cursed himself for a fool.

Tom, TRAVELLING DOWN FROM London on the train, looked out over the Exe estuary. The early-March evening was cold and the reeds rustled in the wind. A heron stood motionless in the rising tide whilst waders bustled over the pale gleaming mud at the water's edge. Waves slapped at the sides of the few moored boats and a handful of rain dashed itself against the carriage window. On the other side of the track, Powderham Castle stood remote and withdrawn in the darkening deer park and the travellers peered from the warm lighted carriages for a sight of the graceful forms that browsed beneath the trees.

Tom reached for a cigarette and gazed unseeingly into the gathering dusk. The conversation that he'd had with Mark II in the bar of the Red Lion that lunchtime had seriously upset him. Mark had been very pleased with himself. It seemed that he had been offered the submariner's job at the Royal Naval College at Dartmouth and he was bragging about his luck to Tom.

'Well, if it's what you want, good luck,' Tom had said, shrugging. 'I wouldn't want it. Too bloody social. And all that business about having to be smart when you're around in the town when you're off duty, and church every Sunday. Good promotional job, though. Felicity will be delighted. Still, rather you than me.'

Mark flushed a little.

'I doubt you'd get the chance, old chap. Not with your Cassandra in the background.'

Tom, who was finishing his pint, lowered his glass and looked at him. 'What d'you mean?'

'Oh, well.' Mark shrugged, still angry at Tom's belittling of his new job and his dig at Felicity. 'They're not too keen on gossip at the College, are they? Everybody sees everything there. Cass would really have to clip her wings.'

Tom stood his glass on the bar and took a step closer. 'You'll have to explain that remark,' he said in a low voice.

'Oh, come on, Tom.' Mark felt uncomfortable. His anger was evaporating and he knew he'd gone too far. Damn Felicity, always going on about Cass! 'You know there are always rumours about Cass: Tony, George and now Stephen, it seems. Nothing in it, I dare say. It's the price you pay for having a beautiful wife. You must have got used to having men falling for her. Come on, have another pint?'

'Thanks,' said Tom, rather mechanically. 'I think I will.'

Some others had come into the bar and Mark, rather thankfully, was able to move away a little. Tom had finished his pint and sandwiches and Mark had taken care not to bump into him again.

I shall have it out with her, Tom thought now, staring out over the inky sea at Dawlish. I'm not going to be made a laughing stock. I've had enough of sly digs and innuendoes. I shall ask her outright.

He felt a bleak depression settle on him at the thought of it and jumped as someone spoke his name.

'Harriet!' he exclaimed.

She was standing smiling shyly down at him. She wore a long flowing navy blue corduroy coat and a navy blue beret on her cap of dark shining hair.

'Where did you spring from?' he asked. 'Sit down.' He caught her by the wrist and pulled her down into the empty seat beside him, glancing sideways as the coat fell open exposing her long lovely legs in their sheer dark stockings.

'I got on at Exeter,' she was saying. 'I've been shopping and then I went to a visit a friend in hospital. You were looking very severe. I was almost afraid to speak to you.'

Tom laughed, realised that he was still grasping her wrist and dropped it quickly. "Rubbish! I was just feeling a bit low.' He suddenly felt very sorry for himself and experienced a great desire to unburden himself to her but she was already speaking.

'Perhaps this evening will cheer you up.'

'This evening?'

'Aren't you coming? I thought Cass said you would be. Perhaps you'll feel too tired to turn out again once you've got in? I shouldn't blame you. It will be a terrible rush for you but the Elliots give such good parties, don't they? Almost as good as yours!'

'I'd completely forgotten.' Tom smote his forehead with the palm of his hand. 'I must be getting senile. Are you and Ralph going?'

'Oh, yes.'

'In that case I shall certainly be there as long as you promise to have a dance with me.'

She smiled shyly, not looking at him. 'I expect that could be arranged.'

'Good. That's settled then.' His depression had lifted and he felt cheerful again but whether it was due to the relief of knowing that there would be no time, after all, for his showdown with Cass or the pleasure of the thought of dancing with Harriet, he didn't trouble to analyse.

CASS HAD NO IDEA that she had received a reprieve. The weekend started with the Elliots' party and then moved into an exeat which coincided with Oliver's ninth birthday. He had had a party on Saturday afternoon and on Sunday the General had come to lunch. By the time the following weekend came round, Mark II's remarks had been put to the back of Tom's mind.

The next week, Cass herself had a narrow escape. Two things conspired to undo her. The first was the unexpected arrival of Stephen
Mortlake. He came after lunch, just as Cass had put Gemma to bed for
her afternoon sleep, and, seizing Cass in his arms, he had vowed his
undying passion and begged that she reconsider her decision to stay
with Tom. In the hope of quietening him down, Cass let him drag her
clothes off and make love to her until he was too exhausted to talk.
Relieved, she was about to get up again when she heard the kitchen
door open and Saul's voice calling her. She sat stock still for two sec-
onds and then, leaping from the bed, dressed in record time, dragging
the recumbent Stephen upright and trying to make him get dressed.
It occurred to her that, now the situation had presented itself, he
might consider forcing the issue by letting her children see him and
she felt so angry that she caught him by the arm and dug her nails into
his flesh:

'If you let them suspect a single thing,' she hissed, 'I'll never speak
to you again, I promise. Get dressed!'

She left the bedroom and went downstairs as Saul was about to
come up to find her.

'Hello, darling,' she said. 'What are you doing home so early?
Aren't you well?'

Charlotte appeared in the kitchen doorway and Cass shooed them
gently back into the kitchen, shutting the door firmly behind her.

'He's got a sore throat,' Charlotte was explaining. 'Mrs Beard
asked if she should phone but I said that if you weren't here we could
go to Grandfather's. I was looking for the gargling stuff you gave me
when I had one.'

'Poor Saul.' Cass gave him a hug, one ear cocked for Stephen. 'Did
you look in the pantry?'

'Yes, I did. I'm sure it's not there. Oh! I know where it is.' She
whirled round. 'It's upstairs in the bathroom cupboard.' And, before
Cass could stop her, she was across the kitchen and opening the door.
Stephen stood just outside. Charlotte gave a little squawk of alarm and
at the same time, upstairs Gemma woke and began to grizzle loudly.

'Hello, Stephen. What on earth are you doing here?' Cass's voice was light and social. Her eyes were cold and wary. She saw that Charlotte was staring at him, less alarmed than she might have been since he was in uniform, dressed in his navy jersey with his stripes on the epaulettes. 'Go up and see to Gemma, darling,' she said to Charlotte and turned back to Stephen. 'I'm afraid Tom's not here,' she said in the same light, carrying voice. She walked towards the front door and he was obliged to follow her. Saul appeared in the hall. 'So sorry, I'll tell him you called.' She almost pushed him out of the front door and turned back to Saul. 'Come on, my darling. Let's go and find that medicine.'

On Friday, Tom travelled down with Tony, who had been to see the Appointer and had been told that he was being appointed to Faslane. They spent some time in the bar getting very mellow and, after a while, Tom said, 'What's all this about you and Cass, then?'

Tony stared into his glass, 'All over now. I'm getting married. I expect you heard.'

'No. No I hadn't heard. There was something then? Between you and Cass, I mean?'

Tony suddenly felt terribly depressed. Liz was a sweet girl but he didn't love her. He didn't want to marry her. He didn't want to be a father. He didn't want to go to Faslane. Why shouldn't other people have some grief too? Why should Cass get off scot-free? A glance at Tom's face made him hesitate. Perhaps it might be a little unwise to admit to his own affair but he could still drop Cass in it.

'Oh, I've always been in love with Cass,' he said. 'Everyone knows that. She knows it. You know it. It's a hopeless passion. Christ knows why I'm marrying Liz! Well, I do know. It's because of the bloody baby. If it hadn't been for that party you gave and seeing Cass carrying on with that wanker, Stephen Mortlake, there wouldn't have been a bloody baby!' He glanced up at Tom slyly. 'I think I'm drunk, old boy. Take no notice of me.'

'Not as drunk as we could be,' said Tom. 'Let's have another.'

When Cass picked him up at the station, she gave Tony a lift too and so the moment of confrontation passed again. When they had dropped Tony, she told Tom that Saul had a bad attack of tonsillitis and that the doctor was calling in after surgery to see how he was and so it wasn't until the Saturday morning that the moment presented itself.

The Wivenhoes had just finished breakfast when Kate arrived. She came into the kitchen carrying a large covered basket and she had just set it on the table and Tom had just pushed the kettle on to the hotplate for more coffee when Charlotte electrified them all by saying, 'Did you tell Daddy that that man came to see him, Mummy? The one who was standing in the hall when we came home early? What was his name?'

Kate saw the expression on Cass's face a split second before Tom turned round and hastily removed the cover from the basket. Out struggled a fluffy golden retriever puppy with floppy ears and huge paws. Charlotte gave a cry and Cass exclaimed and got up to look at him.

'Oh, he's so lovely. Oh, Daddy, look! Oh, is he for us?'

'He is.' Kate was still watching Tom whose face was darkening by the moment.

'What man?' he asked.

'Look, Gemma.' Charlotte tried to lift her up to the table. 'Can you see him? Isn't he beautiful? What shall we call him?'

'His name's Augustus,' said Kate firmly. She simply couldn't bear for her puppies to be called by unsuitable names. 'Gus for short.'

'What man?'

'He's too beautiful for words. What? Oh. Just Stephen Mortlake, darling. He popped in hoping to see you. Put him down on the floor, Kate, so that Gemma can see him properly.'

'Why should he do that? He knows I'm away.'

'I've no idea, darling. He's perfect, Kate. Bless you.'

Tom turned to Charlotte. 'Take him upstairs and show him to Saul. It's unfair to leave him out when he's not well. It will cheer him up. Take Gemma, too.' He picked the puppy up and put him in Charlotte's arms. 'Off you go.' He waited until they'd gone. 'You too, Kate.' He didn't turn round and for once Cass was silent. Kate hesitated and she looked at Cass.

'Out, Kate,' said Tom again, his eyes on Cass's face.

Behind his head, Kate put two fingers against her temple, miming a gun, and, grimacing helplessly at Cass, slipped out into the garden.

'Well?' said Tom.

'I couldn't say this in front of the children, darling, but Stephen Mortlake is a bore and a nuisance and if he goes on like this you'll have to have words with him!'

Taken aback, Tom stared at her and Cass was quick to follow up her advantage.

'Ever since we gave that party he's been pestering me. He phones up and sometimes he calls in. That's what he did on Thursday. He says he's fallen passionately in love with me and God knows what!' Cass folded her arms and shook her head. 'He's driving me mad! Could you speak to him?'

'Well . . . Well, I don't know . . . ' He looked so ludicrously wrong-footed that Cass had great difficulty in restraining herself from bursting into hysterical laughter.

'Oh, well, never mind.' There was a touch of impatience in her voice. 'Thank God he's going back to Gosport so it should all die a natural death. It's probably best that way, I wouldn't want his wife upset.'

'D'you mean you haven't . . . '

'Haven't what?' Cass looked surprised and then incredulous. 'With Stephen Mortlake? Come on, Tom, have a heart!'

'Wait a minute.' He felt that the ground was being cut from beneath him and he made an effort to regain his foothold. 'I travelled down with Tony yesterday as you know . . . '

'Well, if he told you about Stephen you can forget it. Tony's been in love with me for years and now he's gone and got that rather dim girlfriend of his up the spout and he's got to marry her. He's very bitter at the moment. You can't believe anything that Tony says. He likes to think he's the great lover. You know that. And he likes to boast about his conquests—real and imaginary. I'm very fond of old Tony, he's great fun, but to tell you the truth I'm delighted that he's getting married. All this devotion can get you down a bit.'

'But he said . . . ' Tom paused and changed direction. 'Mark II was saying that you and George . . . '

'George?' Cass burst out laughing. 'Oh, it really is too much. Me and old George! There really is no end to what Felicity will say about me! And Mark II repeats it all like a parrot! Of course George has got a soft spot for me. Everyone knows that. But you know very well that Felicity's tongue has been dipped in poison.' Suddenly she looked rather hurt. 'And you've just been taking it to heart, I suppose, and believed everything they've said?'

Tom remembered that at the time he'd been getting at Mark II about the job at BRNC and remembered, too, Tony's sly expression when he said 'Take no notice,' and felt confused. Seeing this, Cass went to him and slipped her arms around his waist.

'I love you,' she said, looking up at him. 'You know that. I thought we trusted each other.'

For one dreadful moment, Tom wondered what he'd do if she asked him if he'd always been faithful to her. Quickly he put his arms round her.

'I do trust you,' he said. 'I just wish you weren't so damned beautiful.'

Cass laughed huskily and pressed closely to him. 'No you don't. You love it.'

He bent to kiss her, running his hands over her hips and around her buttocks. 'I couldn't bear to lose you,' he muttered. 'Oh, Cass . . . '

'You're not going to, you daft old thing.'

'Can we go to bed?'

Cass hesitated. She knew that Tom would only be finally reassured by the physical act and she wished very much to bind him back to her.

'Go on then,' she said. 'Go on up. I'll be as quick as I can. Shut the door or the children will wonder why you're going back to bed.'

She waited until she heard the bedroom door close and then went into the garden. Kate was wandering over the lawn and Cass waved to her.

'Bloody hell, Kate,' she said as she approached. 'That was a close one. No, no bullet,' as Kate raised her eyebrows. 'Talk about quick thinking. No more Russian roulette. At least, not for a bit. Look, can you come in for a minute and stay with the kids . . . '

Sixteen

Alex made himself some coffee, took it along to his sitting room and put it on the gate leg table. He sat down and picked up his patience cards trying to remember what on earth he had done with his evenings before Kate. The Easter holidays were now upon them and Alex was once more living the life of a bachelor. He shuffled his cards and lit a cigarette. He'd started smoking again during the Christmas holidays, finding that it relieved the tension on those occasions when he had wanted to get into his car and drive round to the cottage. He wondered how they would deal with the ten weeks of the summer holidays. He quite understood Kate's rationale, agreed that it was quite likely that Mark might try to divorce her for adultery although he was by no means as sure as she was that the twins would be taken away from her. He had suggested that she divorce Mark for unreasonable behaviour or even mental cruelty but Kate was adamant that no boats should be rocked until the twins had left Mount House; everything was far too local and they started their last year in the autumn so the end wasn't too far ahead.

Alex sighed and drank some coffee. It seemed a very long time to him and he knew very well that Kate hadn't yet realised that the long summer months with their long light evenings would make a significant difference. They couldn't shut themselves away indoors for ever. Of course, one of the things that they did during their evenings together was to talk. Alex had asked her why she had put up with so much for so long and once Kate had started explaining she seemed unable to stop. The floodgates were down and Alex had to ride the tide. He understood her preconceived ideas about marriage and it wasn't difficult to read between the lines. It must have been easy for a man of Mark's character to play on her ideals and her great sense of loyalty. He'd got it made! Alex felt the usual wave of anger. What a fool the man had been! Too idle to make efforts—too selfish to put himself out. Well, he'd lost her although Kate still felt guilty, still needed to be reassured that she had the right to leave him and that she wasn't damaging the twins in some way. Alex calmly talked her through it, evening after evening, as the pain and anger that had gathered over the years slowly washed away in the flood of words. It was exhausting but Alex knew that it was necessary. It must all be done, all got through, before their own life could truly start. There would be scars left, painful places, but time would heal and help as it had helped to heal hurts from his own failed marriage when his German-born wife had left him. Ingrid had got bored quite quickly with Tavistock and Alex's venture with his bookshop. Every penny he had after paying the deposit on the property was tied up in stock and Alex was working hard to make a success of his dream. Ingrid became tired of being short of money and at Alex's preoccupation with the business: Alex, who had seen them working happily together sharing little successes and disasters alike, was disappointed and hurt. When she saw an advertisement for a Personal Assistant who could speak German required by a London- and Hamburg-based company, she had shown it to Alex. He had pointed out that it was a long way from Tavistock. She had said that the salary would support them both until Alex found something. He told her that he already had something; his money and all his ambitions and hopes were wrapped up in the bookshop. He had no desire to live in London—or Hamburg.

In the end she had gone for the interview and got the job. She'd come down at weekends, she said. It was just for a bit. The extra money would be useful. It had worked for a while but then she'd had to go to Hamburg and then there were conferences and finally she stopped coming back at all. Alex had thrown himself into his business which was just beginning to pay when, a few years later, she had written and asked for a divorce. By then he was quite happy to agree, glad that there had been no children. He had come to realise that part of her attraction had been her 'foreignness'—her charming accent, the flaxen hair, her flair with clothes—and that the relationship was probably doomed from the start.

He'd been quite happy to have a succession of women in his life and had no real desire to tie himself down until now. Kate had got under his skin although he still had qualms when he thought of the twins. After all, they could hardly all squash into the flat and he couldn't quite see himself simply moving in at the cottage. There was a long way to go yet.

Alex stubbed out his cigarette, finished his coffee and started to deal the cards.

MRS HAMPTON FINISHED POLISHING Charlotte's chest of drawers and started to replace her collection of china animals, dusting each one carefully as she did so. Her mind was busy. In the Wivenhoe household the Great Education Debate—as Kate had dubbed it—was raging and Mrs Hampton was finding it difficult to hold her tongue.

She'd spoken to the General about it but he, knowing full well that the traditions and advantages of the boarding school system would be concepts of little value to her, had refused to commit himself. After all, he wasn't too sure himself that Charlotte should be sent away to boarding school in the autumn.

'But you sent me,' Cass had cried, sure of his support.

'You had no mother, my darling, and I was away so much.'

'I had a Nanny.'

The General, who knew that Nanny had been as putty in Cass's deft and manipulating hands, had remained silent.

Mrs Hampton put the last china ornament in place and started on the bookshelves. Out came all the old favourites: Beatrix Potter, Richard Scarry, A.A. Milne, Enid Blyton . . .

Why should she have to go? Mrs Hampton shook her head. The child didn't want to and there was no need of it. Her mother didn't have to go out to work, they had a lovely home and Charlotte loved the little ones. She was such a help with them. Mrs Hampton couldn't understand how Cass could bear to part with her. She could tell that her father wasn't too keen for her to go. He'd said as much when he'd been home on leave. She'd heard him when she'd been polishing the stair rods.

'Well, if she hates the idea that much let her stay at home. I thought that you liked the idea of having a girl at home when the boys have to go.'

'I still have Gemma, not to mention Saul for another year or two. Of course I like having her around but I'm thinking of her future.'

'Are you?'

Mrs Hampton had felt a funny little thrill when he'd said that. His voice was cold, like. As if he didn't believe her.

'But of course I am. Charlotte's got a good brain. She can't stay at Meavy for ever, you know. She's got to go somewhere this autumn.'

'I appreciate that. But it doesn't mean she has to go away.'

'Have you any other suggestions? You know how shy and easily hurt she is. D'you think she'd be happy at Tavistock Comprehensive?'

'Surely there are other options?'

'Well, if you're going to encourage her . . . '

'I just can't see why you're so set on her going when she's so unhappy about it. Unless, of course, you've got some other reason for wanting her out of the way?'

'Oh, don't be silly! What possible reason could there be?'

'You tell me.'

There was the sound of chair legs scraping on the slate-flagged kitchen floor and Mrs Hampton, picking up her Brasso and her polishing rags, had scurried up the stairs. Peering down, she saw Tom cross the hall and go out. The front door banged.

Now, a few weeks on, Mrs Hampton replaced Charlotte's books, pulled her Peter Rabbit quilt straight and went on to the landing.

'Hammy?'

She went to the top of the stairs and looked down at Cass. 'I've just finished,' she said. 'Anythin' else special you want done?'

'No. That's lovely. Would you like some more coffee?'

'No, thank you.' Mrs Hampton descended the stairs and followed Cass into the kitchen. 'I'm 'avin' me dinner with Jane today. Jane Maxwell, she is now. 'Er Alan's in they submarines, too. It seems that 'e's been made up to a proper officer. I don't rightly understand the ins an' outs of it to tell the truth.'

'In simple terms,' explained Cass as she took Mrs Hampton's coat from the peg behind the door, 'if a sailor comes up through the ranks and is very promising he can be recommended to be promoted to officer rank. It can be a mixed blessing. They are much older than their brother officers of the same rank and it often means a drop in pay. Still, it's wonderful for Alan. I wonder if Tom knows him. Do I know Jane?'

'Shouldn't think so. She's only just moved back to the village. They've bought one o' they new 'ouses up the Paddocks. She seems a bit nervous about this promotion. She's not sure she's cut out for an officer's wife, like.'

'That can be one of the problems,' said Cass. 'Perhaps I'll pop in and see her. Or ask her up for coffee or something. Tell her I'd love to meet her.'

'I'll do that. 'Ow's my lover, then?' Mrs Hampton paused in the act of putting on her coat to bend down and tickle Gemma's cheek. Gemma held up the doll she was playing with and Mrs Hampton made clucking admiring noises. 'Quiet now, with 'em all gone back to school,' she observed. 'You must be real glad to 'ave this little maid to keep you company.' With this Parthian shot, she kissed Gemma and opened the door. 'See you Thursday.'

Cass made a rude face at her departing back and went to the pantry to pour herself a glass of wine. She knew that she was fighting a losing battle and that she was going to have to give in gracefully. She took a sip, pushed the saucepan of soup on to the hotplate for lunch and took some bread from the crock. Funny how old Tom had made up his mind about it. It had become quite a battlefield with each of them emerging for a light skirmish and then withdrawing to plan the next move.

Cass took another sip. She'd made the fatal mistake of being too serious about it. She should have kept it light and majored on the facts that would have weighed with Tom: that boarding school would have helped Charlotte to become more self-sufficient and that she had a very good brain that deserved a first-class education.

Cass stirred the soup and switched on the toaster. The trouble was that it was impossible to imagine Charlotte as a career girl. She was so obviously wife and mother material that Cass had found herself arguing from a standpoint of weakness and her insistence had made Tom suspicious. The Stephen Mortlake business was too recent and he'd remembered Charlotte's part in it. Cass had managed to allay his fears but he'd begun to feel that her determination that Charlotte should go away to school had something more to it than concern for her future education. Gemma was still very young and Saul would be off to prep school in two years just when he himself, if all went well, would be promoted to Commander and given a Nuclear or Polaris submarine to drive. He was fast coming to the conclusion that while he was at sea Charlotte would make a very good chaperone. Very little would slip past her, especially as she got older.

Cass, who could read Tom like a book, was well aware of these thought processes and decided that for the sake of peace and her marriage, she must give in gracefully. Since there was no local school that Charlotte could go to it would at least mean that there could be no more unexpected arrivals home. She cut some bread, put it in the toaster and took another sip. Gemma had crawled into the puppy's basket and woken him up. He yawned mightily and licked her face enthusiastically. Cass laughed as Gemma squeaked and tried to push him away.

'Up you come,' she said, swinging Gemma into the air. 'Now he's woken up he'll have to go out.'

She hurried Gemma out into the garden, the puppy staggering in the rear, and set her down on the lawn. It would be a sensible move to have a look at some local private schools, she decided. The Great Education Debate had gone on too long and it was time to back down and set Tom's mind at rest. She simply mustn't rock any more boats! She watched the puppy pee and then run after Gemma who had picked up his ball.

'Lunch!' she called. 'Come and have some lunch.' And laughed as they turned and raced across the lawn towards her.

'CASS TELLS ME THAT she's given in over the Great Education Debate,' said Kate as they sat in the warm May sunshine on the little paved terrace outside Kate's sitting room. 'Tom was so relieved that he gave her a huge bottle of scent for her birthday last week.'

'And how will she manage?' asked Alex, who knew all the ins and outs of it through Kate.

'She's sending Charlotte to Lambspark School in Plympton. It's a super little school, apparently, which takes boys up to eight before they go off to prep school and girls to sixteen. They can do O levels but they have to go on to sixth form to do A's. Charlotte is thrilled to bits. One of her friends is going from Meavy.' Kate began to chuckle. 'The beauty of it is that Cass has decided to send Saul as well. That means that she's got rid of two of them at one stroke. Neither of them will be able to pop home from school unexpectedly. Trust Cass.'

'And what does Tom say?'

'Well, he's very pleased about Charlotte and he can't really complain about Saul going. As Cass points out she can't be driving Charlotte to school at half-past eight and seeing to Saul at the same time and, of course, she'd be setting out to pick her up before Saul gets home. Much more sensible that they go together. Anyway, Tom thinks that he's won the battle and that's all that matters.'

'How devious women are,' observed Alex, closing his eyes to the sun. 'Do men ever really get their own way or do they just think they do?'

'Men and women are two quite different species,' said Kate seriously. 'The mistake we all make is in thinking that basically we're the same. We think differently, react differently, require different things. To expect marriage to work is like expecting a fish and a bird to live happily together. Or a bee and a mouse. Totally incompatible really.'

Alex opened his eyes and looked at her. 'Are you trying to tell me something?'

'No. That's as far as I go, really. Because men are different from men and women from women, too. Look at Cass and Felicity—chalk and cheese!'

'And, I hope, you and Cass. Does she behave like she does because she's alone so much?'

'I don't think so. She's just fundamentally naughty. She's been like it since she was twelve. There's no real vice in her. She's one of the kindest people that I know and incredibly generous. She just likes a bit of spice in her life. A touch of risk. We have a joke about it. She called it playing Russian Roulette once and I told her that one day she'll get the bullet.'

'And will she?'

'I sincerely hope not. Cass isn't really immoral, you know. She's amoral. She simply can't help enjoying herself and because it's such fun, in her view it can't really be bad. I honestly believe that she doesn't feel she's hurting anyone. She would be quite understanding if Tom had a fling. Jealousy has been left out of her make-up, you see, so she can't imagine anyone suffering from it. She really loves Tom and actually makes him very happy and she's so much more fun than most upright dreary people who are terribly faithful. For that alone I could forgive her nearly anything.'

'As long as you don't feel the need to follow her example. I promise you that I find you quite enough fun as you are. And jealousy hasn't been left out of my make-up.'

Kate laughed and took his outstretched hand. 'Like I said, women are different from women. I don't have Cass's panache.'

'Thank God for that,' murmured Alex. 'Now that I've met you I'm beginning to have a sneaking sympathy for all those dreary upright people!'

Seventeen

The strain of living a double life was every bit as great as Alex had foreseen and Kate was beginning to wonder how long she could keep it up. She knew that it wasn't fair on Alex to relegate him to a back seat every time the twins appeared but she simply didn't know what else to do. On the occasions when they were all four together Kate was like a cat on a hot tin roof lest the twins should suspect something and Alex, who had hoped that this may be a way of reconciling the twins to the new situation, began to despair. As usual, in these situations, her sense of guilt was well to the fore and she tried hard to make sure that everyone was getting his fair share. It was an impossible hope and Kate felt her temper fraying. When she was with Alex she felt guilty that she wasn't with the twins and when she was with the twins she tortured herself by imagining Alex, all on his own, feeling very much in second place. After all, he had done so much for her. She knew that it was through Alex that she was coming to terms with her sense of failure and guilt over her separation from Mark. Over and over again he showed her a balanced picture, restoring her self-confidence, patiently talking her through it and she was terrified that he might be getting tired of his role as comforter forgetting, once she was away from him, all the other sides of the relationship.

One morning, arriving a little late having taken the twins to Cass, she saw Pam coming out of the shop and her fear had taken the form of an offhand brittleness which puzzled Alex and then, as he jumped to all sorts of conclusions, made him angry. They had had a row and, although they had very quickly sorted themselves out, it had left Kate badly shaken. In order to justify her behaviour she had admitted that she suffered dreadful jealousy from time to time and that she feared that she might lose him. This, she knew, was putting weapons into his hands but she felt that she must hold nothing back. She had been reluctant to leave him, frightened that such misunderstanding could occur and, instead of going straight back to collect the twins, she did as she had so often done at times of crisis. She went to the General.

'I know I'm being unfair to Alex,' she said, sitting at the kitchen table while he made some tea. 'The trouble is that my head is just going round and round and I need someone standing away from us to tell me if I'm trying to have it all ways. My main fear is that Mark could use it as an opportunity to bring me down and get the twins. But secondly, if I'm honest, I have a horror of actually telling the twins. You know, saying the words. To boys of that age, falling in love with someone is something one's own mother doesn't do. I'm terrified that they may see it as something, well, sort of grubby.'

'Oh, my dear.' The General looked at her compassionately. 'It's a very tricky situation, I quite see that, but I can't help feeling that your fears may be unfounded. Surely it's unlikely that Mark would want to disturb his career by any sort of court case? After all, other things may come out that would not be beneficial to him. And why should he want to take the twins away from you? He shows very little interest in them and what would he do with them? You talk of his mother but she's not a young person. Would she want them while he's at sea? It's one thing to have them for a week or two and quite another on a full-time basis. I think that any judge would want proof of a far closer relationship than Mark has with his boys to take them away from a loving and caring mother. And the twins aren't babies, remember. If they were asked their opinion, you may be sure that they'd give it.'

'How comforting you are,' said Kate gratefully. 'It sounds very logical. I thought of him doing it out of spite, you see.'

'But you're not allowing for Mark's character. From what I know of him I can't imagine Mark taking any steps without long and careful thought. He would see that any personal satisfaction he might gain would be far outweighed by future responsibilities. I think you have nothing to fear.'

'And what about the twins?'

The General made the tea and pondered. 'Do they know that your marriage with Mark is quite over?'

'Well, not as such. I think they've guessed but I've glossed over it a bit. It's so easy with Mark always having been at sea. They probably think that he comes home sometimes when they're at school and of course he's never written to them. He writes to me about financial matters and I give them his love and things like that even though he doesn't.'

'Then I think that the first step would be to tell them that your marriage to Mark is over and has been for some time. That should be made clear. They will accept Alex more readily if he is not thought to be the reason for the break up. Children prefer the status quo and rather resent anyone who upsets it. You've made their lives happy and secure within the insecurities of service life and their first requirement will be that you should go on doing it. Your happiness, I fear, will be a secondary consideration.'

Kate laughed. 'Now that I totally believe! No talk of divorce yet, then?'

'Not yet. Let it all sink in and then Alex can start to take his place in all your lives in a more normal way. If that's what you truly want.'

He turned away to make the tea, hoping that his anxiety didn't show. He could see that Alex's display of temper had distressed her and he had a real fear that she might rush into things before she was ready for them.

Kate was silent for a moment, sitting quite straight in her chair, her hands linked loosely on the table.

'I don't know,' she said at last. 'In some ways it doesn't seem real. It's wonderful when the twins aren't there or all the time it's a secret. But it's as if it doesn't belong to real life. Today it was rather sordid. Alex and I screaming at one another and me being jealous. I felt guilty at misjudging him and he said bitter things about me wanting my cake and eating it.'

'Sadly, relationships have to stand up against the harsh winds of the outside world. They have to be tested against the rules and standards of real life, which is why holiday and shipboard romances so rarely work.' The General turned to look at her. 'It's bound to take time. The great thing is to learn from past experience. Not to go jumping from the frying pan into the fire.'

Kate looked at him. She was very serious.

'D'you think that's what I'm doing?'

'Oh, my dear. How can I possibly tell? You've had a bit of a mauling and I want to see you happy. It's so easy, you see, to go from one ex-treme to the other. If you've been denied certain aspects of love within a relationship, the tendency is to grasp these in the next one, ignoring the fact that there will be other drawbacks which may be just as difficult to live with.' He shook his head. 'It's impossible to know what is right for someone else. All I would say is, don't rush it. Give it time. And if it's the right thing for you the moment will come when you'll know. If it's right, it'll come, have no fear. If you are patient and are working for good, the right moment always presents itself.'

'What should I do without you?' Kate took her tea and smiled up at him. 'Let's hope that a right moment presents itself in which I can re-pay all your kindnesses. As far as I'm concerned, you've always been working for good.'

'Oh, if only that were true. I'm sure you've heard the saying "old sins cast long shadows." Lots of cancelling out to do yet.'

'I don't believe it. I shall be looking for the right moment.'

He smiled down at her and Kate saw the likeness to Cass leap up in that much older face. On an impulse, she set down her cup and, jump-ing up, she went to him and hugged him tightly, her face buried in his jersey. He stood holding her, stroking her hair as he did with the chil-dren.

'I love you,' she said, muffled. 'I love you so much I simply don't know how I'd manage without you and it's just occurred to me that

I don't even know your name. All my life you've been Cass's pa or the General.' She leaned back to look up at him and saw that he looked surprised. 'What is your name?'

'My dear, I assumed you knew it. Cass named her eldest son after me, you see. My name's Oliver.'

CASS WAS GIVING A little lunch party: Abby, Liz and Harriet. Abby and Liz were both vastly pregnant, their babies due on the same date. This was not surprising as they had both been conceived on the night of Cass's party. Nobody mentioned the fact that at the time Liz and Tony weren't married. They all knew that they'd been around together since the previous summer and left it at that. Harriet was rather quiet.

They'd reached the coffee stage, that moment of desultory conversation and pleasant idleness.

'William's told me that I must have a boy this time,' said Abby, yawning a little. 'Ever since his father died, he's become very feudal. I don't see why poor old Sophie shouldn't inherit the estate but it's entailed. Does Tony mind what you have, Liz?

'I don't think so.' Pregnancy made Liz look drawn. 'Nor do I, really. I'm just glad that it's due before we go to Faslane.'

'I must say that I'm very glad not to have to move around any more,' said Cass, going round the table to fill up the coffee cups. 'Liz off to Faslane and Harriet going to Gosport. Mind you, I always enjoyed it there. Dear old *Dolphin,* always something going on. We shall miss you. I know that Tom will especially.' She noticed the flush on Harriet's cheek as she bent to fill her cup. 'He always looks for you at parties. You must keep in touch. Come and stay when Ralph's at sea. You too, Liz, although it's a bit of a way from Faslane, especially with a sprog. Never mind, you'll both be back before long.' She sat down again at the table.

'When William came out of the Army to take over the estate,' said Abby, 'I was a bit miffed. Life in the country seemed terribly dreary. But I like it now. I don't think I'd like to be on the move all the time.'

'The excitement tends to wear off after a bit,' agreed Cass. 'We all settle down in the end, though. The question is, where?' She seemed to be addressing Harriet and it was she who answered.

'Ralph thinks he'd like Lee-on-Solent. He's mad on sailing and it's perfect for it there and only just down the road from *Dolphin*.' She looked even more depressed at the thought and Cass drank her coffee thoughtfully.

'I think that Tony will come back here if he can,' said Liz. 'I hope we will. All my family's here and I love Devon.'

'Well, we'll have a little party before you go. Chaps as well. What do you think?' Cass smiled at Harriet. 'Tom would be very upset if you went off without saying goodbye. Give these two chance to whelp down and we'll have a farewell thrash.'

Harriet looked as if she might burst into tears and Cass got up.

'The children seem very quiet. I can always trust Charlotte but I think that we'd better check that all is well. Let's have a wander into the garden.'

ONCE AGAIN, BEFORE THE summer holidays were over, the twins were asked to Cheltenham and Kate, taking the General's advice, gathered up her courage and told them that she and Mark would never live together again.

'The trouble was,' she told them, 'that we weren't suited but we were very young when we got married and we didn't realise it until it was too late. I know it's very upsetting but I hope that he and I can still be friends and that it won't make your lives too difficult. It's not as if you've ever seen much of him and you can still visit him whenever you want to.'

'Does that mean we needn't go to Cheltenham if we don't want to?' asked Giles, looking hopeful.

'Does that mean you're going to get a divorce?' asked Guy, looking wary.

'Yes. No,' said Kate and she laughed. 'Sorry. I mean that there's no talk of a divorce as yet although I expect we shall sometime, and yes, I think that you should go to Cheltenham to see Mark and Granny and

Grandpa. I think that they'd be hurt if you didn't. After all, just because Mark and I don't live together any more doesn't mean that you
need feel any differently about him.'

'Does anyone at school know?' asked Guy suspiciously.

'Will you ever marry anyone else?' asked Giles anxiously.

'No. Yes. Oh, dear. I'm sorry. No, I don't think anyone knows at
school. I've never discussed it with anyone so I don't see how they
could know and yes, I probably will marry again one day but you'll
know all about it and it's nothing to worry about yet.'

'Why can't we just go on like this?' asked Guy, sounding belliger-
ent.

'What if you marry someone who isn't right again?' asked Giles,
sounding frightened.

'We shall be going on like this,' said Kate as calmly as she could.
'Nothing will be changing. Why should it? We've been separated for
nearly two years. I just thought that the time has come when you
should know exactly where we all stand. You'll carry on at school as
usual and we'll go on living here and I shall go on working with Alex.
If I get married again, I shall think about it much more carefully than I
did before. I'm much older now and I hope that I know what sort of
person I can be happy with—and you, too, of course. It will be important that it's someone we all like but it won't happen while you're
at Mount House so don't worry about it.'

She saw Guy relax and smiled at them. 'I don't want to upset you
but I felt it was right you should know before you went to Cheltenham. Mark might have said something, thinking that you knew.'

'I don't want to go,' said Giles tearfully. 'If you aren't going to be
married any more I don't see why I need to.'

Kate's heart sank. 'They all like to see you,' she began.

'They don't!' he cried in a high passionate voice. 'Granny does. But
Grandpa and Dad don't. Grandpa just grunts and Dad says I'm a sissy!'

Kate pulled Giles into her arms and looked a question at Guy who
still wore a closed expression.

'He took us to the fair,' he said reluctantly. 'And Giles didn't want to go on the Big Dipper. Dad said he was a sissy and said he'd have to wait all on his own while we went on it.'

'It was dark.' Giles looked up at her, his eyes huge with remembered horror. 'And there were lots of strange people. He laughed and said watch out that I didn't get kidnapped.' A thrill ran through his body and Kate felt a hot surge of rage and hate twist her gut.

'So he came with us,' said Guy after a moment when Giles seemed unable to speak. 'And he was sick all over Dad's legs.'

'Serve him right,' said Kate lightly. 'Big bully. Do you want to go, Guy?'

He shrugged. 'Don't mind. Granny's all right. Grandpa's boring. Dad's OK if you don't wind him up. I don't like it when he gets in a bate.'

'Surely with Granny and Grandpa there he doesn't get cross?' Kate still hugged Giles.

Guy made a face. 'Not really. It's when we go out on our own with him. He goes on about things. He's OK really.'

Kate thought quickly. She knew that if Mark felt that she was withholding the twins he might become unpleasant and the worse it would be for them. After all, she couldn't stop him seeing them unless she explained why in a court of law. It was an intolerable situation.

'Do you think you could be terribly brave and go this time?' she asked Giles. 'If you don't want to go out with him tell Granny that you don't feel well or something. You see, while he pays your school fees, he has a right to see you. If we divorced it might be a bit different.' She paused, not wanting to go into all the legal ins and outs.

'D'you mean if I don't go to Cheltenham I'd have to leave Mount House?' Giles was staring at her in consternation.

'Not exactly,' said Kate slowly, 'but Mark would want to know why and then it might mean that it would all have to be done legally. I'd have to get the court to order him to pay the fees. The Navy pay a lot of it, of course . . .'

'I'll go,' said Giles quickly. 'Don't go to court. I'll go. It'll be all right, I expect.'

'I'm sorry, darling,' said Kate desperately. 'Guy will be there and it's only for a week.'

'It's all right,' he said dully, pulling away from her.

Kate got to her feet. 'I've got an idea. What d'you say we go into Plymouth to see *Star Wars*? If we get our skates on we just might make it.'

'Oh great!' Their faces lit up, woes forgotten. 'Terrific!'

'Quick then. I'll organise the dogs and afterwards we'll go and have a Wimpy.'

Later, as she sat between the rapt twins who were engrossed in the exploits of Luke Skywalker and Darth Vader, she wondered if she had the right to send Giles to Cheltenham. What were the rights and wrongs in such a situation? Which would be most harmful: to expose him to a bully for a week or to take him away from a school where he was happy and had lots of friends?

She sighed. At least the first step was over without too much trauma and, with Cheltenham behind them, they could go forward on the next stage of the journey.

THE BARBECUE FOR THE twins' birthday had become an institution.

'The trouble is,' said Kate who had dropped in to deliver her share of the goodies, 'that when things happen on a regular basis they mark the passing of time so relentlessly. You start saying things like "this time last year so-and-so" and you realise that you're getting old and that the years are going so quickly.'

'I always did say,' observed Cass, unpacking the basket, 'that it should have been you who was named Cassandra. Nothing but doom and gloom. Anyway, it's been a good year. What with the Great Educational Debate and The Divorce Question all settled, we haven't done too badly.'

'No. And Cheltenham passed without any ructions. I can hardly believe that this will be the twins' last year at Mount House.'

'You've definitely decided on Blundells?' Cass put the packets of beefburgers into the fridge.

'I think so. If they pass their Common Entrance, of course. By the way, I saw Felicity in Creber's the other day. She overcame her fear of contamination to tell me that she's off to Dartmouth. Couldn't resist bragging about Mark II getting the submariner's job. It'll be nice to have her off my back for a year or two. She's got a little clique in Tavistock who cut me dead and then whisper furiously when I've passed.'

'It's based on fear, really. Want a cuppa? Shove the kettle on then. You've broken out, you see. A woman living alone. They're probably all scared that you're going to set your cap at their boring old husbands!'

'You can't be serious!' Kate went to fill the kettle. 'Having escaped one submariner I'm hardly likely to seek out another! I'm not a masochist. Once is quite enough. Coming back with all their clothes ponging of diesel, ghastly cocktail parties . . . '

'Do you remember when you dropped your pâté down Mrs Captain SM's dress?'

'And what about that time we went to sea on Families' Day and you were in the heads when the submarine went to "Action Stations" and that sailor wouldn't let you out until it was all over?'

'I got back to the control room in time to hear the Captain say: "Well, what did you think of that?" and his wife said, "Very nice, dear, but I think John Wayne does it better." '

They rocked with laughter and Mrs Hampton, coming into the kitchen, smiled at them.

'You'd better make that coffee an' go on out into that there sun. My assistant'll be along in a minute and then we've got a birthday tea to prepare!'

Eighteen

A year after Cass's party the effects of it could still be felt. Tony and Liz, tied together by the unwelcome baby, pushed down unspoken reproaches and regrets and lived in an unhappy truce. Even Liz's love was wearing thin and she was beginning to wish that she'd had the courage to remain unmarried and finish her accountancy exams. The baby girl was a whining, fretful little bundle and Tony longed to be back at sea. Liz, plain and tired, doubtful now that she could make him love her, wondered how long she could hold him and in her fear became snappy and withdrawn.

Harriet's infatuation for Tom, fanned by his attentions at the party and at various gatherings thereafter, was threatening to destroy her relationship with Ralph. When they had moved to Lee-on-Solent and she could no longer live on the expectation of seeing Tom, she became moody and Ralph, apparently unable to please her and not knowing why, spent more time in the Mess and on his boat.

Tom himself found the seeds of distrust after the Stephen Mortlake affair could not be so easily done away with and kept his eyes open. At least Charlotte was happy, settling in at her new school and always waiting to welcome him home on Friday evenings. Cass seemed her usual self and there was no sign that everything was not as it should be but still Tom watched.

George, having been dropped in it by Pat, had been confronted by an outraged Felicity and had had his character reviled and his honour impugned. Unwilling to be deprived of future favours and ready to take to himself Felicity's beliefs that he owed her a great deal, he grovelled, abased himself and was finally, after a very uncomfortable period, taken back into her favour.

As for Kate, her affair with Alex having survived the year was still under stress. Since her talk with the General, she had tried to keep her physical passion from colouring all the other aspects of the relationship. The summer holidays had proved a testing time and, riddled with guilt, she made tremendous efforts to make up for it during the autumn term. Try as she would, she was still frightened of any rumours reaching the twins at Mount House and was pathologically worried about she and Alex being seen together publicly out of working hours. Fortunately the short dark winter evenings were soon upon them but Alex was becoming irritated at having to live in this hole and corner way and they had another row, during which he insisted that the boys should be told the truth. Kate, who wasn't sure what the truth was, promised to think about it. It was unlucky that the pressures were forcing Alex to show a much less sympathetic side and Kate began to grow nervous of him, finding that she was watching and waiting for warning signals and desperately thinking up ways and means of maintaining the status quo.

Toward the end of the term, the twins had an exeat weekend and Alex made her promise that she would tell them that they had more than a working relationship. At twelve years old, he told her, they were more than capable of understanding about sex. The thought turned her cold with horror but she knew that out of fairness to Alex, something must be said. To her enormous relief, the twins brought home a friend for the weekend. He was the son of a submariner who had always been one of Mark's friends and when she heard the boys talking she realised that as far as school was concerned, the twins were maintaining the fiction that her marriage was just like everyone else's.

It occurred to her that Mark's status was important to them: a father who drove submarines was surrounded by an aura of glamour and they could identify with all the other naval children at the school. It surprised her that none of the many submariners' children had heard from their parents of the separation or the stories that Mark had told about her and she could only assume that, either they weren't so widespread as she had feared or that they had been discounted. Watching the twins, she knew that she would be quite incapable of causing them any problems or distress and was grateful that no rumours had as yet reached their ears. She could imagine the whispers and remarks that the other boys might make if her affair with Alex became common knowledge and since she was not prepared to think about divorce yet, there was nothing for it but to go on as they were. She knew that she would feel different once the boys were no longer at school locally, if only Alex were prepared to wait.

She went into the bookshop on Monday with a quaking heart and explained what had happened. Alex accepted that it would have been impossible to have any sort of intimate conversation with a third person present and he was very reasonable but made it clear that it was only a postponement. Kate felt that she had a bit of a breathing space but the Christmas holidays were soon upon them and Alex obviously had no intention of spending them in some sort of purdah. She tried for a compromise. Rather than tell the boys the truth, it was agreed that Alex should spend some time at the cottage in the role of very good friend rather than as Kate's boss and they would take it from there.

It started quite promisingly. Alex had given the twins some good presents from the shop so they were already disposed to like him but when he began to appear on a regular basis, the boys were first surprised and then suspicious. To begin with, Alex behaved with circumspection but when he realised that Guy especially was inclined to be awkward he decided to force the pace a little. It really was very unlucky that one of Guy's friends had just been taken away from school because his parents had divorced. He had explained to Guy that his father had refused to pay the fees once the divorce had taken place and Guy assumed that this may happen to him and Giles if Kate divorced Mark. He remembered that Kate had talked of having to go to court over the school fees and red lights began to flash. Coming unexpectedly upon Alex with his arms round Kate confirmed his fears and Guy became openly hostile.

If Alex hoped that Kate would laugh it off and take his part against the twins he had badly misjudged her. She was upset by their distress and cross with Alex for precipitating the confrontation. Guy had already primed Giles and told him terrible stories about having to leave Mount House and probably the cottage and Giles, with unhappy memories of having one man around, was very ready to side with Guy. There was no way that Kate could take Alex's part against such a united front especially at Christmas of all times and a few days before she told him so.

'If only we could go on as we are,' she pleaded as he watched her, stony-faced, across his desk. 'It's only 'til next September.'

'That's not quite the point, is it?' he said. 'The point is that the twins come before me. You're prepared to sacrifice me every time rather than upset them.'

'Oh, Alex . . . '

'It's perfectly true. We've been going on like this for more than a year and you're suggesting that we do it for the best part of another one.' He crossed his arms across his chest in what, to Kate, looked like a gesture of complete rejection.

'What are you saying?'

Alex looked at her. It was unfortunate that Pam had waylaid him that morning and asked if he and Kate were ever going to get together. She'd suggested that Kate's name should have been Rachel and his Jacob and laughed when he looked puzzled.

'She's certainly making you serve your seven years, darling,' she'd said. 'Are you going to enjoy being a daddy?'

Kate was watching him. He uncrossed his arms and thrust his hands into his pockets.

'I've got to think about things,' he said. 'I'm not trying to push you into a divorce but I can't spend another year like the last one. If you're not prepared to be open about our relationship then I think we should call it a day.'

She looked so shocked that he had difficulty in not backing down at once but Pam's thrust had hit a sensitive place and he wasn't prepared to look a fool. Also his defeat at Guy's hands had left him wondering whether he would ever be able to live in amity with the twins.

'I see,' said Kate at last. 'Does that mean I've lost my job too?'

'Of course not.' His voice was irritable, half of him wanting to rush round the desk and take her in his arms, part of him hoping that he might jolt her into changing her mind. 'You won't be in for a bit now anyway and I've got some buying trips in the New Year. Let's see how it goes.'

'If that's the way you want it . . . '

'No, no.' He interrupted her at once. 'It's not how I want it, Kate. You know what I want, I've just told you. If you're not prepared to acknowledge my position in your life it's your decision not mine. Don't blame me for it.'

'Yes, that's fair. I quite see that. And just at the moment I don't feel that I can. I'm sorry. Well.' She tried to smile. 'See you after Christmas then.'

He nodded but didn't move and presently she collected her things and went out, shutting the door gently behind her.

KATE DROVE HOME IN a daze. She felt as if she had been hit on the head and thoughts swirled and dived about in her brain, first one and then another coming to the surface only to vanish before she could bring her mind to bear on it. She struggled to analyse her feelings. It came down to a simple fact: somebody was going to be hurt. If she did as Alex asked there might be many complications with the twins. She tried to weigh this rationally. Would it actually damage them if she insisted on openly living with Alex? She felt that if the rumours reached the school they would certainly suffer. She knew that Giles especially had endured a great deal at Mark's hands—and tongue—and the fact that they pretended that all was still well implied that they needed the security of living within a conventional marriage. Tavistock was a small town and she felt quite sure that somehow rumours would filter back to the school. Her hands gripped the wheel a little more tightly. She simply couldn't risk it. If she and Alex could have married immediately it would be different but even now, especially now, she couldn't envisage them all living as a happy family. Of course, Alex was right. One day the boys would grow up and leave her and she would have nothing. Was it right to sacrifice her own and Alex's happiness for the sake of a few years?

She was deeply hurt that Alex was not prepared to struggle on. Although she knew that she was asking an enormous amount of him, she had hoped that he loved her enough to make the effort and that what she was giving him was making it worth the difficulties. In his place she felt that she would have tried but she knew that this was probably due more to conditioning than anything else, to an acceptance of her role in second place—whether it was to a job or to a man or to her children. It was a question of self-worth. She would have felt it reasonable to be asked to stand back. Alex did not. Even now she knew that she was preparing herself to accept the fact that it had been too much to ask of him, telling herself that—and this was what it came down to—she simply wasn't worth the sacrifice. She was already excusing and forgiving him and feeling guilty that she couldn't make it right for all of them.

She felt a thrust of pure anger, a 'what about me?' sensation that consumed all her emotions. For a glorious moment she felt a charge of strength and defiance. She would not enter into yet another relationship in the position of suppliant, feeling grateful and guilty by turns. She was stuck with this particular situation and she must deal with it as she thought best. Whether her methods were right or wrong was not up for discussion. She would be answerable only to herself. She experienced a wave of relief, of freedom, and in this mood drove on to the Rectory.

Cass was in the kitchen when she arrived, sitting at the table writing a last-minute shopping list. She glanced up as Kate appeared and looked at her questioningly.

Kate pursed her lips and shook her head. 'All over,' she said succinctly. 'All or nothing. It'll have to be nothing, I'm afraid.'

'Oh, lovey.' Cass got up swiftly and went to her. 'I'm sorry.'

'Don't be. I decided on the way over that it's all for the best. Don't be sorry for me or I shall probably break down and howl.'

'A good strong drink,' Cass diagnosed at once. 'A real belter. Would you like it here in peace and quiet? Or would you prefer to join the mob who are busy decking the halls with boughs of holly? The twins are helping Tom with the tree.'

'Oh, I'll go and watch. It'll cheer me up. And Cass, could I have some coffee first? Not instead of that drink. First. I was too nervous to eat any breakfast and I feel quite empty.'

'Absolutely. I'll get the kettle on.'

'I'll do it.' There was a movement in the corner by the dog basket and Oliver, who had been stroking Gus, moved forward.

'I didn't see you there.'

Kate glanced at Cass, eyebrows raised, and Cass shook her head.

'Don't worry.' She answered Kate's unspoken question. 'Oliver's the soul of discretion. He's my best friend.'

Oliver beamed at them with his usual tolerance for adult weakness and went to fill the kettle. Kate strolled across the hall and into the drawing-room. It was a wonderful scene. At the furthest point from the crackling log fire Tom, perched on a step-ladder, was holding a Christmas tree upright while the twins placed billets of wood from the log basket into the brass-bound wooden bucket in which the tree had been placed.

'Not steady yet,' he was saying. 'Needs a few more.'

The twins rolled their eyes and blew out their cheeks at her with expressions of exhaustion and responsibility and she smiled at them and went to the fire. Tom winked and pantomimed a kiss and her sore heart felt soothed and comforted. Charlotte, carefully unwrapping and laying out the decorations, smiled at her but Saul was too busy setting out the Christmas crib on a low table to notice her arrival. Gemma stood beside him, turning the tiny figures over and over in her small hands, fascinated by the carved shapes.

Kate sat down by the fire and watched them all. It seemed puzzling to

her that Cass, who did as she pleased and got away with murder, should
have been blessed with this delightful family and lovely home as well as a
devoted husband who was so good with his children whilst she who had
strived to achieve this very thing, giving out, giving up, had so signally
failed. She had hoped for it with Alex and even that had gone wrong.
Her old despair washed over her for a moment.

'Here's your coffee.'

Oliver stood beside her and she hastened to smile at him. He was not
deceived.

'When you feel sad,' he told her seriously, 'you have to think of
something nice that you're going to do.'

'Is that what you do?' She answered him just as seriously as she took
her coffee, feeling as she always did that he was just as grown up as she
was. Probably more so.

'Oh, yes. Otherwise I get more and more miserable and I can't get
my mind off it, you see. As soon as you feel it coming on you have to
think of something good. It can be anything.' He looked at her con-
sideringly. 'As long as it cheers you up. That's the thing. And then the
thing that's been upsetting you doesn't seem so bad after all. What
would cheer you up?'

'I don't know.' She looked at him helplessly. 'I think you're absolutely right but I just can't think of anything.'

He frowned thoughtfully.

'Mummy buys clothes,' he offered.

'I believe you.' Kate chuckled. 'And a very good idea it is. Something cheerful and cosy, I should think, at this time of the year.'

'Wait a minute.'

He disappeared and Kate sipped her coffee with the uncanny feeling
that she had been talking to the General. Anyway, he had cheered her up.
She felt stronger again and less sorry for herself. What a deadening emotion self-pity was. Oliver was back. He gave her a parcel, something
squashy wrapped in tissue paper.

'It's for you.' He nodded to her to open it.

'For me?' Kate looked puzzled.

'It's for Christmas.' He pulled back the tissue to show her a roll-neck jersey in softest lambswool, the colour of a holly berry.

'Oh.' She fingered the luxurious wool.

'What on earth d'you think you're doing?' Cass spoke above Oliver's head. 'That's Kate's Christmas present! I haven't even wrapped it yet.'

'She needs it now.' Oliver was unmoved by Cass's indignation. 'It's to cheer her up. It'll be too late on Christmas morning. Is it right?'

The blue eyes, Cass's eyes, the General's eyes, looked into her own. She smiled at him and at Cass who was smiling now.

'Absolutely right,' she said.

IN THE SPRING ALEX went away on an extensive buying trip. He intended to travel abroad and combine it with taking a long postponed holiday. When Kate learned that Pam had gone with him, she knew that everything was truly over and any form of reconciliation was out of the question. He left the shop and his flat in the charge of a friend of his who was in the trade and was hoping to set up his own business. Jeremy was a shy, gentle homosexual whose company Kate found infinitely restful.

She missed Alex dreadfully. His companionship, his love-making, had burst upon her like a comet which had cast a revealing light on the dull landscape of her life, shedding a warm and comforting glow and encouraging her to expand and develop in its beneficial rays. Now, just as suddenly, it was gone and she was left to stumble about in the darkness of her old life. At least she had one stroke of luck. Her father had sold the house and land in St Just for a very good profit and, once again, had shared the money with his children. Kate didn't get so much as the others but her debt was wiped out and although she still had to earn enough money to live, a great weight was lifted from her mind.

With Alex so definitely out of the picture, the twins relaxed and life resumed its former pattern. Kate felt the spring to be more melancholy than ever, the cold light rainy days in odd juxtaposition to the

song of birds and blossoming of flowers, and was aware of a deep sad-
ness settling upon her spirit. She remembered how, a year ago, she
and Alex had been in the first deep joy of their love and she ached with
loneliness and loss.

When he returned, he behaved towards her with an easy friendliness which to begin with hurt and repelled her. She tried to find another job but, with no qualifications and the difficulties of school
holidays, nothing was forthcoming and slowly she hardened herself to
being with Alex, unable to touch him, their precious intimacy gone.
Slowly and painfully she adjusted, deciding that when the summer holidays came, she would take the whole time off, have a complete rest
and decide how she planned to go forward. The twins would be off to
Blundells in the autumn so there would be much to be done to get
them ready. She decided to try to do more with the dogs and started
to look at the breeding side more seriously whilst taking up her old
idea of training retrievers to the gun and running obedience classes.
She was considering the possibilities of starting a boarding kennels
when her brother Chris, who was an electrical transmissions engineer, having finished a job abroad asked if he could come for a week or
so. She was delighted to have him and the twins loved every minute
of it.

He took them sailing and to the cinema and for long hikes over the
moor. In the evenings, Kate poured out her ideas and at the end of a
fortnight Chris made a proposal which completely took her aback.

They were sitting at the kitchen table over the remains of a late supper at the end of a long hot day. They'd taken the twins to Torcross to
swim and on to Dartmouth so that Guy could look at the boats—his
great passion—and Giles could wander round the town which he loved.
It had been a happy lazy day and Kate, dividing the remains of the wine
between them, sighed with pleasure.

'I can't remember when I enjoyed myself so much,' she said. 'Bless
you for taking so much trouble with the boys. It's so good for them to
be with a man with no stresses and strains.'

Chris lit a cigarette and inhaled thoughtfully.

'I've been wondering,' he said, 'if we couldn't make a more permanent thing of it. I'm away a lot which means that it's a bit difficult
to keep a place going. You'd like to spread your wings a bit, become
more independent. If you sold this place and we pooled our resources
we could get a bigger place, with outbuildings for kennels and so on.
I'd have somewhere to come home to and would expect to pay a fair
bit towards the upkeep. What d'you think so far?'

'Share a house?' Kate looked interested.

'Why not? I've got some money tucked away and you'd get a good
price for this. We could get somewhere near here with more room.
You could really concentrate on the dog side of things and when I'm
home I could take the boys off your hands a bit. They ought to have a
man about the place.'

'It sounds wonderful. But what about girlfriends? Or what if you
want to get married?'

He shook his head and tapped some ash from his cigarette.

'When Philippa went off I knew that I would never marry again. I
get my entertainment when I'm away. Don't worry—I wouldn't fill
the place with floozies! What about you?'

'I don't think so. You can't legislate for everything in this life but I
don't think I'll take any more chances.'

'Well.' He shrugged. 'If either of us do we'll have to re-think.
Nothing's irrevocable. What d'you say?'

'It sounds as if it could really be the answer.' Kate began to feel excited. 'Oh, Chris, it could just work.'

'Good.' He smiled and raised his glass to her. 'Lots to discuss, of
course. It'll have to be sorted out properly. Tomorrow we'll see
what's on the market, look at prices and so on. Get a feel of things.'

Kate felt elated, as if her life had suddenly taken a new turn. She
grinned at him.

'D'you remember when you brought us down to Dousland in that
van with the twins sitting in their pram in the back? And the General
opened the bottle of champagne?'

'Shall I ever forget it? I forgot where I'd put the screws for their blasted cots and I thought we'd have to bed them down in the chest of drawers.'

'When we get our new house he'll be our first guest,' vowed Kate.

'I'll drink to that,' said Chris.

ONE MORNING IN LATE-OCTOBER, Kate drove through the back lanes to Tavistock. Alex was up country valuing and buying and, as it was early closing day, she had decided to take the dogs to the shop with her, giving them a run on both journeys. It was a clear glowing autumn day, the sky a pure cloudless blue. The rowan berries burned like drops of bright blood, the bracken was touched with fire. As usual at this time of the year Kate felt exhilarated and strong, positive that difficulties could be surmounted, problems overcome. She slowed the car to watch a buzzard circling above her, the air currents bearing him upwards. He seemed a symbol of freedom on this wonderful morning and Kate sighed with pure pleasure. She stopped to walk the dogs on Plaster Moor, enjoying the resilient springiness of the sheep-bitten turf beneath her feet.

The plans that she and Chris had made were going slowly forward and Kate felt at peace for the first time for years. The twins had gone off happily to Blundells, delighted with the new arrangements, and Kate had been able to put her affair with Alex more firmly in the past. She had told him that when she moved she would give in her notice and if he found the idea upsetting he didn't show it, merely saying that he was glad that things were working out for her.

She breathed in great lungfuls of the sparkling air. This weather surely couldn't last much longer and she was glad now she had taken yesterday off, bundled the General into her car and driven him on a full circle of the moor; visiting all the places that he had shown her in those early years.

Crossing to Moorshop, they had taken the Tavistock road to Princetown, turning on to the Moretonhampstead road at Two Bridges, beneath which the East Dart runs, past Bellever Woods and through Post Bridge, over Statts Bridge and up on to the open moor.

They stopped where the road crosses the Two Moors Way, a track ancient in Roman times, to enjoy the panoramic sweep of countryside away to the north where Okehampton lies and, far beyond the moor's eastern boundary, to Exeter.

They made a diversion to Fernworthy Reservoir, hidden away and half circled with forest, before winding down into the old moorland town of Chagford for coffee in the cafe-cum-antique-shop with its room upstairs full of second-hand books. They'd wandered by Hameldown Tor to Widecombe-in-the-Moor, turning off to look at Hound Tor and to spend a moment at Jay's Grave where fresh wild flowers stood in a little pot at the head of the grave. They pondered, as so often before, the mystery of these flowers which, winter and summer alike, were always there. Driving down past Saddle Tor and Haytor they could see the sun shining on the sea away at Teignmouth in the blue distance.

After lunch, they'd taken the lanes behind Ashburton and cut across to Holne, passing Venford Reservoir and pausing at Hexworthy—just beyond the bridge—to watch a dipper on the river, before climbing back up to the Princetown road to have tea at Two Bridges. Lastly, they circled the reservoir at Burrator and dropped down through Sheepstor only a few miles from home where Mrs Hampton was waiting with a delicious macaroni cheese for supper.

It had been a day full of quiet joy, their minds in accord, feeling the other's pleasure in the sheer magnificence of the land: these hills covered with purple heather, these with bracken, and yet others with mile upon mile of bleached tall grasses. They'd marvelled at a dry stone wall that looked like granite lace against a sky of golden light and watched two crows seeing off a buzzard who was always one lazy flap of the wings beyond them. They smiled at the immobility of a moorland pony, shaggy and heavy-headed, standing in the road, indifferent to the motorists and they saw a sheep grazing with a magpie riding on his back.

They ate supper before the study fire, talking peacefully of this and that: Oliver's amazing panache, Saul's determination to be a soldier, the fact that the twins should be so alike and yet so different. Kate sat curled in the corner of the sofa, where Cass always sat, and the General knew that things were on an even keel at last and thought that she looked happier than he had seen her look for many years. She had talked over her new plans with him and he had felt quite sure that she was doing the right thing, relieved to see her set on a course that would bring her a calm, sharing relationship whilst giving her the freedom to be herself. He saw that there were grey hairs in the brown but in the firelight the worry lines smoothed away and she looked contented, confident, as if she had emerged from the dark into the light. The Collect for Advent came into his mind. 'Almighty God, give us grace that we may cast away the works of darkness and put on the armour of light . . . '

When she had gone he wrote a few letters, knocked the logs apart and went upstairs. Before he got into bed, he opened his curtains and looked out on the night; moonless but with a great shawl of stars flung across the deep darkness. The owl was hunting in the Manor Woods and across the fields a vixen barked. He found that the rest of the Collect was still in his mind. ' . . . that in the last day . . . we may rise to the life immortal through Him that liveth and reigneth with Thee . . . ' and he added his own prayer of gratitude. It had been a perfect last day.

Now, the next morning, Kate whistled the dogs and shut them in the back of the car. It really was far too good to be stuck indoors but she couldn't take two days off. The telephone was ringing and she let herself into the shop and, tripping over the dogs, she hurried to answer it.

'Kate? Is that you, Kate?'

'Yes,' she said rather breathlessly. 'Yes, it is. Sorry, who . . . ?'

' 'Tis 'Ammy, my lover.'

'Hammy? Is it . . . ? What is it, Hammy?'

' 'Tis the General, my lover. Now be brave. He passed away in the night. He didden suffer at all, I'm sure o' that. 'Twas a wunnerful way to go. Think of it like that. I'm sorry to be the one to tell you. I've been phonin' since early, like, but Cass was takin' the children to school an' you must've been goin' to the shop. I found 'im when I come in to do 'is breakfast. Must've been 'is old 'eart just give out. I got 'old o' Cass a minute ago an' she said to tell you. She's on 'er way down now.'

'Oh, no . . . ' Kate could barely speak. She felt heavy and slow as if her emotions were slowly congealing in lead.

' 'E did'n suffer. 'E looked so quiet an' peaceful. Will you come?'

'Yes. Yes, I'll come now.'

Mechanically she replaced the receiver, collected the dogs and her bag and, locking up, went back to the car. Mechanically, she drove the car out through the town, through Whitchurch and Horrabridge and on to Dousland and Meavy. She saw nothing now of the glory of the day. Between one moment and the next it had turned to dust and ashes. That was how death was, between one moment and the next. One moment a living breathing being. The next cold, lifeless, the vital spark snuffed out for ever. She thought of him yesterday, gazing out over his beloved moor, watching the dipper, laughing at the pony.

Parking behind Cass's car, she ran into the cottage and, hesitating in the hall for a moment, she called up the stairs.

'Cass? Are you there?' She heard voices and Mrs Hampton appeared on the landing.

'So there you are, my lover. Come on up. There's nothin' to fear.'

But Kate found that as she climbed the steps her heart was hammering with terror. Mrs Hampton took her by the arm; her eyes were red and swollen but her face was calm. 'Don't be afraid. Cass's with 'im.'

As she spoke, Cass appeared in the bedroom doorway. Kate went to her and they stared at each other in horror and grief. With one accord, they turned back into the bedroom and looked at last at the General.

Mrs Hampton had done all that was necessary and he lay as though asleep, his long hands folded on the quilt that covered him. He looked regal and aloof and quite irrevocably gone. The spirit that had given this spare, noble-looking statue its charm and warmth had fled. Kate found that she was clutching Cass's hand and she turned to look at her. Cass's eyes were dark with pain.

'I didn't have time to say goodbye,' she whispered and her lips shook. 'And now it's too late.' She buried her face in Kate's shoulder and began to weep.

Too late. Kate stared beyond her at that quiet compassionless face and felt, like a hammer blow to the heart, the immensity of her own loss. She thought of him: opening the bottle of champagne at Dousland, showing her the moor, listening thoughtfully to her woes. She remembered how he had comforted her when he had told her of her own mother's death and all the other times when he had given her courage. And, behind it all, the generous, uncalculating love. Suddenly she remembered the Christmas tree. She saw again the baubles glowing in the firelight, the tinsel gleaming and the brightly wrapped presents. She remembered the children's rapt expressions, Cass's tear-bright eyes and his own face, full of the pleasure of giving and sharing, and she knew in an almost unbearable agony of pain that something priceless and irreplaceable had gone out of her life for ever. Slowly, lowering her cheek to Cass's hair, she began to cry too, her eyes fixed on his remote, uncaring face.

Part Four

Nineteen

1980-81

Summer was over. In her little cottage next to the church Mrs Hampton put away her blue linen suit in a plastic container and her straw hat into a paper bag. She stood on a chair to place the hat on top of the wardrobe and to bring down the brown felt, also in a paper bag. Climbing down, she pushed the chair back against the wall and, drawing out the hat, gave it a brush with her sleeve. Her winter coat, the blue tweed, was already hanging on the wardrobe door ready to be worn for the service tomorrow, for the nights were beginning to draw in and the mornings were cool. She picked up her stubby brown shoes and carried them downstairs to the warm kitchen to give them a polish. She would have to be early in the morning if she wanted her favourite seat.

HARVEST FESTIVAL AND THE pews were packed to overflowing. Presently the Rector would deliver his well-known Harvest Festival sermon which always contained a jibe at those in the congregation who attended church only on its high-days and holidays and ignored it for the rest of the year.

Every nook and cranny was crammed with the fruits of the field. Flowers in tall vases glowed against the old grey granite, pyramids of apples and sacks of potatoes gave forth a pungent, earthy smell and bowls of brown eggs—no white ones, too much like supermarket eggs—jostled with sheaves of corn for a position by the font.

Jane Maxwell, wedged in beside Mrs Hampton, was unaware of

the significance of the blue tweed and brown felt. Oblivious to her surroundings, she sat quiet and contained, staring sightlessly at the prayer book on the ledge before her.

Cass, across the aisle, craned hither and thither, nodding and waving to friends and acquaintances. Nothing escaped her eye. She noticed Hammy's felt and tweed with amusement and Jane Maxwell's frozen tranquillity with puzzled sympathy. Something seemed wrong there and a touch of guilt assailed her. She'd neglected Jane, hadn't really seen her to talk to since that barbecue back in the summer. Alan had seemed to be finding the transition from Chiefs' Mess to Wardroom easier than was Jane. He was a trifle stiff, his clothes too new and smart, his hair too short, but he had coped very well and had managed not to call Tom 'Sir' too often. Poor Jane had suffered dreadfully. She looked ill at ease in the clothes Alan had chosen for her, she hated the dry white wine Cass gave her and had nothing to say to the Wivenhoes' friends who were frighteningly self-assured, had very loud voices and consumed vast quantities of alcohol. She had withdrawn into herself, avoiding Alan's angry looks and feeling sick inside at the thought of the row they would have when they got home.

'Well, that was a marvellous evening, I must say, with you standing there like a waxwork. God knows what they thought of you. Can't you make some sort of effort?'

'I can't help it, Alan, I just seem to freeze up. I do try, honest I do, but they all seem so affected, you know, the way they speak? And, well . . . so noisy.'

'Who the hell d'you think you are to be judging people? What makes you think you're so much better than everybody else?'

'I don't, Alan, you know I don't. I just feel different. I don't feel we belong.'

'Oh yes we do. Or at least *I* do. Get that straight, OK? I'm as good as Commander Tom Bloody Wivenhoe any day of the week.'

'You know I didn't mean that . . . '

'What did you mean then? You're jealous because I've moved on a

bit. If you'd only join in and have a couple of drinks instead of standing there like a po-faced bloody Sunday School teacher . . . '

Now, on this Harvest Festival morning, recalling this phrase, Jane
grimaced involuntarily.

Cass, seeing the spasm cross her face, felt her fears confirmed.
She would invite the Maxwells round for drinks next time Tom was
home. Or maybe supper—it would be less formal. Meanwhile, though,
she would ask Jane over for coffee. Perhaps she'd get Kate to come
too. Kate had been at the barbecue and had tried to draw Jane out and
make her relax. Hammy caught her eye and smiled at her, nodding
knowingly towards Gemma. Cass nodded and smiled back in total
complicity.

Only Gemma and Saul were with Cass this Sunday morning.
Gemma sat beside her, very aware of herself and deliciously conscious
of her new cord skirt, the colour of crushed raspberries, and also of
the fact that her hair was long enough to be twisted into a knot for the
first time. She was enjoying the feel of the cool air on her exposed
ears, the weight of the coil of hair and even the feel of the pins scraping her scalp. Saul leafed through the hymn book, checking out the
hymns and humming the tunes under his breath. Oliver had stayed at
home with a friend that he had invited for the weekend whilst Charlotte had offered to cook the lunch. She had just had her long heavy
brown hair cut short. Without telling anyone, she had gone with Lucy
Cobbett on the bus to Plymouth and returned looking like an old English sheep dog. Though she declared herself delighted with the result
she seemed reluctant to show herself publicly. Usually she enjoyed
church.

Cassandra smiled to herself at the recollection: Charlotte defiant
and a little scared, and herself, determined not to play the heavy
mother, pretending to be unmoved. Girls of Charlotte's age did all
sorts of things and it was sometimes wise to turn a blind eye. Tom
would be furious. Charlotte's thick brown hair was her one beauty but
it wouldn't be just the loss of it that would upset him. The truth was
that Charlotte no longer looked like a little schoolgirl of nearly fifteen.

Now, in her jeans and oversize sweatshirts, the new haircut empha-
sised the fact that Charlotte was leaving childhood behind her and Tom
would find that very difficult to come to terms with.

Cass craned again to discover the whereabouts of her flower
arrangement and glimpsed it hidden away behind the font as usual. Oh
well, she gave a mental shrug, it was no more than it deserved. She
was not clever with her hands but she liked to keep her end up in the
village, to show willing and join in. She felt that she had a responsibility to the community. As she turned back towards the altar her glance
tangled with that of a man sitting with William in the Manor pew and
she experienced an odd but very familiar sensation: that of recognition between two total strangers. An almost tangible crackle passed
between the two of them and Cass turned away feeling even more vitally alive than before. The stranger's glance proved that she was still
attractive even if she was thirty-five and had four children.

Cass chuckled inwardly and thought briefly of Tom, a Commander
now, who was at that moment manoeuvring his nuclear submarine
with great delicacy in the cold depths of the North Atlantic whilst under attack from a Dutch frigate. This was only a NATO exercise, however, and presently Tom and his submarine would slide away to 'sink,'
in due course, a US aircraft carrier. Since his promotion he'd become
a little more staid, more inclined to want quiet weekends at home instead of the parties and the social round that he had once enjoyed so
much. He still liked to see his friends but less often and in small informal intimate gatherings and Cass was very glad now that they had settled at the Rectory and she had gradually developed her own circle of
friends and entertainments.

She made a show of finding the first hymn for Gemma, pointing
out something to Saul, giving the impression of the devoted mother
with her children. She felt, like a current of warm air, the stranger's
eyes upon her and turned her head slightly to give him the benefit of
her beautiful, grave profile. She wondered who he was. She didn't
remember him from any of Abby's parties and he looked rather
older than William, or even Tom, well into his forties, grey-haired

but very distinguished-looking. There was a well-kept, smooth, expensive look to him and his glance had been keen: both measuring and exciting.

Her gaze rested once more on Jane and she felt a twinge of pity. How awful to be Jane, plain, thin and mousy. She'd never even notice an attractive man, although Alan was rather nice, if formal and over-polite. He was nervous and rather over-awed, poor lamb, thought Cass, casting her mind back to the barbecue. Might be fun to loosen him up a bit, get him a bit tiddly. He probably didn't get much fun with Jane. It was difficult to imagine them in bed together and they had no children.

Cass smiled complacently as she glanced down at her own voluptuous curves and then at the two proofs of her fertility. The choir entered and she rose gracefully to her feet, every inch of her aware of the stranger standing across from her. The boys and men filed into their stalls and the Rector announced the first hymn. The organ swelled and Cass's rich contralto poured forth. We plough the fields and scatter. She did not need her hymn-book; she knew the words by heart but her heart was not in it.

I wonder who he is? Thank Heaven I put on my new Jaeger . . . all good things about us are sent by Heaven above . . .

Mrs Hampton, that little wren of a woman, chirped happily, her heart full of love and peace. How she loved the big festivals of the Christian year, with the old church looking so beautiful and all the dear children. She remembered how the General had loved the early Communion service, always in his place winter and summer alike, and how often she had knelt beside him at the altar rail to take the Sacrament. She was aware of his presence very often. She was aware, too, of Jane's unhappiness. In her opinion Jane didn't belong in that new box of a house with a pocket handkerchief-sized garden on the estate at the edge of the village. She'd known Jane all her life and remembered the old cottage where Jane had been brought up, always over-run with dogs and cats it was, as well as Jane's elder brothers and sisters, and chickens scratching in the garden. Not that Jane could have lived in the cottage even if she'd wanted to. When her father, who'd been cow-man up at Home Farm, had died her mum had moved down near Plymouth to one of Jane's married sisters and Mr Hope-Latymer, young Mr William's father, had sold the cottage. Jane had bettered herself and didn't seem to be getting much happiness from it.

Life seemed much more complicated these days and she felt sorry for these young people who strived for more and more and then never seemed satisfied when they'd got it. She and Jack had been so happy and John was doing so well out in Hong Kong and earning so much that he could afford to help out his old Mum and Dad in so many ways. Yes, she was one of the lucky ones . . . Her voice soared up. So thank the Lord, yes, thank the Lord . . .

Jane's eyes were fixed on the white pages of her hymn-book but her lips barely moved and her voice was little more than a whisper.

CASS WAS TALKING TO the Rector's wife when William emerged from the church porch into the warm September sunshine. She had strategi-cally placed herself by an old stone tablet which assured passers-by that Edith May Trehearne, beloved of Henry Charles, rested in peace and had done so for the last ninety-five years. By stopping at this point where the paths diverged, Cass ensured that everyone leaving the church must pass her sooner or later. In the case of William it seemed very much the latter to the impatient Cass. The Rector's wife was not an easy person to keep engaged in animated conversation.

Gemma, still preoccupied in self-admiration, remained at her mother's side, whilst Saul had wandered off to exchange insults with an erstwhile school chum who sang in the choir. Saul, who had started at Mount House the year before, and was, therefore, now ineligible for this dubious honour, nevertheless enjoyed poking fun at his old friends who still suffered the humours of the somewhat eccentric choirmaster.

When William and his companion finally arrived within her orbit Cass's casual greeting was masterly; indeed she seemed reluctant to let Mrs Tanner go. At length, however, Mrs Tanner was allowed to hurry away to her lunch, giving thanks, as she often did, that she had escaped from the large draughty Rectory to her warm, modern, manageable house.

Cass turned to the men with a charming, if slightly rueful, smile.

'I don't think that Mrs Tanner minds at all that she has to live in that ghastly modern box. Good morning, William.'

'Not everyone likes cold and damp as much as we do, Cass,' said William, who was living in somewhat straitened conditions at the Manor. 'The smell of mice is an acquired taste, you know. And the Tanners couldn't afford the central heating and all the extras you put in.'

'All thanks to my dear old pa,' sighed Cass. 'I still miss him so dreadfully.'

'We all do. This is Nick Farley. He's a lawyer. His firm deals with all our problems and Nick's been helping us out with a boundary dispute. He's staying a few days. This is Cass Wivenhoe, Nick.'

'How do you do?' Cass allowed her hand to rest in Nick's clasp a moment or two longer than was necessary.

'We were wondering if we could carry you off for a lunchtime drink? Abby said to be sure to ask you.'

'Oh!' Cass pretended to debate with herself, eyes fixed on Gemma. 'Well, I don't quite know . . . '

'Oh, do come,' said Nick. He smiled at her and Cass turned to Gemma.

'Darling, d'you think that you and Saul could go home by yourselves? I'll be very quick but tell Charlotte I may be a few minutes late. Good girl. Look, there's Saul, run and tell him. Off you go.'

'Charlotte?' questioned Nick, watching Gemma pick her way between the grassy humps to Saul.

'Charlotte's my elder daughter. She's cooking the lunch.'

'Are you trying to tell me,' Nick lowered his voice slightly as he and Cass followed William out of the churchyard, 'that you have a daughter old enough to cook the lunch?'

'Don't be silly. Charlotte's nearly fifteen.' Cass was never afraid of divulging this fact as the response was always the same. Nick did not disappoint her.

'I don't believe it.'

As they set off towards the Manor, Cass saw Jane Maxwell walking home.

'Hold on a sec,' she said. 'I must have a word with Jane. Jane!' She hurried after her. 'Jane!'

Her preoccupation pierced by Cass's second, more insistent cry, Jane turned and waited for her to approach.

'How are you, Jane? I haven't seen you for ages. Come and have coffee with me very soon. Please,' she said as Jane hesitated. 'Let's make a firm date now. It's a Hammy day tomorrow so what about Tuesday? Yes? Oh, good. See you then. Don't forget. 'Bye.'

Cass hurried back and Jane walked on, seething.

Damn and blast the woman, she thought. I don't want to go and have coffee with her. Why can't she leave me alone? She jumped as a battered Land Rover screeched to a halt beside her.

'Hello then. Been to church?'

'Hello, Phil. That's right.' Jane glanced quickly up and down the lane. Although she had walked some way out from the centre of the village there were still one or two cottages and bungalows in sight. Nobody seemed to be interested but Jane knew her neighbours better than that.

'What're you doing, Phil? You promised me.' The low, furious tones were at odds with the smile still fixed to her lips.

'I didn't promise nothing. Chrissakes, Janey, I can stop and say hello, can't I? We've known each other all our lives. Shouldn't't've bought a house in the village if you didn't want us to meet.' The young man at the wheel seemed charged with vitality. His very hair, thick and dark, seemed to stand on end with it, and his incredibly beautiful, dark blue eyes sparked angrily between long curling lashes.

'I do want to see you. Please, Phil, you know I do. But not here. You know what they're like around here.'

'It would look mighty odd if we ignored each other, old sweethearts

like us.' His voice dropped, caressing and sweet. 'Come on, love, let's
see you smile. I got the key of Long Barn.'

She looked away from the expression in his eyes. 'I don't know.'

'Yes, you do. It'll be OK. Say about four o'clock.'

Jane struggled with herself.

'All right then. About four o'clock. I'll walk across the fields. Don't
come down in the Land Rover mind.'

'Don't talk daft.' He winked at her, pantomimed a kiss. 'See you
later then.'

Jane walked on.

By THE TIME JANE arrived at the Rectory on Tuesday morning Cass had
already had a visitor. Abby had called in on her way to Plymouth.

'I'm doing the Tesco run and I wondered if you wanted anything,'
she told Cass, who had persuaded her to stop for a cup of coffee. 'I
know this is your busy week, getting them all back to school.'

'Sweet of you. Although it's only the girls so far. The boys don't go
back to Mount House until next week.'

'Well.' Abby shrugged. 'You've still got two lots of trunks and
tuck-boxes to do. Sheer hell. Thank God I haven't got to think about
it yet. What will you do with Charlotte when she leaves Lambspark
next year?'

'Don't talk about it.' Cass filled the coffee mugs from the kettle on
the Aga. 'I can see another Education Debate looming. Gemma will
be perfectly happy to go to Meavy with Sophie but where Charlotte
will go I simply don't know. We'd like her to go into the sixth form at
Blundells. Oliver will be starting and they could go together but I
hardly dare mention it. She goes into the most fearful sulks as soon as
I open my mouth. The thought of having all four of them at different
schools fills me with horror.'

'So what did you think of our Nick?' Abby perched at the corner of
the kitchen table with her coffee while Cass scribbled busily on the
back of an old bill with a stub of pencil.

'Perfectly gorgeous,' she answered promptly. 'I couldn't think who he could be when I saw him in church. He looked much too old to be one of William's school chums or Army buddies. Very attractive though, isn't he?'

'Bit old for me,' said Abby provocatively.

'Only in his forties,' protested Cass. 'Forty-five, forty-six?'

'That's twenty years older than I am,' Abby pointed out. 'Anyway, he's married.'

'Is that intended to tell me something?' Cass arched her brows.

Abby laughed. 'Have you finished that list? I must get on.'

'Hold on a sec.' Cass added a few items. 'I think that's it. By the way, what about coming to dinner on Saturday? Tom's home for the weekend and I've got Harriet Masters staying for a few days. You could bring Nick if he's still with you.'

'He won't be,' said Abby. 'William and I would love to come but Nick'll be back home with wifie. I could give you his number if you like?'

'Oh, shut up!' said Cass good-naturedly and grimaced as the door bell shrilled. 'Blast! Here's Jane already, and I'm still in all this muddle.'

'Who?'

'Jane Maxwell. You know? You met her at our barbecue. Her mother was William's old cook or something. She's married to a sub-mariner now. They've bought a house in the village.'

'Oh, her. Rather a dreary creature I always think. What's she coming for?'

'Well, you know how it is. We naval wives must stick together and I don't think she's coping very well with being alone. I might ask if she and Alan would like to come on Saturday if he's home.'

'Oh, bore!' Abby made a face. 'They're such a prim and proper pair, so inhibiting!'

'I'd like to see the person who could inhibit you,' remarked Cass. 'Go and do your shopping and I'll see you later. Don't forget Saturday.'

'As if I would. What a pity Nick won't be around. It's always such an education watching you carry on your little affairs under Tom's nose whilst playing the loving wife. Nick was quite smitten, you know.'

'Oh, go away!' Cass pushed her friend out of the garden door and went to answer the front door in high spirits.

Jane, waiting on the doorstep, was feeling quite the reverse. The hours spent in Long Barn with Philip Raikes on Sunday afternoon had merely served to make her more confused and unhappy.

Phil had been waiting for her when she had stepped tentatively within the door. He had carefully ground out his cigarette before moving forward to take her in his arms.

'Hello, love. All right then?' He kissed her, gently at first but then more passionately. 'Come on over here, I've brought a blanket.'

Ten years before he'd used exactly those words when, as fumbling, inexperienced teenagers, they'd discovered each other in the straw of Long Barn. For nearly three years they'd done everything together, and then Philip had been sent to an uncle in Ivybridge to learn the trade of a plumber. Shortly after that Jane had got a job in the lingerie department at Debenhams in Plymouth and arranged to share a flat with a friend through whom she later met Alan Maxwell, a Petty Officer in the submarine service. She was struck by his cleanliness, good manners and purposeful attitude to life, characteristics that had been very little in evidence during Jane's up-bringing, and it was only later that she became aware of his resemblance to Philip Raikes; taller, perhaps, and heavier built, but his colouring was the same and he had the same vitality. That was a bonus.

Odd, then, that it was the very things that had attracted her to Alan, that, five years later, were to throw her back into Philip's arms. The peace and solitude occasioned by Alan's long months at sea had become loneliness and boredom. The thrill of owning her own home—it was at her request that they had bought the new house in her old village eighteen months previously—had worn off and her immaculate surroundings, once her pride and joy, now seemed sterile and empty.

Besides, Alan's ambition, which had pushed him so swiftly up the ladder, was now a threat to her peace of mind. Parties on the submarine or in the homes of the other officers were a nightmare to her. Her voice and clothes were wrong. They all seemed so frighteningly self-assured and, although they were very kind to her, she knew that secretly they were despising her. It was different for Alan. He was accepted on the strength of his abilities. He'd proved that professionally he was as good as they were and he had managed to pick up so quickly the nuances of social life that still left her bewildered and fumbling. The men talked shop where Alan could more than hold his own; the women were more personal. They talked a language that was unknown to her and—to her amazement—their language was sometimes almost as crude as her old dad's had been. They all drank an enormous amount and sometimes the men became playful and acted very foolishly which their wives thought terribly funny but which embarrassed Jane dreadfully. She simply couldn't understand it or accept it and Alan, preoccupied with holding his own, had no patience with her. They seemed to be drifting further and further apart and it was this loneliness which had made her turn back to the security of a past which she had so readily rejected.

She had met Philip again—now living near Yelverton—coming out of the village shop. It was just after the Wivenhoes' barbecue and Alan had gone back to sea for six weeks, still cross, leaving her miserable and lonely.

Philip's warm greeting and his insistence that they should meet, just for a drink, for old times' sake, both eased her sense of inadequacy and excited her. His admiration was a balm, soothing the sore places of her humiliations, and his dogged pursuit of her flattered the feelings lacerated by Alan's anger and disparagement. She couldn't resist him. They met secretly and more and more often until one day, in looking up old places, they had found themselves in Long Barn.

The inevitable had happened and Jane was trapped. Philip wanted her to leave Alan and come back to him. He insisted that they belonged together, should never have parted and was angry—Jane had been foolish enough to tell him of the wrongs and injustices at Alan's hands—at her husband's treatment of her. Jane, feeling that she was being swept away on some inexorable tide, had begun to feel frightened. Things were getting out of hand.

Now, on Tuesday morning, she looked at Cass, calm and secure, and it was as though a gulf yawned between them. How could someone like Cassandra Wivenhoe ever understand the sort of mess that Jane had made of her life? Any communication between them, except the most superficial, was impossible.

'Jane.' Cass managed to sound both amazed and delighted. 'Come on in. What a marvellous morning. It certainly makes up for such an awful summer, doesn't it?'

Chatting cheerfully she led Jane into the drawing room and hurried off to make some more coffee. She knew quite well that Jane, unlike Abby, would not have been at ease sitting at the cluttered kitchen table, nor would she have welcomed the friendly, if muddy, overtures of Gus, now stretched before the Aga.

Jane, left alone, wondered why people like the Wivenhoes, who were not short of money, should surround themselves with shabby furniture and faded curtains. She looked disparagingly at the ageing Sanderson chair covers—why not those nice stretch nylon ones that could be popped into the washing machine?—and the worn Aubusson rugs. She frowned at the amount of polishing required. You could buy lovely modern stuff already varnished so that it needed only a quick wipe over with a duster. And were those dog hairs on that cushion? As she leaned forward to examine the offending article more closely, Cass reappeared bearing a tray which she placed on a mahogany gate leg table.

'Here we are. Sorry to be so long. Do you know, I can't remember whether you take cream and sugar.'

Since Jane had only been to the house twice this was not remarkable. 'Both, please.' Jane shifted forward to receive the cup and saucer and helped herself from the proffered sugar basin.

'Oh, good,' said Cass. 'It's so nice to find someone else who likes fattening things. People are so Spartan these days, don't you think? Abby only ever drinks it black and it makes me feel so guilty. By the way, that reminds me. I think you told me that Alan's home this week. How about coming to supper on Saturday? We've got a few friends coming in and we'd love you to come too.'

Jane's heart sank. How on earth could she get out of this one? Her brain raced, trying to find an acceptable excuse, but Cass was too quick for her.

'I know you'll want to be on your own together. Tom and I used to be like that in the early years. But you might probably be quite glad of a little outing. I feel that you've been a bit down lately. It's hell, their being away so much, isn't it? Still, one has to make one's own life, too. Now, do say you'll come. Or don't you like any of us?'

'Of course I do, it's not that . . . ' Jane fiddled awkwardly with her spoon. 'It's very kind of you but, well, it's just that I wonder if I ought to check with Alan first?'

'Rubbish. He must know that you have to have your own life here when he's away and be prepared to fit into it when he's ashore. After all, he's hardly likely to have anything planned when he's just arrived back from sea. At least, not that sort of thing.' Cass chuckled and then hesitated as Jane, grasping her meaning, flushed a dark red.

'I'm sorry, Jane, tactless of me. I'm such an old hand that I've forgotten how romantic it can all be.' She paused for a moment while Jane made inarticulate noises and then said, 'Let's have some more coffee. No, don't stand up. Are you absolutely sure there's nothing wrong? You could tell me, you know, I promise I'm quite unshockable and we've all been through it at some time or other.'

I doubt it, thought Jane and pulled herself together.

'No, honestly, I'm fine, Mrs Wivenhoe'—'Call me Cass, please,' protested Cass—'it's just I'm still getting used to Alan's promotion and I do find the loneliness a bit difficult' (and I've got a lover who wants me to leave my husband and I don't want to come to your bloody supper party), 'but I shall be fine when he's back home.'

'Well, of course you will be. But if there's anything I can do meanwhile?'

'Thanks . . . Cass, but honestly, I'm fine. Thanks.' Jane took her refilled cup and smiled bravely. 'And I'm sure we'd love to come to supper.' (Anything to get her off the other track and I can always phone up later and cancel.) 'Who will be coming? Anyone I know?'

'Well, there's Abby and William'—oh, Christ, thought Jane, it would be them—'and there's Harriet Masters, an old friend of ours who's coming to stay for a few days. Frightfully tragic, actually. Her husband was killed in a sailing accident. He'd taken his boat out and a storm blew up and he was washed overboard. It seems that he was struck on the head by the boom. Terrible shock for Harriet.'

'How awful,' said Jane inadequately. 'Poor woman.'

'Quite. They hadn't been married long and there were no children, which was probably a blessing. So there was poor Harriet, all on her own at twenty-seven. Luckily she's got a career to help her along but it was all very dreadful. He was such an experienced sailor too. She's been wonderfully stoic and she's coming to terms with it. Actually, it's odd really. One of the chaps she worked with in London has recently opened an estate agency in Tavistock—you may have seen it, he's called Barret-Thompson. He's asked her to become his partner. I think it would be a very good idea, she's got lots of friends down here, but she doesn't seem to quite know what she wants. Anyway, I'm sure you'd get on very well with her.'

Before Jane could comment the door opened and Oliver put his head in. 'Ollie, darling. So you're up at last. Do you know Mrs Maxwell? This is my elder son, Oliver, Jane.'

'I think we've seen each other in the village.' Oliver advanced with a proffered hand and gave Jane a blinding smile. 'How do you do? Don't get up, I don't want to interrupt anything.'

'Well, actually, I must be going,' said Jane awkwardly, shaking Oliver's hand and seizing the opportunity for escape. 'Honestly. Thanks for the coffee. No, I won't forget Saturday. I'll ask Alan when he gets home and I'll give you a buzz. Thanks a lot.'

Cass gave a frustrated sigh as the front door closed behind Jane and turned to Oliver, hovering in the hall.

'Oh, well, never mind. At least we've broken the ice again.'

'Sorry, Ma. Did I break it up? I didn't realise anyone was here.'

'No, no, darling. It's not your fault. I expect it'll sort itself out. Come on. Let's make some nice, hot coffee. Go and get the tray from the drawing room for me, darling.'

There's something wrong there, mused Cass as she went into the kitchen. I didn't help her at all. I must be losing my touch. Perhaps she just needs Alan home, that will probably sort things out. It will do them good to come to us.

Her thoughts drifted away from Jane and returned to Nick Farley. She was intrigued by him. He'd been very nice to her, allowing the fact that he found her very attractive to show. But he'd been very proper, not a foot out of place, and Cass was surprised how much she had thought of him since their short meeting on Sunday. He wasn't at all like the sort of man she usually felt drawn to: light-hearted, good fun, ready for pleasure. Nick was rather quiet, a serious, thoughtful type. He had watched her with a smile curling his long firm mouth, amusement lighting his hazel eyes, and Cass had felt rather young and giddy. Usually, she took the lead in her affairs, feeling almost patronising in her bestowal of favours upon these besotted males. She felt instinctively that with Nick it would be quite different and the thought excited her. She really couldn't bear the idea of not seeing him again and cursed herself for not plotting with Abby to get herself invited up to the Manor before he left.

Her heart lifted as she remembered that Abby would be coming back with the shopping later on. Cass gave a great sigh of relief. There was still time after all.

A FEW MILES AWAY Charlotte and Hugh Ankerton were sitting on an outcrop of rock on the western slopes of Dartmoor whilst their ponies grazed quietly below them. Though the sun was warm and the view glorious, neither Charlotte nor Hugh appeared to be deriving much pleasure from these blessings. Charlotte, dressed in old denims and an outsize navy blue jersey, her riding hat thrown down to reveal the newly cropped hair, sat hunched over her drawn-up knees. Hugh, a pleasant-looking youth, with long, ungainly limbs, floppy brown hair and spectacles hiding nice brown eyes, lounged a little below her plucking aimlessly at the sheep-bitten turf. Characteristically, he had made no comment on the hair. Invariably he treated Charlotte as one might a nervous animal, gently but firmly and with a great deal of kindness. When the silence threatened to become awkward he cleared his throat.

'I really think you should change your mind about Blundells. You shouldn't get so prejudiced about things. And after all, Oliver will be starting the same term. You'll know lots of people. Guy and Giles will be moving on to the Lower Sixth. There's a lot of Navy.'

'I wouldn't mind if you were still going to be there.' Her voice was muffled.

'I'll tell some of my friends to look out for you. Don't you want to get your A levels and go to a good university?'

Charlotte shrugged her hunched shoulders and picked at some lichen.

'Shouldn't think it makes much difference. I should probably hate it anyway.'

Hugh sighed. He was a near neighbour and just lately Charlotte had developed a tremendous crush on the kindly, sensitive boy. Although he was three years older than she was, he shared her passion for horses and they rode together sometimes. Charlotte kept her pony on their land and he had become used to her hanging about waiting to get a glimpse of him.

He smiled up at her and gave her leg a gentle push. 'Come on. Snap out of it. When are you going to come and see me at Blundells?'

She looked up quickly, her brown eyes serious.

'Do you want me to come and see you?'

'Of course I do. You can look round the school. Wait 'til there's a dance on or something.'

'You've got lots of friends,' she mumbled, head back on knees, knowing his popularity at school. 'Lots of girlfriends.' This was her private torment. 'You won't want me.'

'Of course I shall.' He resisted the urge to stroke her head as though she were an animal and, instead, captured a restless, plucking hand.

'Charlotte!' She looked up, blinking at his change of tone. 'You told me that you'd stopped biting your nails. You promised.' She tried to pull her hand away and he knelt up, holding it tightly. 'Are you still rowing with your mum over going away to school next year?'

The thought of that carefully prepared lunch, burnt and spoiled by the time Cass had eventually returned on Sunday, gave Charlotte the strength to pull her hand away and hide it with the other, under her knees. 'She just wants to get rid of me. She tried before but Daddy stood up for me. She can be really horrid.'

Hugh bit his lip. He had met Cass several times and couldn't imagine her being horrid to anybody.

'Well,' he said helplessly, 'promise you'll come to Blundells? We'll have lots of fun and you might change your mind. You will, won't you?'

'I will if you really want me to. If you don't think I'll let you down in front of your friends.'

Hugh sighed.

'Really, for a very intelligent girl you're sometimes awfully stupid.' He wondered whether to kiss her, decided that she was too young and ruffled her hair instead. 'Come on, up you get. I've got to get back.'

Charlotte scrambled to her feet, grabbed her hat and slid down the rocks after him. The day which had started so black now looked bright and golden, and full of promise.

Twenty

Kate paid the second-hand book seller for the full set of Galsworthy's *Forsyte Saga,* arranged to collect them later when she'd finished her shopping and turned away from his trestle tables. She stood for a moment, feeling in her pocket for her shopping list and trying to remember what she had actually come to buy. It was so easy to be distracted, especially by books. As she stood inhaling the smell of newly baked cakes, fresh vegetables, old books and all the other scents that made up the bouquet of market day in Tavistock, she caught a glimpse of Alex across the hall and her heart gave the familiar little tick of recognition, pain, even fear.

Why fear? she wondered as she made her way through the throng. Perhaps fear was too strong a word and anxiety was more accurate. It was memories of those last weeks: the arguments, justifications, the scenes that needed tact and understanding, the terror of losing all that had become so precious.

Well, she had lost it. Despite her care she had got it wrong, misjudged him and thrown it all away. And even now, more than two years on, it still hurt. She remembered how she had suffered at the thought of him with Pam after that awful Christmas when he had taken her abroad with him. It had been so difficult to accept that he was capable of it: that so soon after the minor miracle of their own love, he should turn back to Pam and carry on as if nothing had happened. That more than anything had been the most difficult to bear.

Probably, thought Kate as she made her way out of the hall at the furthest point from Alex, because it strikes at the most tender part of one's make-up: self-love, self-esteem. Impossible to imagine that another should be preferred to one's dear self. How dreadful it had been, working with him during those following months, unable to touch him or talk to him as she had been used to, with Pam coming in and out, openly proprietorial, flaunting her ownership, as it were. It had hurt so much that he had allowed it. Knowing how she loved him, how capable of jealousy she was, that he had sat back and let her suffer had first surprised and then disappointed her. She had attributed a sort of greatness to him that would have been above such petty, even cruel, behaviour. She remembered the evenings that he had talked her through the pain of her marriage with Mark, the insight, the depth of awareness, and was simply unable to relate this to the Alex who allowed Pam to fawn on him and possess him so publicly. It was almost as if he was stating: Well, you might not love me enough but someone does. So there! It had hurt Kate to acknowledge this weakness in him and it had come as a tremendous relief when she could finally give in her notice and leave the shop forever.

But after all, she thought, pausing to stare in at the butcher's window, he isn't a saint. Why should he be more than human?

Perhaps she was happier alone. No, not necessarily happier but more peaceful. She was used to being alone but now she had freedom with it. There were subtle differences in being alone as a married woman and being alone as an unattached one. And if total freedom also carried with it the downside of loneliness, well, she was used to that too. And in her case it was hardly true. She still had the twins although, at fifteen, they were beginning to grow up and become more independent. And Chris would be home for Christmas, now only a few weeks away.

It had taken nearly a year to sell the cottage and to find and buy the house on the edge of Whitchurch, just outside Tavistock. It was a roomy Victorian family house with a paddock at the end of the garden. There had been enough money to buy and sort out the house but the kennels were still as yet a thing of the future, although there were outbuildings with which to make a very good start. When Honey had her litter Kate, having kept the best dog puppy to use as a stud dog, sold the others at good prices and, although she was well aware that without Chris's financial support she would be unable to cope, nevertheless felt that, slowly, she was getting there.

She finished her shopping and headed back to the Bedford Hotel for coffee. As she stood waiting to cross the road she thought, as she so often did, of the General and one of the things he had been fond of quoting: ' . . . all shall be well and all manner of thing shall be well.' She put her shopping in the car and went up the back steps and into the bar. She spied Felicity in the corner with a couple of her cronies and waved. She received a sour little smile in return and grinned to herself. Felicity didn't change. It seemed like light years ago that Cass had confronted her on the Rectory steps when she had been so upset about George being turned out of the cottage. It had all seemed so important at the time. Kate shook her head. She was beginning to wonder whether anything really mattered at all. She thought about it while she drank her coffee and it was only when she was halfway home that she realised that she'd forgotten to pick up her books.

CASS WAS PREPARING FOR the great festival with a light heart. Hugh Ankerton had invited Charlotte to a sixth-form Christmas Social and, quite overcome and dithering between a mixture of terror and bliss, she had been driven over to Tiverton by Tom, who had gone to see some friends who lived nearby and then fetched her back afterwards. Whether or not Hugh had primed his friends Cass would never know but Charlotte returned in a state of exaltation heightened by the fact that the Christmas holidays were very near and Hugh would be coming home for several weeks. Cass was not deceived. She knew that this visit would by no means persuade Charlotte that she would be happy at Blundells. After all, the twins would be starting in the sixth form with her and if the thought of having Giles at hand was not comforting enough, she couldn't imagine anything else would be. Nevertheless, having Charlotte in a receptive, happy mood might make her open to suggestion and that would be a start.

More to the point regarding Cass's own pleasure was the fact that Abby and William were giving a Christmas party to which Nick Farley had been invited. She was surprised at how very much she was looking forward to meeting him again although Abby had warned her that his wife would be with him. Cass had disregarded that. Wives never figured in her calculations except in the vital assessment of how easy they would be to deceive. However, in her experience, once the husband wished to deceive then, it seemed, nobody was more gullible than a loving wife.

It had been a definite blow to her ego that Nick had done nothing to follow up their two meetings in the autumn. She had been quite sure of his interest in her and day after day, after he had left the Manor, she had waited for a telephone call. He didn't even mention her name in the bread-and-butter letter that he sent to Abby. Cass had been puzzled and decided to put him out of her mind. She had been only partially successful. Having discovered where his firm had their offices in Plymouth, she had, once or twice after shopping, lunched in places which he might reasonably be expected to frequent. There had been no sign of him. On several separate occasions her heart had missed a beat at the sight of a tall, grey-haired man in a city suit but it was never Nick. She felt that she was behaving like a silly girl, like Charlotte waylaying Hugh at the stables, and resolved to do no more of it.

When Abby told her of the party, she felt the old excitement rising. William was still having problems with this long drawn-out boundary dispute and Nick, so Abby said, had the reputation for being the best litigation lawyer this side of Bristol. Anyway, William got on very well with him and had decided to ask him to the party and he had accepted. None of them had met his wife yet and Cass was looking forward to it with rather mixed feelings. She had already determined on her strategy. By no action or word of hers would Nick know that he had occupied her mind for a moment, but if she couldn't make him sit up and take notice then she was really losing her touch.

Cass put her mince pies in the oven with a feeling of anticipatory pleasure. Nick was fast becoming a challenge to her, someone on which to practise all her skills. She smiled to herself as she set the timer. It was an occasion that would require all her expertise and experience and, without doubt, the first requirement in her armoury would be a new outfit.

Tom was merely hoping for a quiet leave. There was always enough to do around the place to occupy his time and he was quite content, the jobs done, to doze in front of the television or catch up on a bit of reading. He was praying that Cass wasn't planning to fill the house with people who would eat his food and drink his booze and bore him to death. It wasn't that he was becoming anti-social as Cass said but just that he was getting older. They'd had a bit of a row when Cass had accused him of that. She had said that he was becoming a bore and he had been stung to retort that it was about time she grew up. She was getting too old to be the femme fatale of every social gathering and he'd said so. He'd told her that she should leave it to the younger women, that it was undignified at her age and merely embarrassed people. Cass had laughed at him but he'd felt guilty afterwards.

He was hoping too that Charlotte's education wasn't going to be a major issue. He was concerned as to where she would go after her O levels and Blundells seemed quite a good idea. He wasn't quite so worried at the thought of her going away as he had been four years before—he felt that she was old enough now to cope with boarding, especially with Oliver and the twins at hand—neither was he quite so anxious that she was there to put a brake on Cass's activities. Despite his disparaging remarks, she seemed to have settled down in the last few years, quite happy with her social round and he had seen no evidence of any extramarital activity. She still liked to flirt at parties but there was no real harm in it. After all, it must be hard for an attractive woman to grow old.

It hadn't occurred to Tom that, even if Charlotte were to witness anything improper, she would never tell him about it. She adored her father and the last thing that she would want to do would be to hurt him. After all, what could he do? There would be rows and fights, which she hated, and it could all result in a separation and divorce and then she might never see him. She was no longer a little girl who might drop Cass in it unintentionally and although her presence might hinder Cass, she would never betray her. Charlotte felt that she did indeed keep Cass under control—up to a point—and she had no intention of going away to school where she could no longer keep an eye on things. Anything could happen and Charlotte was determined to stay put and keep the family together.

Tom, unaware of the undercurrents, felt that there was plenty of time yet before the decision need be taken and made up his mind that he wouldn't let his Christmas leave be disrupted by it.

OF ALL OF THEM, Jane enjoyed Christmas least. Worried that things were getting out of hand with Philip, she had started Alan's leave full of good intentions. At the very least it gave her the opportunity to have a break from Philip, who was spending the holiday with his mother and sister in Moretonhampstead. If only she could have some time alone with Alan, she felt that things might settle down again and be as they were when they were first married, before Alan had been promoted. No sooner was he home, however, than there was a party on the submarine at which, after he had been drinking rather heavily, he announced that he and Jane would be giving a New Year party and that all present were invited. Whilst Jane was speechless with shock and horror, the other officers and their wives had accepted with great enthusiasm. By the time she regained her faculty of speech the thing was done and there was no going back on it. Plead though Jane might—and she did—that he should cancel it, Alan was adamant. He would look a fool, he said, and when Jane protested that he'd been drunk and could say that he'd forgotten a long-standing arrangement that couldn't be put off, he became angry, told her to pull herself together and accused her of being a spoilsport and other things. The invitation had been made and the party would go forward.

All Jane's good intentions vanished into thin air. The thought of the party dominated every waking hour and although Alan, having simmered down a bit and feeling that he'd been the least bit high-handed, told her that he'd help her to organise it, the whole thing was a nightmare to her. Alan had been to quite enough parties to know what was needed and in the end Jane went to Mrs Hampton, who had helped out at enough of Cass's parties, to ask her for some advice on how to deal with the catering. Alan's assurance that all that was necessary was to give people enough to drink and the party would run itself was no comfort to her. She visualised noisy, screaming people, cigarette burns on her precious tables and wine spilt on her new carpet. She could have almost hated him.

By the time that it was all over—and just as dreadful as she'd feared—she was relieved to see him go back to sea and to welcome Philip back into her life.

CASS DID A LITTLE better. By the end of Abby's party she was almost in despair. Nick behaved throughout with the utmost propriety, staying close to his wife and behaving like a devoted husband. She was a short well-built woman, at least five years older than he and making no effort whatever to hide the fact. Her iron grey hair was cut short, her face was unadorned. Her name was Sarah. Cass dismissed her almost at once, seeing in this middle-aged woman no mettle worthy of her steel. She was charming to her and took care to treat Nick with a friendly indifference calculated to re-stimulate his interest. He made no effort to rise to the bait and she began seriously to wonder if she'd misread that earlier interest. However, once or twice she took him unawares and caught him watching her with an expression which Cass could only interpret in one way. On one of the occasions he raised his eyebrows slightly and she stared at him, unable to look away, until somebody spoke to him and he turned to answer him. In the bustle of farewells he carried her hand to his lips and turning it, held the palm against his mouth until she felt that he must feel the blood pounding in her veins. The look he gave her when they parted kept her awake most of the night beside the snoring Tom.

For the first time in her life she felt out of her depth. She barely noticed when Tom went back to sea or the children to school. She haunted the hall, anxious to be within the sound of the telephone's bell. Once she telephoned his office but put the receiver back when the receptionist answered. After all, what could she say to him? And then, one morning in early-February, he telephoned. He said that he would be in Exeter the following day. If she happened to be there shopping perhaps she might like to lunch? Stammering a little, Cass said that she had been meaning to go up to shop. Excellent, he said, and named a restaurant. He added that he was quite sure that she would understand if he asked that their meeting must appear to be quite unpremeditated and that he could trust her to be discreet. She agreed at once and he suggested a time and hung up.

It was the first of many similar meetings, always at his instigation, always in public if secluded places. He was charming, amusing, delightful company. And very attractive.

By the time Easter had arrived, Cass was obsessed, in love as never before and Jane was pregnant.

HARRIET STOOD AT THE bedroom window watching Tom mow the Rectory lawn. He was cross. Harriet could almost feel his crossness emanating upwards from the hunched back, tensed arms and fast-striding legs. Furiously he drove the lawn-mower across the grass, jabbing it violently, if ineffectually, into tall, weedy clumps and only pausing to swipe his forearm across his perspiring brow.

The sweet, piercing joy of seeing him again battled, as usual, with other emotions in Harriet's breast—terror lest he should perceive her love for him, jealousy of his blind love for his wife and rage at Cass's treatment of him. However, for the first time ever, shortly after her arrival earlier that afternoon, she had seen Tom angry.

'Hell's teeth, Cass, not another bloody dinner party! Every time I come home the place is full of people. No, not you, Harriet love.' Pausing behind Harriet's chair, Tom placed his hands on her shoulders as she made a convulsive movement, as if to rise from the kitchen table and flee. 'It's always lovely to see you, you're one of the family. It's all these others, and having to dress up and play the host when I want to relax.' His thumbs idly massaged Harriet's neck muscles as he remained behind her, staring across at Cass who leaned against the old oak dresser.

'Darling.' Cass's voice held a caressing, faintly teasing note. 'Don't think I don't understand. I know how you love it when we're all on our own but life goes on while you're at sea and it's not always possible to drop everything when you come home. I have responsibilities too, you know.'

Harriet almost cried out as Tom's fingers bit into her collar-bones.

'Forgive me if I seem more than usually obtuse.' His voice was very cool. 'But I can't quite see where your responsibilities lie in this particular case. Are you saying that it's your duty to get the Hope-Latymers tight on my booze and to be bored rigid by that tedious Alan Maxwell and his dreary wife?'

Cass retained her expression of amused affection although she raised her eyebrows as if reproving him mentally for his lapse in good manners. Harriet, however, was aware of an inner conflict. Cass was trying to decide whether she should adopt the air of a wronged wife, struggling to keep home and family together in her husband's absence, or to let her hair down and have a blazing row. She decided that Cass would find her decision easier to make without a third party spectator and rose determinedly from beneath Tom's weight.

'I must go and unpack,' she said. 'Will you excuse me?'

Cass seized her opportunity triumphantly.

'Well, I hope you're satisfied, Tom. You've made poor Harriet feel thoroughly unwelcome.'

'I'm sorry, Harriet.' His apologetic hug would have been lovely if it hadn't been so absentminded. 'Honestly, this is nothing to do with you.'

'I know.' She returned his embrace. 'All the same, I must hang up my dress or it will look like an old rag this evening. See you later.'

She paused at the door to look back and saw that Tom was not going to eat humble pie. He had quite forgotten her and was gazing at Cass with a total lack of affection, the kitchen table stretching between them like a battlefield.

Having gained her room and hung up her dress Harriet heard the garden door slam and, a few moments later, the sound of the lawn-mower's engine. Evidently Tom had decided to work off his spleen in frenzied activity.

As he vanished from her line of vision to the lawns at the side of the house Harriet moved back from the window and sat down in a comfort-able wicker chair. The tall room was filled with evening sunlight which turned the ivory-painted walls gold and glinted on the old mahogany furniture. Harriet closed her eyes against it and let her mind rerun the old well-worn pictures: Tom and she dancing at a Christmas Ball: walk-ing with him along some cliffs during a picnic: sitting next to him during dinner parties. Each scene and accompanying conversation was so well-thumbed that it was amazing that she wasn't heartily sick of him. Yet she wasn't. No matter how long the period between their meetings nor how short those meetings were, Tom retained a hold over her imagination that no other man she had met since Ralph's death had been able to loosen.

Harriet, who did not believe in love at first sight, had been quite content with her relationship with Ralph. It had grown out of having certain interests in common and enjoying each other's company, al-though not enough to preclude their having individual hobbies and friends which they continued to pursue after they were married. In fact, Harriet had always rather despised those couples who professed to be so passionately in love that they couldn't spend more than ten minutes apart without getting withdrawal symptoms. So, when she met Tom at that Summer Ball and he had taken her in his arms and kissed her—on the strength, so he explained, of his long-standing friendship with Ralph—she was totally unprepared for the wave of emotion which engulfed her. She had fallen in love for the first time in her life and she got it badly.

The thought of him possessed her. She didn't see him often enough to have any idea of the real Tom. She only ever met him in the framework of social events, where he was at his best, and from which—like any lovesick teenager—she built up a dream which in due course began to destroy the reality of her life with Ralph.

Ralph's death came as a terrible shock and Harriet felt remorse and guilt but no real grief. Self-sufficient to begin with, they had by then drifted so far apart that it was more like losing a very good friend than a husband. Harriet, knowing that she had cut him out of her life, suffered terrible attacks of guilt and had submerged herself in her work, thankful that at least she no longer had to keep up the pretence. Her consolation was that Ralph hadn't been in love with her either and, even in the very beginning, had always spent just as much time on his boat as he had with her. They had congratulated themselves on their sensible, undemanding way of conducting their relationship and mocked gently, in private, the muddled, passionate affairs of their friends.

Tom and Cass had been wonderful after the accident. It had been Tom, urged on by Cass, who had sorted out the legal side of things and had helped her to organise herself financially whilst Cass had, as much as was possible at such a distance, drawn her into their home circle in an effort to shield her against loneliness.

An old friend, with whom she had worked in London, had just opened his own estate agent's office in Tavistock and was urging Harriet to come in with him as a partner. Harriet was tempted. Although the thought of taking a partnership was a terrifying one, she knew that it was time to make a change, to take a new and positive direction in her life. A quiet country town like Tavistock would be a good place to start and, after all, she knew quite a few naval families in the area, the Wivenhoes for one.

Harriet stirred in her chair and glanced at her watch. Heavens! she must have been dreaming. She rose and went into the adjoining bathroom to run her bath, wondering what mood Tom would be in for the party. Her heart fluttered slightly at the thought of seeing him again so soon and, flinging off her clothes, she went into the bathroom and closed the door.

WHEN CASS TOLD TOM that he had made Harriet feel unwelcome she was not merely trying to induce guilt. Nick Farley was once again staying with Abby and William and they were bringing him to the party. Sarah had not accompanied him this time and Cass had been visited with a most uncharacteristic show of nerves at the thought of seeing Nick, here in her own home, at the party. Her confidence that she could continue the flirtation under Tom's eye had evaporated a little. Of course, she and Tom had had rows before but never had she known him so implacable, so unmoved by the explanations that, after Harriet's departure from the kitchen, she had felt it necessary to give him. Indeed, never before had Tom behaved so before another person with the possible exception of Kate. Of course, it was only old Harriet. Cass smiled a little as she sat before her dressing table screwing in her ear-rings. She was well aware of Harriet's feelings for Tom and suddenly she began to wonder if they could be put to good use. Most of us are flattered at the thought of someone being in love with us and Tom, in Cass's opinion, would be no exception. Would he not, at such a disclosure, be distracted not only from his ill-temper but also from Cass's plans for Nick? She decided that the situation was serious enough to give it a try. Her mind worked busily for some time, assembling various pieces of information: one being that Tom had to make a visit to the Ministry of Defence in London and another being that Harriet had to drive back to Lee-on-Solent on Sunday so as to be back in her office on Monday. When Tom emerged from the shower she was ready for him.

'Will you be going up to London by train on Monday, darling?'

'I suppose so.' Tom still sounded grumpy. He hated being addressed as 'darling' when they were having a row.

'You see, I was just thinking. Harriet's got to go back tomorrow and knowing how she hates driving alone and how you hate the train I was wondering if you couldn't go together. Of course she'd be thrilled to bits.'

'I didn't know that Harriet hated driving.'

'Well, it's not so much the driving as being on her own. Of course she'd hate it if she thought we knew but I've spent a lot of time with her, trying to cheer her along, and she's let a few things drop. And, apart from that, just the thought of all that time together, just the two of you! Well, she'd think that she'd died and gone to heaven.'

'What d'you mean?'

'Oh, come on, darling. If you don't know that Harriet's madly in love with you you're the only one who doesn't.'

Through her mirror Cass watched Tom's reaction with satisfaction.

'Harriet? In love with . . . Oh, for heaven's sake, Cass, don't talk rubbish!'

'I assure you, darling, I know what I'm talking about. A woman always knows, especially when her own husband is involved. She's been in love with you for years. I'm only amazed that you never seemed to notice it. Normally I wouldn't have said a word, loyalty to one's sex and all that, but poor Harriet's a bit low this weekend. Of course I wouldn't expect you to notice things like that, but your outburst didn't exactly help, sweetie. I've always tried to make this a second home for Harriet and I hate to think of her feeling in the way. She's such a sensitive girl.'

'Oh, hell,' said Tom. 'I just didn't notice. I'm sorry. But even so, Cass. In love . . . ? Oh, honestly.'

'Well, don't take my word for it. But you just keep your eyes open for a change. And try to be nice to her. I know you always are and there are times when she's been here since Ralph died when you'd rather she hadn't. But make an effort tonight. Life's not easy for her, all on her own.'

'Oh, hell. I'm sorry. I wouldn't upset her for the world . . . '

'Of course you wouldn't, darling, I know that. These things happen. That's why I thought that the prospect of a few hours with you alone tomorrow would cheer her no end. And you wouldn't have to catch the beastly train. Or at least, only from Portsmouth.' Cass paused. 'I'm sure you'd find somewhere to spend the night, perhaps Harriet would offer her spare room . . . ' (Let that one sink in, mustn't push too far.)

'Anyway, think about it. And cheer up, darling. Can't we kiss and make up? I hate to face the evening out of sorts.'

'Yes, of course.' Grappling with this new idea Tom obediently kissed the raised cheek. 'I'm sorry, I honestly didn't mean to upset anyone.'

'Of course not. Let's forget the whole thing, shall we, and have a lovely, jolly evening? I must go and see to the dinner.' And Cass left the room exulting at the success of her plan. So far so good.

WHEN TOM SAW HARRIET enter the drawing room later that evening it was as if he were seeing her for the first time. He had always thought her a very attractive girl but now he really noticed the short dark shining cap of hair, the wide blue-green eyes and the long lovely legs and narrow feet. She wore a Laura Ashley dress in figure-hugging navy blue needle cord with a pattern of dark red flowers scattered across it, sheer navy blue stockings and flat navy leather pumps.

Cass was playing games at present, keeping well away from Nick, flirting in a purely social way with Alan and keeping up the pretence that Nick had been invited to pair off with Harriet. Since Tom— much to Cass's delight—was monopolising Harriet and William was trying to charm Jane out of her paralysing shyness, Nick was left with Annabel who, with great amusement, watched the proceedings through a screen of cigarette smoke.

'You're looking very beautiful, Harriet. Can I get you a drink? Gin and tonic, isn't it?' (Cass must have been making it up. She looks so cool and remote.)

'Am I? Thank you. Yes, please. No ice.' (I sound so stilted. I wish I could be relaxed and natural with him.)

'I want to apologise for earlier, I was an absolute boor . . . Here, take your drink.' (Her fingers are icy cold. Can she possibly be nervous? Perhaps, after all . . .)

'Oh, thank you. Look, please don't apologise, honestly . . . ' (He's looking at me very oddly. I wonder if he started drinking early. He was very upset.)

'It was unforgivable and I hope that you didn't think for a minute that I'm not delighted to see you . . . ' (This is ridiculous, I've known her for years, dammit, and we sound like strangers. If only I could touch her.)

'Of course I know, Tom. Please don't give it another thought.' (Oh God, how good and kind he is. I wish he'd touch me, I'd probably go up in flames.)

'I was wondering if I could beg a lift from you tomorrow.' (I didn't mean to ask that yet. Christ! She looks radiant. As if someone switched a light on. Cass must be right. Christ . . .)

' . . . and so, you see, it was an absolute disaster, so next year we're going to try Portugal. What d'you think?' (And who the bloody hell cares what you think? You are the most boring girl I've ever met. Must have another drink.)

'Well, I really don't know, Mr Hope-Latymer, I've never been abroad.' (Oh God, why did I come? I knew it would be awful. I told Alan that long skirts are out of date now, I feel a right freak. And this awful drink . . .)

'Please call me William, won't you? Have I told you how charming you look? Delightfully Victorian. Let me fill up your glass. No, no, I insist, I shan't be a moment.' (And it gives me a break.) 'Now stay just where you are, Jane. How well the name Jane suits you, very grave and demure.' (And boring, boring, boring. Now where are the drinks? I need a good strong one.)

· 'Yes, all right then, thank you.' (I don't want another bloody drink and what he means is that I'm plain and dull. Look at her sitting there all over Alan. And he's loving it, the way she keeps touching his arm and his knee. God, it makes me sick . . .)

'Come now, Alan. You can't expect me to believe things like that.' (This is too easy. He only needs a little encouragement. And Nick is watching. Mustn't overdo it, though. There's something fastidious about him . . .)

'No, honestly, Cass, I mean it. You don't look old enough to be anybody's mother . . . ' (Why can't Jane relax? She looks so out of place. What the hell am I going to do about her? I wish I wasn't going away tomorrow . . .)

'How very sweet.' (I wonder what he's thinking. I'm not going to throw myself at him. Old Tom's swallowed the bait—hook, line and sinker. Well, it won't do him any harm and Harriet's old enough to look after herself.)

She smiled at Alan and rose to her feet.

'Come along, everybody. Time to eat. Shall we go in?'

THE EVENING FOR CHARLOTTE was a black dismal failure. Cass had been delighted to find that Mr and Mrs Ankerton were giving a party for their daughter who had just become engaged, and Hugh had invited Charlotte. She was just getting to the age when she felt that she should be included in her parents' parties and aware of, although not quite understanding, Charlotte's antagonism towards her, Cass knew that her presence at tonight's party would throw a damper on her flirting with Nick and was deeply relieved when her daughter told her of her invitation to the Ankertons' party.

'Have a lovely time, darling,' she had said, 'and wear something pretty. You can look so attractive when you try.'

The remark still rankled as Charlotte sorted through her clothes on Saturday afternoon. She would be herself. She would not dress herself up and mince around trying to attract men like Cass did. Anyway, Hugh liked her the way she was . . .

Hugh's heart sank as Charlotte hurried out to meet him and climbed into the car. She wore a long black garment that drooped round her ankles and soft leather laced-up booties. A scarf had been tied inexpertly round her head to hide her hair which was in the process of growing out. She was obviously dreadfully nervous and, once they'd arrived, this took the form of an offhand indifference which made it very difficult for Hugh to introduce her and persuade her to join in.

It was aggravated by the presence of a very attractive girl of about eighteen, a distant relation, who had just returned from some years abroad and who was very taken with Hugh. Lucinda, for this was her name, did attempt conversation with Charlotte, whose abrupt answers and refusal to look at her finally made Lucinda raise her eyebrows at Hugh and wander away.

He was getting desperate. He felt very sorry for Charlotte but, after all, it was a party and Lucinda was rather fun. Presently he went off to get Charlotte some food from the buffet. She watched his progress anxiously. Surely he'd gone quite deliberately to where Lucinda was selecting her supper? Why did he stand so long talking to her instead of just grabbing some food and coming straight back? She watched him laughing at something Lucinda said and the way her fair hair shone and how slim she looked in her elegant flowered dress.

As despair and jealousy swept over Charlotte she suddenly felt unbearably hot in her heavy clothes and, leaping up, she fled out into the cool spring air.

When, some time later, Hugh found her they had a terrible row. Hugh, refusing to recede from his position that he was merely being friendly to a guest and relation, nevertheless tried, unsuccessfully, to reassure her. Finally he drove her home where she cried herself to sleep.

ON SUNDAY MORNING TOM and Harriet left for Hampshire, Tom driving.

On Sunday afternoon Cass went out for a walk with the dog and the announced intention of checking the cottage she was caretaking for the Mallinsons who were abroad. She had mentioned this publicly at the party and arranged with Nick privately that he would meet her there.

On Sunday evening Alan Maxwell was picked up by a brother officer and driven down to Plymouth dockyard. They were sailing very early the next morning.

Charlotte spent the day in bed.

Twenty-one

During the night someone had moved Harriet's bedroom window. Drowsy and relaxed, she was aware that the morning light, flooding in from somewhere at the foot of the bed, should be coming in from her left. She rolled over lazily and saw a rumpled, empty stretch of bed and a blank wall. For a moment she stared, half raised on her elbow. 'Hell!' she said as she flopped back on to her own side of the bed.

The previous day's journey back to Hampshire had been uneventful. She and Tom were two old friends discussing, amongst other things, Tom's family and the offer that Harriet had received from Michael Barrett-Thompson, her friend in Tavistock. About this Tom was very enthusiastic and he got so far, during lunch, as to suggest where she might live when she moved down. Later, as they passed through Fareham, they stopped to pick up some Chinese take-away before driving into Lee-on-Solent. The sea lapped quietly against the deserted beach and the Isle of Wight floated mistily on the horizon.

There seem to be no question that Tom would stay anywhere but in Harriet's semi-detached Victorian house in its peaceful tree-lined street. He drove the car into the garage while Harriet hurried indoors to turn up the central heating and put some wine in the fridge. Suddenly she was nervous. The tranquillity of the day had gone and she felt brittle and shy.

'Which room can I have?' Tom appeared in the kitchen doorway, calm, unhurried, holding his naval grip.

'Oh, yes.' Flustered, she tried to think clearly. 'I'm in the little room at the back. I know it sounds odd but I hate big bedrooms and big beds if I'm on my own . . . ' (God, what was she saying?) 'The big one at the front. The bed's not made up.' She plunged into the fridge, grateful for the blast of icy air on her burning face.

'Right.' Tom hefted his grip and was gone.

While he was upstairs Harriet warmed plates, set a match to the fire in the sitting room, stood the gate leg table before it and laid it ready for supper. She dashed off for a quick pee and a tidy-up in the downstairs loo. Still no Tom.

Back into the kitchen to fetch the cheese, no bread, of course, but plenty of crackers. Where on earth was he? She poured herself a large gin and tonic and, gulping it back, heard Tom's footsteps on the stairs.

After that things became hazy. Two gins and tonic and several glasses of wine removed the feeling of tension and she relaxed into her chair, enjoying the Chinese food, revelling in the fact of his presence and knowing that what would follow was inevitable, that she had been waiting for it for years. When, much later, Tom rose to his feet, she rose too, as if pulled by an invisible string.

'Come here, Harriet love,' he murmured, and she went to him slowly as though wading through water.

He put an arm about her and helped her up the stairs to his room, murmuring almost inaudibly to her. She stood, dazed and docile, whilst he stripped her jersey from her and unbuttoned her shirt. Then, with a swift movement he pushed her flat on her back on the big double bed. She remembered thinking, as her fingers felt smooth sheets and blankets beneath her, so that was what he was doing, before giving herself up completely to pleasure.

Now, on Monday morning, she sat up, swung her feet out of bed and came face-to-face with herself in the dressing-table mirror. From its corner hung a large white sheet of paper.

'Harriet, love,' the sprawling writing was barely legible, 'have to dash off or I'll be late in London. Will be back later today. Hope to get a few days off. Love, Tom.'

She telephoned the office to say that she was unwell and wouldn't be in for a few days and went into the kitchen. Whilst she made coffee one niggling thought disturbed the surface of her dreaming bliss. Why was she so surprised that Tom had been so good at it, so experienced, so aware of what gave pleasure? After all, he'd been married a good many years, why shouldn't he be? After a while she realised that it was because he had seemed so relaxed, so easy, in the role of lover. She had always imagined him as being faithful to Cass but there had certainly been nothing in his behaviour last night to indicate that he had felt uneasy at committing adultery. After all, Cass's reputation was fairly well-known and certainly no one would have criticised Tom for getting his own back a little. It would hardly be surprising if, over seventeen or so years of marriage, he hadn't strayed a little. And really, there was no reason at all why it should matter. But somehow, it did.

JANE MET MRS HAMPTON on the steps of the village shop.

''Ow are you then, Jane? I 'ear that 'usband of yours went off again yesterday. What about poppin' in for a cuppa tea?'

'Yes, yes he has.' She'd been surprisingly sorry to see him go. He'd been very nice to her after Cass's party, more like the man he'd been before the promotion. 'Well. All right then, thanks, but I was just going to get some shopping.'

'Well, you do that an' I'll go an' get the kettle on. No 'urry.'

Funny, Jane thought later, how particular these old dears were. Mrs Hampton's tea service was of the finest bone china, the teapot was silver. A cake stand bearing a feather-light sponge and a plateful of tiny, hot scones stood beside a low table drawn up to the brightly burning fire. Not for her, thought Jane, a mug at the kitchen table with the cake tin open beside it. She had a brief mental vision of Cass and Abby in just that situation, as she'd seen them not long ago. Ah, but they didn't feel the need to impress, did they? Did Mrs Hampton? She'd picked up her fine ways at the Hall, parlourmaid was it, or tweeny? Anyway, she knew just how the gentry did it.

Mrs Hampton appeared with the hot water jug and sat down.

'Now then. Milk?'

'Yes, please.' Jane took the cup and saucer and fiddled awkwardly with the silver sugar tongs. Why not just some granulated and a spoon?

'So 'ow long's 'e gone for this time?'

'Not too long.' The sugar went in with a plop. 'Only a couple of weeks and then he's leaving.'

'What! Not leavin' the Navy?'

'Oh, no. Just the submarine. Seems he's got a shore job coming up. A nuclear sub in Chatham. It's in refit.'

'Chatham.' Mrs Hampton nodded thoughtfully. 'Nice county, Kent. My Jack was there durin' the war for a bit. He was Army, mind. Went up an' stayed with 'im for a few days' embarkation leave. What a time that was. Yes, you'll like it up there—if you're goin', that is!' She regarded Jane, birdlike, head on one side, eyes bright.

'What d'you mean?' Jane's cup clattered against the saucer and she put it back on the table.

'Mean?' Mrs Hampton passed Jane the scones and offered her home-made raspberry jam and clotted cream. ' 'Ave one of these.'

'Well.' Jane regarded the food whilst nausea, her constant companion, made warning signals off. 'I don't know.'

'Feelin' a bit off, are you? Sick perhaps?' The bright eyes seemed to bore into her and Jane felt a twinge of fear.

'No. No, of course not.' She took one, helping herself to jam and cream. 'They look delicious. Just thinking about my waistline.' Stupid thing to say as it drew Mrs Hampton's eyes straight to it.

'No, what I meant, Jane, was that some of these wives don't go round with their 'usbands, do they? That may be right when the children start school an' the marriage is good an' steady. 'Tisn't wise in the early years.'

'Don't you think so?' Jane chewed and swallowed valiantly.

'A woman should be with 'er 'usband, 'tis only right an' proper. 'Usbands tend to stray unless they'm watched. Stands to reason, they won't come 'ome so readily if it means a long journey, they'll find their comforts closer to 'and. Wives stray too, o'course, don't they?'

Jane caught her breath, choked, eyes streaming, and fumbled for her handkerchief.

''Course, you can't go to sea with 'em, stands to reason,' Mrs Hampton passed Jane a large linen napkin, 'but you can be waitin' on the dock when 'e gets in. Men 're lazy creatures. They don't generally go botherin' after other women if they're 'appy at 'ome.'

Jane mopped her eyes and gulped at her lukewarm tea, fighting rising nausea.

'And what if it's the other way round?'

'Well, women d'get bored easy if they'm left alone too long. An' then 'tis off with the old an' on with the new.' She paused. 'An' then again, with some, 'tis more a case of off with the new an' back on with the old, isn't it? Either way, 'tisn't wise. An' then, o' course, a woman likes a bit of security, especially when there're babies on the way . . . '

'Oh, my God . . . ' Jane stumbled to her feet, clutched her stomach and vomited dreadfully into Mrs Hampton's clean grate.

CHARLOTTE, JUST BACK FROM her ride, was standing at the kitchen table reading Cass's note when Hugh pulled up in his old Morris 1000.

She stood, hardly breathing, listening to the familiar clunk of the engine and the way the driver's door rattled when it was slammed. She'd looked for him when she'd ridden out but there had been no sign of him and his car was not in the usual place. She dropped the note and fled into the garden to meet him.

'Hi.' He smiled uncertainly. 'Just came to see if you were OK and, well, to say goodbye.'

'Goodbye?'

'Yes.' He forced a cheerful note into his voice. 'Back to school to-morrow, remember? I wanted to see you before I went.' Accurately judging her mood to be one of remorse he went forward confidently and put his arm around her shoulder. 'How about making me some coffee?'

'Yes, OK.' She turned back into the kitchen. 'It's come so quickly.'

'Yes, hasn't it?' Hugh tried to harden his heart against her stricken look and failed miserably. She was only a child really. 'You must come up again this term.' Fool, he told himself, make a clean break. This was even more desirable now he knew that Lucinda lived only ten miles from Bristol where he hoped to be going to university in the autumn.

'Will there be another Social?' Oh, why had she fought with him when time was so short?

'Bound to be something on in the summer term. Have you been out riding?' A nod as she put coffee into the mugs. She couldn't trust her voice. 'Usual place, I suppose. Don't forget to keep off the path past the quarry. The fence along the top was broken down in that storm and the quarry's flooded.'

'Oh, don't go on. You sound like Ma.'

'Well, we care about you. Where is your mum?'

'Out.' Charlotte indicated the note indifferently. 'Doesn't know how long she'll be and can I get Gemma some tea? She's with some man, I expect.'

'Honestly! Must you be so dramatic? What man?'

'Dunno. But I bet she is. Somewhere.'

TOM ARRIVED BACK JUST as it was getting dark. Harriet had been waiting for him, all on edge, for at least an hour. The question was, how did one behave to the husband of one's best friend when, overnight, literally, said husband had become one's lover? Would he refer to it directly, pretend it hadn't happened at all or carry on where he'd left off? He'd had all day to think about it, regret it, perhaps. He might not even turn up. She would probably get a polite little letter in a few days' time, carefully worded . . . The door handle turned quietly and he was standing there smiling at her.

'Hi.'

She leaped up and stood rooted to the spot. 'Hello. I—I didn't hear you arrive. The taxi . . . '

'Oh, he dropped me on the front. I walked the rest.'

'How did you go this morning?'

'Same thing. Phoned from here for the taxi, met him on the front. Don't want to advertise the fact that I'm here.'

'No. No, I suppose not. I hadn't thought of that . . . ' (It's rather sordid somehow, oh dear . . .)

'Well, I'm thinking of you, love.' (Have been all day. Who'd have thought that cool, calm Harriet would be such a hot one. Couldn't wait to get back . . .) 'I don't want to ruin your reputation.' (Or mine, come to that. After all I know plenty of naval families in Lee.)

'Yes, of course. I just wasn't thinking.' (Well, not about that anyway. I hope he's got some time off.) 'Had a good day?' (God! I sound just like a boring wife. But what on earth would a mistress say?)

'Blow all that! Come and say hello properly. Aah! That's better.' (She's gone all shy and nervous again, soon take care of that.) I've been looking forward to this all day, no concentration whatever. Mmm.'

'Oh, Tom, I've missed you too.' (Oh God, I do so want him.)

'Just one more. Mmm. Now let me see. Where had we got to when I had to rush away this morning? Shall we go upstairs and try to refresh our memories?'

Much later, struck by a wonderful idea, she raised her head from his shoulder.

'Tom! Why don't we go to Tavistock for a few days? I could see Michael and we could look for places to live. Oh, do let's!'

'You must be crazy, love.' He pulled himself up, reaching for his cigarettes. 'Tavistock is less than half an hour's drive from home. Cass often shops there. No chance of that, I'm afraid.'

Harriet felt as if she had been doused in cold water. She was plunged back into reality, and very cold and bleak it was, too. Well, what did she expect? That Cass would cease to exist? That Tom would up and leave his family? And would she really want him to? She pushed this last disturbing thought away and moved to the edge of the bed.

Tom, inhaling on his cigarette, watched her collect her discarded clothes and thought quickly. That one had been a bit close and he'd been a bit clumsy. Should he persuade her back to bed and take her mind off it? On the other hand he was absolutely starving . . . Compromise.

'Is there anywhere else you'd like to go, love? I don't care where we are as long as we're together. We could stay here if you wanted.' (As long as we keep a low profile.) 'Must you go? Have you had enough of me already?'

'Of course not!' She turned back quickly. 'Don't be silly!' (And I mustn't be silly, I don't want to lose him . . . oh, dear. I've got a lot to learn.) 'I just thought that some supper might go down well. I've got some nice juicy steaks.'

She leaned over to kiss him and his hands moved up under her dressing-gown as he murmured appreciatively.

'Well, I suppose so then. But only on the condition that we come straight back here afterwards. I've never known anyone like you, Harriet.'

At last he let her go and then lay back on the rumpled pillows to finish his cigarette. He would have to play this one very carefully indeed.

'Hello? That you, Jane?'

'Hello. Yes, it's me. I told you not to phone me here, Philip. Alan might answer it.'

'Yeah, but he's gone, hasn't he? And I haven't seen you in two weeks, have I? How'd it go, then? Did you tell him?'

'Tell him what?'

'Come off it, Jane! You know what I mean. Obviously you didn't then. Why not?'

'Dunno, really. Didn't seem to come up.'

'For Chrissakes, Jane! What's that mean? Didn't come up! Not likely to, is it, not without you bring it up? You promised you'd have it out with him.'

'I know, but somehow I couldn't. It's not that easy and anyway I don't feel well enough to cope with it all.'

'Oh, Jane. But we gotta do something.'

'I know. Where are you now?'

'I'm in Yelverton. Look, I gotta go up to Okehampton to pick up some parts. What say you come with me?'

'Oh. Well, I don't know.'

'Come on, the drive'll do you good. It'll be lovely over the moors today.'

'I'd have to meet you. You can't come here. Oh, God, I don't know if I should.' A pause. 'Phil, Mrs Hampton knows.'

'Knows what?'

'About us, the baby, everything!'

'Bloody hell. These old dames don't miss nothing. Well, she's all right, she won't go talking.'

'I know. But if she knows who else does?'

'I dunno. What's it matter anyway? They'll all know soon enough. Look. I gotta go. I'll meet you in the usual place, OK? 'Bout half-two.'

The phone went dead. Jane replaced the receiver and walked slowly to the window, her arms folded across her stomach. How kind Mrs Hampton had been to her, and was she right? Should she, Jane, stick to Alan, try to make a go of it, learn to accept his job? Certainly, for the baby's sake it was the right option. But what of Philip? He made her feel so alive and so carefree, or he had, before all this trouble had started. But would she continue to feel carefree in a tumbling-down old cottage, not knowing where the next penny was coming from and wondering how she'd manage? If it was just me, thought Jane, but there's the baby now. I don't even know whose it is. She'd had to tell Philip that it was his. She'd sworn that she and Alan weren't sleeping together anymore. Philip's temper was a byword locally and Jane was a little frightened of him, especially when he'd been drinking.

As yet, Alan didn't know she was pregnant. She'd have to tell him sooner or later but it was as if she were waiting for something to solve the problem for her. She had no strength left. Apathy enfolded her. She wanted someone to tell her what to do, even do it for her, but without anger and shouting. If only, calmly and peacefully, it could all be put right. But how?

A shaft of golden sunlight slanted through the window, piercing the grey gloom that enfolded her. She would go with Philip to Okehampton. Why not? At least if she moved in with Philip she'd have company, not these long, empty hours of boredom. Would she, though? Unbidden came the thought that Philip was mostly out on jobs, off on trips like this one to Okehampton, never knew how long he'd be, and, of course, he liked to go down to the pub of an evening. And I'd have to stay at home with the baby, thought Jane. I'd still be on my own . . . Oh, hell! She turned away from the window and went to get her coat. At least today she could have company and tomorrow could look after itself.

KATE SAT AT THE kitchen table, her hands wrapped around a mug of coffee, trying to decide whether she should take the plunge and start showing Oscar at some of the larger dog shows. Her breeder friends all advised it. Once he started winning, then other breeders would want to use him. It was essential, they told her, if she wanted to make a name and make some money.

The flump of the letters arriving on the doormat disturbed her reverie and she got up and wandered into the hall. Three envelopes lay there. Kate picked them up and turned them over idly. One looked interesting with its London postmark and the name of a firm of solicitors in the corner. Perhaps some unknown rich relative had died and left her some money. Kate carried the letters back to the kitchen and slit open the long white envelope. She read the letter through without taking in a single word and, with her heart beginning to thump, read it through again. After all, it was quite simple. Their client, Mark Webster, was seeking a divorce on the grounds of an irretrievable breakdown of the marriage. He would continue to support his sons until they had left school. After that, he would consider that his responsibilities were at an end.

Kate felt for her chair and sat down. She tried to collect her thoughts and decide how she should feel. It was hardly a surprise that after five years he should want his freedom. Perhaps he wanted to marry again? Kate examined the thought carefully and diagnosed her reaction with as much self-honesty as she could muster. There was a twinge. Yes, there was certainly a tiny fluttering at the pit of her stomach. Could it be jealousy? Kate didn't think so. Never for a moment had she regretted her decision to leave Mark, never had she wanted him back. No, this was more a sensation of shock that there would be an official finality to what had once been between them, the love that they had once known, the shared moments, the fact that, for a moment in space and time, they had been linked together. Now, it would be judged, a few strokes of the pen would sever it and it would be wiped out.

After a moment another thought struck her. She seized the paper again. Yes, there it was: no support for the twins once they had left school. How would she manage to get them through university, keep them clothed and fed until they had qualified in order to find jobs? It was cold fear now that clutched at her stomach and she stood up and automatically pushed the kettle on to the hotplate.

She made some more coffee and sat down again, willing herself not to panic. Was Mark legally able to stop supporting his sons when they finished school? Giles wanted to read drama and theatre studies, his great ambition being to direct films, and Guy wanted to study engineering. Kate imagined telling them that they wouldn't be able to and felt quite desperate. Were the twins to be punished and deprived for her mistakes? She took a gulp of coffee and strove again for calm. It was stupid to panic until she knew all the facts. She must talk to someone who could advise her. Chris had left the name of his lawyer to be contacted if an emergency should arise and he was obviously the person to whom she should speak. Kate finished her coffee and pushed back her chair, Oscar and his future career completely forgotten.

WHEN TOM HAD LEFT Harriet to rejoin his submarine he was uncertain as to when they would be able to spend more time together. In the end they had spent their few days together in Harriet's house with only an occasional sortie in the car. After all, if you're a naval officer Hampshire is a dangerous county in which to have an affair. It had been a blissful time and now Harriet felt flat and lonely. She had pushed away any long-term thoughts of the relationship but her resolve to move to Tavistock and join Michael was slowly strengthening.

'After all,' Tom had observed, 'it would be a lot easier for us to meet if you were only half an hour away across the moor. Quite legitimately, of course. Burst pipes, blocked gutters . . . Oh, Harriet! I'm really going to miss you.'

Now, more than a week later, she slumped in an armchair, coffee untasted on the table beside her. She felt it would be quite impossible to carry on with her life as if nothing had happened. No. It was a time for positive action and, sitting up, she opened the small address book that she had dug out of her bag and pulled the telephone towards her.

A soft voice with a West Country burr informed her that Michael was on the other line. If she could hold on a moment?

Impatiently Harriet tasted her now-lukewarm coffee. She mustn't lose her nerve. After all, she needn't commit herself to anything, just a chat . . .

'Harriet! How marvellous! How are you?' Michael's voice, exploding suddenly into her left ear, made her jump and spill the coffee.

'Michael! Hello. I hope I'm not interrupting anything.' She scrubbed at the table with her handkerchief.

'Of course not. Where are you? Dare I hope that you're down here in the Wild West?'

'No, no.' Harriet felt warmed, her spirits lifting at his obvious enthusiasm. 'But I could well be soon.'

'Really? That's fantastic. Have you thought over my offer?'

'Well, yes, I have. No, no, hang on. I haven't come to any decision yet, except that I want to move down to Devon and I want to carry on working.'

'I should think so! And I need you, Harriet, remember that. So what are your plans?'

'Well, I thought I'd come down and have a look around at houses, see what's going and prices, etc.'

'Well, you've certainly come to the right man for that!'

'Yes. And then we could have a long chat about my coming in with you.'

'Sounds good to me. So when?'

Harriet could visualise the tall, loose-limbed form, crouched over his desk, dark hair falling across his forehead, horn-rimmed spectacles slipping down his nose, whilst the pencil in his free hand doodled on the blotter.

'Heavens! I had no idea you were so dynamic. Well, let me see . . . ' She thought quickly. She was taking some time off and could easily ask for extended leave. 'What about tomorrow? I could be down by tea-time. Could you book me in somewhere?'

'Splendid. But can't you stay with me? I've got plenty of room, you know.'

'Well.' She hesitated.

'Oh, come on, Harriet.' His chuckle seemed to reverberate down the line. 'I shan't jump on you if I see you in your dressing gown.'

'No, no. I know that.' She was embarrassed that he might think that she considered herself irresistible. 'It's just your reputation I'm think-ing about. Up and coming tycoon and all that and I imagine that Tav-istock, like most small towns, has its share of gossips?'

'Oh, quite. But I happen to live out of the town up on the moor. The only raised eyebrows will belong to the sheep or the ponies. Now let me tell you how to get there.' He gave her detailed directions, which included where she would find the key to the cottage.

As she replaced the receiver Harriet experienced a moment of sheer terror. What on earth was she doing? Nothing, yet, she told herself firmly. Just going to Tavistock to look at houses and having a talk with Michael is nothing to panic about. After all, I've been thinking of making changes for ages now. It's really nothing to do with Tom. At the thought of him her terror faded and she felt full of strength. She must clean the house, pack, get the car ready. As she put the coffee mug in the sink in the kitchen she thought of how Tom and she had embraced almost where she now stood, before he had left. You never know, she told him silently, next time you come home I might just be down there waiting for you.

Twenty-two

Oliver was lounging at the kitchen table when the telephone rang.

'Phone, Ma!' he bellowed, making no attempt to rise from his chair. Presently the bell was silenced and he heard Cass's voice in the hall, exclaiming with pleasure.

'Who can it be?' Oliver asked Gus, who was sitting at his feet and receiving pieces of toast dipped in tea. 'Don't slobber, you disgusting animal.'

'Well.' Cass appeared. 'That was Daddy. The boat's in at Devonport for a few days—some engine problem—so he's coming home while they sort it out. What a nice surprise. And here's another surprise!' She brandished a postcard at Oliver. 'It's from Harriet. She's staying with a friend near Tavistock.' She smiled to herself. 'Quite a coincidence.'

'Why?' Oliver pushed Gus away with his foot and slumped over the table, head on arms. 'Why is that a coincidence?'

'Oh, well. It just is, darling.'

Cass was longing to know what, if anything, had happened in Lee. Since that weekend Tom had not been home and she had heard nothing from Harriet, not even her usual bread-and-butter letter or telephone call to thank Cass for the weekend. That in itself was significant. Cass could well imagine the difficulty of composing such a letter in the circumstances. Since her own wonderful Sunday afternoon with Nick in the Mallinsons' cottage she was even more obsessed by him. Never before had Cass conducted an affair with a very experienced man who was a great deal older than she was. Her previous lovers were all naval officers, all men of her own age and all much of a type. A few months of knowing Nick had shown her that, although to begin with, military life tended to make young men grow up quickly, give them responsibility and mature them faster than their peers outside, it also protected them from ordinary life. Many of them found it difficult to cope without a book of rules and without the safety of the hierarchical parameters. To help them to deal with nonmilitary situations they often tried to categorise civilians into senior officers, junior officers and lower ranks and then treated them accordingly which often caused resentment. They were used to a social life and a working environment which encouraged them to drink too much and often behave in a childish and irresponsible way when they were off duty. All this to Cass—having been brought up with the Army and having married into the Navy—was the norm and Nick was an overwhelmingly new experience. He fascinated her. His very differences made him interesting and, because they were new to her, the more acceptable and desirable. She was like a child with a new and absorbing toy and nobody was going to take it away from her.

To know that Tom and Harriet were having an affair would ease her conscience. It would also keep Tom occupied. But how on earth was she to find out? She felt fairly confident that Harriet would give the show away quite quickly but she wasn't so sure about Tom. It occurred to her that if she saw them both together, especially if they weren't expecting to meet each other, she'd know at once. 'Love and a cough cannot be hid.' She'd read that in a book and it was probably true. She looked again at the postcard and realised that she had the means to hand. It seemed a bit cruel but at least she'd know where she stood. Nick, whom she had found to be a tender, exciting lover, had suggested a few days away together and Cass longed to go. Everything would be that much easier if she knew that Harriet and Tom were involved with each other. She turned the postcard thoughtfully in her hands. She would invite Harriet for tea on Sunday, by which time Tom would be home. Neither would know whether Tom's telephone call or Harriet's postcard had come first so she could pretend that it was all a great surprise. With luck, they'd be too shocked to think it through properly. Cass couldn't help smiling.

'What are you grinning at?'

'Nothing. Take your arm out of the butter and go and get dressed. It's nearly eleven o'clock and Daddy will be home for lunch. Someone's dropping him off. Have you got any plans for the weekend, darling?'

'Nope!' Oliver hauled himself out of his chair and wandered to the door. 'I shall sleep and watch television.'

'Honestly, Ollie! Anyone would think you were fifty. A good long walk with Gus would be much better for you. Children these days are so lazy. When I was your age . . . '

'Oh, Ma, don't start on that! I bet at my age you were wearing a mini-skirt and lying about smoking pot. "If you go to San Francisco," ' he sang, in a ghastly falsetto, whilst swaying his hips and rolling his eyes, ' "Be sure to wear some flowers in your hair." Were you a hippie, Ma?' He vanished into the hall and Cass burst out laughing. She was pleased with her little plan. She studied the postcard again. Harriet had put a telephone number at the top and Cass decided to telephone now before Tom arrived.

She dialled the number and waited. A man's voice spoke in her ear, a lovely deep warm voice.

'Oh, hello. Have I got the right number? I want to speak to Harriet Masters.'

'Yes, she's here. Who's calling please?' He made no effort to cover the receiver. 'Harriet, it's Cassandra Wivenhoe for you.' There were fumbling noises and then Harriet's voice.

'Hello, Cass. You got my card then?'

'Yes. It was a lovely surprise. Are you staying long and are we going to see you?'

'Well, I shall be here for a week or so . . . '

'Splendid. We're hoping that you'll come and have tea tomorrow.'

'Oh. Tomorrow? When you say "we," do you mean . . . ? Have you . . . ?'

'Well, the boys are home for the weekend, but you know what it's like here, lovey, anything could happen. Oh, and do bring your friend, he sounds rather nice.'

'Well, I don't know. I'd have to ask him. Hang on a minute.' Silence. 'Hello Cass? Yes, thank you. We'd both love to come. About three, then?'

'Lovely. See you tomorrow. 'Bye.'

Cass stood in the hall for a moment. For a fleeting moment she wondered if she might be opening Pandora's box. Then she thought of Nick and her doubts fled.

TOM, JOLTING ALONG IN Lieutenant Harrap's Citroën Diane, was barely listening to the stream of chatter issuing from the lips of Angela Harrap who was driving them home. She and Peter were obviously delighted to have the Captain travelling with them and Angela was doing her best to play the part of a loyal naval wife whilst indicating, subtly, that she was an attractive woman in her own right and found him just as attractive. Shifting in the uncomfortable passenger seat, Tom reflected that he'd seen it done better. Anyway, he preferred a different approach. He remembered a woman at a cocktail party telling him that she considered that his job as Captain was purely an ego trip and that it disgusted her to see all his young officers, who did all the real work, fawning over him and treating him like some sort of deity. He'd taken her out to dinner afterwards, and later . . .

Tom smiled reminiscently and glanced sideways at Angela: slight, dark, long legs stretched out to the pedals. Not unlike Harriet, he thought and his heart contracted. He'd tried to phone her last night from the Mess and at regular intervals thereafter and, finally, had assumed her to be away and given up. Certainly Cass had been right. When the first nervous moments had passed, Harriet had displayed a depth of feeling that Tom would never have guessed at. How well she had hidden it from him all this time. It had been rather touching and terribly flattering and it would have taken a stronger character than Tom's to resist such an opportunity. After all, Harriet was a widow now and a free woman and was quite old enough to take responsibility for her actions. She knew that he was a married man and must realise that there was no future to it; nevertheless, it would be pleasant to have a compliant eager mistress living not too far away. Harriet was an old friend and there would be plenty of reasons for going to see her. He'd been tempted to rush off to Lee this morning but it was probably sensible to stay close to the boat. The First Lieutenant had been left on board but, nevertheless, Tom could be recalled at any time and, with the boat in his home port, it would be odd if he asked to be contacted anywhere else but at his own home and embarrassing if Cass discovered that the boat was in. He wondered when he would see Harriet again—they had agreed not to write to each other—and turned to smile at Angela. Dammit! He'd probably have to invite them in for drinks.

As THE VOLVO, WITH Michael driving, climbed up from Meavy on Sunday afternoon Harriet had a presentiment that the afternoon was going to prove a disaster. How could she face Cass now? It was one thing to tell oneself that Cass deserved some of the same treatment that she'd served out but quite another to feel justified in being the one redressing the balance when one was a mile or two from her front door. She remembered all Cass's kindnesses of the past years: the hospitality, the support after Ralph's death, and her spirit writhed within her. It didn't help that she was now pretty sure that Tom was not the poor wronged husband that she had always believed him to be. He was taking it all too calmly, too naturally for that to be the case. During the years of blind infatuation she had talked herself into believing that it was almost her duty to rescue him from Cass, that she had a perfect right to show him what real love and loyalty was all about. When her conscience had pointed out that it was to Ralph and not to another woman's husband that these admirable qualities should be displayed, she excused herself on the grounds that she had never really been in love with Ralph nor he with her and so it wasn't the same. How easily we delude ourselves, rationalising and excusing our own failings, whilst seeing the weaknesses of others in such a clear, harsh and unforgiving light.

She had told herself that the reason she had sent a postcard to Cass and put a telephone number on it was because she knew that Cass's feelings would be hurt if she found out that Harriet was in the area without having let her know but the truth was that she hoped that Tom might find it and get in touch. Why had she promised not to write or ring? Surely a letter to the submarine would have been quite safe? Tom had been adamant, disquietingly so. It was another pointer that he knew quite well the rules of this particular game and had no intention of breaking them. Realising that she was being a very poor companion, Harriet pulled herself together and looked about her. Almost there: her heart jumped with nervousness.

'It's off to the right here,' she said, hoping that her nerves didn't show in her voice. 'Just up past the church here and it's those big gates. Just drive straight in. Oh, God. There's Cass in the garden.'

'Harriet. How lovely.' Cass, who had been waiting to intercept them, hurried to the car and hugged Harriet as she climbed out.

Would she be hugging me like this, wondered Harriet, if she knew that Tom and I had slept together? Everything has changed and I'm not going to be able to behave as I have done in the past. I shouldn't have come.

Michael was shaking Cass firmly by the hand and they were moving towards the house. Cass was wearing a blue twill skirt with a crisp white shirt and Harriet had never seen her look so well. She seemed to glow with superabundant health and well-being. Beside her, Harriet, in jeans and a sweater, felt positively dowdy, though Michael, in brown cords and a Guernsey, seemed totally unmoved. It was apparent that Cass approved of him and, as they went through the front door, she took an arm of each and guided them towards the sitting room.

'Darling!' she exclaimed, pausing in the doorway. 'Look who's here!'

She felt Harriet's arm stiffen beneath her fingers as Tom, who had been half asleep, rose from the sofa, the Sunday paper falling from his hands.

'Harriet!' He croaked rather than spoke her name and his face told Cass all that she needed to know.

To Harriet the shock was total and she could neither move nor speak.

'Isn't this a lovely surprise?' Cass smoothly bridged the awkward moment. 'Tom phoned just after I spoke to you yesterday morning. He behaved so badly last time that I was afraid to tell him you were coming. But I know he always likes to see you, Harriet. And how nice to meet Michael. This is my husband Tom. Harriet's staying with Michael at Tavistock, darling.' She let this sink in, whilst Tom and Michael shook hands. 'And now, what about some tea?'

ON MONDAY MORNING TOM, having watched Cass out of the house, came quietly downstairs and into the kitchen. Where was that post-card? He must, absolutely must, contact Harriet. It had been the worst afternoon Tom could ever remember, with Cass playing the role of the devoted wife, Harriet brittle and unapproachable, the friend Michael, detached, observant—and how close a friend was he, dammit?—even the children had conspired to make it hell. Gemma, conscious, as always, of an audience had clung to him, sat on his lap, kissed him repeatedly instead of ignoring him as she usually did. And Oliver . . . well, to be fair, Oliver hadn't been too bad. He had played the dutiful son entertaining his parents' fuddy-duddy old friends and it was he who had mentioned the postcard. It had, apparently, a Victorian reproduction picture for which Oliver had invented a rather amusing caption. He had told Harriet about it and how he liked doing the same thing with the cartoons at the back of *Punch*. The postcard had been fetched to prove his point and Harriet's address remarked on. Now where the hell was it? Not on the hall table at any event. And then Charlotte, who was so moody lately one hardly dared speak to her . . . At the recollection Tom shook his head in disbelief. She had breezed in, face wreathed in smiles, positively bubbling over, helped people to cakes and tea, chatted brightly. They couldn't have presented a more united family front if they'd been practising all year.

Tom reached up to the high shelf above the Aga, a favourite place for bits and pieces.

'Are you lookin' for somethin', sir?'

Tom jumped, barked his knuckles and swore. Mrs Hampton stood behind him looking concerned.

'I'm sorry, sir. I didn't mean to startle you.'

'That's all right, Mrs Hampton. I didn't hear you.' He nursed his bruised hand. Damn the woman, creeping about instead of getting on with her work. 'Don't let me interrupt you.' He left the kitchen quickly to resume the search elsewhere.

Mrs Hampton watched him go and then took from her apron pocket the postcard she had found whilst turning out the drawing-room. Halfway down the side of the sofa it had been. She studied the picture thoughtfully and then reversing it read the message. After a moment she placed it where Cass always stood postcards and the like—on the high shelf above the Aga.

UPSTAIRS IN HER BEDROOM Charlotte, who had a day off to revise for her O levels, moved to and fro sorting out her clothes. Since Hugh's telephone call yesterday morning to invite her to a school fête next weekend followed by a party she had been overflowing with joy. She was not to know that she was being invited because Lucinda couldn't go, and she was happier than she had been for many months. She had allowed herself to be taken to look at several schools—including Blundells—and had agreed to think seriously about boarding. Her name was down provisionally, her place dependent on the result of her exams in a few weeks' time. She had decided that sulks and moods were getting her nowhere and that, at present, it was best to be com-pliant. She was waiting for Tom's leave, for an opportunity to talk to him seriously about how she felt. Slowly Hugh was making her feel that to take her A levels and go to university was a sensible, adult thing to do and she longed to do and be all the things he would want. She knew that she'd behaved badly at his sister's party and wanted to prove to him that it had just been a bad moment and that she was perfectly capable of being sensible. She was still unhappy at the idea of being away from home but Guy and Giles would be starting in the sixth form at the same time and Hugh had suggested that she might like to visit him in Bristol and altogether it seemed about time that she considered her future carefully. She was still concerned about Cass, sure that she was up to something, although she wasn't quite sure what and she was keeping an eye on her. Meanwhile there was Hugh and next weekend and the long summer holiday to look forward to.

So Charlotte sang to herself as she planned what to wear in five days' time when she saw Hugh.

HARRIET LAY IN BED gazing sightlessly at the ceiling. She had heard Michael leave and even now, several hours later, couldn't summon up the energy to get up. What was the point? She felt sick with horror every time she thought about yesterday's tea-party, re-living it over and over again, as if it were a film being projected on to the ceiling above her. What had seemed so romantic all these years and had been so delightful an idyll for those few days in her own home in Lee, had rather a different guise when looked at in the cold light of day. Cass, surrounded by her family, had made her feel cheap, grubby. And Tom's face . . . Harriet groaned aloud and pulled the sheet over her head in an effort to shut out the pictures. She jumped violently as the shriek of the doorbell tore through the cottage followed by the barking of Michael's dog. She found that she was trembling as she pulled on her dressing-gown, thrust her feet into slippers and hurried down the stairs. Maybe Cass had come to confront her, or maybe Tom himself. She dragged open the front door and gazed in bewilderment at the postman.

'Parcel to sign for.'

Silently Harriet took the proffered pencil in nerveless fingers and signed shakily, aware of the postman's interested gaze.

'Sorry to get you up, missis.' He was smiling openly now. Oh, God. He must think that she and Michael . . .

'No, no. I was up, actually. Mr Barrett-Thompson isn't here at the moment. I'll give it to him when he gets back.' She could see that he didn't believe a word of it. Well, who cared?

She shut the door, put the parcel on the hall table and went into the kitchen. Max, the huge Newfoundland, emerged from the utility room off the kitchen and looked at her. His tail waved languidly in greeting before he sat down with a deep sigh, resting against the door jamb. Max never stood when he could sit, or sat without leaning against something.

'Oh, Max.' Harriet looked at the great dog with his benevolent expression and kindly eye and her misery seemed to overwhelm her. Kneeling beside him she threw her arms round his neck and, burying her face in his abundant coat, burst into tears. Max was quite equal to this sort of thing. People were always hugging and stroking him, exclaiming at his size, remarking on his coat and admiring his general demeanour. He found the burden of being so wonderful very tiring and he sighed again deeply.

Harriet stood up, wiping her eyes on a tea-towel, and Max, worn out by his output, lay down with his head between his paws.

'I must pull myself together,' Harriet told him and he cocked an eye at her. Was she moving towards the biscuit tin? No, merely toward the kettle. He rolled on his side and prepared to sleep. Barking at the postman always exhausted him.

Harriet made coffee wondering how Max, even while unconscious, managed to exude comfort. Whilst she was drinking her third mug of coffee the doorbell shrieked again causing her to start and bang the mug against her teeth.

Max struggled up from his short course in death and essayed a bark or two. Really! Couldn't a dog get a minute's peace? Harriet had got the door open and was staring at Tom. Seeing a strange man, Max felt a bit more effort was called for on his part, but he was ignored. They were too busy gasping at one another.

'How on earth . . . ?'

'I remembered his name and looked him up in the book.'

'Why didn't you phone?'

'Wanted to check he wasn't here . . . '

'But how . . . '

'Stopped off at his office. Saw him through the window. Didn't wait to find a phone-box. Oh, Harriet . . . '

'Oh, God, Tom. Yesterday was so ghastly . . . '

And so on, and so on. Humans were so emotional, so exhausting. Max returned to the utility room and, flopping down, resumed his slumbers.

'FOR HEAVEN'S SAKE RELAX, love. Talk about a cat on a hot tin roof.' Now that they'd made love again Tom was back in control. His urgency to track Harriet down had surprised him and he had a feeling that he was being rather swept along, out of control.

'I just feel that we shouldn't have done it here, Tom.' With her passion temporarily abated, Harriet felt guilty and confused. 'After all, it is Michael's house.'

'Well, we're not in his bed, are we?'

Tom's calmness had the opposite effect on Harriet who now felt edgy. There was a tendency for her beautiful romantic affair to look sordid and she simply couldn't bear it.

'No, but still, let's get up. He might arrive at any moment.'

'Why?' Tom made no effort to move. 'Does he usually come home for lunch?'

'Well, no. But I was upset last night and I didn't get up for breakfast this morning and he might just check.'

'Why should he check? You're sure there's nothing between you?'

'Oh, yes, Tom, honestly.' Harriet was now feeling positively irritable. 'We've been through all that. And he doesn't know anything about us, either. But I was very quiet on the way back last evening and he must have guessed that something was wrong. He's much too nice to ask questions but he might just come back to see if I'm OK.'

Harriet pulled away from Tom's caressing hand and got out of bed. 'I'm going to get up. Oh, God! Oh, Christ! Here's his car! Oh! Quickly, Tom, get up!'

'Hell's teeth, woman, calm down. Stop pulling me.' Tom was moving as slowly as he dared in an attempt to maintain his dignity. 'I'm dressing. Go on down and chat to him. I'm allowed to come and see you, dammit. Pull yourself together and go on down. Tell him I'm in the loo. For heaven's sake, Harriet, you can tidy up later. He won't come into your bedroom, for God's sake. Go on, Harriet.'

She almost fell down the narrow staircase, sobbing dryly, hot with shame.

'Michael!' She arrived in the hall as he opened the front door.

He stood for a moment, pocketing his key, surveying her flushed face, dishevelled hair and the hastily donned jersey and then turned towards the kitchen door where Max had appeared with a weary 'here we go again' expression about him.

'I see we've got visitors.' Michael's voice was calm. Max sniffed at him and his tail waved tentatively. Something wrong here. Michael stroked his ears and spoke gently to him, but Max was not deceived. He sat down, leaning against the fridge, in case he should be needed to give comfort and support.

'It's Tom.' Harriet sounded breathless. 'He had to come to Tavistock and he thought he'd return our call. He's just dashed up to the loo.'

'Ah. Is he staying to lunch?'

'No.' It came out much too quickly and she turned as Tom came into the kitchen. 'You can't stay to lunch, can you, Tom? Didn't you say you were on your way somewhere?' She signalled furiously to him behind Michael's back.

'That's right. Hello, Michael. Hope you don't mind my popping in. Messages from Cass and so on. Actually, why don't you come with me, Harriet? I'm sure you remember the Harraps, don't you? They'd love to see you again. I can drop you back later.'

One look at Michael's face decided her. She couldn't face him just yet.

'That would be lovely. Is that OK, Michael?'

'Of course. You don't have to ask permission, you know. You're my guest, not my prisoner.'

'No. I realise that. Well, I'll just get my bag.' She vanished.

'Well, nice to see you again, Michael.' Tom followed her.

Michael stood motionless, listening to Harriet's feet running upstairs, down again, across the hall. The front door slammed and a car engine started up. Presently he sat down at the table.

Recognising his cue Max rose and came to sit by him. He leaned against his leg and put his heavy head on Michael's knee. It was one of those days.

WHEN MICHAEL ARRIVED HOME that evening Harriet was in the kitchen, busy at the Aga.

'Hello!' she said, without turning round, her voice brittle and gay. 'Sold lots of houses? I'm making us a special dinner.'

'That sounds good.' Michael's voice was noncommittal. 'Hello, Max. Don't get up, old chap.'

Max hauled himself up into a sitting position supported by the dresser and wagged his tail. He flattened his ears and his tongue lolled out which was what Harriet called 'Max laughing.'

'I took him for a walk,' she said, in the same light, social tone. 'I thought he needed exercise.'

Max looked at her reproachfully. Needed exercise! Great Scott! He'd been on the go all day, what with one thing and another. He'd only just settled down for a real snooze after Michael had gone back to the office when Harriet had appeared in a state of nervous tension and dragged him out to walk for miles on the moor. It was a dog's life! He looked at Michael for sympathy, but he was looking at Harriet. Max pulled in his tongue and lay down. There was no justice in this life.

'Harriet.'

Harriet's heart began to thump and she busied herself with pans and plates.

'Yes?'

He didn't speak again and she was forced, at last, to turn to look at him. He was leaning against the dresser, ankles crossed, with a cigarette in one hand and the other thrust into his trouser pocket.

'How long have we known each other, Harriet?'

'Heavens! I don't know!' Her laugh sounded artificial, even to her. 'Years I should think.'

'It's eight years. I'd just passed my Chartered Surveyor's exams.'

'What a memory you've got! Why do you ask?'

'I was wondering why you're behaving like a stranger.'

She turned quickly to the Aga, pretending to move a saucepan.

'Harriet.'

Reluctantly she turned back.

'Are you having an affair with Tom?'

The directness of the question took her breath away.

'Yes.' She couldn't look at him.

'Did you come here just to be close to him?'

'No!' It burst out of her. Had she? No, not just that. 'No. I wanted,' yes, this was true, 'I wanted to work with you. Be near you.' She found that she could look at him again.

'Oh, Harriet!' He stubbed out his cigarette in exasperation and sat down at the kitchen table.

'Michael, don't be cross. I can't seem to help myself. I've been in love with Tom for years but he never seemed to notice me until now.'

'You mean you were in love with Tom when you met Ralph?' His interruption cut across her explanation and he sounded shocked.

'No, no. I'd never met him then. Actually I rather fancied you, if I'm honest, but you were always tied up with that Joanna woman and . . .'

'Wait a minute!' She was struck by his grimace of pain. 'Are you serious?'

'What, about fancying you? Oh, yes. But you couldn't seem to detach yourself and I decided, in the end, that you didn't really want to.'

'It wasn't that easy. She was very determined, as well as being neurotic, suicide threats and so on. I managed it in the end.' He gave a bitter smile. 'I remember the morning I came into the office to tell you I'd made the break. You greeted me first, with the news of your engagement to Ralph.'

She looked at him in horror.

'But, Michael! You never told me you cared about me like that.'

'I couldn't until I was free, but I tried to give you hints about how difficult it was . . . '

'But I thought it was because you were so besotted about her that you were always telling me about her. You know, sort of warning me off.'

They stared at each other aghast.

'I never thought you were really available,' said Harriet, at last, 'and after that there was Ralph. And then I met Tom.' Her voice trailed off.

Michael raised his head. 'Tom wasn't available either.'

'I know.' Harriet sounded miserable. 'I just went up like straw. From the moment I met him I was just, well, obsessed by him.'

'So that was why, after Ralph died, I couldn't get anywhere with you. Because of Tom?'

'I suppose so. Although, well, to be honest, Michael, I wasn't aware of your trying. You just behaved like an old friend, a brother. I couldn't have managed without you.'

'I seem to have got it wrong all the way round, don't I?' Michael got up and went to the dresser to fetch some glasses. 'Well, perhaps it's third time lucky.'

'What d'you mean?' Harriet passed him the wine.

'Just this. Just so's there no mistake this time—I love you, Harriet. I've loved you for more than eight years and I don't want to miss out this time round because I'm standing back being brotherly.' He poured the wine and raised his glass to her. 'Just bear it in mind, will you? And now I'm going up for a shower.' Taking his glass, he left the kitchen.

Harriet sat down suddenly at the kitchen table.

Well, now you know, she said to herself. Oh, hell! This was all

I needed. Her gaze roamed around the kitchen and alighted on Max, snoring by the dresser, sympathy oozing from his inert form.

'Oh, Max!' she wailed. 'What am I going to do?'

He opened a bleary eye in alarm. Not again! No, really, this was too much! Rising as quickly as his bulk would allow, he vanished into the utility room and wedged himself behind the freezer and Harriet was left alone.

Twenty-three

Alan delved in his pocket for his key, raised his hand to the fellow officer who had given him a lift from the dockyard and, picking up his grip, went into the house. He called a few times, put his head into the living room and the kitchen and, finding them empty, went upstairs to change. It was quite possible that Jane was staying with a friend or had gone to see her mum but it was unlikely. She tended to stay put when he was at sea, making the excuse that she couldn't drive and public transport was so inconvenient. It was so silly having a car unused in the garage for months on end but, since she was so nervous of the idea of driving, Alan had let the matter drop hoping that the sheer difficulties of getting about may encourage her.

All her things were lying about in their usual places in the bedroom and the bathroom so she evidently didn't plan to be away long. There was no need to panic yet, after all she wasn't expecting him, but he felt a little worried. He'd been phoning since the evening before and wondered with whom she was staying. He decided to have a cup of tea and then make a few telephone calls. He'd just filled the kettle when he heard the key in the lock.

As Jane let herself in at the front door Alan appeared in the living-room doorway.

'So there you are! Where have you been?'

White-faced, throat dry, Jane gaped at him in horror. He gave a short laugh.

'Well, you don't look overjoyed to see me. Where were you last night?'

'I was over Sharon's.' (God! Supposing he's checked!) Fright made her aggressive. 'How was I supposed to know you'd be home? Haven't got a crystal ball, have I?'

'I know that.' He looked at her curiously. 'Are you OK? Sorry if I startled you. We're in for a couple of days unexpectedly. Didn't know myself, so I couldn't let you know. Got in late last night. I tried phoning then and again before I left this morning but there was no reply and I was just going to check around. You don't look well, love. Sure you're OK?'

His tone was genuinely concerned and Jane felt swamped with guilt. She'd let Philip persuade her to go for a picnic up on the moor yesterday. He'd drunk too much cider and they'd almost had a collision with another car on their way back to his cottage for a cup of tea. She hated it when he drank too much and got violent, swearing and shouting and saying he'd kill Alan. He'd refused to drive her home and it was, by then, too late and too far for her to walk. His lovemaking had been rough and painful and Jane had been awake most of the night with gut-ache. Supposing she lost the baby? She knew three months was the danger period, the doctor had told her so, and she'd been surprised, last night, at the terror she'd felt at the thought of losing it. Once she'd have been only too pleased, now she felt differently. This morning Philip had been sullen when she insisted that he dropped her at the other end of the field path and she'd felt a moment of real anxiety that he might insist that he take her right home. She could feel her zero hour coming closer and closer and felt almost annihilated with fear.

Alan, surprised by the look of her fragility and unhappiness, went to her and took her coat.

'Come on, Jane. Come in the kitchen and I'll make you a cuppa. What's that Sharon been up to? You look all in.'

His kindness was the last straw and overwhelmed by exhaustion and fright she burst into tears.

'Jane, love!' As he caught her to him the pain, as her swollen, tender breasts came into contact with his rib cage, made her cry out and thrust him away. He released her abruptly and suddenly guessed the truth.

'You're pregnant!'

It was a statement, not a question, and Jane turned away, sobbing harder.

'Why didn't you tell me?'

When she didn't answer he went to her and, leading her like a child, took her into the living room and placed her in a corner of the sofa. Then, sitting beside her and turning sideways, so that he could see her, he picked up her hand and chafed it gently between his.

'Is it that bad?' he asked gently. He took her chin in his fingers and turned the drowned face to his. 'Did you think I was going to beat you? Oh, I know I said I didn't want kids yet but, if you want the truth, I'm thrilled to bits.'

She looked at him properly for the first time. This was the old Alan, the Alan she hadn't seen for months and months, not since that wretched promotion had changed their lives.

'I've been a bit difficult lately, love,' he said, as if he'd read her thoughts. 'I know that. You'll have to try to forgive me for it. It was a big thing for me, you know, being made up, and, frankly, I was terrified. But I've found my feet a bit now and things are settling down. But I need you, Jane. I can't do it without you.'

Jane stared at him in amazement—Alan the confident, the brave—and saw tears in his eyes.

'Alan!'

'I'm sorry.' He bent his head over their joined hands. 'These last few months have been a strain. And what with coming home and you not here and now this! It's all a bit of a shock.' He tried to laugh, patted her hand and swallowed hard. 'I'm going to make that tea.'

Jane remained riveted in her corner. Who'd believe it? Alan in tears over her. Suddenly she wished with all her heart that she knew the baby was his. It could be, but she'd never be sure. Did she have the courage to tell him or, if they stayed together, would it always be there between them?

Suddenly she realised just what she had done and how much she might lose.

HARRIET STROLLED DOWN THE high street outwardly serene, her mind in turmoil. Michael's outburst the week before had left her in a state of shock from which she was only now beginning to emerge. He had made no further reference to Tom or his own personal feelings, merely behaving as he had before, but for Harriet that was now impossible. Everything had changed and she didn't know whether she was on her head or her heels. Fortunately Tom had gone back to sea which solved the immediate problem of how to see him whilst she was living with Michael. However, several things were becoming clear, one of which was that she couldn't continue to stay in his cottage. But where should she go? Secondly, could she, knowing how Michael felt, accept his offer of a partnership?

She stopped to look into Creber's window. She must buy something for dinner, but what? Even that decision was beyond her. Gradually she became aware of activity beyond the display of cheeses. A hand seemed to be waving at her and now the owner of the hand was moving to the door and hurrying out on to the pavement.

'Harriet! It is you, isn't it? Yes, of course it is! Heavens, it must be years since I saw you.'

'Kate Webster,' said Harriet slowly. 'Good Lord! Yes, years and years.' She stared at Kate, taking in the grey hairs, the old jeans and rather grubby sweatshirt. 'I'm sorry. Just for a moment I didn't recognise you.'

'I know!' Kate grinned back at her. 'Shocking, isn't it? We only met on social occasions when I was forced to dress up. But once I was free of it all, I never looked back.'

'Free . . . ?' An old rumour filtered through Harriet's mind, something to do with running off with another man . . .

'Shall we have some coffee?' Kate was saying. 'Or, better still, would you like to come back for some lunch?'

'Oh, that would be wonderful!' Harriet's tone was heartfelt. 'I'm in a dreadful muddle and I desperately need someone to talk to.'

'Heavens!' said Kate cheerfully. 'Nothing too frightful, I hope? I was so sorry about Ralph,' she added in a changed tone. 'It was an appalling tragedy.'

'Yes.' Harriet remembered receiving a kind letter from Kate which she'd never answered. How long ago it seemed and what would Kate say if Harriet told her that even then she'd been in love with Tom Wivenhoe?

'Could I come to lunch, Kate?' she asked. 'I'd love to talk to you and to hear all your news, too.'

'Good. I've finished shopping and the car's just across the road.' She gestured to a rather ancient estate car parked opposite. 'Where's your car?'

'Parked up in Chapel Street.'

'Let's go straight home, I'll bring you back in later.' Seizing Harriet by the arm, Kate plunged across the road to the car, in the back of which reposed a large, regal-looking golden retriever.

Shooting out under the bonnet of a large lorry and turning right by Creber's, Kate headed the car towards Whitchurch.

'What luck that we should meet like that! Are you staying with Cass?'

'Not this time.' Harriet thought of Tom. 'I'm staying with a friend at Peter Tavy, not Navy. Just 'til I find a place of my own. I've been offered a partnership in an estate agency in Tavistock but I'm in such a guggle I don't know what to do about it.'

'A man?' Kate raised an eyebrow.

'Two men,' amended Harriet.

'Heavens! Well, I always say that if there's anything better than one man it's two men, ad infinitum. Here we are.'

She pulled in through a gateway, came to a halt beside a pleasant

Victorian house and, getting out, opened the tailgate, allowing the big dog to jump out.

'Oscar's just become a father and he's frightfully pleased with himself. Come and see his babies.'

She led the way between the house and the clematis-covered garage into the walled back garden, which stretched for some considerable distance before it reached the paddock. The high wall, covered with roses and honeysuckle, gave the back garden a feeling of absolute privacy and on the lawn, in a large run, seven golden puppies played.

'Oh! Aren't they sweet!' exclaimed Harriet. 'Oh, Oscar, aren't you clever?'

The dog pranced beside her, showing off, and then went to peer through the wire at his progeny, who were squeaking and tumbling over each other in their excitement.

'Hello, Honey.' Kate bent to stroke the mother who had been lying in the shade. 'Harriet's come to see your babies. You're the clever one really, aren't you? Oscar just had the fun of it all. You did all the work.' Honey allowed Harriet to stroke her but when Oscar pushed in between, demanding attention, was quite happy to go back to her place in the shade. Kate bent over the puppies, hesitated for a moment and then swiftly picked one from the mêlée and put it into Harriet's arms. 'There you are. Nearly six weeks old. They'll be going off to their new homes in ten days.'

'It's beautiful.' Harriet looked in awe at the huge paws and floppy ears and stroked the soft, fluffy hair.

'Come and have some lunch. I've got some delicious pâté and you'll need a spoon for the Brie. Oh, yes, and some lovely crusty bread.'

Harriet, still clutching the puppy, followed her through a utility room into a large, cluttered, delightful kitchen where it was apparent that Kate did most of her day-to-day living.

'Sit there,' commanded Kate, pointing to an old sofa, with shabby chintz covers, which stood beneath the window, 'and tell me all while I get the lunch.'

Somehow the weight and warmth of the puppy, who had gone to sleep, was comforting as Harriet slowly and painfully brought forth everything that had happened since the moment she had met Tom to Michael's revelation a week before. Meanwhile Kate pottered up and down covering the huge pine table with delicious food, buttering bread and pouring wine.

'I don't know why I can tell you all this, Kate,' said Harriet, at last. 'I never thought I'd be able to tell anybody.'

'It's probably because you know that I, too, have erred,' she answered lightly, although she was secretly shocked to hear that Tom was so deeply involved. She wondered if Cass knew. 'Unfortunately good people are really rather tiresome and holier than thou and one seldom feels like unburdening one's soul to them. What's worse is that so often good people are good because they've never been tempted or because they've simply been luckier and it's no real credit to them at all. I'm not excusing myself, mind you. I did leave Mark. I didn't go off with a man but I did commit adultery although we had separated by then. It wasn't quite the way Mark reported it in the Mess, but he had to go on living with his friends, so I suppose it was fair enough. Are you actually saying that you think Tom might seriously think of leaving Cass?'

'I just don't know.' Harriet stared miserably at the comatose puppy. 'He makes no mention of it but we are rather in the early stages yet. I don't know if I'd want him to. Oh, Kate, I don't know what I want. Do you think that I should give Tom up?'

Kate put some knives and forks on the table wishing that, of all the people in the world that there were to confide in, Harriet had chosen someone else. She was absolutely certain that Tom had no intention of leaving his family for Harriet but she wondered if it were best for her to see Tom in his true light and then she might turn to this Michael who sounded a very nice man. It was in no one's interest to have Harriet mooning after Tom. She wondered if Cass knew what was going on. Since her move to Whitchurch she saw Cass less often and she'd been so busy taking Oscar to shows, hoping to get him established as a stud dog, that it must be weeks since she'd been in touch with her at all.

'Don't get worked up about it all.' Kate decided to stay calm until she'd seen Cass. 'Take your time. The first thing is to get you settled in your own place. A friend of mine's looking for someone to house-sit when she goes abroad. Her usual woman's let her down so she's pretty desperate. You could go there until the autumn which would give you time to sort yourself out. Take up Michael's offer to work with him, but not on a permanent basis until you see how it goes. Get your house in Lee on the market and look about here while you're house-sitting. If you definitely decide that this is where you want to live it's much more sensible to buy your new house with the money from the old one in your pocket. You'll have to give your notice in though, won't you?'

'I shall do that anyway. I don't want to stay in Lee, whatever hap-pens between me and Tom. I think that I'd like to work with Michael but it's got so complicated now.'

'Well, give it a chance to uncomplicate itself. Now put the puppy on the sofa and come and eat.'

THE CHARMING LITTLE COTTAGE at Moortown was just what Harriet needed: somewhere of her own where she could relax and think things through. She agreed to a moving-in date and steeled herself to tell Michael. She hadn't seen or heard from Tom since that awful Monday. Perhaps she could let him know of her new plans through Cass.

Michael took it remarkably well.

'I think it's a very good idea,' he said, as they stood in his garden, watching the sun set beyond the Cornish hills. 'You can't stay here in-definitely, much as I should like it, and I'm delighted to hear that you're going to go on giving it a try at the office. I really do need someone very badly and I would like it to be you.'

'That's very nice of you.' Overcome with relief Harriet slipped her arm through his. 'Thanks for making it so easy.'

He smiled down at her, pressing her arm against his side. 'Rubbish! Did you think that I was going to scream and shout at you? I just want you to be happy, you know, and if it includes me, so much the better.'

She smiled back at him but something in his eyes made her turn away in confusion and look out towards the outcrop of Bodmin Moor, ink blue against the pale sky.

'I hope you'll come and see the cottage. It's absolutely tiny and not a bit like this place.' She sounded rather breathless, the words tripping over one another.

'Certainly I shall come. And Max, too, of course.'

'Heavens!' Harriet chuckled. 'I don't think it's big enough for Max, he'll fill the whole ground floor.'

They both looked down at Max, stretched full-length on the grass at their feet. Suddenly Harriet knew that she was going to miss them both quite dreadfully and was overwhelmed with emotion. She'd worked herself up to telling Michael her news, wondering if he'd take it silently, coldly, indifferently, and here he was being marvellous. If it weren't for Tom, she thought suddenly, I could almost go back to feeling for him just as I did all those years ago. Her control deserted her.

'Oh, Michael!' she said unhappily. 'What's the matter with me? I don't really want to leave you at all but I feel I've got to sort my life out. And there's Tom. Ohhh! I'm in such a muddle.' She abandoned herself to the luxury of tears.

Max sat up, tail wagging uncertainly, and looked at Michael who, after a moment, took Harriet in one arm whilst he felt in his pocket with his free hand for his handkerchief.

'Come on, now. Don't get worked up.' He pushed the handkerchief into her hand. 'You're only going a few miles across the moor, you know. We can be there in ten minutes. Much too close really. We shall be there so often you'll be sick of the sight of us. Don't cry, please, Harriet. There's nothing to cry about.'

'Sorry. I'm sorry,' she gulped into his handkerchief, scrubbing at her face, the tears still flowing. 'Oh, Michael, I do love you, really, but Tom gets in between. Oh, what shall I do?'

'I know, I know.' He stroked her hair, holding her tightly. 'Don't worry about it. There's plenty of time, no one's rushing you. You'll get it all sorted out. Please don't cry, Harriet.'

She clung to him, not wanting to let him go, and suddenly realised that her feelings were not purely emotional.

'Michael!' She stared up at him, aghast, her face swollen and blotchy. 'Michael, I want to go to bed with you.' She saw his face change, felt his arms stiffen. 'Oh, God! What have I said? I'm sorry, I'm sorry, how awful of me and I must look so ghastly and anyway you wouldn't want to . . . oh, hell!' She began to cry again.

To Michael, it was one of the worst moments of his life. He had no desire whatever to make love to Harriet in her present confused, emotional state, with the memory of Tom, who was, no doubt, a wonderful lover, fixed in the forefront of her mind. However, anything less would probably undermine her confidence and threaten his hopes for their future. He had to convince her that he loved her and he had to do it in bed. He took her back into his arms.

'I thought you would never ask. Harriet, you know I love you. Shall we go inside?'

She strained back to look up at him.

'Michael! Are you sure? You're just being nice, aren't you? I know I must look awful.'

'You underestimate yourself, Harriet. I shall be fulfilling a lifetime's ambition, but you must stop crying or we'll be waterlogged.'

She managed a feeble smile and allowed herself to be led into the house. He paused at the foot of the stairs, his arm still round her. 'Go on upstairs while I lock the door and turn the dinner down, then we shall be able to relax. My room, OK?' She stared at him, remembering Tom and she in her own room. He read her thoughts and bent to kiss her, smiling. 'Up you go! I'll be right with you.'

She vanished into the twilight of the upper landing and Michael went into the kitchen where he stood gazing mindlessly at the Aga. Terror gripped him. He'd never be able to do it! Not just like that, to order, as it were. He longed for a drink but she'd smell it on his breath. Not even time for a cigarette! No use, he'd have to do it cold. With a groan of despair he turned away and climbed the stairs to Harriet.

JANE, PEELING POTATOES AT the kitchen sink, felt strangely happy. It was months since she had felt like this, light of heart, confident of the future. She and Alan had enjoyed their few days together, re-establishing their relationship and planning for the baby. Jane had agreed to go with him to Chatham, to let or even sell the house, spend as much time as possible together, even if it did mean moving regularly. It would be fun at least until the baby was old enough to start school, then they'd think again. If only she could be certain that it was Alan's baby. Reaching for another potato Jane pushed the thought away. No good dwelling on it, that way lay madness. It was her punishment for playing around and she'd just have to live with it. But Alan must never know! Her heart contracted with fear at the mere thought. And Philip! What was she to do about him? How could she possibly tell him what she planned to do? He would try to kill her, or Alan, or probably both of them. Either way Alan would certainly find out the truth. There must be a way out of this terrible muddle. She finished preparing the casserole and put it in the oven. Mrs Hampton had been prevailed upon to come to supper and Jane resolved to put the problem to her. Since their last talk, Jane had put tremendous faith in the old lady she had known all her life.

When, however, several hours later, the casserole was cooked and Mrs Hampton arrived to eat it, Jane discovered that things weren't quite that simple.

'You must certainly go with 'im, Jane,' agreed Mrs Hampton, shaking out her napkin and looking with approval at the prettily laid table. 'I'm that pleased that you've made it up, what with the baby comin' an' all. But I don't know 'ow you'll keep it from young Philip, that I don't.'

'He mustn't know.' Jane ladled generous quantities of casserole on to her guest's plate. 'But you know what it's like here! It'll be all over the village in half an hour once the house is up for sale. Everyone will know, including him. And what'll I tell him? He'll kill me!'

'He's got a very nasty temper, that we do know.' Mrs Hampton accepted the plate appreciatively. 'This looks very nice, Jane love, very nice. Can't you just go off quick like an' sell the house later?'

Jane sat down with her own plate and looked at Mrs Hampton thoughtfully.

'You've got an idea there. Just go off without anyone knowing. That's what I'd like to do, but how can I explain the secrecy to Alan? And how can I sell the house when I'm up in Chatham?'

Mrs Hampton shook her head, perplexed.

'I can't tell you that,' she said at last. 'It do seem impossible without that Alan knows what's goin' on.'

'I can't tell him,' gasped Jane, laying down her fork. 'How can I? And just when everything's going nice again. Oh, I can't!'

Mrs Hampton looked at her with compassion.

'I know, love. But without that I just can't see 'ow 'tis to be done. 'Ave you thought,' she added casually, spearing a piece of potato with her fork, 'of 'aving a chat to Mrs Wivenhoe, perhaps?'

'To Cass?' Jane's mouth hung open. 'Cass! God, no! What, you mean tell her about this? About Philip and the baby and everything?'

Mrs Hampton nodded, her mouth full.

'You must be kidding! Sorry, I don't mean to be rude, but how could I? Cass, of all people! She's so . . . well . . . so . . . oh, you know!'

'No, I can't say as I do.' Mrs Hampton wiped her mouth with the napkin. 'Just because she's gentry you think she's better'n you are. 'Tisn't true. Between you an' me, this is, mind, but 'er morals ain't no better than a tomcat's.' She smiled at Jane's stunned face. 'When you're in trouble 'tis no good seekin' out the bible-punchers. 'Tis the ones who've been in trouble their-selves that you need. They've 'ad to get out of scrapes an' such, an' they're a sight more sympathetic, too. I reckon Mrs Wivenhoe's got 'erself outa plenty of scrapes.'

'I don't believe it!'

Mrs Hampton smiled.

' 'Tis between you an' me, mind. She's one o' they sorts who can't 'elp theirselves, I reckon, but this I do know. Go an' tell 'er your troubles an' you'll 'ave a friend. She'll be more use to you than I can be, I promise you.'

'You've absolutely floored me.' Jane shook her head in disbelief. 'Cass! It can't be true!'

'Take my word for it. Go an' see 'er an' ask 'er to 'elp you. This is very tasty, Jane. Worthy of your mother. What a cook she was!'

When Jane cleared away the plates her brain was seething. Could Mrs Hampton possibly be right? She remembered Cass's earlier concern for her, the good-natured attempts to help her, and recalled Cass saying, 'Are you sure there's nothing wrong? You could tell me, you know. I promise you I'm quite unshockable. After all, we've all been through it some time or other.' It was almost as if she'd known. And anyway, thought Jane, what have I got to lose? Only my marriage, she told herself hysterically, and my baby, and possibly my life!

Twenty-four

Cass replaced the telephone receiver and wandered out into the hot, peaceful garden. The summer holidays were well under way and she was enjoying a day of comparative and welcome peace. The children were all employed in enjoying themselves elsewhere and she was quite alone. When Kate had telephoned and invited herself over there had been no reason or excuse to put her off. However, she felt strangely disturbed at the thought of seeing Kate, probably because she knew that she was the one person in the world from whom it was impossible to keep her true feelings secret. She had hardly seen her since she moved and, in her absorption with Nick, had hardly missed her. But now she was coming over and Cass dithered between throwing a cloak of secrecy over the affair with Nick or revelling in the relief of telling her the whole thing. The trouble with that, of course, was that it would only work if the confidante was of like mind and was going to sympathise. Cass had a very realistic idea of how Kate would receive the news and she wondered if it were probably best to put on a jolly front and pretend that everything was as usual. On the other hand, it would be so wonderful to pour it all out, to discuss it all with Kate as she had discussed other things on so many other occasions, to laugh and giggle with her and behave like an irresponsible child.

The strain was beginning to tell on Cass. Nick's elusiveness, his refusal to be tied down, was very wearing. Cass had been the one in the past who had always called the tune, granted the favours, and being kept on tenterhooks was both novel and exhausting. She could not be sure of him for a second and she knew that if she didn't abide by his rules she would lose him. Yet, when they were together, he treated her with a depth of passion that she had known with no other lover. Then all her frustrations were swept away and she felt as though every one of her faculties and senses was at full stretch. Nor was it just a physical relationship. During those lunches and other public meetings they talked about everything under the sun. He was erudite and amusing and listened, fascinated, as she talked about her life and her family. With Tom and her other lovers, she knew that she could control events but now she was out of her depth. Nick was too old and too experienced to be treated like a lovesick boy and, anyway, it wasn't in his character. There was nothing of the child about him and even in the high moments of their passion, Cass knew that it was still Nick who was in control. It added a new dimension to love-making, leaving her feeling shaken and weak. She felt, for the first time in her life, clinging and helpless and she revelled in his tall strength and his power over her.

How to explain it all to Kate? She had a very good idea that Kate had gone through exactly the same process with Alex. She had been knocked sideways by it all. The fact remained that when it came to a choice between Alex and the twins there had been no contest. And Alex wasn't a married man. She knew that Kate would not encourage her to put her marriage at risk for a man who was obviously very attached to his wife. Sarah was the big fly in the ointment. He never discussed her with Cass but she couldn't help but wonder why he remained with an older, plain and apparently rather dreary woman when he could have had almost any woman he chose. It was a mystery.

Cass turned back to the house. Kate would be here at any moment so at least she could get the kettle on. As for the rest, she would have to play it by ear.

KATE WAS DRIVING THOUGHTFULLY across the moor. She couldn't decide whether to present Harriet's dilemma to Cass or to pretend that

she was assuming that all was well and see what transpired. It would
be an ironic manifestation of poetic justice if it were to be Tom, after
all this, who broke up his marriage. Kate shook her head. She simply
couldn't believe that after all this time it could come to that. However
Tom and Cass might behave, they had a very stable relationship and a
great deal to lose. Surely they wouldn't throw it all away? Kate wished
that the General were still alive. Although she couldn't have discussed
this particular situation with him, he had a knack of saying things,
quoting passages that on reflection had great relevance to life and had
the effect of clearing her brain. She missed him every bit as much as
she had known she would and still caught herself talking aloud to him,
usually when she was walking on the moor. The mere thought of him
was enough to calm her fears and give her thoughts a sensible direction. When she drove up the drive and parked by the front steps she
was still thinking of him and, when she slammed the door and looked
round and saw Cass standing by the door, all her inhibitions fell away.

They grinned at one another and the next moment were hugging as
they had for the past twenty-four years. Kate held Cass away from her
and knew at once that she was in the throes of something momentous.
She looked at her for a long moment.

'I have a horrid feeling that whatever it is, it's a great deal worse
than Russian roulette,' she said, and Cass burst out laughing.

'I should have known that I couldn't fool you,' she said. 'Come on.
Let's have a drink. I don't think that coffee will be nearly strong
enough.'

'Oh, Cass. What's going on?'

Cass went ahead into the kitchen. She fiddled with mugs and
spoons and then, abandoning them, she turned to look at Kate who
had sat down at the table.

'With my track record I don't expect you to take this seriously but
I've met someone and,' she clasped her hands, rubbed her face and fi-
nally shook her head, 'well, I've just fallen for him. Really, I mean.
Don't you dare laugh, Kate.'

But Kate was showing no inclination to laugh. She watched Cass compassionately knowing that this was exactly what she had always feared would happen. Cass's lighthearted amours had carried with them the risk of backfiring and injuring her. Kate felt no desire whatever to laugh.

'Does Tom know?' she asked.

'Tom,' said Cass with a little snort, 'is far too wrapped up in Harriet Masters to have the least idea about anything else.'

Well, that at least answered the question about whether Cass knew or not. Kate hesitated a little.

'Is it because of that?' she began tentatively.

'Good grief, no,' said Cass at once. 'I pushed Tom into Harriet's arms to keep him off the scent. You know she's always had a thing about him.'

'Oh, Cass.' Kate put her head in her hands. She rubbed her forehead with her fingers and looked up to see Cass watching her. 'What are you going to do?'

'I don't know. Nothing desperate at the moment. I love him, Kate.'

'I'm sure you do,' said Kate gently. 'Just don't do anything in a hurry. Don't go throwing the baby out with the bath water. You've got so much to lose, Cass.'

'You don't need to tell me that.'

Kate had never seen quite that mixture of despair, joy and fear on Cass's face and she got up and went to her.

'Remember your old pa,' she said, putting her arm round her. 'Remember how he used to tell us "think each problem through twice and then don't do it"? I know it was a joke but it's not a bad rule.'

At the mention of the General, Cass began to weep. Kate pushed her into a chair.

'You're right,' she said. 'This calls for something stronger than coffee. Hang on. I'll get us a drink.'

HARRIET OPENED THE CUPBOARD that housed her clothes and gazed at them despairingly. She was sick to death of them. Michael had suggested that he drive her back to Lee-on-Solent to collect some of her belongings. They could pack the back of the Volvo with the smaller items and arrange to put the rest into store until she decided what to do with them. The house was already up for sale and, apparently, great interest was being shown in it. Harriet, however, was filled with a tremendous apathy. The mere thought of the drive to Hampshire was horrific to her, let alone all that packing up . . . Michael would help, of course. Michael. Harriet shut the cupboard and sat down on the bed. He had been wonderful to her, had made love to her with such tenderness that she'd been near to tears, but for himself it had been an appalling failure. In the end he'd given up, dressed and, bleak-faced, had gone downstairs. When she'd joined him, wrapping herself in his dressing-gown, he'd been hunched beside the Aga. He looked so vulnerable and unhappy that her heart went out to him.

'Sorry about that.' He didn't look at her.

'Michael, please! It couldn't matter less. And anyway it was wonderful for me. You mustn't blame yourself. After all, it's not your fault if I don't turn you on.'

'For God's sake!' She jumped as he rose with a violent movement and slammed his hand down on the table. 'It's not your fault. OK? I'm just not very good at it. Not like Tom, for instance, who I expect is wonderful in bed.'

'Michael!' She stared at him aghast.

'Sorry. I'm sorry. That was unforgivable.' He rubbed his hand across his brow. 'I'm in a disgusting mood. I think I'll go and walk it off.'

Ignoring her pleas he went into the utility room where she heard him talking to Max. Presently the back door slammed. After a few moments she went to sit where he had been sitting, huddling against the Aga for warmth.

Now, sitting on the bed in the cottage at Moortown, she realised that she'd hurt him terribly. She knew she shouldn't have asked him to do it, especially when she had known in her heart that he didn't really want to. It had been an act of total selfishness. She knew now that subconsciously she had hoped that it would help her make up her mind and it had all backfired on her. Michael's love-making had been a continuation of his caring and all that he felt for her, she'd been pleasured in every way possible, and she'd just lain there and loved it. With Tom it was like sharing a performance with an expert at the height of his powers, exciting, yes, and satisfying but not so moving. And what did any of it prove? That Michael was in love with her and Tom was not? And more to the point, how did she feel herself? Just when Tom was at last within her grasp, after years of longing for that very thing, she was now wondering if, after all, she was in love with Michael. It was like some terrible joke. She wondered if Michael could possibly continue to love her now that he knew about Tom. And, if he did, then why had their love-making been so disastrous for him?

Michael had continued to behave exactly as usual, just as he had after the Tom incident, but Harriet hated to feel that there was anything unsaid between them. Certainly there had been no suggestion of further love-making and Harriet, who was no psychologist and had no idea of Michael's fear of being found inadequate after Tom's sexual feats, could only assume that perhaps he didn't love her after all. And, given that it was Tom she was supposed to be in love with, should that matter?

Perhaps a trip to Lee with Michael would be a good thing. They would have the opportunity to talk things over and if they stayed overnight on neutral ground—after all Michael need never know that Tom had ever been to her house in Lee—perhaps things may straighten themselves out. Was it possible to be in love with two men at once? Harriet sighed and started to get dressed.

IN THE END, JANE telephoned Cass and asked her to come over. She said that she had a problem that she didn't know how to solve and was hoping that Cass could help her. Cass, who now knew that she had Kate's support and sympathy, if not her approval, and was rather surprised at the measure of relief at having been able to share everything with her, was only too pleased to help a fellow sufferer and agreed to come to coffee the next morning.

She hesitated as she approached the gate. Was Jane a back-door person? When visiting most of her friends it would not occur to Cass to knock at the front door and then wait politely to be let in. Much more likely would be for her to let herself in through a back or kitchen door calling: 'Hi! It's me!' Jane, however, was not what she would term a friend and Cass couldn't imagine Jane walking into anyone's house uninvited, however well she knew them.

As it was, the problem was solved for her. As she advanced up the drive the front door opened and Jane stood waiting for her.

'Hi!' cried Cass, her glance travelling over Jane's clothes and hair and wondering, as usual, where on earth she had found those awful old jeans—and that jersey. How she could go out and choose things like that was beyond Cass's powers of imagination. And why did her hair look as if it had been attacked by a knife and fork? She could be quite attractive if she tried.

'Hello. Go on in, it's the room on your left.' Jane shut the front door behind her wondering, as usual, why Cass always had to dress up. She obviously spent a fortune on her clothes which seemed so pointless stuck out here in the middle of nowhere.

'What a cosy room!' Cass turned to beam at Jane who was well aware that her lounge-diner could have been dropped into Cass's drawing room quite easily and with room to spare. 'I had no idea these houses were so nice.'

You've only seen one room, thought Jane sourly, and then pulled herself together. She'd get nowhere if she let her antagonism overcome her.

'Yes, they're quite cosy but a bit on the small side. Actually the house is one of the things I want to talk to you about but I'll make the coffee first.'

She went off to the kitchen while Cass did an inventory of the small, neat room. Three-piece Dralon-covered suite at one end . . . a round coffee table with a glass top inset . . . television on its own table . . . various pot plants . . . a ghastly picture of a shoreline with big breakers turning to white horses. Cass shuddered and glanced through to the dining area. One oval teak dining table . . . four matching chairs (more Dralon) . . . another ghastly picture—this time of an Italian child with tears trickling from its improbably huge eyes. How incredibly clean and highly polished everything was; perhaps she ought to have Jane cleaning for her instead of Hammy. On second thoughts, that wouldn't work now that Alan had been made up. One couldn't have one officer's wife cleaning for another officer's wife—not at all the thing!

'Come and sit down.' Cass jumped as Jane, with a loaded tray, spoke from the doorway.

'Right.' Cass sat herself down in one of the armchairs. 'Gosh, that looks good.'

'Yes,' Jane surveyed the tray glumly, despising herself for bringing out the best china and baking some special biscuits. She'd even bought lump sugar, though she hadn't any tongs. The fresh coffee smelt delicious as she poured it from the glass jug. Why not just the usual instant in a mug?

'Thanks,' Cass accepted the coffee and took two biscuits. 'Now, come on, what's all this about? I'm dying of curiosity.'

Silly cow, thought Jane, but at least it makes it easier than pretending it's a purely social visit. 'I'm in a mess.' Might as well come straight to the point. 'The only other person who knows anything about it is Mrs Hampton and she told me to ask you for advice.'

'Did she really?' Cass arched her brows. 'It all sounds very mysterious.'

'When Alan got made up,' began Jane, somewhat desperately, 'he became different somehow, bad-tempered, like, and sort of, well, unapproachable. He began to nag at me, said I'd never make an officer's wife, criticised my clothes, you know what I mean?'

Cass nodded silently—and who could blame him? she thought—and sipped at her coffee.

'Well, things went from bad to worse. We were always rowing and I was very miserable.' She paused and swallowed. 'Alan'd gone off to sea and I met up with an old boyfriend. We'd nearly got married backalong but somehow it didn't happen and when we met up again, well . . . '

Cass nodded. 'I know,' she said, 'it was nice to find an old friend when you were so unhappy, someone who knew you well and was still fond of you.'

'Exactly!' cried Jane with relief. Cass made it sound very normal. 'He was such a comfort, see? We could talk about old times and he made me laugh.' She paused again.

'How important that is,' remarked Cass thoughtfully. 'One is always so attracted to people who make one laugh. And so you found yourself in bed with him?'

'Well, yes.' Jane was taken aback, she hadn't expected Cass to get to the point quite so quickly.

'Understandable.' Cass helped herself to another biscuit. 'And now what? Do you want to leave Alan and go back to the boyfriend?'

'No! No, it's not that. I thought I did for a bit but it wouldn't work, I can see that now. It's taken me long enough to find out, mind, but I know it now. It's Alan I want. We've talked it over and he's changed again—come more like he used to be. We're going to try again, see?'

'So what's the problem? Are you afraid to tell the boyfriend?'

'I'm pregnant.' Jane placed her untouched coffee back on the tray. 'Alan thinks it's his,' she said, 'I've let him think it's his.' She looked at Cass defiantly. 'It could be his! There's a fifty-fifty chance, see? Anyway, what else can I do? I'm not having an abortion.'

'Of course not.' Cass refilled her cup and ladled in cream and sugar absentmindedly. 'I'd have done exactly the same in your place. We'll just have to hope it doesn't have ginger hair or something or Alan might smell a rat.'

'I don't think there's any danger of that, they've both got the same colouring. In fact, they're very alike. Probably that's what attracted me to Alan in the first place, his being so like Ph——' She paused, 'Like this other man.'

Cass seemed not to have noticed the slip. 'Of course, it still may be a problem genetically. After all, you don't know what the grandparents were like.' She caught sight of Jane's puzzled face and stopped. There was no point in worrying her unnecessarily. 'Yes, well, that's OK then, but I must say that if that's the case I can't see what the problem is.'

'You see it's OK with Alan. He doesn't know anything about . . . this other man and he thinks the baby's his. That's all right, but if . . . the other man finds out that I'm finishing with him he'll probably do something dreadful. Oh yes he will!' This in answer to the faintly quizzical expression on Cass's face. 'You don't know him. He's rough! And he's got a really terrible temper, he's been in trouble with the police and allsorts. If he finds out he's quite capable of coming over and doing something bad, 'specially if he's had a few drinks.'

'But I don't see how he can help but know?' Cass frowned in an effort to understand. 'I assume you let this chap think that the baby was his and that you were going to go off with him. If you stay with Alan he must find out.'

'Yes, but you see, he needn't!' Jane leaned forward, regaining her self-control. 'Alan's been appointed to Chatham. He joins in a few weeks' time and I want us to get away quick before Philip finds out.' It was no good, in her eager intensity the name slipped out. She did not notice and if Cass did she made no sign.

'Right, I see what you're getting at, but how on earth . . . '

'Exactly! You see the problem. I've got to sell or rent and get Alan away without anyone knowing. But how?'

Cass sat still, concentrating hard. 'Do you plan to move into a married quarter?'

Jane shrugged. 'Dunno.'

'OK. Now look, I think I can help.'

'Really?' Jane gaped at Cass in astonishment. To be honest she hadn't seen how Cass could possibly help but so far Mrs Hampton had been right. Seeing Cass giving her all to Jane's problems, showing nothing but a willingness to help and offering no criticism, made Jane look again at her guest and she felt her dislike beginning to thaw.

'I think so. I know a couple who want to rent a place around here. They're Navy, but they don't want a married quarter. The husband's already living in the mess in *Drake* so they could move in at any time. They're so desperate that they'll take what I recommend and they'll jump at this house. So that's this end sorted out. Chatham's not so easy but I know quite a few people in the area and I may be able to find you a hiring there. I'll make some 'phone calls this evening. Now, when's Alan home next?'

'Not for a few weeks, unless it's unexpected, and then he's got two weeks' leave before he goes to Chatham.'

'Right! Then what we've got to do is to have everything tied up so that you go to Chatham more or less the day after he comes home on leave so he doesn't have a chance to go around telling people that you're off. It means you can't take any furniture, of course, so you'll have to go to a furnished place. D'you mind that?'

'I don't mind anything so long as we get away in one piece,' said Jane, fervently.

'How will Alan take it?'

'Dunno. After all, he wouldn't be able to hang around down here to sell the house. It would be up to me anyway, wouldn't it?'

'OK. So you tell him that being preggers you don't feel up to all that and you've had this offer to let that you couldn't refuse but it has to be let furnished and you have to be out by a certain date or you'll lose it. You leave a key with me and when this couple arrive I'll let them in and sort all that out for you. We'll get something legal sorted out. I'll ask Martin, our chap, about that.'

Jane stared at her and a twinge of resentment returned. She would be the sort who would call her solicitor by his Christian name but you had to hand it to her, she'd got all her marbles.

'All we've got to do now,' Cass continued, 'is to find you somewhere in or near Chatham, otherwise it all falls to the floor. It's so infuriating that wives aren't allowed to apply for quarters and so stupid too. After all, if the Navy hadn't appointed Alan to Chatham you wouldn't be going. Still, that's the rule and by the time Alan can apply, your secret would be out of the bag. Never mind. I'm sure we'll manage. So! Is there anything else?'

'Well, no, you seem to have it all sorted out,' Jane gestured, help-lessly. 'I don't know what to say.'

'Don't say anything. What are friends for? I'll let you know what happens when I've made a few 'phone calls. In fact, I might hurry home now and make a start. No time to lose.'

'Well, if you're sure . . . ' Jane stood up, awkwardly. 'It's really good of you. I'll pay for the calls, of course.'

'Oh, don't be daft!' Cass gathered up her bag. 'I'll let you know as soon as I've got some news. Thanks for the coffee.'

Jane watched her walk down the garden path. Even now she couldn't like her. She had a strange sensation of fear, shuddered and then shook herself mentally as she shut the door.

'Pull yourself together,' she said, 'it's the baby making you feel fanciful. Old Cass wouldn't hurt a fly and she's solved your problem anyway—well, almost. I think I'll make myself a decent cup of in-stant.'

Twenty-five

Charlotte never found the opportunity to talk to Tom. On the occasions when he was at home he was preoccupied and, although he was still affectionate, it was evident that his thoughts were elsewhere. It was impossible, whilst he was in this mood, to arrive at that state of intimacy with him that would have been necessary for the opening of her innermost heart. He would disappear for hours on end and when he arrived back he would be evasive as to where he had been. Charlotte recognised—after years of living with Cass—a disturbing pattern in his behaviour and began to feel worried. However, a conspiracy between the twins and Hugh, designed to keep her up to the mark and off to Blundells without any last-minute panics, kept her busy and full of plans for the new term. The sixth form, they assured her, was quite different from school as she had known it so far, and Hugh promised her visits to him in Bristol in an effort to show her that she had her own life to lead and that it was time she started to grow up. Since Cass seemed to be living a very muted life at present, with only the occasional dashes off to Exeter to lunch with some girlfriend or other, Charlotte was coming to the decision that she must take a chance and leave her parents to their own devices. Such golden things were promised her and she couldn't seriously believe that her father was playing around.

She went off with Oliver quite happily, prepared to overcome her shyness and fear of new things and strange people, and armed with the promise from Hugh that, on her first exeat, he would come down and take her out.

For Charlotte that weekend was like a dream come true. On Saturday morning she and Hugh went riding. In the evening they went into Plymouth to a cinema and finished the day off with a Chinese meal. On Sunday they took a picnic and drove first to Dartmouth, where they wandered by the river and through the town, quiet now with the tourists gone, before driving along the coast to Slapton Sands. The wonderful autumn weather, which seemed as if it would last for ever, was quite warm enough to make picnicking on the beach delightful. Hugh was a good companion. He made her laugh with stories of his tutors and fellow students and she was fascinated by his description of university life.

A few hours later, when he dropped her off at school on his way back to Bristol, Charlotte's cup was running over. He had told her that he wouldn't be down again for several weeks, essays to catch up on, financial pressures, etc., but she didn't mind. She was beginning to form a plan. Why shouldn't she go to Bristol to see him? He'd always suggested that she should, although he hadn't actually mentioned it recently, probably because he felt she couldn't afford it either.

Later still, re-living the hours spent with Hugh, another thought emerged. She would go to Bristol without telling him and take him by surprise. She hugged the idea to her, delighted with it. He would be pleased at her initiative and it would show him that she could look after herself. The other girls in the sixth form were almost frighteningly self-assured. They travelled all over the place and went to parties all on their own and thought nothing of it. Well, she would show them—and Hugh—that she could do it too. She decided to wait until half-term. It would be easier to organise from home.

Hugh had been very popular at Blundells and several girls who were now in the Upper Sixth had had crushes on him. They regarded Charlotte with a certain amount of envy when it appeared that she was, more or less, his regular girlfriend. Hugh—modest young man though he was—had known that Charlotte's stock would increase quite dramatically if she were to be seen as his protégée, as it were. It was to encourage her, to assist her over the first difficult hurdles, that he'd invited her to the school and let it be known that she was a special friend. It was the best he could do for her, apart from the odd treat when he was down for the weekend. He looked upon her as a younger sister of whom he was very fond and towards whom he felt very protective. Some instinct had led him to keep his growing friendship with Lucinda private and he was relieved now that, since it might very well have queered Charlotte's pitch there, she had never been to Blundells. He was strongly attracted to Lucinda and she to him and he was hoping that, as soon as Charlotte had found her feet, her infatuation for him would die a natural death and they could all get on with their own lives. He considered her preoccupation with her mother's infidelities morbid and had felt that it would be much healthier for her to get away to school and see that she could have a life of her own. It would bring other things into line and give her a sense of proportion. Hugh knew Cass and liked her enormously. He was aware of her great charm and secretly wondered if Charlotte was jealous of her beautiful mother. She certainly adored her father and when, during the holidays, Charlotte had begun to suggest that he, too, might be playing around, Hugh felt that it was time for action and, enlisting the twins, who viewed him with a certain amount of awe, he had set about directing her thoughts in a different channel.

Charlotte was very aware of the envy and interest her friendship with Hugh was causing and revelled in it. The whole class knew that Hugh was down from Bristol for the weekend—some of them had seen her being dropped off—and she had every intention of telling them what a fantastic time she'd had with him. She could already imagine how wonderful it would be if she were able to brag about going to Bristol to visit him.

'Oh, I'm going up to Bristol at half-term to see Hugh.' She could imagine herself saying it casually to the other girls.

Charlotte began to make plans.

CASS SAT AT THE kitchen table looking at her unopened letters. Gemma had gone off to school with Sophie and Gus lay stretched out by the Aga. The house was full of silence.

Cass drew the letters to her, slit the envelopes and, placing them in a neat pile, opened the top one. The address merely read: At sea.

Dear Cass,

Hope all is well at home. This is just a quickie as I want to catch the chopper. It seems that we'll be in next weekend as the boat has finished work-up and we're ready for the 'biggy.' Looks as if I might miss Christmas this year. Boring, isn't it? Never mind, it's years since I was at sea for Chrissy, so I can't complain. Anyway, looking forward to the w/e, should be in by Friday lunchtime. I'll cadge a lift out. See you then,
    All love as always to you and the kids, Tom xx

PS: Seen anything of old Harriet? Expect she's gone home by now.
                                                    Love, T.

Cass smiled at the postscript and opened the second envelope. The address was a Tavistock one and Cass perused it closely.

Dear Cass,

Couldn't get you on the phone so I thought I'd drop you a line to say that I've settled into my temporary new home— address as above. I've almost certainly decided to go into partnership with Michael—the chap you met that weekend—so I'll be looking about for a permanent place as soon as the house in Lee has sold. Love to see you any time, hope you're all OK.
                                                    Love, Harriet

PS: I suppose Tom has gone back to sea? Hope for your sake that it's not for too long!

Cass smiled again and reached for the third letter. This had no address at all and was typed.

My dearest darling,

This is breaking all the rules and I rely on you absolutely to destroy it as soon as you've read it. I was truly sorry that I had to cancel our few days away. I don't think you realise how much you mean to me. I've never known anything like this in my life before. I thought I was much too old to feel as I do but I'm like a boy of eighteen. I must see you again soon. Sarah is away next w/e. Please can we go away then? I shall phone you.

There was no signature. Cass's face changed as she read it and she pressed it to her lips. 'Oh, Nick,' she murmured, 'oh, my darling.' She read the letter again and then crumpled it into a ball. Almost immediately she straightened it out and read it a third time. 'Darling,' she said again and, folding the letter into a small square, put it in her pocket. The fourth letter came from Chatham.

My dear Cass,

You're in luck but then you always did have the luck of the devil. The Jacksons—remember them, he was on *Valiant* with Tom?— are going off to Canada on a two-year exchange in a fortnight and their people have let them down, so they're desperate. If you can vouch for this couple they'll let them have the place, of course they may even know them. The name doesn't ring a bell. Are they submariners? Anyway, I'll put their telephone number at the end so you can phone them direct. Must dash to pick Thomas up from school. How's your Thomas and all the Smalls? Not so small now, of course. Terrifying, isn't it? Must get together soon—but how?

All love,
Jenny

The last letter bore the crest of *HMS Drake* in Devonport.

Dear Cass,

I just don't know how to thank you enough. Annie and I were getting quite desperate. She can't stand the thought of a quarter, and hirings and lets are like gold dust. She told me to tell you how grateful she is and that when we've moved in we'll stand you dinner. I've described it to her as best I can from your description—I don't quite understand the secrecy and silence bit—and she says that it will do fine. The village sounds super and, of course, it will be marvellous to be on the Moor. Let us know where we go from here.

Bless you, Cass. Regards to Tom,

Martin

Cass gave a little nod of pleasure and her expression grew thoughtful. She took the small square of paper from her pocket and, unfolding it, read it again.

'Oh, Nick, darling. I love you,' she murmured. 'How on earth can I do anything with Tom coming home? And half-term as well. Oh, hell!' Her gaze roamed over the table as if seeking a conclusion and fell on the letters. Well, at least it looked as though several other people's problems were being solved, and putting her letter resolutely away she went into the hall to telephone Jane.

KATE SAT IN THE warm October sunshine, drinking a cup of coffee and worrying about Cass. There was no doubt that she was in a bad way. Kate had never seen her like this before and she was truly anxious for her, much more anxious than she was about Tom. It seemed unlikely that his affair with Harriet would last very long. Already Harriet was in two minds, dithering between Tom and Michael, and it would be quite out of character if Tom were to be regarding the relationship in a serious light. Kate was well aware that he had enjoyed one or two flings before now, which was all to the good in light of Cass's tendencies, and it was reasonable to assume that he intended Harriet to be no more than a passing fancy. She remembered Tom's attitude towards her when she had left Mark. Several times he had implied that he was available should she need a man, obviously feeling that he would be doing her a favour, implying that she must be pretty desperate now that she was without a man of her own to satisfy her physical needs.

Kate, remembering Cass's voice on the phone earlier, shook her head. It seemed that this Nick had asked her to go away for the weekend and Cass had every intention of going despite the fact that Tom was home for the weekend and Charlotte and Oliver started their half-term two days before it. Kate had begged her to put it out of her mind, to wait for another occasion. But Cass was adamant. Kate's heart ached for her. There was no doubt that she was in love with this man and Kate, remembering only too clearly how she had felt about Alex in those early months, knew that Cass was beyond listening to advice or heeding caution.

'I don't care if I do get the bullet this time,' she had said. 'Please, Kate. Don't go on about it. Just tell me you'll have Gus. And the children too if I can't get them farmed out. I think that Tom will go and stay with Harriet. I'm leaving her letter in a very obvious place. I hope he does and then I shan't feel guilty.'

'Oh, Cass . . . '

'I know, I know. Don't nag, there's a duck. Oliver's going to my aged aunt. D'you remember her at my old pa's funeral? She's his sister. She was just back from abroad when Daddy died and she took an enormous fancy to Oliver. Says he's just like Daddy when he was young and of course he's an Oliver, too. Anyway, he's going off to her, all being well, and Gemma's staying with Sophie. Charlotte's talking about going up to a school friend in Bristol. Saul doesn't come home 'til later. The thing is that I want to shut the house up so that Tom has every excuse to go to Harriet. I know it sounds silly but it'll make me feel better about it somehow if he's with her.'

'It sounds as if you've got everything organised. Where do I come in, apart from having Gus?'

'Well, with luck you don't. I just need to know that if anything goes wrong with the children's plans I can call on you.'

'Of course you can. But, honestly, Cass . . . '

'No, no. It's no good butting, Kate. I'm going and that's all there is to it. I'll let you know if I need you. Bless you.'

Kate sighed and stood her empty coffee cup on the terrace. She remembered how long the holidays had seemed when they kept her from Alex and how she had burned and longed for him. Even now she missed him: missed that feeling of being alive in every nerve, every corpuscle tingling and alert to the loved one's touch. It was like a terrible illness, throwing past and future into dim unimportance, only the fever of this moment mattering, burning one up, so that one was prepared to consign duties, responsibilities, even loved ones, to the flames. The trouble was that it was so often no more than a passing fever and when one recovered it was sometimes too late to regain all that one had lost.

There was simply nothing she could do. Cass did not want the cold hand of common sense laid on the fiery brow of her passion and if she refused to have the children, Cass would merely find someone else—Abby probably—and carry on as before. Kate certainly had no intention of antagonising her. She wanted to be on hand, keeping the lines of communication open, so as to be ready for every eventuality. Perhaps a whole weekend with this Nick might do the trick, get him out of her system. Kate found herself thinking of the General. What would he have advised? She felt that in some way that she was letting him down and despair filled her.

'Please don't let anything happen to her,' she found herself saying but she did not know to whom she prayed.

CASS WENT ABOUT HER last-minute arrangements methodically, cancelling milk and papers—making it as uncomfortable for Tom as possible—and eating up all the leftovers. She wrote to Saul telling him that they would be away and phoned Abby to confirm that Gemma would be with them on Friday, coming with Sophie straight from school. Oliver had been collected from Blundells by Aunt Maria's handyman-cum-chauffeur and Kate picked Charlotte up with the twins, dropping her off at the Rectory and collecting Gus at the same time.

Up in her bedroom, Charlotte, in a frenzy of nerves, packed and unpacked several times. Excitement was fast giving way to anxiety and twice she had almost phoned Hugh to tell him of her plans. Each time her hand had dropped away from the receiver and, after a moment, she had returned to her bedroom for another bout of packing.

'Don't be so wet!' she muttered fiercely to herself. 'Have the courage of your convictions! Hugh's always telling you to have more initiative. He'll be pleased! Anyway, you don't need his permission or approval to go to Bristol.'

When the round nylon carry-all had finally been filled to her satisfaction she sat down on her bed and drew a guide book to Bristol from her rubbed and shabby leather satchel. She studied it closely, tracing with her finger the roads between the small hotel, the address of which she had located in the back of an AA book, and Hugh's Hall of Residence, only a few minutes' walk away. Both, however, were miles from the station. She'd have to take a taxi.

Charlotte had never been away from home alone before and she felt a twinge of apprehension, quickly suppressed. Luckily her allowance had hardly been touched these past months and there was plenty in her account to cope with a weekend in Bristol.

She didn't know whether to be hurt or relieved by Cass's indifference to the whole escapade. To be fair, she had told her mother that she was staying with a school friend's family in Bristol and had answered Cass's questions with exaggerated patience. Yes, the train went straight through with no changing. Yes, someone would be meeting the train. No, she didn't need any money, and for goodness' sake, don't fuss, Ma! Yes, she'd organised a lift to Plymouth with Mrs Haynes, who was going in shopping and who had agreed to drop her at the station. Anything else? Cass had hesitated. Since she had no intention of giving Charlotte a telephone number or address in case of emergency she could hardly ask for one in return. She decided to let the matter drop. After all, Charlotte would be quite safe with her friends.

Charlotte put away the book, counted the cash that she'd drawn out over the past few weeks from her building society account in Tiverton, and decided that, on the whole, she was relieved that Cass hadn't probed further and discovered the truth. She may have put a ban on the whole thing if she'd known that Charlotte wasn't going to friends or she might have wanted to phone the hotel and check it out. Much better as it was. After all, what could go wrong?

CASS DOUBLE-CHECKED THE TRAIN timetable to make certain that Charlotte would be well on her way to Bristol by the time that she, Cass, left for Shropshire. She found Harriet's letter and re-read Tom's, praying that the boat wouldn't come in early.

Lastly, on Friday morning, with everyone gone, she phoned Jane.

'Hi, it's Cass. Everything OK? . . . Good. So it's just a question of keeping a low profile locally for a couple of weeks? . . . Fine. Look, I'm off for a couple of days, back sometime Monday. You don't anticipate any problems before then? . . . Right . . . Oh, don't mention it. Isn't it marvellous how everything worked out? Must be meant . . . Quite. Now, no panics, bad for the baby, OK? I'll phone as soon as I'm back. Take care. 'Bye.'

She replaced the receiver and stood for a minute, thinking of Nick. Only a few more hours and she would be with him . . .

Twenty-six

At the time that Cass was talking to Jane, Kate was walking on Plaster Down. The dogs gambolled in and out of the leat as the sun sucked up the last shreds of the thinning mist and shone warm on Kate's back. Her thoughts twisted and turned, part of her mind on Cass, part on her own situation. She had discovered, through the naval grapevine, that it seemed unlikely that Mark would get his third stripe and intended to leave the Navy within the next few years. This wasn't terribly surprising. If Mark was not to be promoted to Commander, then he would be unable to drive a nuclear or polaris submarine and his sea-going days were over. She knew how much he would hate pushing a pen at Northwood or the MOD for the rest of his working life. There was a rumour that he intended to go to Canada. He had struck up a friendship with a Canadian Engineer Officer over on exchange some years before and, according to Kate's source, he had offered Mark a job in his father's company where he himself now worked.

'Let him go,' Chris had advised. 'Have done with it all. We'll manage with the boys. If their father has gone abroad, they'll be eligible for grants and things so stop worrying. There's a few years to go yet. It's not worth fighting it and dragging it all up again.'

Kate had agreed with relief and prayed that Chris was right. She never heard from Mark. He paid a sum of money monthly for the twins' upkeep and settled the bills that the school sent in. Occasionally he wrote to the twins but never to Kate. Sometimes she wrote to him telling him of the boys' achievements and to arrange the yearly visit to their grandparents so that it coincided with his leave but, in the main, silence prevailed. She knew that, despite his fifteen years, Giles was still nervous of Mark and neither of the boys looked forward to their yearly holiday with their father so perhaps it would be a relief to all parties to have the last threads cut. Kate wondered briefly how Mark's parents would take the defection of their only son and turned her thoughts to Cass. She would have set off by now and Kate sighed. She called to the dogs and turned to retrace her steps. She would be very relieved when the weekend was over and Cass was safely back again.

As CASS DROVE UP the motorway towards the Severn Bridge she was aware that her present feelings were entirely new to her. She felt as if she had cast all her cares and responsibilities away and was possessed of a great happiness. None of the sensations she usually experienced at this stage of a relationship were present. No sharpening of wits ready for the cut and thrust of flirtatious backchat, no keen anticipation of new sexual technique, none of the thrill of knowing that she was successfully deceiving not only Tom and her friends but another wife or girlfriend: just this deep joy.

The day reflected her mood. The sun shone, warm and mellow, on glowing leaves and berries not yet torn from their moorings by harsh winds or beaten down by fierce rain. This glorious weather seemed set to last for ever.

Once through Ludlow she pulled in to consult the map Nick had sent her. Concluding rightly that she could get herself as far as Ludlow he had drawn the map beginning at the turning off at Wootton and it was marked with strange and delightful names—Chapel Lawn, New Invention, Clun.

'"Clungunford, Clunbury, Clunton and Clun / Are the quietest places under the sun," ' he had quoted to her during one of their lunches. 'Of course you've read Houseman. You're going to love Shropshire, my darling.'

From what she'd seen of it she felt that he was right. However, she made several wrong turns before she found the narrow lane that wound on beneath the shoulder of the hill and finally brought her to Nick.

Leaving the lane where it started a sharp upward climb, she swung the car on to a narrow track that doubled back on itself, sloped down to a stream and stopped. Beyond the stream stood a little wooden house, rather like a Swiss chalet, painted black, with green window frames and a green door. A thread of blue smoke drifted from its twisted chimney and a wicker chair stood on the verandah. The house nestled into the side of the hill beyond which the sun was now disappearing and, even as she looked, the door opened and Nick hurried out.

'Thank God, my darling,' he called. 'I was beginning to worry.'

Her heart leapt up in her breast. How tall and straight he was, how distinguished, and he wore such delightful clothes. His cords were a loden green, his Viyella shirt matched them perfectly and his cashmere sweater was the colour of porridge. His brogues gleamed like chestnuts and he looked expensive, well-preserved and charming.

He crossed the wooden footbridge and came round to the car window. For a moment or two they smiled at one another and when she put out her hand to him he raised her fingers to his lips. She gave a little shiver of pleasure as his hazel eyes looked into hers and then he moved back.

'Look.' He indicated an open-fronted barn, built back into the hedge where his own car was already parked. 'Put her in there beside mine.'

Once out of the car Cass realised that the place was a perfect hideaway. Both the house and the barn were impossible to see from the lane and she turned to Nick with a smile.

'It's perfect,' she said. 'Is it just as lovely inside?'

He exhaled deeply with relief.

'Thank heavens you approve,' he said. 'I lost my nerve as the day wore on and I was sure you'd hate it. It's a bit primitive, I'm afraid. Careful now! The bridge is a bit rickety. It gets a hell of a beating in the winter when the water pours down off the hills and the stream becomes quite impassable. Not that one would want to be here in the winter anyway, the house gets no sun then and it would be damp. There now!'

He led her on to the verandah, pushed wide the green-painted door and Cass looked in upon a charming scene. The house consisted of just one big room, one corner of which was partitioned off to make a tiny kitchen. Against the back wall, which was windowless, stood a wood-burning stove and above it was a deep balcony that stretched the width of the house and on which stood a low, wide bed, piled high with gaily coloured blankets, a small painted chest and two spindly chairs. Wooden steps led up to it from the extreme left side and beside these, on the opposite wall to the kitchen, was a door leading out to a small lean-to which contained a shower unit and lavatory. The floor was covered with a huge square of carpet and several comfortable armchairs were pulled up to the stove, behind whose glass doors flames danced. At the entrance to the kitchen a gate leg table stood, laid for tea with two chairs beside it.

Despite the fact that the sun had now completely vanished the room was still full of light. There were large windows on the east and west walls as well as those opening south on to the verandah and, despite the cosy atmosphere, the room also felt light and airy. Although it was apparent that it was furnished with cast-off pieces, it was also apparent that the things had been of high quality and were, even now, well cared for, clean and pleasant to the eye.

'It's perfect,' Cass repeated when she could find her voice. 'I feel I've wandered into fairyland.'

'Darling Cass! How like you to be so generous. It's all very basic, really. Of course, you turn it into a palace.'

'Oh, Nick. You are an idiot.' She turned to him and they embraced for the first time. He kissed her tenderly and then, releasing her, led her to an armchair by the stove.

'Sit down there and relax while I make the tea. You must be exhausted after that long trip. Bless you for making it. I couldn't have waited another day. If only we could have travelled up together but I'm sure you were right to point out that it would have been madness.'

Cass, who had thought that the idea that they should travel separately in case of some disaster had come from him, smiled back at him.

'I couldn't have waited either. I've missed you so much.'

He blew her a kiss and disappeared behind the heavy velvet curtain that screened the kitchen. Cass stretched luxuriously, admiring her long, elegant legs in the cream ribbed tights and feeling absurdly pleased that the green tweed of her skirt blended so well with the green of Nick's trousers. She watched him finish laying the table with a practised hand.

'You'd like some tea, I hope? Nothing too much, just some teacakes and a sponge. I've booked us in for supper at the Bear in Ludlow. I discovered that they have a nice, quiet little room and the food is delicious.'

'I thought that everyone went to the Feathers in Ludlow,' observed Cass, a delicious languor stealing over her. It was lovely to be sitting here whilst Nick prepared tea and talked of their supper plans.

'We're not everyone. Now come along and have some tea. I'll leave you to pour while I get your case in. Where are your keys?'

'Oh, Nick.' She fumbled in her bag and passed the keys over. 'You've no idea how wonderful it is to be fussed over. You'll spoil me.'

'Quite impossible, sweetie!' He kissed her lightly and went out.

Cass moved across to the table. The food looked delicious, homemade. Perhaps he'd bought it in Ludlow. How nice it was not to be leapt on at once, not to have one's clothes torn off and have to perform without so much as an exchange of pleasantries. Nick was so civilised. Perhaps it's because he's older, thought Cass, sitting down and lifting the teapot. After all, he must be in his late-forties, quite a lot older than Tom. Well, whatever it is I like it. She smiled at him as he returned and waved a teacake at him.

'Delicious!' she cried. 'Hurry up, or I'll eat them all.'

'Don't you dare!' He climbed the little staircase and placed her suitcase on the bed. 'Anything to be hung up?'

'Oh, yes please,' she said. 'If we're going out my skirt should be hung up to let the creases drop out.'

'Don't move!' he called, as she made as if to push back her chair. 'I'm quite capable of hanging up clothes.' He lifted out a skirt in soft, donkey-brown suede. 'Is this it?'

'Yes. There are hangers in the case. And, would you mind? There's a silk shirt, too.'

'Yes, I've got it. And the hangers. What an efficient girl you are.' He dealt with the clothes, hanging them on a peg on the wall. 'Anything else?'

'No, that's fine for now. Come and have your tea.'

'I'm coming. Oh, thanks. Now, I want to hear about everything that's happened to you since we last met.'

WHEN TOM ARRIVED HOME and found Cass's note, it came as a very pleasant surprise to find that he could have a whole weekend with Harriet without any difficulties or explanations. That she would not be as pleased about it as he was never occurred to him for a moment. In their encounters so far, even before their affair, she had been eager, willing, compliant and grateful and he saw no reason why this should not continue. He found her letter, telephoned her at once and, in tearing high spirits, told her the news.

Harriet replaced the receiver and stood for a moment paralysed with panic. He had sounded like a stranger to her and she felt it impossible that he should be about to enter her life, her cottage and, finally, even her own body as though he were anything else. His voice had sounded full of excitement and something else. After a while Harriet realised what it was. He had sounded like a naughty, small boy who was about to perpetrate some dreadful trick on his elders, as though the whole thing was a lighthearted joke. At that moment something shifted a little within their relationship. Always in the past Harriet had seen Tom as the older man, the senior officer, the next generation. He had always seemed so much more mature than Ralph and she had always felt flattered by the attention that he had showed her, his predilection for her company. Ralph's deference towards him had underlined the feeling and he had always made her feel rather young and inexperienced and shy. It was he who had made all the moves in the relationship so far and Harriet liked his air of command. She didn't want to feel she was someone he was amusing himself with whilst congratulating himself on pulling the wool over Cass's eyes. She did not wish to enter into a kind of conspiracy with him as if they were two small children defying and hoodwinking their elders. She wanted to think of him as strong, confident and desirable and it was a different Harriet that went to greet him. She opened the door and he bounded in, enveloping her in a huge hug.

'What wonderful luck!' He was jubilant. 'Fancy the boat coming in unexpectedly just when Cass is away for the weekend. I can have you all to myself. I can't believe it!' He was too hyped-up to notice her reservation. 'I had a shower, grabbed a bag and came straight over. Thank God Cass left your letter lying about. Let me look at you. Mmm. Delicious. But you've got too many clothes on.'

He slipped his hands up beneath her jersey and she felt a spurt of irritation.

'Hang on a minute!' She made herself smile at him. 'You haven't told me what you think of my cottage yet.'

He gave a perfunctory glance round.

'It's great! But you're nicer. Oh, Harriet, I've missed you. Come and give me a kiss!'

'Tom!' She began to laugh, mainly with exasperation. 'You're impossible! Is this what Cass has to put up with when you come home from sea? You've hardly said hello.'

He began to look sulky.

'I didn't realise that you'd want to go through all the formalities,' he said, rather childishly. 'I hoped you'd feel as I do.'

Careful! thought Harriet.

'I probably do feel as you do,' she replied calmly, 'but you've had a bit of time to get used to the idea. I haven't heard from you for weeks and suddenly here you are. I need a moment to adjust.'

'After all, we did agree not to write.' Tom sounded aggrieved. 'I didn't even have your address. If I'm in the way I'll push off.'

Harriet had never seen Tom's peevish side and began feeling he was a stranger. Over the years she had built up a picture of an idealised figure which she now realised had nothing to do with the real man. Panic stirred again and she pushed it down.

'Don't be silly. It's lovely to see you and I'm as thrilled as you are. It's just a bit of a shock, that's all. It seems so long ago that we were together that I was beginning to think I'd dreamed the whole thing.'

'I'm sorry, love.' He was all penitence. 'I'm a selfish bastard, I know.' Admitting it, apparently, seemed to excuse it, even make it acceptable. 'I haven't stopped thinking about you for weeks and when I saw you it was just too much. You'll have to forgive me.'

This time she didn't avoid his embrace and a few moments later they were in Harriet's bedroom, her clothes scattered across the floor.

Afterwards, Harriet made omelettes whilst Tom sat at the kitchen table watching her.

'The problem is,' she spoke her thoughts aloud, 'that I suppose we daren't go out together.'

'I must admit it is a bit close to home.' Tom poured himself another gin and tonic. 'It's marvellous to have you down here but it's going to be a bit tricky. Still, you won't be here forever, will you?'

'What are you suggesting?'

'Well, only that this is a temporary move, isn't it? When you buy your own place you can be a bit further out, you don't need to be so close, do you?'

'Close to what? I shall be working in Tavistock, remember.'

'Quite, but you don't have to live right on top of the office, do you? Surely you won't mind a bit of a drive to and fro.'

'Anything to oblige.'

'What does that mean?'

'Well, I wouldn't want to put you out. Don't worry about any inconvenience to me.' She turned some sliced potatoes cooking separately in another pan, wondering what had come over her. Sex—or should she call it love-making?—had left her irritable, empty.

'Hang on a minute.' Tom got up and went to her, turning her by the shoulders to face him. 'What's the matter?'

'Nothing.' She tried to twist away from him. 'Look, let go, or the omelette will burn.'

'Sod the omelette! I want to know what's going on. You've been behaving strangely ever since I arrived. What is it?'

'Oh, I don't know.' She stopped struggling and relaxed in his grip. 'I suppose I feel you're taking me over a bit too much. You come in, out of the blue, expect to lay me at once, practically on the hall floor, and then start telling me where to live. It just seemed a bit much, that's all.'

His hands dropped abruptly away from her.

'I see. Anything else?'

'What else should there be?'

'I don't know.' He sat down again at the kitchen table. 'Perhaps I should have said "who" else?'

'Who else? What d'you mean?'

'Well, if I had to guess I'd suggest that chap you were living with the last time I was home, Michael, is it?'

To her horror she found herself blushing.

'Rubbish! I've known Michael for years. Why does it have to be someone else? I've told you exactly what it is. Or is it that you prefer to think that it's someone else rather than your own behaviour?' What am I saying! she thought aghast. What am I doing?

Tom stood up and moved his chair back under the table.

'OK. I can take a hint. Why didn't you just say so at once? I don't know what's happened, Harriet, but you've changed. You always seemed such a warm, gentle, feminine person but now I'm beginning to wonder if I know you at all.'

'For warm, gentle and feminine read infatuated, weak and ready to be used! I don't think we know each other at all, Tom. I think we've had a very idealised view of one another which was bound to dissolve once we came into close contact. The point is, do we want to get to know the real people underneath?'

'I don't know.' Tom shoved his fists into his pockets. 'This is a hell of a shock.' He managed to look both pathetic and cross. 'I was so looking forward to being with you.'

She felt both impatient and sympathetic but the inevitable feelings of guilt stirred.

'Well, you still can be. I just want it to be real and not pretend.' She went to him and slipped her arm through his. 'We're old friends, that must count for something. Shall we try again?'

'If you really want to.' He looked down at her and she saw that she'd shaken his confidence as well as annoyedp him. The guilt became stronger.

'Of course I do,' she lied. 'Where shall we start?'

'Let's go back to bed.' He looked much happier; more in control, of himself and the situation, and, unlike Michael, he had no doubt as to his abilities in the bedroom. 'It's always a good place to start.'

Biting back a retort Harriet switched off the hotplates.

'You don't want to eat first?'

'I couldn't. I just want you. Oh God, you gave me a fright, Harriet. Come over here.'

She went to him praying that she could put up a good performance. It was going to be a very long weekend.

FOR CASS THE WEEKEND passed in a haze of sunshine, mellow wines, good food and love-making. Nick was tender, exciting, thoughtful and untiring. If this is an older man, thought Cass at one deliriously exciting moment, you can keep all the young ones!

They walked across the Long Mynd hand in hand and embraced, knee deep in heather, with the sunshine warm on their shoulders and the wind tugging gently at their hair. They explored Offa's Dyke and Clun Castle and drove to Bishops Castle and Shrewsbury. In the evenings, Cass exchanged her tweed skirt and Aran jersey for the calf-length suede skirt and long, supple leather boots; a soft, woollen shawl flung round the silk shirt. Nick wore a fine wool grey suit with a silk shirt and tie and thus attired they sallied out to eat. They made a handsome couple. They had decided to make the small room at the Bear 'their' place and went there on each of the three evenings. They called the waiter, George, by his Christian name and delighted in his special attentions.

'You'd think he'd known us for years,' whispered Cass, lifting a little spray of flowers put specially by her plate, as George left the room with their order.

'People don't have to know you years to love you, my darling. It's instantaneous. Look how it was with me.'

'Nonsense!' They'd already discussed this ad nauseam.

'What can I do to make you believe me? Wait 'til we get back home, I'll show you then!' And they smiled at each other, delightfully, secretly, in the candlelight.

On Sunday night, however, clasped in Nick's arms, Cass watched the firelight flickering in the room below them and felt miserable.

'Nick,' she whispered and felt his arms tighten around her, 'I don't want to go home tomorrow. I want to stay here with you.'

'Darling.' She felt his lips move against her hair. 'I'd like that too, but you know it's impossible.'

'Why?' She felt his chest move as he chuckled.

'You know very well why, my love.'

'I don't. There's no real reason why we can't always be together like this.'

'It wouldn't be like this. I'm a partner in a busy practice and I have to work. And what about our families?'

'You haven't got a family.'

'I have Sarah to look after. I could hardly abandon her, could I? She's older than I am, you know, and she's been a loyal wife.'

'Yes, but you say there's nothing between you any more, you have separate bedrooms and different interests. Wouldn't she give you your freedom if she were well provided for? We're so good together, Nick.'

'Ah, my darling. Don't you think I haven't thought about it? Of course I have. But it's not something to be entered into lightly, you'd probably tire of me in a fortnight.'

'You know that's rubbish!'

'How sweet you are. Come here, my darling, don't let's spoil our last evening. We must be together again very soon and meanwhile we'll think very hard of what is to be done.'

And, as his lips touched hers and his hands moved against her skin, Cass felt that she'd give up family, friends, everything, if Nick and she could stay like this forever, in the little magic world she'd found here in the Shropshire hills.

I WONDER, THOUGHT HARRIET, as she lay beside the sleeping Tom, how I could have been so obsessed by him for so long? The thought of him has dominated my life for years, like some long illness. It ruined my marriage and has all but destroyed any happiness I might have found with Michael. What a fool I've been, like a lovesick infatuated kid of fifteen. How am I going to tell him it's all over when it's only just started?

It was early Sunday morning and the weekend had indeed been a long one. They had patched things together on Friday evening but, for Harriet, the vital spark had been extinguished and without it she found the pretence an enormous strain. Tom, however, seemed to have been taken in by her efforts and for that she was grateful. He had decided that the idea of a mistress near to hand was very attractive. He had always taken his pleasures where he'd found them but now he was getting older a more permanent arrangement would have many advantages. Harriet had given him a rather nasty shock but he was already putting that down to feminine megrims or PMT. Nevertheless he felt that a few treats were in order. So he'd taken her to Exeter on Saturday and, praying that he wouldn't see anyone he knew, had given her lunch.

Later that evening they'd gone out to dinner at Grumpy's in Tavistock, Harriet in terror that she should see Michael but Tom, by now, very blasé about the whole thing. As it happened it all went very smoothly but Harriet was finding it increasingly difficult to behave as though she were at the beginning of a relationship when she knew, in her heart, that she was at the end.

I should have told him at once, she thought now, edging cautiously across the bed. It would have been fairer. I'm just a coward.

'Where are you off to?' Tom put out an arm and caught her round the waist. 'Sneaking off when I wasn't looking.'

Oh, for God's sake, not again! Harriet bit back the words but resisted firmly.

'Must go to the loo.' She prised away his hand. 'Shan't be long.'

'Mind you're not.' He rolled over and seemed to go back to sleep.

She picked up her dressing-gown and slippers and went out quietly. She could not, simply could not, face any more sex. Her whole body ached with it. He seemed indefatigable. They'd made love before rising on Saturday morning, on their return from Exeter and having arrived home from Grumpy's. Thank heavens he had to be back on the boat this afternoon!

Twenty-seven

On Monday morning Mrs Hampton and Jane Maxwell met by chance again on the step of the village shop. This time Mrs Hampton was going in and Jane was coming out.

'How's everythin' goin', my lover?'

'It's worked out like a dream.' Not usually given to demonstrative ways, Jane clasped Mrs Hampton's forearm and shook it. 'You were right, you know, about Mrs Wivenhoe—Cass. She's just sorted everything out like magic. She seems to know everyone. I've wanted to come and tell you but I'm staying in as much as possible. See what I mean? In case I see Phil. That's why I'm out so early.' Her voice dropped to a whisper, though there was no one in earshot. 'He keeps phoning up. Threatening to come to the house.'

Mrs Hampton drew Jane to one side as someone opened the shop door from inside.

'You haven't told him?'

'God, no! Told him I wasn't well and the doctor said I had to rest or I'd lose the baby. Last time we were together he was a bit, well, rough like. He'd had a few. So I told him it was his fault and I've got to stay in bed. Only a week or so to go now, thank God.'

Looking at Jane, Mrs Hampton began to wonder if she were, after all, doing the right thing in encouraging her. Of course it was right to be faithful and loyal to your husband, no question about that, but she couldn't, somehow, see Jane placed happily amongst the officers and their wives.

The simple truth of the matter was that Jane had tried to better herself. Mrs Hampton didn't hold with it. No harm in improving your lifestyle, broadening your outlook, stretching the brain, as long as you didn't pretend. Once you started to pretend you were all set for misery. And Jane did pretend. Mrs Hampton was well aware of Jane's refinements; her speech—which tended to slip when she was excited or relaxed—her clothes and her home were all proof of this to those who knew her of old. Mrs Hampton sighed, filled with foreboding. Well, it was too late now. She'd made her bed and she would have to lie on it. She was as likely to have as much happiness with one as with the other.

'I'm glad to see you lookin' brighter,' she said. 'You looked right worried when I saw you last.'

'Yeah, I know.' Jane gave a self-conscious little laugh. 'I was out of my mind. But I'll be all right now, though. As long as I can keep out of his way.' She looked, almost fearfully, up the village street. 'Silly, isn't it?'

'When d'you think you'll be off?'

'I'm waiting to hear from Alan. Could be as soon as this weekend. Dunno how he'll take it. All sudden, like. I shall be glad when it's all over.'

''Course you will. I 'ope we'll be able to say goodbye proper like.'

'I'm gonna miss you.' Looking at Mrs Hampton's comfortable shape and kindly face representing, for the moment, her childhood and roots, Jane felt an overwhelming sense of loss and fear: she would miss Mrs Hampton, her mum and sister down near Plymouth, the village and the friends of her youth. Although she had tried to separate herself from them, rise above them as it were, they had been there, within call, part of her daily life. She was going among strangers—she included Alan—and leaving her own people.

Mrs Hampton saw the panic in her eyes and guessed, rightly, the reason for it.

'Everythin'll be fine, my lover. It'll all blow over an' then you'll be 'ome again with a new member of the family to show us all. 'Twill go like a flash.'

'I suppose so,' said Jane slowly. 'I hope so. I don't want to go away forever.'

'An' why should you? 'Tis your 'ome. Young Philip'll get over it an' 'twill be good for you to get away an' see somethin' of the world. We'll still all be 'ere, waitin' for you.'

'You'd better be.' Jane tried for a lighter note. 'We'll stay in touch, though, won't we? I'll be able to ring you up for a chat, like. It'll be strange at first.'

'We can write too, can't we? Taught you that at the village school, didn't they? Well, then! An' you'll 'ave your Alan with you. 'Tisn't as if he's at sea. You'll 'ave a lovely time. Little outin's in the car. 'Tis a pretty county, Kent. Oh, you'll 'ave a wonderful time! An' then there's the baby to look forward to; you'll be rushed off your feet.'

'Yeah, I know, really. I'm being silly. It's the baby, I reckon, makes you all emotional like. You can't come over for a cuppa?'

'Not this mornin', my lover. I've gotta go over to the Rectory. They've all been away for the weekend so I may be able to get on a bit before any of 'em's back.' She felt compassion, however, at Jane's expression. The days are long when you're in hiding. 'Course I could come in about teatime. 'ow's that suit you?'

'Oh, yes! That'd be great! I'll go home and do a bit of baking. It'll make a change from knitting.'

'Thass right, love, keep yourself busy. I'll see you later on, then.'

They parted and Mrs Hampton entered the shop. Having bought one or two items, which, since they were to be used for the cleaning of the Wivenhoes' home, she put on Cass's bill, she crossed the green and went up the Rectory drive. The kitchen door was locked but she had her own key and, letting herself in, hung her coat up on one of the hooks in the passage, changed her shoes and went into the kitchen.

Charlotte sat at the kitchen table staring at a bowl of uneaten corn-flakes.

'Well, there! I didn't know anyone was 'ere. When did you get back?' She looked more closely at Charlotte. There was something wrong with the child.

'And 'ow was Bristol then?' she asked when Charlotte showed no disposition to speak. 'Did you manage to see Hugh?'

Charlotte shook her head and her lips trembled. 'He wasn't there. They said he'd gone away for the weekend. With friends.' She paused, rubbing her hands over her mouth and gazed wildly round the kitchen. 'But I saw him. I went out for a walk and I saw him. Them.' She stared at Mrs Hampton. 'He was with a girl. That Lucinda that was at the party. They didn't see me. They were all over each other, in public, kissing, his hands were all over her. And then he saw me.' Her face twitched uncontrollably, as expressions of horror, distaste, anger and misery chased across it. 'They came up to me and started talking. Hugh didn't know what to say but she didn't care. She laughed and said they were having a naughty weekend at her brother's flat, just the two of them. She had her arms all round him. And he . . . he . . . ' She choked over her words. 'He spoke to me as if I were just some friend or other. Asked who I was staying with. I told him I was with Ma and he looked . . . he looked . . . relieved!' She wrenched the last word out painfully and, as she did so, she collapsed across the table, arms outstretched, her head upsetting the bowl of cereal, milk splashing over her face.

Mrs Hampton, who had been shocked into silence by this recital, pulled herself together and hurried to her, hauling her upright and wiping Charlotte's face with the apron she still held in her hand.

'There, there, my lover, gently, gently now. Let 'Ammy dry your face. Ssh, now, quiet now.' The abandonment of Charlotte's grief terrified her and she rocked her against her bosom while the tears poured out of the girl's eyes into her open mouth, stretched wide in a silent scream. She lay like a great rag doll in her arms. Desperately Mrs Hampton looked round for inspiration. She would phone Kate. Kate would know how to handle it.

'Look my lover, look, sit up properly now. Up we come.' It was like dealing with a drunk person. 'Look, come over 'ere, then, where 'tis comfortable.' She led Charlotte, reeling, to the rocking chair and propped her in it. 'I'm gonna make you a nice 'ot strong cuppa. Sit there, now. That's it.' She went to the Aga where the kettle, probably put on by Charlotte earlier, had almost boiled itself dry, refilled it and glanced back at her. The girl sat, slumped in the rocker, tears trickling from beneath her closed lids.

Mrs Hampton slipped into the hall and picked up the telephone receiver.

AT LUNCHTIME ON MONDAY, Harriet paused outside Michael's office and peered through the window, looking beyond the revolving photographs of desirable properties to the brightly lit interior. There was no sign of Michael. He might be closeted with a client in his office, out taking on a new property or doing a survey. She was conscious of a feeling of great disappointment.

Yesterday afternoon, after Tom had left, she had washed her hair and soaked in a hot bath for some time before dressing in clean clothes and changing the sheets on the bed. Then, after a general clean round, she had driven up on to the moor and, parking at Sampford Spiney, embarked on a long, refreshing walk. She felt that she wanted to slough Tom off, to rid herself, as it were, of the feel of him, the smell of him and his presence generally: she wanted to cleanse herself of him, mentally and physically. Her obsession for him was over as if it had never been and she could only marvel at and regret all those years she had spent mooning after him. What a fool she'd been. She thought of Ralph and felt a wave of remorse and self-disgust. With her mad infatuation colouring her emotions the marriage had stood no chance. She knew now that she had never been in love with Ralph; nevertheless, she knew that they would have done much better if she had not clung to her stubborn idealistic love for Tom. She thought of him, dying alone in the water, and felt horror, guilt and real sorrow. She knew that it had been an accident, Ralph was not the suicidal type, and she knew too that he had not been in love with her, but they might have been as happy as most people are and certainly a great deal happier than they had been.

It was all over. There was no point in looking back. At least she had come to her senses before any more lives were spoiled. She thought of Michael. She needed desperately to see him but knew that it must wait until tomorrow. She did not want to see him on the same day that she had been with Tom.

'I'm being silly,' she said aloud to herself, as she trod the short sheep-bitten turf, 'but I want it to be a completely new start.'

So now she stood, hesitating, until one of the girls inside saw her and waved. That decided her; she opened the door and smiled.

'Is he in?'

'Yes, he is. And there's no one with him.' Tessa had a delightfully warm West Country drawl—Michael believed in employing the locals—and a round smiling face beneath fuzzy blonde hair. 'Go on in, I would. I've just taken him his coffee. Would you like one?'

'Yes, please.' Harriet smiled at Rebecca who, at present, wore the glazed expression of one plugged into a dictaphone and knocked at Michael's door.

'Come in,' he shouted.

He was standing at a filing cabinet and turned as she entered.

'Harriet!' His pleasure was quite genuine and she felt enormous relief. During the sleepless hours of the night terror had gripped her. Supposing that, now that she had discovered that she couldn't live without him, he realised that he didn't care for her after all? Or perhaps he might have a car accident going to Tavistock in the morning . . . or she might . . .

'Hello.' She was aware that she was grinning foolishly but could do nothing about it. 'I thought I'd come to see you.'

'I'm delighted. Sit down, won't you? How was your weekend?'

'OK,' she said awkwardly. 'Any chance of taking you out to lunch?'

'We can do better than that!' he answered promptly. 'I've got to take on a property near Moretonhampstead. Why not come with me? The house is empty so you can help me measure up. We can get lunch at a pub somewhere. How about it?'

Harriet glowed with pleasure.

'Sounds marvellous. I'd love it.'

'Good. I'm hoping that you'll be able to come in full-time this week. We're terribly busy. We really need you, don't we, Tessa?' He smiled at the girl who came in with Harriet's coffee.

'We certainly do! Even if it's only to give him someone else to nag at. It'll give us a break.'

They all laughed and Tessa withdrew.

'Let me finish this report and I'll be with you.' Michael drew some papers towards him. 'It won't take me a moment and then we'll get off.'

'Suits me.' Harriet sipped her coffee—thank goodness Tessa could make decent coffee, so important that one's workmates could—and let her gaze roam round the office.

Michael sat at ease, in a huge Windsor chair behind his equally huge mahogany desk which was covered, as usual, with papers, files and forms. Pens and pencils stood in a green Wedgwood pot and two china dishes, designed to hold sweetcorn, held paper clips, elastic bands and the like. His personality was stamped everywhere. The room, unlike the modern front office, was part of the old house behind and had once been someone's sitting room. Michael had retained and used the lovely old Victorian fireplace and several prints of the same period hung on either side of it. The opposite wall was lined with books and the whole effect was that of a study more than an office. Harriet noticed that a pair of gumboots stood beneath an old-fashioned hat-stand on a worn, but still lovely, Persian rug. The window opened on to a side yard used by the people next door and to which Michael had access should he so wish. He looked up and smiled at her and her whole being glowed with happiness.

He loves me, she thought. Let joy be unconfined!

'Heavens!' He gave a start of dismay. 'I've just remembered! Minutes before you appeared Kate Webster phoned. She sounded in a bit of a state. She's at the Rectory. Apparently the girl—what's her name, Charlotte?—has been taken ill and Cass is away. Anyway, she says can you phone?'

Harriet's spirits plummeted. Kate, no doubt, wanted to know

where Tom was and, with Cass away, Harriet was the only other person who might know. The grubbiness of the whole affair swept over her and she felt ashamed. She didn't want to speak to Kate or to see Cass, or indeed any of the Wivenhoes. It was all over. But, said her conscience, Cass was very good to you when Ralph died. Perhaps Charlotte's really ill and with Tom away at sea . . .

'Oh, hell!' she said.

Michael raised his eyebrows.

'Do you anticipate trouble?' he asked.

'Not really, I suppose. But,' she looked directly at him, 'frankly I want to put the Wivenhoes behind me. All of them,' she added pointedly.

He looked at her for a long moment.

'You're sure?'

'Absolutely and totally sure.'

He reached across to her and took her hand.

'I've been an absolute idiot, Michael, but it's all over now. Really.' She moved in her chair, stretching out her feet so as to lean across the desk. They struck something warm and solid which emitted a loud grunt.

'Michael!' She leapt up with a cry of alarm and bending down peered under the desk. 'Oh, God, it's Max!' Relief, joy, sheer happiness overwhelmed her and she knelt to stroke him. 'It would be you,' his injured expression seemed to say. 'I might have guessed.' She hugged him as he emerged majestically, pausing to allow Harriet her moment of emotion before moving to the filing cabinet, against which he sat, leaning heavily.

'Oh, Michael,' she sat down again, keeping a strong rein on her feelings, all big moments with Michael seemed fraught with danger, 'it's nice to be back! Is Max coming with us?'

'That was my intention. He can have a run on the moor. Well, a walk. Max rarely works himself up to actually running.'

They both laughed, relieved that Max was there to prevent the situation becoming overcharged with emotion.

Later, thought Harriet, finishing her coffee. There'll be plenty of time for that later.

KATE DROVE HOME FROM the Rectory in a state of very real anxiety. She knew that Cass had not known that Charlotte was planning to stay alone in Bristol with the sole purpose of seeing Hugh. Kate had only found out because the twins had told her. The whole sixth form knew about it and when Kate had casually asked Giles which school friend she was staying with, he had been surprised and had told her Charlotte's plans. Giles had implied that Hugh had arranged everything and so Kate had not felt worried but now things seemed rather different. She and Mrs Hampton had got Charlotte to bed and when the doctor arrived he had given her a sedative. He had known Charlotte for quite a few years and knew that she was highly-strung so he had believed the story they had told him about boyfriend trouble and had advised that she stay in bed for a day or so.

Mrs Hampton had been deeply upset and shocked that Cass had let her go off on her own and Kate had been obliged to assure her that Cass had been under the impression that Charlotte was safe with a school-friend's family. Having allowed her to do a rather sketchy clean round, Kate had finally sent her off knowing that she would rather be there on her own when Cass finally arrived home.

It was Cass's reaction that had disturbed Kate. She hardly seemed able to take in Charlotte's escapade, her shock and misery. It was as if she were unable to take it seriously, as if her own problems were too great to be able to take on board the situation that had arisen. Once she'd ascertained that Charlotte was safe in bed, sedated and everything under control, she rather lost interest in the whole proceedings. She viewed the whole thing in a dismissive light and was certain that Charlotte would recover in no time. These childish infatuations were painful but part of growing up.

Kate, knowing how deeply Charlotte felt about things, was not so sanguine. For one thing, she wondered, under these circumstances, how difficult Charlotte would find it to return to school. According to

Giles, her friendship with Hugh was the cornerstone of her existence and it would be rather humiliating to have to go back and deal with the inevitable questions. Charlotte was not the type to bluff it out or even to admit it and fling herself on her friends' sympathy and understanding. She would want to die of shame. Kate, remembering what persuasive powers had been needed to get her there in the first place, wondered if she'd ever go back. These things hit the young so hard and poor Charlotte would suffer agonies.

Cass had pooh-poohed this thought and told Kate that she was overdramatising the situation. Kate, who sincerely hoped that she was, decided that she could do no more and asked Cass how her weekend had been. Her face had taken on a look of beatific bliss.

'It was heaven,' she had breathed. 'Pure heaven.'

Even more alarmed, Kate said that Harriet had rung briefly to say that Tom had gone back to sea and that she had no idea when he might be back. Also, she had added rather cryptically, she didn't expect to see him again, but Cass didn't appear to have much interest in Tom or Harriet either. She was completely distracted and glanced at her watch from time to time as if she were waiting for someone. Some sixth sense told Kate that she was waiting for a telephone call—probably from Nick—and when the telephone rang and Cass leapt from her chair and ran to answer it, Kate felt her suspicions were confirmed. It was Abby checking that Cass was back and when she returned to the kitchen it was obvious that she was disappointed.

Kate decided that there was no more that she could do and decided to leave her to it. She told Cass what directions the doctor had given for the medicine and said goodbye. Perhaps if Cass had seen Charlotte, crying and distraught and finally hysterical, she might have taken it all more seriously. Kate realised that she should have taken Gus back with her but decided that it gave her a good excuse to call again tomorrow, to see how things were progressing.

As she pulled into the drive, she realised that she was afraid. She tried to analyse it but could come to no conclusion. If only she had someone she could talk to. She thought automatically of the General but knew that in this particular situation she could not have enlisted his help.

She sighed and got out of the car. She'd go again tomorrow and see how things were.

ON TUESDAY, AFTER KATE had gone, Cass went up to check on Charlotte. She looked down at the sleeping face. In repose she was startlingly like Tom; the same blunt features, the heavy brows and hair and stubborn mouth. At this time, in her mother's eyes, this was not particularly to her advantage.

Cass left the room and closed the door behind her. She stood for a long minute in thought, her hand still on the door handle and then, as if having made up her mind to something, she went to the telephone table and, taking out the Plymouth directory, hunted through the *M*'s. Presently, she dialled a number.

She waited for it to connect, her free hand clenched into a fist and pressed against her heart which seemed to be most irregular in its behaviour, beating now fast, now slow. There was a click.

'Murchison Marriott. Good afternoon. Can I help you?'

'Oh, yes. Hello.' She felt as though she were suffocating. 'Could I speak to Mr Farley, please?'

'One moment. I'll check. Who's calling, please?'

Cass hesitated for a second.

'This is Mrs Wivenhoe. Yes, Wivenhoe. That's right.'

'One moment.' There was a long pause. 'You're through.'

'Hello? Nick?'

'I'm sorry. This is Mr Farley's secretary. Can I help you?'

'Oh, I'm sorry. I thought . . . Yes, please. I'd like to speak to Mr Farley. It's . . . well, it's rather important.'

'If you'll hold on one moment, I'll see if he's free. He may have gone to lunch.'

Lunch? thought Cass. He can't have gone to lunch. Please let him be there.

'Hello.' Nick's voice in her ear took her off guard and she sank into the chair beside the telephone table, weak with relief.

'Nick, oh, thank God! I was terrified that you might not be there.'

'Good morning, Mrs Wivenhoe. What can I do for you?'

'Oh, for heaven's sake, Nick! Do we have to be so formal? Is there someone there?'

'I'm afraid that's quite correct. I agree it's tiresome but there's very little we can do at present.'

'Nick, please! I've got to see you. It's terribly important. Can we make some arrangement, I don't care where, but it must be soon. Later on today.'

'It's so difficult at present, though I quite see your point.' His voice changed suddenly and became low and cross. 'We did agree, Cass. No calls to the office. I just can't risk it.'

'Oh, please don't be angry. I'm at my wit's end, darling, truly. I had to speak to you and I can't phone you at home. We should have made some definite plan yesterday. Don't be cross, I miss you so much.'

'My darling girl, I'm not cross, but we've got to be careful. You know, a lawyer has to be like Caesar's wife. I just can't take risks. Now, I've got a few minutes. What is it?'

'I can't explain on the phone. I must see you.'

'Don't you think I long to see you, too? But it's not that easy.'

'Couldn't we meet somewhere, on your way home from the office, by chance, as it were?'

There was a silence and she knew he was thinking. Her whole body strained towards him.

'Very well. Do you ever go to the Skylark at Clearbrook? So they wouldn't be surprised to see you there alone? Good. Now I often, well, once or twice a week, pop in for a drink on my way home. We'll meet there at about, say, six. I might be a bit later. Depends on the traffic.'

'I'd wait for ever, Nick, you know that.'

'Silly girl. You won't have to do that. But remember, Cass! We're just friends, OK? A lot of people know us around there and I'm right on my own doorstep. So no histrionics.'

'You do sound fierce. Not like the Nick I know at all. You don't sound as if you love me a bit.'

'Would I be risking this if I didn't?' It was the old familiar caressing voice and Cass shivered with pleasure.

'Oh, darling, if only you knew how I love you . . . '

'Then that's all arranged, Mrs Wivenhoe.' His voice cut her short. 'We'll do the best we can in the matter. Goodbye.'

The receiver went down with a click and Cass stood for a moment, bereft, weak with love for him. At last she replaced her own receiver and glanced almost automatically at her watch. It was after one o'clock. She would be seeing him in less than five hours from now.

THE NEXT DAY, CHARLOTTE sat in bed, propped up by pillows, trying to summon up the energy to go to the bathroom. She felt weak and apathetic and, although she was constantly aware of Hugh's perfidy as she might have been of a toothache, it was as if the pain of it was deadened slightly; not by indifference but rather by a lack of energy to concentrate on it.

She gathered up her willpower and pushed back the quilt. If she didn't get up she'd wet the bed. Pulling a large and rather smelly Peruvian shawl around her shoulders she padded to the door and opened it. At once she heard her mother's voice. Something, perhaps the hurried muffled tones punctuated by lengthy pauses, warned her that Cass was talking on the telephone and wouldn't want to be overheard.

Silent as an Indian, Charlotte moved across the landing and, crouching, stared down between the banisters.

Cass was perched on the chair in the hall, hunched over the telephone. Even from this distance Charlotte was aware of the intensity emanating from her which seemed to charge the very air of the quiet hallway. The voice rose and sank.

'No, but, darling . . . I know, I lost my head, but this time . . . honestly . . . it's really important . . . '

Charlotte watched her. She was talking to a man, no doubt about it, and it was not Tom. If it was Daddy, thought Charlotte, she would have been standing up, gesticulating theatrically, watching herself in the mirror that hung over the telephone table. Charlotte had seen it many times before and listened to the conversations. 'Hello, darling, how marvellous to hear you . . . where are you . . . oh, don't say you're not going to make it . . . what a pity . . . oh, yes, fine . . . the usual chaos . . . absolute trauma yesterday . . . well, of course, we'll miss you terribly . . . ' And afterwards she'd go upstairs humming, not in the least put out, and later, after another phone call she'd be off, all dressed up, in the car.

Charlotte shut her eyes, resting her forehead on her knees, as a futile anger possessed her. She wanted to hurt Cass, to punish her. It seemed to her confused mind that everything that had gone wrong was directly or indirectly Cass's fault. She hadn't been there when Charlotte, having got herself back from Bristol by train and out from Plymouth by taxi, had finally arrived home. The house had been shut up, cold and empty, and she'd spent the night there all alone, waiting for her mother to come home. And now she was home, she didn't really care about how Charlotte was suffering. She was still more concerned with making assignations with her latest lover.

Charlotte stood up abruptly and Cass glanced up sharply and bent lower over the receiver for a moment, cupping her hand about it before she replaced it and stood up.

'Is that you, Charlotte? Are you OK, darling? Anything you want?' She peered upwards into the shadows.

'No, thanks. I'm fine.' Charlotte moved into view at the top of the stairs. 'I'm just going to have a bath.' As if you cared, she added silently.

'Would you like some breakfast now you're up?' Cass came halfway up the stairs. 'Is there anything that you feel you'd really enjoy?'

'No,' said Charlotte, unwilling to relinquish the idea of Cass's indifference to her misery.

'Just a cup of coffee then?' Cass advanced a few more steps and smiled at her. 'Feeling a bit better?'

'Not really.' Charlotte felt a weary indignation at the suggestion that this could be hoped for under the circumstances.

'Oh, well.' Feeling nonplussed. Cass looked at her daughter and then shrugged. 'I'll make some coffee anyway. Enjoy your bath.'

She turned away and Charlotte went into the bathroom and slammed the door.

Twenty-eight

Nick Farley sat at his desk, idly turning a pencil between his fingers as he stared out over the chimney pots of Plymouth.

His detractors—Nick didn't have enemies—said that he had arrived at his elevated position through his wife's connections but that, nevertheless, he was a thoroughly nice chap, reliable, marvellous old world manners, very useful at dinner parties: a delightful man, they would say. And so he was.

His office, like Michael's, reflected a bygone age. Tall, glass-fronted bookcases reared up towards the lofty ceilings with their ornate plaster cornices, a satinwood bureau gleamed beside the Adam fireplace, whilst one or two originals in oil hung against the dark wall panelling.

As one of the senior partners, he saw only selected clients; pacing across the polished floor to meet them, the Waterford decanter and glasses waiting on their silver tray. Yes, life was very good.

Nick frowned a little, sighed deeply, and rising, walked to the window, where he gazed out over the city, absentmindedly jingling the coins in his pocket. It was unfortunate, it was damned disappointing, but Cass would have to go. She was becoming a nuisance—worse, a threat. He shook his head and pursed his rather thin lips. Dammit! Who would have thought that he could have misjudged her so completely?

Nick picked the partners for his romantic little affairs very carefully indeed. He usually selected women of a certain age; bored, lonely, neglected, guaranteed to be grateful for some flattering attention, overjoyed to receive a little pleasure in civilised surroundings.

After a while—how long depended on how well the woman behaved herself—he would regretfully, charmingly but very firmly, declare the affair over. Since he always made certain that the woman had as much to lose as he had, no fuss, or at least not an unbearable amount, was made and he usually managed to remain on good terms with his former mistresses. Only once had he misjudged it, when he had selected a young girl who had lost her head and had caused rather a nasty moment. He had dealt with it cleverly and now it looked as if such tactics might be needed again. Who would have believed that such an experienced dallier as Cass—he was well aware of her reputation—would start behaving like a girl of eighteen? Although, to be fair, he'd been rather bowled over himself, certainly enough to have actually written her—well, typed, he wasn't that stupid—a note.

He felt cold sweat prickle on his back. He must have been mad! He exhaled self-pityingly and walked back to his desk. And it could have been such fun! She was a charming, attractive companion, very good in bed . . . He shook his head again. It just would not do. Twice this week she'd telephoned, trying to make arrangements to see him on the flimsiest pretexts, hinting of dramas and problems that didn't exist. He'd had to tell her that he wouldn't accept any more calls. His reputation was very dear to him and he wasn't prepared to risk it for anyone. When he'd met her at the Skylark she'd behaved with far less restraint than usual. He'd noticed one or two looks from the regulars and he was beginning to regret the weekend in Shropshire.

The intercom on his desk buzzed and he leaned over to press the button.

'Yes?'

'Mrs Stretton is downstairs, sir. Your twelve-thirty appointment. Shall I ask her to come up?'

'Just a moment Susannah . . . Mrs Stretton?' He paused, puzzling over the name. 'Do we know her?'

'No, sir. She's a new client. Said Admiral Hartley recommended you and you agreed to see her. Apparently it's all rather urgent.'

'Oh, yes. I remember your telling me. Very well. Wheel her in.'

He ran a comb quickly through his hair, straightened his tie, made sure that his desk was clear and was still on his feet when Susannah knocked and opened the door.

'Mrs Stretton, sir.'

'How do you do?' Nick moved forward and stopped, thunderstruck. The door closed behind Susannah and Cass smiled at him.

'Surprise!' she said and burst out laughing.

'What on earth d'you think you're doing?' His face was stiff with displeasure and he ignored her outstretched hands.

'Oh, darling! Don't be so stuffy! It's a joke. You were so funny about how I mustn't phone and mustn't come to see you here that I decided to penetrate the inner sanctum. Well? Now that I am here aren't you going to kiss me?'

Nick looked at her smiling face and felt only an urge to slap it very hard. However, he dared not make a scene. It was most unlikely that anyone would walk in whilst he had a client with him but nevertheless . . . He took a deep breath.

'I'm really very cross with you, you know,' he began, moving round his desk, away from her. 'It really is a very silly thing to do and you might easily be recognised. That doesn't matter. Anyone is allowed to visit a lawyer's rooms, but not under an assumed name. Anyway, why Stretton?'

'Don't you remember Church Stretton? In Shropshire? I thought you might have guessed. Don't be so boring about it all, Nick. I wanted to see your office—or do you call it "chambers"?—and you in it. Are you going to take me out to lunch? I'm in my city clothes as you can see.'

For the first time he looked at her properly. Her severely cut suit with its double breasted jacket and straight skirt was made of expensive grey flannel, her sheer stockings were pearly grey and her feet

were shod in narrow black suede pumps. Her crisp white shirt had a
mandarin collar and her golden hair was swept upwards into a loose,
shining knot. She looked wonderful.

'I can't,' he said flatly. 'I'm having lunch with the senior partner.
I'm sorry but it's quite impossible.' He watched her disappointment
with satisfaction.

'Surely you could cancel it!' she cried. 'After I've come all this way
specially. Oh, Nick, can't you put him off? You can have lunch with
him any time.'

'It's out of the question.' He allowed his impatience to show. 'I
can't just cancel lunch for no good reason.'

'Aren't I a good reason?' She came close to him, trying to make
him touch her, and he felt a renewed urge to use physical violence.

'Not quite good enough, I'm afraid.' He forced a laugh. 'I might
think so but I don't think John Marriott would, necessarily. Of course,
he hasn't seen you.' He tried for a little of his usual manner. 'If he did
he'd probably want to take you out himself.' He kissed her quickly.
'Now then. We've time for a glass of sherry before I have to go.' He
freed himself from her clinging hands and went to the decanter. 'You'll
approve of this. Now, what's the news?'

Ten minutes later he shut the door behind her with a gasp of relief,
his mind fully made up. Cass must go and the sooner the better. Going
to his desk he pressed the switch that gave him a line out and began to
dial.

On the same morning, but slightly earlier, Harriet and Michael set
out, at last, for Lee-on-Solent. It had become necessary for Harriet to
see her solicitor, sign the contract for the sale of her house and tie up
various loose ends.

As the car breasted the hill, Dartmoor lay spread out before them,
the bracken burning a fierce orange, the purple heather looking like
patches of smoke.

Harriet caught her breath.

'Wonderful,' she said. 'I shall never get used to it. It's always wonderful and different.'

Plumes of shadow chased across the stony tors as high cloud passed across the sun.

'But will you like it in the winter when the winds howl and everything is obliterated by driving rain?' wondered Michael. 'The weather's been exceptional since you've been here. At the first sign of West Country weather you'll probably be back off up-country to civilisation.'

'I shan't,' she declared. 'I shall love it whatever it does. Do you ever get tired of it?'

'Never! But then I'm a West Country man, you know. I'm not a townie.'

'Pig!' She laughed. 'Neither am I. Or, at least, not any more. I've been very happy at Lower Barton.'

'I wanted to talk to you about that.' Michael slowed and pulled out as a solitary sheep ambled into the road. 'Would you like, perhaps, to start afresh: somewhere new for both of us? If we pooled our resources we could get quite a decent place, you know.'

She turned to look at him in surprise.

'D'you know, I hadn't thought of it.'

'I wondered if we both might prefer a home that had no previous associations.'

She felt a spasm of guilt. Was he thinking of that dreadful morning when Tom had appeared at the cottage? Perhaps it had spoiled Lower Barton for him and he was merely being tactful. She pulled herself together. If that were the case, surely, during the last few days, she would have seen some sign of it since she had spent most of them at the cottage? She had lived with him as a friend, now she was living with him as a lover. In fact there was very little difference except that Michael, sure of her for the first time, had found that his difficulties in bed had quite disappeared.

'Well? Now that you have thought of it, what d'you say? There are some rather nice properties on the market at the moment and I'd have no problem in selling the cottage.'

'I'd say that I'd rather we stayed at Lower Barton. I'm sure we'll never find anything half so nice. But only if it's what you want too?'

'I'd rather stay. We can change the decorations, of course, and you'll want your own furniture but, to be honest, I'd be very sad to leave it.' He smiled without taking his eyes from the road and reached for her hand. 'Happy?'

'Blissfully!'

CASS ARRIVED HOME FROM Plymouth feeling helpless and miserable. She simply didn't know what to do. For her, the weekend in Shropshire had been a turning point in her affair with Nick. For him there seemed to have been no change at all: quite the reverse. This week he had been almost cold and unsympathetic. He was totally uninterested in Charlotte's disaster and showed no disposition to behave any differently from before their perfect weekend. Cass, who had imagined some change—although she hardly knew what—was bitterly disappointed. The trouble was that she had no power over him, nothing that she could offer him was enough to tempt him. For the first time Cass was on the receiving end and she didn't like it a bit. In her calmer moments she couldn't decide exactly what it was that she wanted. She couldn't really imagine life without her children or Tom or even living anywhere but at the Rectory. Nevertheless, these things paled into insignificance when she thought about Nick and she couldn't now imagine being without him either. If she were honest, what she wanted was for him to leave his wife and set up on his own somewhere. Then they could meet whenever possible, re-creating another Shropshire here in Devon. To be fair, Nick had given the impression that nothing but kindness kept him with his wife and Cass, therefore, could see no reason why he should not provide handsomely for Sarah and lead his own life. He could still visit her, help her with problems or emergencies, she needn't feel alone. But Nick wouldn't hear of it. He fielded these questions with all the cleverness that the legal profession had taught him and Cass felt helpless and confused.

Changing from her city clothes into an old tweed skirt, a sweater and some sensible shoes she went into the garden to do some tidying up. She was aware of a change in the air. The brilliant champagne freshness had been replaced by a sultry heaviness, though the sun still shone.

She tied up some chrysanthemums and snipped a few dead heads, watched by Charlotte from her open bedroom window, and made a half-hearted attempt to sweep up some leaves. In this she was defeated by Gus, who would plunge into the pile, catching the leaves in his mouth and tossing them into the air before turning round and round in circles to fall panting in the middle of them. He was enjoying himself so much that she didn't have the heart to stop him and was standing, leaning on her rake watching him, as a car swept into the drive and halted a few feet away.

Cass watched in surprise and then horror as a short, rather dumpy woman with cropped grey hair climbed out and came across the lawn towards her. She wore navy blue cords with a navy Guernsey and a scarf knotted loosely around her neck.

'Sarah,' breathed Cass and her heart gave a sickening thud. 'Sarah!' It came out more strongly this time, as a greeting, though she remained rooted to the spot.

'Cass, my dear. How lucky to find you home. I came on the off-chance. How are you?'

'I'm . . . well.' Cass let go of the rake to accept the proffered embrace and each kissed the air the statutory two inches from the other's cheek bone.

'I'm glad. What weather! But I think this spell is almost over. I smell a change in the air. All alone?'

'Yes. Well, there's Charlotte.' Cass glanced up towards her window. 'She's not too well at present. Gemma's gone to tea with a friend.'

'How lucky you are to have all these lovely children.' Sarah moved purposefully to a little wooden seat. 'Shall we sit down for a moment?' Cass followed her, dazed. 'I want to talk to you about Nick. He's got a problem.' She smiled and squeezed Cass's arm. 'It's you!'

Cass stared at her speechlessly.

'This is very difficult, my dear, but it's got to be said and he's asked me to say it. He doesn't want to see you any more. He feels you're getting serious and you'll be hurt.'

'He asked you . . . ?'

'I know. But Nick hates hurting people's feelings, especially women's. It upsets him dreadfully but he feels that it's necessary for you to know the truth.'

'He asked you to . . . '

'I know it's unusual. In most cases it all ends quietly with no ill feeling, but this time . . . '

'In most cases? Sarah . . . '

'I'm sorry, my dear. You weren't the first, you know, and you won't be the last. Nick likes a little romance in his life. Oh, it's all quite harmless but he can't resist it.'

'Sarah! Stop this, please! Are you telling me that Nick . . . that Nick . . . '

'Nick thought that you would understand the situation and accept it for what it was. He wouldn't have dreamed of hurting you. I think he felt you knew the rules. After all, Cass, if we're honest, you do have a certain reputation yourself.'

She stared at Sarah, seeing for the first time the determined chin and the steel in the grey eyes.

'I don't believe you,' she said flatly. 'None of this is true. Nick wouldn't do this. You're bluffing.'

'Oh, my dear.' Sarah gave a little laugh. 'I can see that I shall have to be brutal. Nick phoned me about one o'clock and told me the whole thing. I knew there was someone, of course, I always do, I didn't know who it was. He said that he'd taken you to our place in Shropshire . . . '

'Your place?'

'Funny little shack, isn't it? He likes to say that he borrows it, makes it look less premeditated. And I'm sure you went to The Bear and met George? He takes them all there.'

'I don't believe this!'

'Anyhow, he says that since you've been back it's got much too serious. You've been into the office, I hear, with an assumed name. Really, my dear, that was very foolish of you. Nick won't take any risks, you know. And he'd never leave me. He does very well but our private income comes through my family and he wouldn't want to give up his little luxuries. He's a very selfish man, vain too. But then, none of us is perfect.'

Cass looked upon Sarah's ruthlessness and wondered how she'd ever thought her colourless and insignificant.

'Well, he asked me to come over and explain things to you. I know you'll try to understand.'

'He sent you to me?' It was all that Cass could say.

'Let's face it, my dear, he's a weak character. He looks to me to help him out of his difficulties. Always has. We've had a very good life together, once I got used to his little distractions.'

'But how can you live like that? I just can't understand . . . '

'Can't you, Cass? How does Tom manage?'

There was a dreadful silence and then Cass struggled to her feet.

'You'd better go, Sarah. Please go. Tell Nick he has nothing to fear from me. I shall never speak to him again. I simply can't believe this is happening!'

'I'm sorry you're taking it like this. We both hope that we shall all remain friends. After all . . . '

'Friends!'

Sarah stepped back at the look on Cass's face.

'After all,' she repeated quietly, 'we have a good many mutual acquaintances and I imagine you wouldn't like any gossip. Think about it. I must be off. Goodbye.'

She crossed the lawn, climbed back into her car and drove away, leaving Cass where she stood.

———

LATER THAT EVENING JANE received a telephone call from Alan.

'Hello, love. How are you? How's the sprog?'

'OK. We're fine. Is the boat in?'

'Yep! And I'll be home later when I've finished off here. Could be very late, mind. I've got a lift, though.'

'Oh, that's great. Listen, Alan.' She swallowed nervously. This was the big one. 'Thank God you've come in. I've found someone to rent the house. No, listen. It means we don't have to sell unless we're really sure we want to. I'm ever so pleased about it. Only trouble is they want to be in by'—she did a quick mental calculation—'Tuesday at the latest.'

'Tuesday? That's a bit quick, isn't it?'

'I know. That's why I'm so glad you're in. They've got to be out of where they are, see? And they have got somewhere else but they want this place. They're ever such a nice couple, no children, really ideal. I wouldn't have to worry about them wrecking the place and you know how difficult it is to find nice people!' She gabbled on breathlessly, willing him to believe her, to agree.

'Well, OK, love, I can see the advantages, but can we be packed up by Tuesday?'

'Well, we've got to leave a lot of the stuff anyway, as it's a furnished let. And I've been doing a bit myself, praying you'd be in on time. Cass Wivenhoe says she'll finish anything off for us and send things on and that. Honestly, Alan, it's just like a miracle. I'm ever so pleased.'

'As long as you're happy, Jane, I don't really mind. But don't forget we've got to go somewhere when we get to Chatham. I suppose we could stay in a Bed and Breakfast 'til I get a married quarter sorted out . . . '

'Well, I've arranged that too! See, Cass knows this couple in Chatham who've just gone abroad on an exchange. Their people let them down and they want someone in their place. It's all ready, we can move straight in. Cass says it's a really nice cottage, just out a bit, in the country. Sounds much nicer than a quarter. Please, Alan. I think it's sort of meant, the way it's just all happened. I'm sure we could be ready in time.'

'OK, love, if it's what you want.' She could have fainted with relief. 'Turning into a proper naval wife, aren't you? Bit of luck we got in today then, wasn't it?'

'Oh, yes!' she lied. "That's what I mean, it's meant to happen this way.'

'Fine. Well, we'll get ourselves sorted out tomorrow, then. Must go, there's a queue forming. See you later on, love. 'Bye.'

Jane sank into a chair and closed her eyes, horrified by the ease with which she had told so many lies. Soon, soon they'd be gone! No more skulking indoors, frightened to answer the phone in case it was Philip, fobbing him off with excuses that didn't make him suspicious. She'd been packing the car for days, going secretly from the kitchen door that led directly into the garage, so that none of the neighbours should see. They could be off on Monday, with luck. With a deep sigh of relief she hauled herself to her feet and went in to the kitchen. After all that she desperately needed a cup of tea.

ON SUNDAY, AFTER CHURCH, Cass strolled down to the Mallinsons' cottage, leaving Gemma to go home alone. Charlotte had said that she felt up to cooking the Sunday lunch. She was still in a very nervous state and had positively refused to return to school on the Thursday. In despair, Cass had telephoned the doctor and asked his opinion. He had told her that a few more days wouldn't hurt but that she should be perfectly fit to go back the following week. Cass felt that the longer Charlotte stayed away the harder she would find it to return and rather unwisely told her so. She explained, sympathetically enough, that when these things happened it was best to face up to them and get on with life at once. She likened it to falling off a horse and getting straight back up on to it again, a parallel she felt sure that Charlotte would understand. Charlotte had stared at her in a stony and stubborn silence and Cass knew herself to be defeated. She had told Charlotte that she could stay home until the weekend but that she must go back to school on Sunday evening. Charlotte continued to stare at her and Cass had left her to it. She was still battling with her own pain over Nick's desertion and the way that he had deceived her. She had been so certain that it had been as special for him as it had for her. To know that she had been just one more poor duped female was almost too much to bear and she lay awake at night, staring into the dark, shattered by the turn of events and occasionally shedding tears. She remembered his tender love-making and whispered endearments and ached to feel his arms about her. At these moments, she would turn on to her face and cry in earnest into her pillow. By morning, she felt too exhausted and too miserable to cope with Charlotte's unreasonable behaviour and was grateful that only Gemma was at home. Oliver had already been taken back to school by his great-aunt's henchman and Cass had been obliged to telephone and explain to him that Charlotte wasn't well but that she would be back soon. The twins, too, had returned, under pain of death should they so much as breathe a word about what had happened in Bristol.

On Saturday evening, when Cass told her to pack her things for school, Charlotte had announced that nothing would induce her to go back to Blundells, that she would be an object of pity and scorn. There had been a row at this point but Charlotte remained obdurate and had refused to speak another word since.

At least, on Sunday morning she had stirred from her apathy enough to suggest that she could cook the lunch, although she had looked very oddly at Cass when the latter had announced her intention to check the cottage.

'I haven't been over for ages,' she explained, almost defensively. The child was behaving most peculiarly and it would probably be a good thing when she'd finished those tablets. They seemed to have a very strange effect on her. 'I shan't be late for lunch, it's only a ten-minute walk, fifteen at the most!'

Mrs Hampton waylaid her at the church gate to ask after Charlotte.

'By the way,' Cass glanced round and lowered her voice, 'I've got a message for you from Jane Maxwell. Alan's home and they'll be off tomorrow. I think you know that it's all very hush-hush?'

'I do indeed, my lover. Well, I am pleased. An' all thanks to you, I 'ear!'

'Rubbish! But she said that if you happened to be passing and popped in, she'd love to say goodbye.'

'O' course I will. I'm that pleased for 'em.'

'Good.' Cass smiled at her. 'See you in the morning then, thank goodness! You seem to be the only person that Charlotte will talk to at the moment, and I'm hoping you'll have a chat with her tomorrow. She simply refuses to go back to school this evening and I'm at my wits' end. She says that they'll all laugh at her. We've had a bit of a row, I'm afraid, but what can I do? I can't take her by force. I wish Tom was home. Kate's been over and tried to reason with her but she just won't have it. She says she'd rather go to Tavistock Comprehensive. There's just a chance she'll listen to you. You've always been so close.'

Mrs Hampton looked dismayed.

'There now! I'd quite forgot! I can't come in tomorrow. I meant to tell you Friday but it went outa me mind, what with Charlotte an' everythin'. I've gotta go down the 'ospital for me check-up. It's that ol' leg o' mine. Mrs Drew's takin' me down in the mornin'. Goodness knows how long it'll all take. You know what them consultants is like. Could take all day.'

'Don't give it a thought. You can talk to her any time. It looks as if I'm landed with her. Let me know how it goes. It might be better if she came down to you. You could invite her down for tea and have a little heart to heart.'

They parted and Cass set off on the bridle path that led, amongst other places, to the cottage. The earth was bone dry beneath her feet but today the sun was obscured by a high mist although it was still warm. Change was in the air. She approached the cottage from the back and climbed the stile into the garden thinking of her assignation there with Nick after her party all those months ago. Her heart gave a great throb of pain. She still couldn't quite believe it and hoped against hope to hear from him, telling her that it had all been a dreadful mistake. But she knew in her heart that it was all too true. Sarah's revelations had shocked her; Nick must have told her everything and that hurt almost more than anything else. She remembered the pity and contempt in Sarah's eyes and felt a thrill of humiliation and pain. How could he have exposed her to that?

She unlocked the front door and went in. It smelt musty and unused and she decided that it might be time to start up the central heating for the winter. It wouldn't do any harm, either, to let Hammy in with a duster. She passed through, opening windows, and went to look at the central heating boiler. After five minutes it was still a mystery to her and she knew that she'd have to get someone in. She went into the sitting room and looked at the pad which was kept by the telephone. Here, Paul had written various instructions and telephone numbers which he had considered might be useful to her in her capacity as caretaker. Yes, here indeed was an entry: P.R. Plumbing, and a local telephone number. Well, it was Sunday, but it was worth a try. She dialled. After some time a sleepy voice spoke in her ear.

'Hello? Who is it?'

'Oh, hello. I'm sorry to bother you on a Sunday but I've got a bit of a problem. I'm at Brook Cottage, the Mallinsons' place, just outside . . . '

'Yeah. I know where it is. I put the central heating in for 'em.'

'Ah. Well, that's the point. They're abroad at present and I'm caretaking for them. The place is getting very damp but I haven't a clue how to start the wretched thing up. I suppose you couldn't come over and get it going for me?'

'What, now?'

'No, no. But as soon as possible. It really does need some warmth in the place.'

'Yeah. Well, I could be over that way tomorrer, as it happens. I could do it then, it's only a five-minute job.'

'Could you really? That would be marvellous. What sort of time would that be?'

'Well, I dunno at the minute. I'll have to check with someone else I gotta see. I'll phone you in the morning.'

'That'll be fine. Look, I'll give you my home number so that you can phone me there. OK?'

She gave him the Rectory number then, having given the place an airing, shut all the windows, locked up and walked home to lunch.

Twenty-nine

During the night the wind had risen and though for most of the next morning the sun shone fitfully, great pillows of purple cloud banked steadily up in the west.

Holding open the drawing-room door just a crack, Charlotte watched Cass take the telephone call. She strained to hear the conversation.

'Oh, hello . . . So you can come? That's marvellous . . . About half-past three? Commander Mallinson, that's right . . . Oh, don't worry! I'll wait . . . Fine, 'bye.'

To Charlotte's feverish imagination it sounded like an assignation at the Mallinsons' cottage. She was convinced now that she had been right all along in imagining that her mother was involved with somebody. It was just as well that she had refused to go back to school. If there was to be no Hugh for her then she simply couldn't face the mock sympathy, the whisperings that would result when her peers found out. She might just as well stay at home and make sure that at least the family remained safe and all together. It was time for action. Her brain seethed with ideas.

Cass left the Rectory just after a quarter past three. This time, in view of the weather, she took the car, parking it on the hard standing in front of the Mallinsons' garage. She hurried through the garden and into the cottage, glad to be out of the wind. There seemed to be a storm brewing.

The plumber arrived some ten minutes later and parked a rather battered van beside Cass's car. She let him in and he nodded to her, going through to the kitchen where the boiler was housed with the air of one who knew his way about.

'Won't take long, Missis.' He put his tool-bag down on the kitchen floor and glanced meaningly at her mug of coffee. 'Cold, innit? That's our summer over, I reckon.'

'I'm afraid you're right.' Cass smiled at him, rather liking his looks. He reminded her of someone but she couldn't think who it was. 'You're very welcome to a cup of coffee but you'll have to drink it black. I didn't bring any milk, I'm afraid.'

' 'Tis better than nothing, as long as there's sugar.'

'Plenty of sugar.' Cass produced another mug, spooned in coffee and sugar, poured on boiling water. 'I wasn't sure how long you might be so I thought I'd keep myself warm while I waited.'

'Ta!' He took the mug and gulped down a mouthful. 'That's better. Now, let's have a look at this.'

He set down the mug and opened the boiler door. Cass perched idly on the edge of the kitchen table, sipping her coffee and observing his crisp black hair and the warm tan of his skin with approval. She was just opening her lips to remark on his likeness to Alan Maxwell when the kitchen door swung back and Charlotte almost fell into the room.

'Caught you!' she cried, with a sound between a laugh and a sob. 'I've caught you . . . ' Her voice died away as she took in the scene, seeing the young man in overalls at the boiler.

'What are you doing?' said Cass, annoyed and half-suspecting what was in Charlotte's mind.

'I've caught you,' began the girl, feebly now, aware that the plumber was staring at her in surprise. 'Caught you before you left, I mean.' She tried to pull herself together, seeing that she had mis-judged the situation completely. 'I ran across the fields.'

'Yes, but why?' Cass's temper was rising now and she had quite for-gotten the plumber. This thing between them was coming to a head and she, for one, was ready for it. Charlotte had been treating her as

though she were an enemy, as though she were to blame for the deba-
cle in Bristol, and Cass had been hurt by it. All the misery and humiliation of the last few days rose to the surface of her mind and real
anger, something she rarely experienced, was erupting out of them.
'What's all this about?'

Charlotte gazed into her mother's face with dismay. In all her life
she had seen Cass lose her temper probably no more than half a
dozen times and she always found it very frightening. Everything was
going terribly wrong. Her overwrought brain had conjured up images as she had run across the fields, having been presented with the
perfect excuse to come to the cottage. She had imagined Cass in
her lover's arms and she, Charlotte, denouncing her and extracting
promises of fidelity for the future whilst Cass grovelled at her feet in
humiliation. What had gone wrong? She closed her eyes tight to shut
out Cass's expression of anger and contempt and searched desperately for a way out. Of course! She gulped with relief. She already
had her excuse.

'It's the Maxwells!' she cried, opening her eyes. 'Jane phoned just after you'd gone. She wanted to say goodbye to you. They're leaving for
Chatham and she wanted to say thanks for everything and she'll phone
when she gets to their new place. They were leaving that minute, she
said, but I thought if I ran you could phone from here . . . '

'What rubbish!' shouted Cass, getting off the table. 'Why not tell
her to phone me here? Or why didn't you phone? It was just an excuse . . . '

She broke off as the plumber elbowed her unceremoniously aside.

'Wait a minute,' he said. He seized Charlotte by the upper arms,
his face screwed up with a mixture of puzzlement and rising anger. He
looked as if he was attempting a violent mental exercise. 'What do
you mean, "just leaving for Chatham"?'

Charlotte stared at him in surprise.

'Tell me!' He gave her a little shake as though to jolt the words
from her. 'Did you say Jane Maxwell is just leaving for Chatham?'

'Yes, I did.' Charlotte gazed at him in alarm. His entire concentration was focused upon her. 'She's going to live there with her husband. Why? What's the matter?'

'The bitch!' he whispered, loosing his grip on the frightened girl. 'The bloody bitch! She's been lying to me. Fobbing me off! I should've guessed. She's going off with that bastard. With my kid!'

He stood quite still for a moment and then with a supreme effort he seemed to pull himself together. The doors banged open as he flew out and Cass gave a cry as realisation struck her like a physical blow. Her hands flew to her face as she saw, as if etched on the air before her, the name that was printed on the notes she had found on the telephone table. Philip Raikes. P.R. Plumbing.

'Philip Raikes,' she whispered. 'Oh, my God, it's him . . . You idiot!' She turned on Charlotte. 'You bloody idiot. D'you see what you've done? Come on, we'll have to try to stop him!'

She seized Charlotte by the arm, dragging her with her. They raced through the garden, the wind tearing at their hair, out of the gate, in time to see Philip Raikes turning his van. He could have been drunk the way he was driving. As Cass reached him, he straightened the van up and tore off down the lane, mud and gravel spurting from beneath the wheels.

Cass leapt for her car.

'Get in!' she shouted to Charlotte, who was near to tears. 'Get in!'

Charlotte scrabbled into the passenger seat as Cass dragged the keys from her pocket and started the engine. As the car leapt into the lane Charlotte turned to Cass.

'What is it?' she pleaded, her voice trembling with fear. 'What have I done? Please, tell me!'

'That man,' Cass jerked her head towards the vanishing vehicle, 'has been having an affair with Jane Maxwell. She's having his baby and he wants her to leave Alan and live with him.' She changed down with a shrieking of gears and took a bend on the wrong side. 'He's threatened to kill her if she stays with Alan and, it seems, he's quite capable of carrying out the threat. We'd managed to arrange to get them both away without his knowing. They're going to Chatham. And you, you stupid little fool, have blurted it all out in front of him.' She clashed the gears again, putting on another spurt as she saw the van reach the junction and pause. 'God knows what he means to do but . . . '

She too, had reached the junction and slammed into first gear but, even as she let out the clutch, she gave a little cry for the Maxwells' distinctive yellow car had appeared over the brow of the hill. Charlotte, who at such a bald stating of the facts had covered her face with her hands, dragged them down at Cass's cry just in time to see the van career across the road and smash at full speed into the yellow car. There was a noise of tearing metal and splintering glass as Philip was flung, first through his own windscreen and then the Maxwell's, to die in Jane's lap as she sat, covered with fragments of glass and rigid with shock and horror, watching his blood soak into her skirt. After a moment, or a lifetime, Jane was aware that the low moaning noise that had been issuing from Alan's lips had stopped and he lay slumped sideways, his face grey, blood pumping from his leg. She lost consciousness.

'No,' Cass was crying, as if pleading with somebody. 'No.'

She fumbled with her door handle, almost falling into the road, before she started to run towards the tangled vehicles. Charlotte followed her, begging her to stop.

'Go and get help!' Cass turned on her, her face crumpled with horror and fury. 'You see what you've done! Now go on into the village and get help. Go into Mrs Drew's. Tell her to phone for an ambulance!'

They reached the cars together and Cass gasped at the dreadful sight. Charlotte, choking with sobs, and with one appalled glance at the carnage in the car, stumbled on in the direction of the village. As she did so the storm broke above her head and the rain poured down.

CASS REPLACED THE TELEPHONE receiver and stood for a moment, leaning heavily against the hall table.

'How are they?'

She turned to look at Kate whom she had telephoned earlier, telling her the dreadful news and asking if she would come and keep her company. Cass gestured futilely.

'I suppose it could be worse.' She made it sound as if she couldn't imagine how. 'Philip was killed more or less outright.' A spasm of horror crossed her face. It would be a long time before she could forget that scene: Philip dying, with his maimed and bloody head pressed against his unborn child—if it were his child . . . Not that it mattered any more. 'Jane's suffering from shock. She's lost the baby but they think she'll recover. Alan's side of the car took the impact. He tried to swerve away when he saw the van heading for them. They think he'll lose a leg. Oh, Kate.' Her eyes swam with tears.

Kate took her arm and led her into the drawing room, pushing her down gently into an armchair. Presently she returned with a glass containing gin and tonic.

'Here,' she said. 'This might help.'

'Thanks.' Cass looked wan. 'I could do with a drink. Heavens!' she grimaced as she sipped it. 'That's a strong one.'

'Cass.' Kate perched on the edge of another chair. 'D'you know where Charlotte is?'

'No.' Cass shook her head. 'I assumed she was upstairs. I haven't seen her since I sent her off to raise the alarm but I must talk to her. Nobody need know why Philip Raikes rammed the Maxwells' car. There's no reason why it shouldn't have been a perfectly ordinary accident. I told the police that he'd been to turn on the central heating and we happened to be following him back. His van seemed to go out of control as he turned on to the road. It was a very old van so I'm hoping that they'll assume something broke or snapped or something. Only Jane and I and Mrs Hampton know anything about the other thing. And Charlotte, of course. That's why I must speak to her. I don't want her blabbing it all out and the police are bound to want a statement from her.'

'Well, she's not upstairs. Gemma's in bed asleep but Charlotte's nowhere around. D'you think she's OK?'

'I haven't the least idea!' Cass took another sip, looking more like her old self. 'She's probably with Hammy. I'd better phone and check. I wish Tom was here.' She was suddenly aware of how deeply she needed him. Tom was good in a crisis. All his service training came to the fore. He was calm, efficient, completely in charge. 'Why can't they ever be around when you need them? What's the time?'

'It's after ten. That's why I'm so worried about Charlotte. D'you think . . . ?'

The phone began to ring.

'Oh, hell,' said Cass wearily. 'What now?'

'I'll get it.' Kate went out and Cass heard her answering. She was too exhausted to try to hear the words. She rested her head on the back of the chair and shut her eyes.

'Cass. It's Mrs Ankerton.' Cass opened her eyes and stared up at Kate. 'She says that Charlotte took her horse out earlier and it's just come back without her. She said that she had no idea that Charlotte had been there or she wouldn't have let her go in this weather. She's terribly upset about it. She can't think what can have happened to her.'

'I AM THE RESURRECTION and the life, saith the Lord: he that believeth in me, though he were dead, yet shall he live: and whosoever liveth and believeth in me shall never die.'

Cass and Tom walked behind Charlotte's coffin, following it into the old granite church. None of their other children was at the funeral. While she was waiting for Tom to come home, Cass and Kate had driven to Blundells.

'There's no question of Oliver coming to the funeral,' Cass had said when Kate had suggested that he would be devastated at the news. 'I talked to his Housemaster about it and he agreed that it would be cruel. Oliver would have to go straight back to school and how would he feel, lying awake in the dormitory remembering . . . imagining . . . ' Her lips shook and she swallowed hard, gripping the wheel as if it were a lifeline.

Kate, who had let her drive knowing that it was better for her to have something to concentrate on, looked away from Cass's grief-ravaged face and stared out of the window recalling Giles's horror when she had telephoned him to warn him that they were coming and why.

'I feel the same about Saul,' Cass was saying. 'He's too little. It won't seem quite so real if he doesn't come to the funeral.'

When they arrived at Blundells, Oliver was already in the twins' study. Gently, carefully, Cass told him that Charlotte had been thrown from her horse and had been killed outright. She had not been wearing her hard hat. Oliver was shocked and silent. Hugging him tightly, she explained to him that it would be better for him to stay at school and that Giles and Guy would be there if he needed them. He could telephone her at any time and if he really felt that he must come home he would be allowed to. When she had gone, Giles put his arms round Oliver and held him while he cried.

Afterwards she drove to Mount House to see Saul. Alone with him in the headmaster's study, she told him that Charlotte had died in a riding accident. He watched her, not knowing how to react or what was expected of him. Somehow he couldn't take it in and, as Cass had guessed, it didn't seem real to him. She had hugged him and told him that he must be brave but that he could go to Matron or one of the masters if he felt he couldn't cope. It was better, she said, for him to go on as usual and not to dwell on it. He would be home very soon for half-term anyway. When she had gone everyone was very nice to him and great care was taken that there should always be someone at hand, ready to offer comfort.

Gemma was staying with Sophie. She was hardly old enough to understand it all and Abby kept her occupied, giving the two little girls treats and outings.

Harriet, hearing of the tragedy through Kate, sent flowers, feeling that it would be tactless to be there in person. She felt a terrible sense of guilt. Had Charlotte known of her affair with Tom and been affected by it? The girl had always been very fond of her father.

Had Tom been with her, Harriet, when he should have been with his family?

'Deliver me from all mine offences . . . ' Hugh Ankerton stood at the very back of the church, not wishing to be seen. His mother and father, Lucinda, all of them had been loud in their protestations that it was nothing to do with him. But he knew differently. He knew that the story was that Charlotte, already in a nervous state, had been over-set by the sight of a dreadful accident and had gone out on her horse in a terrible storm, up near the quarry where the fences were still down. She had been thrown and her body had been found in the water at the bottom of the quarry. Ah! But why had she been in that earlier ner-vous state? And why had she ridden up on that slippery, dangerous path, knowing as she did—for had not Hugh himself warned her?—what a risk she was taking, especially in a storm? If only I'd told her about Lucinda, he thought, instead of letting her find out like that. If only I'd written to her afterwards. Hugh bowed his head, swallowing his tears.

'Hear my prayer, O Lord . . . ' Mrs Hampton stood with Kate and mourned privately. If only she'd been there on that Monday as usual, Charlotte might not have gone running to the cottage with the mes-sage and none of it would have happened. She saw in her mind's eye the child's bedroom: the Peter Rabbit quilt, the soft toys ranged in chairs and on the window seat, and Charlotte's collection of china animals and much-loved books. She thought of her as a baby and as a little girl, thumb in mouth, head bent intently over a book: she re-membered teaching her to cook, the barbecues that she had loved so much and the day she had been made Head-girl. Hot tears scorched her wrinkled cheeks.

'Thou hast set our misdeeds before thee: and our secret sins in the light of our countenance . . . ' Tom knelt, stood, sat mechanically, staring straight ahead, his throat aching with unshed tears and trying to prevent his imagination from showing him, in dreadful clarity, Char-lotte's broken body lying in the muddy water at the bottom of the quarry. She had been his favourite child, not least because she had loved him so much. Even as a baby . . . He jerked his mind away from Charlotte as a baby. He had hardly seen her during his last leave. He'd been too busy pursuing Harriet to give any time to her. He knew that Charlotte had wanted to talk to him but, dreading another Education Debate, he'd avoided her, putting her off. Had she perhaps hated school so much that . . . ? He wrenched his mind away from that thought. What a selfish fool he'd been. Supposing he'd lost everything? Cass was so remote, so withdrawn. If only she would give him some small sign that she still cared, that their life together was not shattered forever.

'Comfort us again now . . . ' Kate stared at Cass's back, knowing how she suffered, guessing her thoughts. She had heard them over and over in the last few days and had done her utmost to comfort her but Cass was beyond comfort. Although she could not be held responsible for the accident, she knew very well that Charlotte had suspected that she might be meeting a man. And the whole trouble was that her suspicions were grounded in fact. If she had been a different woman, Charlotte would not have come to the cottage that afternoon. A good mother would have checked out the trip to Bristol more thoroughly. She would have been at home when Charlotte returned in her distraught state, not in the arms of a lover in the Shropshire hills. Her concern for Charlotte in this past week had been quite eclipsed by her own despair about Nick.

'I'm not fit to be a mother,' she cried at one point and Kate had put her arms about her and held her as she sobbed. 'You always warned me that one day I'd get the bullet. But why did Charlotte have to suffer? It wasn't her fault.'

'For as in Adam all die, even so in Christ shall all be made alive . . . ' Cass gazed up at the east window where Mary held the Infant Jesus on her lap. She saw the pride and tenderness in the painted face and the smooth limbs of the Child. It made her think of Charlotte as a baby and she remembered her own pride and Tom's joy in his new daughter. The pain clawed at her heart but she continued to gaze, her eyes staring against the tears that threatened: anything rather than let her eyes rest on

Charlotte's coffin standing before the altar. It didn't bear thinking about: not the dank earth and the worms and the darkness . . .

'Behold, I shew you a mystery. We shall not all sleep, but we shall all be changed . . . '

She tried to pray but her thoughts scurried hither and thither and she was unable to form even one coherent idea. Tom stood beside her as distant as another planet: withdrawn, silent, locked in his own mystery. She had not been the one to break the news to him. He had been at sea and the Navy had done it for her. By the time he had got home it was as if his emotions were lying beneath a thin coating of ice and they had behaved like strangers to each other: polite, kindly, gentle, as though they were viewing each other through a thin plastic membrane. Each longed to break through, to seek comfort from the other but were prevented by their secret guilt. Their passions and desires seemed to have been expunged as if they had never been: such pointless, shameful schemings they seemed now that pay day had come round and they had to meet the bill.

'Oh death, where is thy sting? O grave, where is thy victory . . . ?'

The coffin was being carried out now. Tom stood aside for Cass and as she passed into the aisle her eyes met Kate's. She understood the unspoken request and moved to walk beside Cass, their hands meeting for a moment, holding, pressing in a shared love. They emerged into the churchyard which was swept and buffeted by a boisterous autumn gale, the tall trees bowing before the wind that swept clean and pure, down from the moor. As they reached the open grave where Charlotte would lie, only a few feet from her grandfather, Kate, unable to bear the anguish in Cass's face, looked away for a moment, up at the clouds that bellied and raced like huge spinnakers, white and golden before the wind.

'Man that is born of woman hath but a short time to live and is full of misery . . . '

KATE AND CASS EMBRACED wordlessly and Cass watched as Kate went down the front steps and climbed into the car where Hammy observed them compassionately from the passenger's seat. As the sound of the engine died away, Cass turned back into the house and shut the door behind her. How different was a wake for a child from one for an old person. The usual trite clichés—'he'd had a good innings,' 'it was a merciful release'—simply didn't apply. It had been an agonising afternoon with everyone aware of the fragility of human life and its transitory nature.

Cass began to wonder where Tom was. They had hardly spoken to each other all afternoon and when they had it had been in that brittle way in which they had communicated for the last few days. Cass checked the study and the kitchen and wearily climbed the stairs, almost hauling herself up by the banister. Having gained the landing, she turned towards her bedroom, taking the pins out of her hair as she did so. Her head was splitting and she could hardly see. A noise, muffled, distinct, caused her to pause. She listened, aware of the wind still howling and roaring round the house.

There it was again and it was coming from Charlotte's room. Her heart gave a flutter of fear and she pressed her hands against her breast. Suddenly she crossed the few feet of carpet and gently pushed open the bedroom door.

Tom stood by the window, his head bowed. In his hands he held Charlotte's teddy bear, Winnie-the-Pooh, made by Hammy years before, his corduroy worn thin and rubbed from huggings. Cass heard the sound again, a painful, tearing whimper of pain and her heart contracted with love. The shell that had been forming over her emotions cracked and fell away in the face of Tom's anguish and in the knowledge of his pain and her love for him.

'Tom!' she cried sharply and then, more gently, 'Tom.'

He turned to her, his eyes swollen and streaming, his mouth stretched in an ugly soundless cry, and she opened her arms to him. The generosity of her gesture and her expression told him that all could be forgiven between them and that their grief could be shared. He stumbled towards her, still holding the bear, and she gathered him tightly to her breast.

'Darling,' she murmured. 'Oh, darling.'

She held him as he mourned, gazing beyond him at the square church tower, dark against the bright turbulent sky and, quite suddenly, it were as if she saw her father standing before her. He was young again, upright, smiling, and in his arms he held a child. He smoothed its hair and touched its cheek and she seemed to hear him speak. The voice was his but the words—words that he had used so often—were the words of Dame Julian of Norwich.

' . . . and all shall be well and all manner of thing shall be well.'